He checked his watch. Ten past eight. He would wash up and then give Helen a ring. Even now, after twenty-three years of marriage, the thought of hearing her voice gave him a charge of anticipation. For a moment he imagined her picking up the phone, barefoot on the smooth flagstones of the main room, under the broad beams of the oak ceiling. He switched on the radio: a local disc jockey introducing Sixties' hits – The Searchers and 'Sweets for my Sweet'. Tom hummed, at the same time trying to remember the words he had once known better than the National Anthem. As he washed the whisky glass, the telephone on the sideboard rang.

Chris Kelly has produced, written and broadcast many different television and radio programmes for thirty years, including most recently *Kavanagh Q.C.* and *Food and Drink*. He spent a number of years living in Cambridge, where he was a co-owner of the acclaimed Midsummer House Restaurant. He now lives in North London with his wife.

Taking Leave

Chris Kelly

CORONET BOOKS
Hodder and Stoughton

Copyright © 1995 Chris Kelly

First published in Great Britain in 1995
by Hodder and Stoughton

First published in paperback in 1996
by Hodder & Stoughton
A division of Hodder Headline PLC

A Coronet paperback

The right of Chris Kelly to be identified as the Author of the Work
has been asserted by him in accordance with the Copyright,
Designs and Patents Act 1988.

10 9 8 7 6 5 4 3 2 1

British Library Cataloguing in Publication Data

Kelly, Chris
Taking Leave
I. Title
823.914 [F]

ISBN 0 340 61744 6

Typeset by Avon Dataset Ltd, Bidford-on-Avon, Warks

Printed and bound in Great Britain by
Cox & Wyman, Reading, Berks

Hodder and Stoughton
A division of Hodder Headline PLC
338 Euston Road
London NW1 3BH

For my wife, Vivien, who proposed,
guided, and encouraged.

CHAPTER ONE

Behind the tinted visor of the mask, Henri Gazin felt unbeatable. His head encased in black metal like a knight in a history book, he had never known such a strong, calm sense of purpose. This was how it must be in the cockpit of a grand prix car, he thought; focused on nothing but the road ahead; no doubts, no fear; cool, controlled; more alive at this moment than ever before. He looked down at his gloved hands, holding them out to check their steadiness. Though there was no sign of a tremor, they seemed remote; like the gauntlets of nuclear scientists he'd seen on television, arms pushed through holes in a glass shield. He half-clenched them, enjoying the power generated by years of manual labour. Sharp and ready, he reached behind his seat for the shotgun.

Easing on the motorcycle helmet had only taken seconds. Now, as he got out of the van, closing the passenger door with care, Henri glanced across at the driver. Félix's older helmet, in scuffed dark blue, made his body seem even more unprotected than usual, like a snail half out of its shell. But Henri knew that the young estate agent's thin frame was deceptive. Félix was as whip-like and streamlined as a stoat. Henri made a thumbs-up signal. Returning it, Félix was unable to disguise his tension.

The house ahead of them was typical of the farm cottages in the Auxerrois. Long and low, with a sagging, pantiled roof, it comprised two cowsheds flanking a central living room, with a barn at the right-hand end. The faded 'For Sale' sign, the missing tiles, cracked windows and jagged scars in the plasterwork gave it a broken-backed, neglected look.

Making sure the van was hidden from the road by a tall stand of lilacs, Henri pointed at the weathered barn door. Félix jerked his head back to indicate the car, a grey Peugeot 203, parked at the roadside, but Henri repeated his firm gesture, the shotgun balanced in his other hand. As they left the heat of the afternoon for the musty shade of the stone-built barn, a swallow skimmed low over their heads, escaping to blue freedom.

Henri stooped as he crossed the cobbled floor of the cowshed adjoining the barn, noticing the old iron plough at rest in the corner. Though dull now, the swept-back blades of its long snout reminded him of a shark. Once, when he was four or five, his father had shown him how to use one; how to keep the furrows straight behind the straining horse; how to clean the bright, slicing edge with straw. That was about the time his mother had died . . . when the nightmares began.

A sudden dustfall on his helmet and a restraining hand on his arm made him pause. Turning, he saw Félix pointing to the beams above their heads. The girl. She must be waiting for them to join her. Or perhaps she hadn't heard the van? Either way she was caught in a snare. There were no witnesses to raise the alarm. No bodyguards to save her. Henri couldn't believe how well the plan had worked.

Overhead, in the large room she meant to make her own, Julia Walker found herself smiling. Tall and tanned, with the assurance bred of a privileged upbringing, she hugged her secret, as yet confided to no one. Four months ago, her Aunt

Loretta had died in Chicago, leaving her seventy-five thousand dollars. Peanuts; but in Burgundy peanuts still went a long way. Staying at her parents' château was fine as far as it went, but she craved independence. She wanted to entertain the sort of friends for whom she might otherwise have to make excuses. 'Oh but Dad, he's not at all like a pit-bull when you get to know him.' She wanted to smoke a joint when she felt like it, without antagonising her French stepmother, and walk naked on the flagstones as the dawn sun spied through the knot-hole in the shutter.

Telling no one, Julia had contacted a real estate agency in Beaune: Cabinet Lamotte. This was the first house they had shown her. That unforgettable day, she had known it was the one the moment she crossed the threshold. Despite the brown paint muddying the oak beams, and the wallpaper from hell, she saw its possibilities at once. A glance through the wrought-iron lattice of the back door at the plum trees in the waist-high grass had confirmed the choice. To her astonishment, her offer of one hundred thousand francs looked like being accepted. Pangs of guilt almost drove her to bleat: 'Here, have more!' but she resisted the impulse. Now there would be plenty left over to make the old house feel loved again.

Eager to return and plan the restoration in detail, Julia had fixed the appointment for four o'clock. The young realtor to whom she spoke was the one who had introduced her to the property. Arriving early, she had clambered in through an unhinged window at the back. For a few moments she had lingered in the main room, removing her slip-ons and feeling the age of the stones beneath her bare feet. Then, like an exploring child, she had climbed the rickety staircase leading from the further cowshed to the first floor. When the house had formed the heart of a working farm, this was where the hay had been stored. And a little further on was the big bedroom, where Julia stood now, looking out to the low line of hills beyond Lacanche. Here the farmer and his wife had nested, safe from the keen winter cold, the heat from the cattle rising to blanket them. In the corner were signs of more recent occupants; small bones and dry droppings left by owls. Julia had heard a vehicle arrive a couple of minutes ago but, assuming it was the man from Cabinet Lamotte, had not bothered to check. Besides, now that she had the house to herself, she was reluctant to break the spell. Even this necessary professional visit already seemed like an intrusion. Touching the uneven stones of the wall with a gentle hand, she resolved to get rid of the realtor as soon as possible.

Hearing a sound from the main room she called, in fluent French: 'Monsieur, I'm up here! In the Marie Antoinette suite!' To her surprise there was no reply. When she crossed to the grimy window facing the road, she could see her own Peugeot but no other car. Had she been mistaken? No, she was sure of it. The sound of an engine drawing closer and cutting out had been unmistakable. Puzzled, she left the bedroom and went through the hayloft to the head of the stairs. After a pause she called: 'Why the silence, monsieur? Did they turn my offer down after all? That's not a problem you know. We might find another few sous. Or perhaps you're admiring my Aubusson tapestries? Is that it?'

Still no reply. Impatient now, Julia went down the dusty steps. At the bottom she could see a pair of faded jeans and black sneakers. What was this jerk playing at, she wondered? For a Frenchman to be speechless there must be something wrong. A second later she saw what it was. The visitor – wiry, perhaps five foot six or seven – was wearing a ridiculous, blue, motorcyclist's helmet. Julia's first reaction was to laugh. He looked like a kid caught dressing up. Could this be a realtor? Even in the Bronx they didn't dress like that. But then the urge to tease him froze in her. Behind him was a taller man, thicker-set, his shoulders heavy under a navy T-shirt, his arms weathered red to just above the elbow and, beyond that, white. This more menacing figure wore a sinister black helmet with a smoky visor, obscuring even his eyes. And in his raised hands was a shotgun, its double barrel fixing her with a cold, hard stare.

'Well, guys, you certainly know how to show a girl a good time,' Julia said in English, with more confidence than she felt. Then, in French: 'Don't tell me. You came to read the meter.'

The single word Blue Helmet uttered was muffled by his helmet.

'How's that again?' Julia said.

'Turn!' Blue Helmet roared, describing a clockwise movement with his gloved hand.

'Asshole,' Julia muttered, turning her back to him and facing up the stairs. No point in hollering, she thought. No one for miles. Besides, the guy with the gun looked liable to use it. Fumbling with nerves, Blue Helmet pulled a pair of handcuffs out of his jeans' pocket.

'The hands!' he shouted.

'What?' Julia said.

'The hands!' he repeated. 'The hands behind the back.'

Julia considered making a run for it and maybe diving out of an upstairs window, but realised it was hopeless. By the time she got there the psycho would have blasted her with buckshot. Abandoning the idea, she obeyed Blue Helmet's order.

After several clumsy attempts, during which he cursed the inventor of handcuffs, Félix managed to snap them shut around the slender, sunburned wrists. Just as he was about to make his victim turn again, and lead her to the van, he felt a sharp prod in the back. Taking his eyes off Julia, he twisted his body to see Henri making frantic gestures towards the front door. There, through the dirty, frosted glass, a dark shape was visible – a shape which seemed to be leaning in the attitude of a listener.

'Shit!' Félix said.

There was a firm knock, audible even through the helmets.

'What do we do now?' Félix said, panic rising.

Hearing the knock and the men's confusion, Julia yelled 'Help!', in French.

Félix reacted fast, clamping a hand over her mouth before glancing at Henri for an answer. The figure at the door seemed more upright, more alert. Henri pointed with the shotgun up the stairs. Then he indicated his chest and gestured in the direction of the intruder. Taking this to mean that he should keep Julia out of sight while Henri attended to the visitor, Félix crowded and manhandled the resistant girl up the stairs. Midway, she managed to raise a foot against the wall for leverage, refusing to budge further, and bit his hand with all her force. Under the helmet, stifled with heat and anxiety, Félix winced and cursed.

Below, in the main room, Henri was unaware of the sounds of struggle as he crossed to the door. There was another loud knock, followed by an English voice saying:

'Hello!'

With his free hand, Henri took hold of the knob. There, framed in the doorway, was an attractive, dark-haired woman wearing white jeans, trainers, and a denim jacket. Henri guessed she was in her early forties. He watched her eyes change as she registered the gun, the half-smiling mouth falling slack with bewilderment. Before she had time to think of escape, he grabbed her hard by the left arm and pulled her into the house, kicking the door shut behind her. Henri could see by the woman's expression, the angle of her frightened glance, that she was hearing something from the area of the staircase. Inclining his head, he too could now make out the sound of a violent scuffle. He tightened his grip and turned to see Félix grappling with the girl – who was visible only from the waist down – holding her tight from behind and forcing her against the wall as, in desperation, she tried to kick backwards at his legs.

The scheme, which a few short minutes earlier had seemed to be going like clockwork, was already coming apart. Henri tried to think. If the girl somehow got the better of Félix and made a run for it, this could end in disaster. There was nothing for it but to deal with this other woman and then make sure the American couldn't escape. Meanwhile the newcomer was saying something. Through Henri's visor she looked like a fish gulping for air. Her face was very pale now, and her eyes were bright with alarm. She reminded him of someone . . . the chestnut hair and the full lips. Whoever it was, the memory was unwelcome. As he dragged her towards the cowshed through which he and Félix had entered, he considered shooting her. No one was likely to hear the gun. The nearest house was half a kilometre away. The body might not be found for weeks. Félix had arranged the meeting with the American without telling anyone where he was going. But maybe they should discuss it first. He and Félix were a team. That was the best thing about this whole plan. It was the only team Henri had ever belonged to.

The woman was stubborn. Despite his rough handling she wasn't crying. Instead she was shouting something he couldn't understand, though it seemed plain that she was cursing him. He tasted a bitterness like bile in his mouth. Taking the rifle barrels in both hands, he raised the weapon and jabbed the woman hard with the butt on the side of the head. She seemed to fall in slow motion. He was surprised how light and small she looked as she landed on the cobblestones of the cowshed, one arm trapped under her body. It only took a moment to bind her hands with baling wire and tie his stained handkerchief round her mouth. Not until then did he begin to wonder what on earth she was doing here. Not sent by Cabinet Lamotte to view the house at the same time? That would be a chance in a million. The place had been on the market for three years or more. No one but stupid foreigners wanted these places. Maybe she was a friend of the American's? That must be it, though at present Henri couldn't work out what that might mean for the operation. Félix was the man for that. He had a brilliant brain.

As Henri went back into the main room, it seemed that Félix's strength was being tested to the limit. With ferocious determination the girl had fought and manoeuvred herself round to face her captor at the foot of the stairs. Now, as Félix gasped for breath, she raised her knee and doubled him up with a vicious blow to the groin. Quick to use the advantage she had gained, she made a dash for the door, finding running an unnatural movement with her hands tied behind her back. Henri knew he had only one chance to save his dream. If he failed now, he would be plunged back into emptiness for ever. Hurling aside the shotgun, he rushed at the girl with bull-like power. Her teeth were showing, and the muscles in her neck were taut, as she yelled with rage and frustration. He cannoned into her just as she reached the front door and tried in desperation to nudge it open with her outstretched chin. Seeming to have no more substance than a sack of straw, she was sent sprawling across the flagstones. Unable to break her fall, she hit her head against the angle of the stone fireplace. Henri noticed her legs twitching as she lay, like a dog in sleep.

Close by, Félix was still kneeling, his hand on his crutch and his forehead touching the floor. Henri helped him up, guiding his limping friend to the foot of the stairs. He urged Félix to sit on the second step and was almost tender as he helped him off with the blue helmet. The estate agent's face looked grey, his thin hair matted with sweat. His mouth pursed, Félix groaned. With a backward look at the unconscious American, Henri also took off his helmet. Feeling for a handkerchief to mop his brow, he remembered it was now in the woman's mouth. Instead he used the back of his hand.

'How is it?' he said.

'The cow,' Félix said.

'What do you think? Could she be a friend of the American – the woman?'

'How the hell do I know? She could be anyone for all I know.'

'Félix, this is important. Help me. We have to know how she got here.'

'My balls ache like . . . it's killing me,' Félix moaned.

Henri realised he was getting nowhere. Retrieving the shotgun, he put it into Félix's hands. 'There,' he said, 'don't be afraid to use it. But don't kill the American. We need her alive.'

'Why? Where are you going?' Félix asked.

'Outside . . . only for a moment.'

Henri put on the hot, black helmet and crossed to the door, pausing beside the girl to retrieve her car keys, shaken from her jeans' pocket as she fell. When he had satisfied himself that there were no witnesses, he took a few cautious paces on the parched, sloping stretch of grass in front of the house. At once his eyes were drawn to a maroon and cream Citroën 2CV, parked by the roadside and half-obscured by the lilacs. Another six steps and he saw the crude fleur-de-lys painted on the driver's door, and the flat rear tyre. So that was it. The woman must have had a puncture and, seeing the Peugeot, assumed there was someone in the house. But what terrible luck for him and Félix! What an incredible coincidence! It was as if someone knew their plan and had decided to wreck it for them.

First the cars must be got out of sight. It was like Le Mans out here! And the job would have to be done fast. If there was trouble indoors, Félix was in no fit state to handle it. Henri ran back to the barn, flung open the doors, and drove in the van, leaving enough room to its right for the Citroën. He then raced over to the 2CV, hoping the keys would still be in the transmission. They were. Not wanting to damage the wheel-rim under the punctured tyre, he had no option but to take it easy up the slope and into the temporary garage.

Next, the Peugeot. As he broke cover from behind the lilacs, Henri saw a familiar tractor passing, and drew back. That was close! The tractor driver was Alain, a fellow farmer from St Luc-des-Prés. That showed just how careful they would have to be. Alain wouldn't have recognised the helmet but he sure as hell would have known the body underneath it. Suppose he'd stopped? Asked questions? Henri was no good at inventing stories. Félix was the one for that, and just now he had other things on his mind. The lesson was learned. From now on, extreme care. Making sure the coast was clear, Henri ran to the Peugeot. With no need for restraint, he started the engine and roared across the grass, enjoying the brief surge of power, the sense of being in control. Braking hard behind the lilacs, he switched off, disconnected the mobile telephone, and plucked it from its cradle.

Exhilarated by this decisive action, Henri re-entered the house through the barn. In the cowshed, the woman was conscious. Her white jeans were soiled now as she sat with her knees raised and her head against the wooden trough, which ran the length of the room. On the side of her face was a large purplish stain, like a wine-spill. But still she was defiant, looking up at Henri with fear and confrontation in her eyes. She was their biggest problem, he thought; except that there was an easy answer to it, if Félix would agree. For the moment he put it out of his mind, forcing her to her feet and securing her tied hands to an iron ring with another length of wire.

Next door, Félix looked more tense than his prisoner. Holding the shotgun as though it was porcelain, he was trying to outstare the girl. She had managed to raise herself to her knees, and there were two lines of blood running from her nose to her mouth. As Henri approached he saw there was also blood high on her forehead and in her wheat-coloured hair. She looked shocked and angry.

'Are you completely crazy?' she said in French.

There was no reply.

'You! I'm talking to you! Are you mad? Do you know who my father is?'

Henri nodded.

'When he finds out he'll have you hunted. Do you understand? They'll come looking for you and they'll kill you. Think about it. Is this something worth dying for? Mmm?' Then, in English, she shouted: 'Take that stupid mask off and answer me, you malodorous bastard.' Though there was still no answer from her captor, Julia thought she heard a sound from the cowshed next door. Could that be the woman whose white jeans she had glimpsed across the room during the struggle?

Henri motioned a request to Félix. The estate agent took a handkerchief out of his pocket and, still walking as though recovering from an illness, handed it to Henri. Holding the fabric taut, Henri stooped to tie it round Julia's mouth. With a twist of her head, she refused to co-operate.

'It's disgusting,' she said.

Henri wanted to take hold of her hair and force her to turn, but the thought both repelled and frightened him. The hair was strong, with a life of its own. Her blood would be on his hand and he might never be able to wash it away. Like the nightmare . . . Instead he stationed himself behind her and, catching her unawares, placed the gag fast, with a deftness learned from dealing with stubborn animals.

There was a torrent of incoherent rage as, summoning the last of her strength, Julia rose from the floor. Glaring at the runt with the gun, she wondered whether he was prepared to use it. Now might be the time to find out. Only four yards or so separated her from the door. It was too ridiculous. Only four yards between her and sunlight, birdsong, people doing normal, everyday things. To hell with it. She was sick of playing the victim. Might as well go like Superwoman. For a moment she appeared to relax, even smiling at the guy in the blue helmet. She could see his dumb frown behind the Perspex. Then, with an explosive burst of energy, she darted for the door.

Henri was more agile than he looked. Seeing the movement out of the corner of his eye, he swung to his left, took a pace and kicked out his right leg, tripping Julia in mid-stride. The force of the check lifted her off her feet and flung her headlong. Though she tried to twist her body and break the fall, she gasped with pain as her shoulder once more struck the flagstones. Now he was standing over her, his belly bulging under the T-shirt. It was the first time Julia had ever wanted to hurt someone; to do physical damage. She resolved to nurture the feeling and use it to survive.

Henri put his foot under her body and swung her round. Dragging her to the cupboard under the window by the leg of her jeans, he took off his belt and tied her to the central strut. He could see that contact with the grit on the floor had raked the skin on her side and arm. Pinpoints of blood appeared on the exposed flesh. He registered the fact as though it was a natural sign like any other – like dew on the hedgerows – and had nothing to do with suffering.

There were big decisions to be made. The arrival of the second woman had changed everything. At the foot of the stairs, raising their helmets and speaking in whispers, Henri and Félix reviewed the options.

'The woman?' Henri said.

Félix shrugged. 'We'll have to take her with us. Keep them separate but take her too.'

'Two to guard, two to feed . . . What's the point? We only

want the American. Why not . . . ?' Henri raised an imaginary revolver and closed an eye.

Félix shook his head. 'The nights are light. Disposing of a body . . . Besides, somebody passing could hear the shot. Ask questions. That's how it begins. It's too dangerous.' He paused. 'Anyway, killing wasn't part of the arrangement. That wasn't the plan. Never. You know that.'

Henri seemed unconvinced, but let it drop for the moment. 'But all these cars. What are we going to do with them?'

'What do you mean, "all" these cars?'

'The woman's crate was at the side of the road too. A puncture. It's got a big drawing on the door. I put it in the barn with the van.'

Félix thought for a moment. 'Well, there's only one more than we expected, that's all. It's not a big thing. What we do is you drive her and the American separately to the place. Do the loading in the barn, like we planned. Paul will be ready to help you at the other end. Phone me on the mobile when it's done and I'll drive the American's Peugeot into Beaune. Park where it won't attract attention for a while, up by the city wall, beyond the key-cutter's. Then I'll come back to the place in mine. Yes?'

Henri nodded. He was relieved that Félix had recovered, feeling more secure when his friend took charge like this.

'Then there's just the 2CV,' Félix went on. 'All we can do is leave it here until it's dark. Paul can take charge while we come and dump it.'

'Maybe up on the high road, between Bligny and the canal?' Henri suggested. 'I know some places no one ever goes up there. Chaudenay-le-Château . . . around there.'

'Excellent,' Félix said. 'Very good idea.'

For a moment, before beginning his task, Henri basked in the compliment.

* * *

Two hours later, Robert Ryaux was enjoying his third glass of red wine at the Café Claudette, behind the Place Monge, in Beaune. The *patron*, Dédé, had served with him in Algeria. Whenever Robert was in town – not often in summer because of the tourists – he would drop in for a chat about old times, the absurdities of politicians, the ailments of advancing age, sex and the young, the price of petrol. They discussed these and other topics not with righteous indignation but with a keen sense of the ridiculous.

Robert had come from spending a long half-hour with his mother's notary, Maître Debelfort. The widow Ryaux was selling a small farmhouse to a Dutch family and Robert had volunteered to handle the legal side. At eighty-three she could do without the worry. The meeting had given Robert a thirst. Lawyers always had that effect on him. It was something about their cold, white hands, with manicured nails; their shiny shoes; their smug air of knowing better.

Robert drained his glass and rose to go. 'Right,' he said, 'to arms.'

'Sit down,' Dédé said, already uncorking the bottle. 'The *patron*'s buying.'

'My God,' Robert said, feeling for his heart. 'I'm not sure the old ticker will take the shock.'

Dédé poured. 'There, that's one to tell your grandchildren about.'

'The quality of this stuff, I'll be lucky if I see them again.' Draining the glass, Robert rose once more. This time there would be no detaining him. 'So long, my old friend,' he said. 'Soon, hunting!' He aimed at an imaginary duck and fired with both barrels. 'Paf! Paf!'

'Missed! Hit the postman again!' Dédé said. 'All right, Robert. Till the next one.'

As he made his way towards the old Renault, Robert found himself thinking of Helen Bellman, who was eating with them that evening. She and her husband Tom – an English schoolteacher – had bought the small house next door five years ago. Since then the English couple had spent every Easter and summer in St Luc-des-Prés, becoming well-liked members of the community. Helen and Robert's wife, Yvonne, had hit it off at once. With Robert and Tom, friendship had taken longer to grow. But now the teacher and the former policeman enjoyed each other's company. Robert looked forward to Tom's arrival at the end of the week. Then 'the quarter' (their affectionate term for the northern edge of the village) would once again be alive with its full complement.

Turning off the Beaune ring-road for Bligny-sur-Ouche, Robert climbed up through the vineyards, past the steep road leading to the Hautes Côtes. Once over the brow, he began the long, gradual descent to Lusigny and the valley of the Ouche. Here the road ran straight as a telegraph pole for more than a kilometre, flanked by woods on either side. With a pleasant evening in prospect, Robert began to sing, his rich baritone overflowing the small car. In the distance a grey Peugeot was approaching. Robert thought he recognised the number plate. Yes, without doubt, that was Mademoiselle Walker's car. Her father, the retired American publisher, had asked his advice when they bought it for her. Robert waved. But who was that at the wheel? Not Mademoiselle Walker, that was certain. Hers was a face once seen, never forgotten. Mademoiselle Walker was a beauty. No, this was a man, youngish by the look of him. No time to register his features before he was visible only in the rear-view mirror. A friend of the family, perhaps? Let's hope he's friendlier to them than he was to me, Robert thought.

Sitting on the cool, hard floor in the high-ceilinged, stone room, Julia Walker forced herself to be positive. If she was to live through this, she must find the will to direct her mind down

constructive lines. She must memorise every detail which might
be useful later. Above all she must not put a term on her
captivity, but try to endure it a day at a time. Her side was
sore, her head hurt, her shoulder ached, the gag stank of sweat,
but she was alive. And logic dictated that it must suit her captors
to keep her that way. If sex had been the motive for the kidnap
– and the mere thought of it made her want to retch – something
would have happened by now. Besides, these guys didn't seem
the sort. If anything the bigger of the two, the slob with the
black helmet and the bulging belly, had been almost squeamish
about touching her. The other had been in too much pain to
bother. Somehow the memory of kneeing him in the balls gave
her strength. These men were amateur, vulnerable, beatable,
she told herself.

No, it had to be money. Despite the fact that the family
kept a low profile, it was well known in the area that Julia's
father had been big in newspapers and magazines, both in the
United States and across Europe. He lived in a château, drove
a Mercedes sports, among other cars, and entertained on a scale
not seen in the district for many years. It was therefore
reasonable to assume that he could well afford a ransom.
Kidnaps might be out of fashion, but the desire to gain
something for nothing was not. Spotting the main chance, the
realtor must have roped in an accomplice and suggested they
move fast. By keeping the purchase to herself, Julia had made
it easy for them.

How much would they demand, she wondered? And what
would be her father's reaction? Much as he loved her, he was
not a sentimentalist. Far from it. When he had been active in
business his ruthlessness had been legendary. Dishonesty,
inefficiency and complacency had been punished with a swift
blade. Allied to formidable presence and charm, this adherence
to high standards had won him resounding success and universal
respect. Julia knew her father would be outraged by the crime

itself, as well as by the loss of his only child. There would be no question of paying up and not pursuing the kidnappers. He would never rest until they were found and punished. She wished they knew what a tenacious adversary they had. Assuming they had any intelligence at all, which on the evidence so far seemed doubtful, at the first opportunity she would tell them . . . and keep on telling them, like the Chinese water torture.

But what of Madeleine, her stepmother? Though more durable than her slight figure might suggest, she had a weaker hold on her emotions than Julia's father. Madeleine's overriding fear would be for Julia's physical well-being. Beneath the cool, elegant exterior, her imagination would work overtime, permutating the dreadful possibilities. Madeleine had personal experience of mistreatment. She had once revealed to Julia that her first husband had been a drunk and an abuser.

Julia found that dwelling on these thoughts made the waves of pain more bearable. She wondered how the other woman was, the one whose lower half she had glimpsed at the cottage. It had been quite clear at the time that the unexpected arrival had caused consternation. Later there had been the muffled human sound from the direction of the cowshed. And when Julia had been led from the main room through the cowshed to the barn, the jerk in the black helmet had put a sack over her head. Was that to prevent her from seeing someone, as well as to blind her to the route they took? But where was this someone now, and why had she not been bundled into the van alongside Julia? God, perhaps those half-witted bastards had shot her; left her there, broken, on the grey cobblestones.

At the château close to the village of Bessey-la-Cour, Madeleine Walker was nearing the end of a telephone conversation. Even on this warm evening, she looked fresh in her cream linen jacket, worn without a shirt. The gold necklace bearing grey baroque pearls was lustrous against her skin. Looking out on to the courtyard, with the ruins of the old tower among the tall trees to the west, she spoke in a tone which was not intended to be overheard.

'Perhaps tomorrow,' she said in French. 'Oh, I don't know. Maybe around three. I have things to do. Yes. If I can't, I'll call you. Me too. *Au revoir*.'

She replaced the receiver and crossed the hall; the clicking of her heels the only sound in that echoing space, with its great marble stairway, while the polished flagstones recorded her progress in a fleeting, indistinct image. In the yellow sitting room, its three handsome front windows framing a view of the formal garden with its topiary birds, and the old communal wash-house beyond the high wall, William Walker was reading a book with a blue cover. Slight and fit for a man in his late sixties, he was smiling as Madeleine entered.

'Darling,' he said, 'do you have any idea what Louis XVI wrote in his diary the day the Revolution broke out? Mmmm? Go ahead, have a guess.'

'Help?' Madeleine suggested.

'Not bad,' Walker said. 'It was one word but it wasn't that one. What he wrote was . . . wait for it: "Nothing!" It's rather magnificent, don't you think? I think we would have to call that understatement, wouldn't you say? His world collapses, his country is in turmoil, the guillotine beckons and "nothing!" – big zero.'

'Was he mad, or only stupid?'

'Neither. He was a hunter. A man, perhaps fortunately, burdened with little imagination. He'd shot nothing that day, so "nothing" was what he recorded in his diary.' He paused. 'And what have you recorded in yours today, my darling? Here, come and sit down. Let me fix you a drink.' He rose to make good the offer.

'I was stood up,' Madeleine said.

'Stood up?' Walker said, with exaggerated concern. 'By whom? Who had the audacity?'

'Mrs Bellman . . . Helen, the Englishwoman from St Luc-des-Prés. We were going to talk about the performances next month. I'm surprised. She seems so reliable. I just hope she isn't going to let me down. I've arranged the seating and everything . . . the lights, posters, tickets . . . everything.'

Bringing over a Campari on ice in a cut-glass tumbler, William Walker handed it to his wife. 'There, don't say I don't look after you.' He sat beside her, taking up his own glass of Jack Daniels from beside the yellow silk sofa. 'Well, maybe something came up?'

'Perhaps. It's just that it seems unlike her not to say . . . not to telephone. Ah well . . .' Madeleine smiled, raising her glass in a small toast.

'If it's any consolation, my darling,' Walker said, 'you're not alone among your compatriots in finding the British unreliable partners.' He took a sip of the bourbon. 'Talking of unreliable partners, is Julia favouring us this evening?'

'Who knows?' Madeleine gave a tiny shrug. 'Maybe, maybe not.'

Six kilometres away, in St Luc-des-Prés, Robert Ryaux looked at his watch. 'Seven twenty-five,' he said.

His wife Yvonne, a stout woman with a firm grasp on reality, was carrying a casserole to the table. 'I told you; we eat,' she said. 'She must have been held up somewhere. It's not serious.'

'All the same,' Robert said, 'it's two days now.'

'So? Helen goes where she wants.'

'Maybe it's a lover,' Robert joked. 'A big farmer. Or the wood merchant from Arnay. I've seen old Vauliquet sizing her up.'

Yvonne gave him a look which left him in no doubt as to her opinion on that theory. 'Vauliquet's just an old barrel. Talk sense, man.'

Robert started to get up from the table.

'Where do you think you're going now?' Yvonne barked.

'To have a look in their house. Just to see if there's anything
. . .'

Before he could finish, Yvonne was pointing to his chair.
'If you don't park your backside there this minute, this lot
goes out to the chickens. Understand?'

Robert understood.

Félix had driven the van up to a sheltered cart track overlooking
Chaudenay-le-Château, while Henri had taken the 2CV.
Together they had fitted the spare wheel, peeled off the licence,
removed the number plates, and painted over the fleur-de-lys
in a matter of minutes. Compared with the unwanted
complications of the afternoon, this phase of the plan felt tight
and efficient. They had spoken little, absorbed by what they
were doing. In the nine kilometres they had travelled from the
house, neither of them had seen a single other vehicle. Farming
families went to bed early, ready for a dawn start.

It was ten past one in the morning. When the moon was
released from cloud, objects and creatures were sharp-edged;
the ruins of the château itself, the long piles of graded logs,
the white Charolais cattle in the fields. The only sounds were
the chatter of crickets, the occasional call of an owl, and a dog
barking far below in the valley. Félix inhaled the sweet smell
of grass. In a few moments Henri would join him on foot and
the first, difficult phase would be over.

On a steep gradient, Henri had switched off the engine of
the 2CV. Even though the road was deserted, there was no
point in making unnecessary noise. Henri wished this part of
the operation would take longer. Here he understood what to
do and how to do it. You knew where you were with machinery.
With people, it was different. Like animals, they were
unpredictable, and stupid. Except Félix. He was neither. Félix

was clever, and he cared. When Henri had carried out his mission and climbed up through the woods to where his friend was waiting, he felt sure Félix would be pleased. Turning off the road, he stopped the car at the head of a wide, rutted path between the trees. By the fact that it was overgrown, he judged that it had not seen a vehicle in a long time. When he had extended the stiff, horizontal handbrake, he rummaged in his pocket and took out an old, brass petrol lighter which had belonged to his father. The ridged wheel felt rough under his thumb as he leaned over and used the flame to light up the glove compartment. With his other hand he rifled through the contents, which included a map of Paris, a box of English matches, with some spent ones among the unfamiliar pink heads, several credit card slips, and a half-empty tin of powdery boiled sweets. Having pocketed the slips and the matchbox, he noticed something shiny at the back of the hollow. Henri held the light closer and reached in. First he took out a dented silver bracelet, which he also put in his pocket, and then a small silver torch with a crack in its glass. Round the barrel was wound a dirty piece of Elastoplast with what appeared to be writing on it. Smudged and grimy, it was impossible to understand. He slipped the torch under his belt, took one last look round the interior, extinguished the lighter, and got out of the car. Then he released the handbrake with a slow, deliberate movement, and gave the bodywork a shove to speed its descent. As it gathered momentum the 2CV, stripped of its identifying marks, creaked and rattled on its driverless lurch down the track. Turning away, Henri smiled to himself at a job well done.

CHAPTER TWO

Tom Bellman poured himself a generous measure of Talisker. Every day he savoured this moment, enjoying the small physical sensations; the way the oily malt whisky eddied in the heavy tumbler; the reassurance that the bottle was still two-thirds full; the crack of the ice as it met the spirit. He knew purists disapproved, but this was how he liked it; fire and frost made to marry, under protest.

He settled in the leather armchair, taking the first, considered sip; letting the peppery weight of the scotch linger on his tongue. It was the one swallow that did make a summer, he thought, smiling. And it banished at a stroke the grind and repetition of the day; urging shuttered minds to open wide enough for a glimmer of knowledge. Normally Helen would have been sitting opposite, lending a patient ear to his litany of frustrations. He remembered one evening she had quoted a line at him in mock reproof – an English inscription they had found on a curious stone tablet in the hilltop village of St Romain: 'With moderate blessings be content.'

Tom reflected on his blessings. They were more than moderate, and on the whole he was content with them. Head of St Bede's French department at fifty-one, he would go no further in his profession, but he didn't lose sleep over that. There was more to life than introducing recalcitrant teenagers to the austere charms of Corneille. Tom's marriage had come through earlier storms to a deep and unbreachable understanding. His children, Daisy and Frank, were only an occasional drain on the exchequer. And eventual retirement in Burgundy beckoned, among wild flowers, and ancient stone-built towns, and vineyards. Not a retirement of snailing around in grey shoes and a Panama hat, but a chance to revive old interests and develop new ones; to take better photographs; to nose out the heraldry of the region; to know as much about the place as there was time and energy to know. This time Helen had gone across five days before him, as an advance party. Now, just three more days and he would join her for their long-awaited summer break in St Luc-des-Prés. Roll on . . .

Tom and Helen had last spoken on the telephone two nights ago, when she was about to take a stroll round the village. This after-supper exercise had become a ritual when they were together. He had cautioned her not to talk to strange men and she had told him to stop being an old woman. She also mentioned that she had delivered their car, the beaten-up 2CV, to a garage near Beaune for a service, coming back by bus. She had made him laugh describing how, quite unconcerned, the driver had made an unscheduled stop for a very public pee.

Tom poured another Talisker, promising himself a half-bottle of Juliénas with his Lean Cuisine. He switched on the television. Two women were sitting at a kitchen table, talking about their husbands. The audience laughed at every second clanking line. He changed channels. An earnest young newsreader was affecting concern over famine victims in Somalia. Change. A bovine oaf with a tattoo mimed a crass lyric. Change. An actor in gaiters was pretending to be a farmer, yanking on the teats of a cow as though they were bell-pulls. No change.

Later, the Juliénas reminded Tom of the fierce autumn heat on an afternoon high above Beaujolais, where the grape-pickers had that day begun the *vendange*. Colourful against the parched earth and the green ranks of vines, they had given him and Helen a sense of wellbeing, and continuity. For centuries, at this time of year the landscape had sprung to life in the self-same way. Steel vats might have replaced oak, but no microchip could match the strength and dexterity of human hand and muscle. Tom had wondered whether hundreds of years hence the scene would remain unchanged. Against all the evidence, he suspected it would.

Not much beaujolais, however, was consumed in St Luc-des-Prés, except by foreigners. Friends and neighbours – like Robert and Yvonne Ryaux – preferred swapping anecdotes over unlabelled bottles of rough red, bought in bulk. Tom loved evenings at the Ryaux'. The good humour never flagged, and an endless succession of visiting relatives provided constant cross-currents in the conversation, punctuated by Robert's resounding laugh. His aged mother would often sit in on these sessions, responding with the smile of a spontaneous teenager to her son's robust but affectionate teasing. It was a far cry from Bury St Edmunds, Tom thought, where families hugged their isolation as though they lived in nuclear bunkers. He checked his watch. Ten past eight. He would wash up and then give Helen a ring. Even now, after twenty-three years of marriage, the thought of hearing her voice gave him a charge of anticipation. For a moment he imagined her picking up the phone, barefoot on the smooth flagstones of the main room, under the broad beams of the oak ceiling. He switched on the radio; a local disc jockey introducing Sixties' hits – The Searchers and 'Sweets For My Sweet'. Tom hummed, at the same time trying to memorise the lines he had once known better than the National Anthem. As he washed the whisky glass, the telephone on the sideboard rang. Turning down the music, he answered it.

'Hello.'

'Good day, Tom. How goes it?' It was the rich, unmistakable voice of Robert Ryaux, speaking French with a Burgundian accent.

'Fine, my friend. Much better in three days. And you?'

'Yes. Listen, Tom, Yvonne thought I shouldn't trouble you . . .'

Tom switched off the radio. A dog barked, emphasising the stillness in the kitchen.

'It's funny, this, because I was just going to ring Helen,' he said.

'Well, it's about Helen that I'm calling.' Robert sounded subdued.

Tom's mouth felt dry. 'What is it?'

'A couple of things. Like I told Yvonne, they may be nothing at all . . .'

'Go on.'

'Tom, we haven't seen Helen for two days now. Neither her nor the little car. I just looked in the barn, even in the house, but nothing. The door is unlocked, some windows are open, but . . . nothing, no one.'

'Well the car was due in for a service. I knew about that. But it should have been back by now. Maybe something cropped up.'

'That's right,' Robert agreed. 'Sometimes it's like that. She has things to do, places to go, people to see. But also Monsieur Walker called me. It seems Helen didn't arrive for a meeting with his wife at the château yesterday afternoon. Madame Walker said she must have misunderstood the arrangement. You know about that?'

Tom felt a clutch of alarm. Helen had never misunderstood an arrangement in her life. She had told him about the proposed meeting two nights ago. It had meant a great deal to her. She and Madeleine Walker were planning a week's performances of *A Midsummer Night's Dream* by a Bury drama group at the château in August. Helen was hoping this long-cherished project would turn into an annual event. Meanwhile, though from such contrasting backgrounds, in organising it she and Madeleine had become friends. For Helen, letting her down would be unthinkable.

'Yes,' Tom said, unable to disguise his nervousness. 'Yes, I knew. It was important for Helen. And you mean she didn't telephone to explain?'

'Not a word. And like I say, unfortunately we haven't seen her to ask her. She was coming to eat last night but she didn't arrive. It wasn't a problem of course, but with the other thing . . .'

Tom tried to take it all in. Punctual to an almost neurotic degree, Helen had missed two appointments within a few hours, one of them with a woman of considerable influence, without letting anyone know. What the hell was going on?

'Are you still there my friend?' Robert said.

'Yes, yes, I'm still here but I just don't know what to say. Helen never lets people down. Never. In twenty-three years she's never done that.' Thinking back over what Robert had said, he went on: 'And you mean Walker just called you about Helen? That seems a strange thing for him to do.'

'No, not just Helen,' Robert said. 'There was something else.'

Tom sensed his control eddying away.

'Tom, yesterday the Walkers' daughter, Julia – you know . . . ?'

'Yes, of course. The beautiful girl.'

'Well, she was kidnapped.'

'My God. Where?'

'We don't know. Her car is missing. A man telephoned the Walkers this morning. He wanted ten million francs. I telephoned you this afternoon but you weren't there.'

'I was at the school. This is terrible, Robert. I can't believe it . . . , it's such a quiet little corner. How are the Walkers?'

'Very concerned, of course. He's tough, Monsieur Walker, but madame . . . she's very upset, even though she isn't the mother. The pig who rang told them not to contact the police or he would . . . well, you know what these animals say. The Walkers want me to help.'

'How? Oh, with the investigation you mean? Yes, I understand.' Tom felt overwhelmed by this new revelation, on top of Helen's inexplicable non-appearance. The world, which ten minutes ago had seemed ordered, offering hope, had now taken a sickening lurch into chaos. What was he to make of it? What should he do? Could he afford to wait the three days before he was due in St Luc anyway? His immediate instinct was to go at once; leave everything – work, everything – jump in the car and drive through the night.

Robert's next statement confirmed his inclination. 'Monsieur Walker wants to see me,' the ex-policeman was saying, 'to discuss this affair, tomorrow afternoon.'

Convinced now that any action was better than none, Tom felt calmer. 'You don't think there could be any connection . . . Helen and Julia? In any case, what could it possibly be?' he said, half to himself.

'I don't know, my friend. I doubt it. For Helen it's not so serious. I'm sure. But I don't know. I'm only wondering if it might be useful for you to talk to the Walkers as well? Maybe they can help. To talk to everyone. Get to the bottom of this thing.'

Tom did a rapid review of the complications. Only two days remained of the term. He felt sure that, in the circumstances, Gerald would let him go. Anyway, to hell with Gerald. The evidence, which seemed compelling, suggested that Helen was missing. Beside that, nothing else mattered. 'I'll be there,' he said. 'Tomorrow, before lunch, I'll be there.'

* * *

The moment he had put down the receiver, he dialled the French code and the eight figures of his own number in St Luc-des-Prés. Maybe the whole thing was just a chain of misunderstandings, unexpected changes of plan, bizarre coincidences. That quite often happened, even to the most conscientious individuals. The distinctive French dialling tone mocked him. Still he let it ring. Maybe Helen was in the garden. Maybe she had sprained her ankle and was unable to get to the phone. Maybe . . . But after two or three minutes, and with reluctance, Tom accepted the fact that, for the moment at least, Helen was elsewhere. No, he mustn't delude himself. It seemed she had been elsewhere, out of contact, for two whole days . . . since their last conversation, in fact.

The first, the obvious assumption, was an accident. Perhaps after she had collected the 2CV from the garage, Helen had been involved in a collision, suffering slight concussion? Tom rang Robert back and asked him to look up the numbers of the two nearest hospitals, in Arnay-le-Duc and Beaune, as well as the big one in Dijon. What did they call that . . . ? The Bocage, that was it. Robert also volunteered the numbers of the gendarmeries in Bligny-sur-Ouche and Beaune, urging Tom not to be alarmed. He was sure there was a simple explanation. Perhaps, in half an hour, Helen would walk into the Ryaux' house, fit and well, with a colourful story of mishaps and telephones out of order. Tom heard himself humour this comforting theory, more to go along with Robert's efforts to distract him than because he believed it.

Tom started with friends and other neighbours in Burgundy, including Monique and Zazie, whom Helen often visited. Though delighted to hear from Tom, Monique had no news of Helen either. The day before yesterday they had planned to drive into Autun together for lunch, but Helen hadn't appeared. It had been a loose arrangement and Monique assumed there had been a last-minute hitch, but since then they hadn't spoken. Roland Viggars, the wayward old puppeteer, who had enlivened many an evening for Tom and Helen with Rabelaisian stories of touring Europe with his wooden troupe, was no wiser. Through a torrent of good-natured ribaldry, all Tom could make out was that if Helen did turn up, Roland would invite her into his bed. Even in his anxious state, Tom couldn't help laughing. The thought of Roland managing anything that called for moderate effort after the second bottle was hilarious. As he hung up, he remembered an evening when the zestful satyr had farted with such abandon during a lively account of disaster in Zurich that he had fallen off his chair.

Next, Tom steeled himself for the hospitals. A matter-of-fact woman in Dijon said that yesterday there had been a fatal accident in the region. Stifling panic, Tom pressed for details. To his relief the woman said the victim had been a truck driver, heading north from Bourg-en-Bresse with a load of chickens. He had fallen asleep near Pouilly-en-Auxois and plunged off the A6. Feathers all over the road, she said. And he was only twenty-eight. Tom thanked her. Apart from that neither local gendarmes nor accident departments had any reports of a recent major accident, nor of anything concerning an Englishwoman.

By now it was ten-thirty. Again Tom tried his own number in St Luc-des-Prés, with the same result as before. He was tempted to leave for Folkestone straight away. Would there be ferries at this time of night? There must be. Freight must cross the Channel at all hours. In any case there was the tunnel, which he tended to forget because Helen, who suffered from claustrophobia, had made him promise not to use it. They both preferred the sleek, fast Sea Cat, which sliced through the narrow straits in a mere thirty minutes, offering decent coffee, duty frees, and pleasurable anticipation. But what if, soon after he set out, Helen rang to explain everything? What if she had driven to Paris, or Auxerre, or Dijon at short notice and had been so carried away she forgot to ring? Or she couldn't get to a phone box? Or she had broken down in the middle of nowhere? Could that be it? No, of course not. She would have been in touch by now. Unless . . . unless someone had prevented her from being in touch. But why? A sensible, middle-aged woman? Tom saw her now, in his mind's eye, warm, vital, engaged in life and not an onlooker. An attractive, middle-aged woman; to Tom, beautiful. Could it be that? Sex? Tom locked the repellent thought out of his mind. Helen was resourceful. She could take care of herself. And as for any connection with Julia Walker, whom she had met perhaps twice, where was the logic in that?

Tom realised he was letting his imagination run further than was good for it. He would spend the night here and if there was still no reply when he rang the cottage in St Luc again at . . . what time? Seven? No, six o'clock in the morning, he would call the Headmaster, (Gerald wouldn't be very pleased about that) and put his foot down hard for the coast.

In the double bed that seemed so empty, he was hot and restless. He had exchanged Helen's pillow for his own because it still bore the scent of her hair. For the past few days he had thought of her being apart from him, but not of her being at risk. Now he was tormented by fears that she was helpless, lonely, afraid. The demons he had earlier managed to suppress reared again out of the night . . . Rape, murder, violence, cruelty . . . Heartless, mindless, soulless acts of degradation happening everywhere, every day; the dark, vicious, pitiless evil, deep in the shadows of the cave.

Sweating, he threw off the sheet and looked at the alarm clock. Three-fifteen. An hour later in France. Tom reached out and dialled the house in St Luc for the third time. Again the tone was unrelenting. He decided he could wait no longer. He would set out at once and ring Gerald from the port. Bundling jeans and shirts into a holdall, he tried to be disciplined about leaving. Notes for the milkman, the paper-shop . . . who else? Never mind. He could contact the rest when he got there. Switch off the central heating, lock all the doors, take the perishables out of the fridge, put the rubbish in the bin . . . He looked in the bathroom mirror. Unshaven, hair wild, eyes red-rimmed. Tom, he thought; is it finally happening? The thing you read about and think 'poor sod' – is it finally happening to you?

By the time he joined the M11 outside Newmarket, the sun was breaking through the July haze. The beauty of it made his eyes fill for a moment. Too much scotch, he thought. Emotions too near the surface. He could picture the same dawn in Burgundy, the broad summer landscape enticing the heat like a lover. But where was Helen seeing it? From the isolated wreckage of the Citroën? From a makeshift prison in a strange town? Was she blindfolded and not seeing it at all? Tom put on a cassette of Harry Connick Jr to distract himself. It was a favourite of Helen's. Finding it too sentimental, he changed to an old Muggsy Spanier.

As he crossed the soaring Dartford bridge, Tom thought he wasn't a single person any more. He was no more than a half searching for its complement; no longer whole without it. Was that unhealthy, he wondered? Was that degree of dependence absurd? George Galbraith had said so once, meaning to be honest rather than offensive. 'You can't live your life like a bloody Siamese twin,' he had said; 'joined at the hip. People have operations for that. What happens when the other half drops off the perch? Are you supposed to snuff it as well? Bollocks to that! Man's a hunter, a loner. Put your faith in you, mate. It's all you can count on.'

At Folkestone there were a surprising number of holidaymakers getting an early start, and the inevitable pantechnicons that looked capable of sinking the stoutest vessel. A pale fat man was yawning and stretching, revealing the hairy suet of his belly. Catching sight of him, his carrot-haired partner turned back to the windscreen and shut her eyes. Was that despair, or just a sleepless night, Tom wondered? Then again, maybe she wanted to treasure the vision.

Lucky enough to get one of the two last tickets remaining for the crossing, Tom made calls from a public telephone in the departure lounge. Full of irrational hope he once again dialled his own French number. The unrevealing tone repeated itself. Next he rang Robert Ryaux, who wouldn't know how to be downhearted. Like Tom, he would have been up since dawn, busying himself about the place.

'Good day, my friend.' Sure enough the Frenchman sounded full of energy.

'Good day, Robert. I'm at Folkestone. Any news?'

'Unfortunately not. I've just been to your place. It's the same. Forgive me but I even looked in the bedrooms. Of course it's possible Helen came back very late and left very early. The car still isn't in the barn.'

'No. I rang several times.'

'Perhaps she's planning a little surprise for you. Something to please you.' Robert went on, trying to cheer him up. 'There was no news from the hospitals or the cops?'

'Nothing,' Tom said. 'Anyway Robert, I'm on my way. I should be in St Luc at about two o'clock.'

'Great,' Robert said. 'Good journey.'

The headmaster of St Bede's, Gerald Maynard, whom Robert had never much liked, was sympathetic. He said Tom must take as long as he needed. He would find someone else to do Tom's invigilating and exam marking, or if necessary tackle them himself, though his French was rusty. He wanted to be kept in touch with developments and said if there was anything else he could do, Tom knew where he was.

On the crossing Tom dozed for a few minutes, feeling worse

when he woke. Even in that brief sleep, he had an anxiety dream. In it he was being chased across an ice-floe which cracked and parted from its neighbours, just as he reached the edge. He snapped awake with a violent shudder to find the carrot-haired woman staring at him. As their eyes met, she shut hers again. Tom imagined them swivelling like an iguana's, under the lids with their pale ginger fringe. The thought made him bilious, and he heaved himself up to find a cup of coffee.

In France, as usual, the roads seemed as uncluttered as those of a nation with three million inhabitants rather than sixty. On this first leg to Paris, he and Helen would always feel as carefree as kids let out of school after a boring term. They would test each other on the words of Sixties' songs, and compete in naming the states of the Union and their capital cities. Exasperated at his inability to win, Tom had also introduced the listing of Scottish football clubs but, despite her lack of interest in the game, Helen had soon mastered those too. Queen of the South was her particular favourite. She was better read than him, and he often thought she should have been the teacher. Admiring her was part of his love for her. At the beginning he had been frustrated by her reluctance to make more of her talents, until he realised that she didn't feel the need. It was enough for her that their quiet, private development made her feel more complete. Tom was torn between encouraging these thoughts of her, which crowded in on him, and keeping them at arm's length, for fear they overpowered him.

At the big service station, where he and Helen always stopped for a cappuccino and a ham sandwich, Tom felt drained of energy. He supposed it was a reaction, combined with lack of food and the early start. Nevertheless he had to get a grip. This was just the beginning of who knew what? He was going to need every atom of his strength and determination to see it through. Unless of course Helen was sitting there smiling when he got to St Luc, with the one plausible story he had failed to foresee? But after another abortive phone call, that hope too began to evaporate.

When, three and a half hours later, he saw Burgundy spread to the horizon on all sides, vast and fertile, Tom felt a mixture of emotions. The view, foreign yet familiar, never failed to make his heart leap, and yet on this occasion the smiling face might conceal a dark design. Though not the scenery for secrets, its natural openness might have been abused by human malevolence. Pulling off the A6 at the slip-road for Pouilly-en-Auxois, Tom was on the last lap. Passing the turning to the pottery run by an English couple, where Helen had treated him to a cup and saucer the colour of cornflowers, he thought how he and she would stop for a beer in Arnay-le-Duc – the first of the holiday; the ritual toast to a happy stay. Outside Chez Camille, Helen's favourite restaurant when they were in funds, an earnest family of four were easing out of a new Mercedes, looking as though they faced a firing squad rather than a lunch to remember.

Six kilometres beyond Arnay, on the Chagny road, the tiny lettering on the sign at last proclaimed St Luc-des-Prés. Tom signalled, climbed to the crossroads, and turned left for the village. Like dark sentinels, two hawks perched on telegraph poles took off at his approach. A tractor towing a trailer came towards him, filling most of the road. The driver waved and grinned, as each made space for the other. It was Jean-Jacques, Robert's friend, who sometimes came over for a game of *boules* on summer evenings.

Tom pulled up in front of the house. Though long and low, it was substantial. Flanking the main room paved with flagstones on the ground floor were a bedroom, and a large kitchen adjoining the barn. Upstairs, under the pantiled roof, were three more bedrooms and space for another. Tom tried the dull brass knob on the green door – the locals called the colour 'the English style' – lingering for a moment on the forlorn chance that it might be snatched open from the inside to reveal Helen smiling, and calling out: 'Surprise, surprise!' But there was no such welcome. Tom went in. On the stone mantelpiece to his left stood a jam jar full of wild flowers, and on the maroon velvet seat of one ramshackle armchair lay the wide-brimmed straw hat Helen often wore for gardening. Tom picked it up, running his fingers round the brim. Unable to bear the unaccustomed silence, he called out:

'Helen! Helen, darling!' The stillness was more profound than before.

The bedrooms were bright with sun, the open windows a reminder that Helen had touched them a short while ago. Sitting for a moment on the edge of their cast-iron bed, in the big room with a balcony overlooking the garden, Tom rubbed his eyes. Now he felt weary and without direction. For the first time in his life he faced a problem with no circumference. Unlike a lack of money, or an unhappy child, an illness, or a career disappointment, it couldn't be defined, and therefore couldn't, in theory, be remedied. Better not to dwell on it too much for the moment; tiredness distorted everything.

As Tom opened the great double doors of the cool barn, he noticed three swallows' nests high on the left-hand wall, under the hay platform. Like the rest of the house, the space spoke not of presence but of absence. The only trace of Helen's car was a blotch of oil patches on the earth floor.

In the kitchen, both the window at the courtyard end and the French windows leading to the little wooden gallery and the garden were open. More than any other, this room was a reflection of Helen's taste. Dried flowers hung from the beams – not polite bunches bought in shops, but Impressionist clusters of colour Helen had picked and prepared herself. All the cups and plates on the ancient country dresser had been bought in local junk shops. Many were chipped and cracked, and none matched any other, but they all chimed with the happy mood of the house. The rectangular oak table, with one leg shorter than the rest, and six odd chairs, had all been picked up for next to nothing in the dealers' quarter of Beaune, behind the railway station, or at Emmaus, where the proceeds went to a community of the homeless. The pictures and baskets and yellow enamel storage tins also testified to an eye for a pleasing bargain. This was not the lifeless taste of an interior designer, but the flair of an enthusiast confident in her style.

As Tom took a Stella Artois from the fridge, he heard a familiar, resonant baritone calling from the main room.

'Hello, Mister Professor!'

'Come in, Robert!' Tom said, replacing the bottle. Beer was no drink for his neighbour, who now stood framed in the doorway; a ruddy, round-faced figure, with a prominent belly under a blue, workman's shirt, a strong straight back, and an outstretched hand. Robert Ryaux would still have boyish zest at eighty, Tom thought.

'My friend,' Robert boomed. 'You had a good journey?'

'Not bad, thank you Robert. Quick enough. I'm really delighted to see you. A little *canon*?'

'But of course.'

Tom took an unlabelled bottle of red wine from the rack, uncorked it, and filled two water glasses. '*Tchin, tchin.*'

'*Tchin,*' Robert echoed, taking a deep gulp. 'Well,' he went on, 'this is a bad business, Thomas.'

'Nothing yet?' Tom asked.

Robert shook his head. 'I drove many kilometres this morning looking for Helen's car, and Mademoiselle Walker's but . . .' He gave a slight shrug.

'That reminds me,' Tom said. 'I meant to check with the garage that Helen had picked it up. A moment, Robert.' Tom went through to make the call, returning less than five minutes later.

'Well?' Robert said.

'It was a young mechanic. He said a woman collected the 2CV the day before yesterday, in the afternoon. I asked him whether it was the same woman who brought it in, an Englishwoman? He said yes, she was English.'

'Did you ask him how she paid?'

'There was no need. Helen has an account there.'

'That was the afternoon of the kidnap,' Robert said, thinking aloud.

'I'm frightened, Robert. My mind keeps racing round in circles.'

'Fear is useless,' Robert said. 'It serves no purpose. We will find her, believe me. It's certain.' For emphasis, he topped up Tom's glass.

At quarter to four, when Tom had been round to see Yvonne, he and Robert drove to the Walkers' château. Even in a crisis – perhaps more than ever in a crisis – Robert remained irrepressible. Tom knew he was as aware as anyone of the seriousness of the situation, and yet the former policeman refused to waste energy on what he would regard as self-indulgent worry. For him the only thing to do was find the enemy and defeat him. The rest was wind. It was an attitude Tom envied. As Robert whistled at the wheel, Tom could imagine him in tight corners, earning the admiration of his men; raids on dark Parisian ghettoes, confronting armed drug-pushers. Perhaps Robert had whistled then too, as he put the fear of God into them.

For the first four years of their acquaintance, the two had not been close. While not by any means hostile, Robert had been less ready than his wife Yvonne, to involve himself with the English couple. Despite his ebullience, there was about him a reserve when confronted with the unfamiliar. Combined with Tom's undemonstrative Anglo-Saxon manner, this had brought about a relationship which, though not altogether uneasy, lacked warmth.

And then, in the course of a single evening the previous summer, it had all changed. At the time Yvonne had been away visiting a sister in Carcassonne, while Helen had gone to Maligny for an evening of Molière performed by English undergraduates on tour. Deciding to give culture a miss, Tom had been passing his neighbour's door when, to his surprise, Robert had invited him in. On the table was an unopened bottle of whisky with two glasses. As the level of the liquid sank and sank over the next three hours, the conversation became more animated and confiding. Tom made Robert laugh with accounts of eccentric teachers and unruly kids while, with enormous gusto, Robert had told stories of serving with the army in Algeria; a tour of duty which had allowed him to retire early from the police force. When the discussion turned to hunting, one of Robert's passions, he amazed Tom by bringing through from the ground-floor bedroom two tear-gas grenades and his old service revolver. This, he said, was the only way to deal with foxes. Toss in a grenade and, when the pest emerged, plug it between the eyes. Tom was appalled, but such was the unsentimental relish of the telling, that he couldn't help laughing. It was simple. To Robert, living in a farming community, the fox was vermin, to be dispatched fast and without pain.

The ice was broken. After that, Tom and Robert would sometimes go out for evenings together. A favourite haunt was the bar overlooking the square in Bligny-sur-Ouche. There, well fortified, they would offer free advice to referees handling televised football games, and Robert would tease the wood-merchant, Raymond Vauliquet, whose partiality to red wine had obliged his family to ban him from using the mechanical saw after eleven a.m. These sessions had encouraged Tom to be more outgoing – a development which had pleased Helen, for his sake.

Robert was still whistling when they turned down the lane leading to the château. As they passed the rose-coloured public wash-house, still maintained though no longer used, Tom reflected that it was an extraordinary friendship. Different backgrounds, different attitudes, in many ways different worlds; the practical and the clumsy; the uncomplicated and the ironic; the demonstrative and the wry. And yet, perhaps because of the contrast, it worked. Each had something to give the other. Robert called Tom Mr Professor, while Tom nicknamed him Mr Commissioner. Above all, one thing was indisputable, Tom thought, as Robert pulled up in the courtyard of the château: there was no man on earth with whom he would rather face the unknown.

Madeleine Walker herself met them at the door. Tanned, in a yellow dress, with elegant flat shoes, she looked cool and serene, despite the anxiety in her eyes. Leading them across the polished hall to the drawing room she made easy conversation, for all the world as though they were visiting VIPs. Nevertheless, Tom felt awkward. Their plight might be similar but the power and influence at the Walkers' disposal gave him a momentary feeling of hopelessness. He wondered what was the point of being here when he might be out looking for Helen. But looking where? At that moment Robert caught his eye and winked.

In the drawing room, with its exuberant flower arrangement in a large ornamental urn, overlooking the geometrical gardens, they were joined by William Walker. His bearing and manner proclaiming him to be intelligent and discerning, he looked a man ill-equipped to deal with violent reality. Those of his close acquaintance, however, including Madeleine, knew otherwise. Success in publishing had made him more enemies than friends. But unlike the enemies, the friends were in very high places, and notable for their loyalty to his qualities – steadfastness, courage, principle. Nevertheless, he was apt to strike strangers as hard and judgemental. Robert, whose acquaintance with Walker had begun three years ago at the August fête in St Luc, was used to this carapace. Tom, who despite Helen's friendship with Madeleine had met him only once, at the Walkers' charity barbecue the previous summer, still found him forbidding.

Inviting them to sit down, Walker came straight to the point. 'So, Mr Bellman. It seems we may share a problem,' he said.

In reply, Tom found himself trying to say several things at once. 'What, in the sense that Helen and Julia are both missing you mean? Well, yes, I suppose we do, but beyond that I haven't thought . . . I mean there can't be anything else linking them, can there? It's absolutely terrible what's happened to Julia but unfortunately the motive's clear enough, isn't it? Whereas with Helen . . .'

Robert shifted his bulk on the sofa, ill at ease in such opulence, and unable to follow the English conversation. Realising this, Madeleine interpreted for him.

'What enquiries have you made?' Walker asked.

'Well, everything I can think of really,' Tom said. 'From the other end, anyway. Local hospitals, the gendarmerie, friends. There are other people we know here but it's just unthinkable that Helen wouldn't have been in touch by now. And then the meeting with Madame Walker,' he went on, turning to Madeleine; 'Helen's just never let anybody down in her life. Never.'

Madeleine Walker gave him a small, sympathetic smile.

'Let's just try and be objective for a moment here,' Walker said. 'What facts do we have? The facts are that in a small, peaceable, rural area, two women go missing, probably within twelve hours of each other. One, Julia, we know has been kidnapped, but we don't know by whom.'

'Doesn't get us very far does it?' Tom said.

Robert nodded as Madeleine translated for him.

Noticing, Walker said: 'I'm sorry, Robert. This is stupid. Let's do it in French.' Speaking in an accent more workmanlike than polished, he went on: 'No, I accept it doesn't get us very far. But suppose for one moment that rather than being isolated incidents, these two events were somehow related.'

'I'm sorry, I don't see what you're getting at,' Tom said.

'Simply this. We can't rule out the possibility, and I put it no stronger, that Julia and your wife went missing at the same time.'

'And in the same place?' Robert asked.

Walker nodded. 'It's a possibility we can't dismiss.'

Tom was dumbfounded. 'But that's ridiculous,' he said. 'What on earth would they be doing together? They've only met . . . I don't know, a few times. I'm not all that sure they've even spoken to each other.'

'Yes. On several occasions,' Madeleine said. 'When Helen came to see me.'

'But why . . . ?' Tom was too confused to formulate his thoughts.

'I have no answers, Mr Bellman,' Walker said. 'Maybe a chance meeting? A shared interest we weren't aware of? A mutual friend? I don't know. All I'm saying is that the alternative – two women missing, here, simultaneously in separate incidents – is just as hard to accept; maybe harder.'

'But did the kidnappers say anything about anyone else?' Tom said.

Walker shook his head. 'But of course they wouldn't, would they? Especially if this development was unforeseen.'

After a moment's silence, while he pondered Walker's theory, Tom said: 'What are you planning to do then?'

Walker leaned forward. 'Make that "we", Mr Bellman. What are we going to do?'

Tom was somehow encouraged and flattered by this inclusion from a man used to going his own way.

'Well, let me tell you,' Walker went on. 'These people are making the usual threats about what'll happen if we contact the police. I think they're bluffing, but we're talking human lives here and I'm not about to take any chances. Absolutely none. This is a small community and they'd very soon spot unusual activity. Or be told about it. Now I know some gentlemen . . . some very experienced gentlemen . . . whom I could draft in to help me. If you will it's one of the few useful legacies of my time in business. However, these gentlemen do not know the lie of the land. Neither are they familiar with the language. Either way there is a distinct danger that they would stick out like quarterbacks in a farmyard.' Walker allowed himself a small smile. 'Our friend here, on the other hand,' he turned to Robert, 'our friend Robert knows every blade of grass. He's a highly respected member of the community, and he's familiar with police methods.'

All three looked to Robert for his reaction. He remained impassive. 'If you accept, Robert, we could make the best possible start without causing suspicion. Further down the line it may well be necessary to organise back-up, of one sort or another. But for the moment, discreet enquiries, listening to gossip, watching movements . . . you know what I'm talking about; basic intelligence gathering. That's what'll smoke these bastards out, not battalions in blue with guns and klaxons. I'm sure of it. What do you say?'

Once again, attention shifted to Robert. After a moment, he nodded, twice. 'It's been a long time,' he said, 'but I'll do what I can.'

'That's magnificent,' Walker said.

'Thank you, Robert,' Madeleine said.

'It goes without saying we'll make a suitable arrangement . . .' It was plain that Walker was about to mention money.

In reply, Robert rose from the sofa. 'I don't want it,' he said. 'I wouldn't accept it. I'll do all I can for you and madame . . .' he turned to Tom, who had also taken his cue to get up, '. . . and Tom. And, more importantly, for the young women.'

It touched Tom to hear Helen bracketed with Julia in youth, though once more it seemed to underline her vulnerability.

'The kidnapper said they'd call tomorrow morning with details of how and where they want the ten million francs delivered,' Walker said. 'Meanwhile, of course, I demanded proof of life.'

Madeleine cast her eyes down at the cold phrase.

'They agreed?' Robert said.

'The man . . . he sounded young, but who can tell? . . . said: "in due course". Big of him, wasn't it?' Walker let the anger show through. 'But remember, Mr Bellman, it's in their paramount interest to see that the hostage – or hostages – remain in good shape.'

Looking grave, Tom nodded. 'When you next make contact,' he said, 'will you please ask, specifically, about Helen? If I could just know she's . . .'

'Of course,' Walker replied without hesitation. 'You have my word.'

As Tom and Robert took their leave, Robert asked the Walkers whether they had any idea who it was he had seen driving Julia's car the previous afternoon on the Beaune road. Puzzled and concerned, Madeleine replied that when she was in Burgundy, or indeed anywhere else, Julia tended to live an independent life, introducing them only to the friends she wished them to meet. Pressed for a description, Robert explained that apart from his evident youth and his sunglasses, the driver had been a speeding blur. Nevertheless, he said, the direction the Peugeot was travelling in might prove significant.

As he and Robert crossed the courtyard to rejoin the car, Tom was preoccupied with everything Walker had said. Seeing the need to distract him, Robert smiled.

'Now it's you who must learn, Mr Professor,' he said.

'What do you mean?'

'An investigator needs a partner. You will be my partner.'

'That's ridiculous. This should be handled by professionals. I don't know the first thing about the methods.'

Robert considered for a moment. 'You understand the method of buying a beer?' he said.

Tom shrugged. 'Sure,' he said.

'Excellent. We'll start with that.'

CHAPTER THREE

When Julia woke the sun was up. Through the one window high in the rough stone wall she could see the first promise of a warm summer's day; a day when she might have driven to La Rochepôt for lunch with friends, or gone antiqueing in the dealers' ghetto of Beaune. On her last foray she had seen several things she coveted for the cottage, including a magnificent rustic sideboard in faded walnut, with dull brass handles like fists holding tiny batons. Instead here she was, bound, bored, and sore, her bladder bursting. In the far corner was a piebald enamel bucket, but how was she supposed to manoeuvre with tied hands? Raising herself, she clambered to her feet and, stiff from the hard floor, tried kicking the massive door. She could feel the jolt of the impact the length of her spine. Yelling half in pain and half to attract attention, she kicked again. The hollow boom reverberated in the space beyond the door, and the sound of the cries dispersed like smoke. Perhaps the thugs were still in their fetid beds, confident that their prisoner was secure. But the other woman must be able to hear her? If so she might be comforted by evidence of a fellow human being. If she was alive to be comforted . . . Julia held the thought at arm's length and resumed her barrage.

After several painful minutes, just as she was about to give up and try later, she heard the snug insertion of a key in the great cast-iron lock. At the same time a young voice shouted in French.

'Stand back, mademoiselle. I'm going to count to three and then I'm going to fire. I have a shotgun. So stand well back.'

There was no sensible option but to obey. It must be an empty threat, Julia reasoned. Firing through doors made no sense whatsoever. But she doubted whether logic was the kidnappers' strong suit, and it was impossible to know how violent these strange, edgy misfits might become. Best, therefore, to assume the worst. Stepping backwards, she retreated to the corner. The warning hadn't sounded like either the man in the black mask, or his skinny accomplice. Its tone had been more tentative, and the Burgundian accent thicker. Apprehensive, in spite of her determination to be strong, Julia waited for the blast.

As she had suspected, it never came. Instead the key turned and the door opened to reveal a short, somehow lopsided figure with what looked like a coarse, grimy flour-bag over his head. Irregular holes had been cut for his eyes and further gashes for the nose and mouth. The images that immediately sprang to Julia's mind were Halloween, and the famous photograph of William Bonney – Billy the Kid – the one where he stood there, knowing his fame, with that incongruous, tall, battered hat; unable to belong – both dangerous and pitiable.

Holding the shotgun steady, the gaoler re-locked the door and pocketed the key. As his attention shifted back to Julia, face and flour-bag were not quite aligned and he had some difficulty re-locating the eye-holes. Tight-lipped, Julia sealed an involuntary smile.

'What do you want?' the unlikely desperado said.

'I have to use the bucket,' Julia said, her voice muffled by the gag.

'So, use it.' He motioned with the shotgun.

'Look, asshole, think about it . . .' Julia began in English, before switching to French. 'Untie my hands.'

'Don't t-t-tell me what to do. I give the orders.' For the first time his stammer was apparent.

Julia felt the blood rise, but forced herself to sound measured. 'OK, OK. Untie my hands . . . please. Otherwise, you'll have to do it. Right? You'll have to lay down your popgun and you'll have to take down my jeans and pants. And if that doesn't turn you on, I'll die of water retention. Understand? And you'll be blamed. No money. No nothing. And the rest of your life in the slammer. Now, is that what you want? Mmmm?'

After a short pause, the young man took one hand off the gun, indicating that Julia should turn round. Resting the butt on the floor and leaning the barrels against the small of her back, he clenched the weapon between his knees and unlocked the handcuffs. Released for the first time in over twelve hours, Julia felt an excruciating seizure of pain in both shoulders. Clenching back a groan, she inched her arms to her sides, knowing that though the urge to take on this pathetic adversary was powerful, her body could not comply. In an agony of cramp, and feeling the nudge of the gun between her shoulder-blades, she walked over to the bucket.

'You want to watch, like a dirty little boy?' she said, as the crumpled figure showed no sign of turning away. 'You've never seen a woman before, and you want to watch? Just wait till I tell your friends out there how you were so desperate for a cheap thrill, you had to watch a woman take a pee.'

To Julia's relief the taunt worked. The mask was turned to the wall, while the gun kept its blind eyes pointing in her direction.

'Are you going to tell me your name?' she said. 'Now we're sharing this intimate moment? You know mine, I guess.'

There was no reply.

'Only, if we're going to be spending some time together . . . I wonder what it is? Something strong, probably. Georges, maybe? Or Jacques? Something you can respect. Not like these wishy-washy names – Emile, and like that. Mmmm? Are you going to tell me?'

'Shut your mouth,' the man said.

'Well, that's very friendly, I must say. That's the reply of a man who isn't very sure of himself. And that's strange because you look like a man who's *very* sure of himself. A man who understands . . . Henri, maybe? Won't you tell me? Please?'

'They t-t-told me,' the man began and then cleared his throat; 'they told me not to.'

'They "told" you? Who are they to "tell" you anything? Mmmm?' Julia rose from her squat. 'Just a couple of guys. No different from you. Except a little less mature maybe. You do what you want. They can't "tell" you anything . . . Charles! Could that be it?' Julia said, zipping up her men's jeans. 'You can turn round now . . . Charles.'

The man faced her. 'It's not my name,' he said.

'Oh, OK. Well, now we're getting somewhere. Great. That's eliminated one; now there's only about . . . how many? . . . a couple of hundred to go. A small step for man . . . Gaston? How about Gaston?'

'T-t-turn round,' the man said. 'Face the wall.'

'Could I just have a little stretch first?' Julia made her voice sound plaintive. 'My shoulders feel like they've got knives in them. Do you ever get cramp? You know what I mean, that really sharp pain . . . ?' She was babbling now. Anything to postpone the constriction of the handcuffs; anything to establish some sort of spurious rapport with this misshapen oaf.

The attempt failed. As she held out her arms, rotating them from the shoulders, the man became agitated, advancing two steps and jabbing at her with the gun.

'Don't talk. Just shut up and t-t-turn round.'

Letting her arms drop, Julia shrugged and did as she was told. 'OK. You're the boss. But it's a shame. I was beginning to think we had something in common. Sometimes you need a friend, you know?' She winced as he replaced the handcuffs, which had chafed the skin of her wrists. 'Someone just to listen,' she went on. 'Nobody listens these days. Have you noticed that? Everybody talks but nobody listens. It's a selfish world, Gaston. All out for themselves. If you could just find one person who cared enough to hear what you have to say . . . to hear what *you* think for a change.' She sensed from his silence that the anger had subsided and he was absorbing what she said.

When, at length, the man spoke, his voice was subdued. 'I'm not Gaston,' he said. 'My name is Paul.'

Less than twenty kilometres away, beyond the Canal de Bourgogne, over hills and parched farmlands, on the high ground rising from the valley of the Ouche, Tom Bellman was sitting in his kitchen. It had been a warm night in the big room under the pantiles. Mosquitoes had flown sorties in the darkness, alighting only long enough to inject their target. Tom scratched a red swelling on his knuckle. Helen would have known where to find the tablets that slotted into the device on the electric plug, keeping the enemy squadrons at bay, but Tom had no idea where they were kept. Filling the stained metal percolator, he reflected that he had never felt so lonely in his life. If, the day before, there had been any doubt about Helen's disappearance, now there could be none. Her silence said it all. And if he was feeling lonely, what must she be going through? At least he had friends, neighbours. He wondered whether he should break the news to Frank and Daisy. Well, Daisy; Frank, last heard of in Guatemala, was still on his year out, before going to Manchester University. What the hell was he doing in Guatemala, Tom thought? Talk about mosquitoes. Trust him to go somewhere off the map. He pictured Daisy in Stobart's, the London saleroom where she worked, among self-possessed young women called D'Este and Auriole. Open, whole-hearted, funny Daisy, who did the job for rotten money because she loved good paintings and was ravenous to learn. What was the point of upsetting her, with nothing definite to say? Tom would wait another day or two. By then there might be no need. Helen might well have been found, shaken but unharmed. Hang on to that thought, Tom told himself. Whatever happens, always hope. Meanwhile he longed to hold Daisy; to hug her tight, and tell her he loved her.

Taking his cup back to the deep, rustic sink with the dripping tap, he passed a photograph of Helen and her sister Nancy in an antique oval frame. They were smiling in the sun. Tom remembered the picture being taken there, in the garden, two summers ago. Looking through the gallery at the plum and greengage trees, the ruined bake-house in the apple orchard, he noticed a pair of Helen's gardening gloves left on the edge of the wheelbarrow. It was this waitingness of things that he found unbearable; things that she wore, or had touched, or made, seemed depleted, lacking any purpose without her, seemed to need her for their meaning and existence.

Just as he was wondering where to begin, Tom heard a familiar whistle from the main room. When he turned, Robert was in the doorway, nosing the aroma of coffee like a retriever. Under his arm was a folded map.

'First coffee, second the hunt,' Robert said. 'Good day, my friend. You slept well?'

'No,' Tom said. 'But it doesn't matter. Half of me doesn't want to. It feels like time wasted.' He poured black coffee into a mug and handed it to Robert.

Sitting down, Robert laid the map on the table and opened

it out. Next he took a well-worn leather flask from his pocket and poured a measure of cognac into the steaming drink, offering the same to Tom, who declined.

'Aah, this is what they're missing, those frogs in the font,' Robert said, after taking a deep draught.

'Frogs?' Tom frowned.

'The old crones in black, hanging round the church door like bats. Frogs in the font I call them. What they want is a drop of this, the real holy spirit. Put some sap in their branches.' Robert grinned. 'Now,' he went on, 'like we said, this morning we comb this part of the map.' With a plump finger he indicated an area to the south east, between Beaune and Bligny. 'That's the route Helen usually took home isn't it, the D970?'

Tom nodded. 'And she'd have had in mind the meeting with Mrs Walker. They're off the same road.'

'Excellent,' Robert said. 'And as soon as they're open we'll call at the garage where Helen left the car. See what they really remember. By then Monsieur Walker should have heard something.'

'There's a lot of square kilometres here, Robert,' Tom said, studying the search zone.

'There's a lot of square kilometres in the Atlantic, Mr Professor,' Robert said, 'but they found the Titanic, my friend.' With that he took another gulp of the fortified coffee.

Tom smiled. Though the analogy bore little scrutiny, it was presented with the verve of a man who didn't know the meaning of submission. 'And you think the kidnappers are still in the area?' Tom said. 'They could be anywhere.'

'They're here all right,' Robert said. 'My nose tells me. We've been through this before. These animals, they know this little corner. It's obvious. They knew about the Walkers and they knew where to find the girl. And if they know it, they're in it. In any case, why go further when there's plenty of space here? It just makes things more complicated.'

Tom saw the logic of the theory, but there remained in his mind a sickening doubt. 'I still can't see why they'd be together. Helen and the Walker girl. It's been going round in my mind all night. I can't make any sense of it.'

'Listen,' Robert said, as he rose and re-folded the map, 'you only know the sense of these things when you have the answers. Criminals are not philosophers. They do the thing – maybe they plan it, maybe they don't – and, if they're not caught, they do something else. Sense has nothing to do with it.'

Tom thought about this. 'I'd still feel a lot happier if we had the police on the case,' he said.

'We have,' Robert said with a beam, clicking his heels at mock attention and saluting. 'And if we need more, in say, two days, we know where to find them.'

Without her Rolex, a present from her stepmother, which had been taken from her the previous evening by the man in the black helmet, Julia found it impossible to gauge the passing of time. The glow from the window grew richer, and the air warmer, but how long had the process taken? Some while after the encounter with Paul, the door had opened again to admit the smaller of the two original kidnappers, Blue Helmet. He had brought with him a tin tray bearing half a baguette and a cup of milk. Untying her gag so that it rested round her neck, he had secured her ankles with a length of baling wire before unlocking the handcuffs. She could see his small red-rimmed eyes through the scratched Perspex of his mask, as he watched her bite the stale bread. For a moment she had considered a hunger strike, but soon realised it would be more sensible to maintain her energy. Escape was the first priority. She must be ready to take advantage of even the smallest opening, reasoning that the kidnappers couldn't afford to damage the goods.

Unlike Paul, his younger colleague, this gaoler would not be drawn into conversation. Julia asked him the time, his name, the whereabouts of the other woman, but nothing prompted a reply. When she had eaten as much as she wanted of the baguette, and drunk the milk, he re-tied the gag and blindfolded her, locked the handcuffs and, leaving her legs free, pulled her towards the door. Unsure what he intended, she tried to dig her heels in, but that only made him tug harder. Off balance, she half-walked, half-stumbled out into what she sensed was a less constricted space. Beyond that they entered what appeared to be a passage. Perhaps twenty metres further on she cursed as she stubbed her toe on a solid object.

'It's a staircase,' Blue Helmet said.

'Well thanks for telling me.' Muffled by the gag, Julia's response was robbed of its irony.

At the top of the steps a heavy door opened on to what Julia guessed was a large, tall space. Blue Helmet tugged her by the sleeve, urging her across the stone floor. Julia measured the distance in paces – fourteen. When they reached their destination, Blue Helmet grasped her by the shoulders, directing her to stop and turn one hundred and eighty degrees. His hands felt less than confident as he re-tied the baling wire, and removed the gag and the blindfold.

Facing Julia were Paul, holding the shotgun, and the man in the ridiculous black helmet. The latter held a Polaroid camera with which he seemed to be having some difficulty. In a curious way Julia felt more caged now, with the three of them present, than she had in her cell, even though the room was, as she had suspected, enormous. To her left was a huge window with all the glass missing, looking out across an overgrown space to a high wall in bad repair. Hungry for details she noticed the cracked plasterwork of the ceiling which showed traces of having been decorated with a motif of leaves and branches. Ribs, radiating from a high central point, ended in bosses, each of which bore a coat of arms. What was this place? Some sort of château?

Since Black Helmet was still distracted, and Blue Helmet had gone to help him, Julia braved the pain in her shoulders and upper arms to take a surreptitious look behind her. There the main feature was a massive stone fireplace, with an ancient mirror above the broad mantelshelf. Though the silvering behind the mottled glass had flaked with age, she could still see the distorted group of three, like some punk parody of a Dutch master. Since they were preoccupied, she dared to angle her head further, revealing the ghost of her own image, staring like a stranger from another century. She was startled by the whiteness, the dark red stain in the hairline, and the parallel stripes of blood from the nose. Jesus, she looked fifty – dark-eyed with fatigue and uncertainty. And what was that? Now she noticed a round, tarnished metal object lying on the mantelshelf. Intrigued, she felt a momentary boldness.

'Hey. If you're going to take my picture, I want these off.'

Only Blue Helmet looked up. The others were too absorbed in their problems with the camera.

'These handcuffs,' Julia went on. 'I'm absolutely not having my picture taken trussed up like a chicken.'

Seeming to decide that the small concession would buy a moment's peace, Blue Helmet walked across and did as she asked. 'Afterwards they go on again,' he said. 'And don't try anything.'

Nodding, Julia waited until the three men were again distracted. As Paul stretched to point something out on the camera and Black Helmet yelled at him, in a movement half-shielded by her body, she reached up for what she now saw was a bracelet. Her first intuitive, independent action since her capture, it gave her a small feeling of liberation. The movement had not gone unnoticed, though its purpose had not been spotted.

'What are you doing?' Black Helmet shouted. Through the visor he sounded like a long-distance telephone call.

'Just getting the circulation going,' Julia lied.

'Well stand still and keep your gob shut,' Black Helmet said.

Behind her back, Julia slipped the bracelet onto her left wrist with a pleasant sensation of defiance. She was sore where the handcuffs had inflamed the skin but this lay lower, on the heel of her hand. It was a meaningless triumph in the context of her plight, but a triumph none the less.

'Right,' Black Helmet said, advancing with the camera in one hand and a newspaper in the other. 'Here. Take this. Hold it in front of you with the date showing.'

Looking down at the tabloid, Julia arranged it so that the front page covered her chest, her right hand high on the newsprint, and her left held low, nearer her waist.

'Good. Now, absolutely still.' Black Helmet's visor was steaming up as he looked through the unfamiliar viewfinder.

Her mind hazed by lack of sleep, Julia had only now grasped the full significance of the photo-call. If this was all for her father's benefit, what was the appropriate expression? Would fear make him act faster? Since at this moment she didn't feel fear, but rather anger, discomfort and frustration, she doubted her ability to act the emotion without mugging like a heroine of the silent screen. How about a nonchalant smile, to insult her captors and give her family heart? No, that seemed somehow tasteless. Just look straight. Just look this stupid, ignorant, ugly bastard right in the piggy, steamed-up eye.

'Loiseau at Saulieu. Now there's a chef,' Robert was saying, warming to his theme with relish. 'That man's a genius. Do you know, to make a sauce he will reduce six litres of red wine to one. Six to one! My God, that's magnificent. My cousin took me there once – François; the wine-grower from Nuits-St-Georges. I tell you Thomas, I thought I was in paradise.' He mimed passing money through his fingers. 'But sous, my friend. Many, many sous. For the price of that meal you could buy Arnay-le-Duc. All of it, including Josette in the butcher's.' His eyes took on a faraway look. 'Oh, what a woman. Impeccable. When I watch her wrapping calves' liver I have to stop myself vaulting the counter.'

Tom couldn't help laughing. They were on their way back to Beaune having explored the wooded country further towards Bligny. Though they had plunged down rutted tracks between the trees and swung off the main road towards Montceau-et-Echarnant, the searching had revealed nothing. Throughout, however, Robert had kept the mood buoyant with reminiscences of his childhood. Stories of toads and lizards being put down his shirt-front as he lay in the meadows by the Ouche, and how the priest once caught him baring his backside in the cemetery, to shock the prim spinster Guibaudet. Robert described her as having a nose like a bacon-slicer; but the disappointing thing was that she hadn't been shocked at all.

The small garage lay between Bouze-lès-Beaune and Beaune itself. Tom explained that Helen used it in preference to larger, perhaps more efficient places because the proprietor, Gustave, had once been kind and helpful over a breakdown, and tended to be relaxed about bills. Tom teased Helen that it was because the old boy fancied her rotten. Though she knew it was true, Helen would tell him not to be daft and make an abrupt change of subject.

As Robert pulled in to the forecourt, a young man at the side of the corrugated-iron workshop threw away a cigarette butt.

'If the idiot had chucked that near the pumps,' Robert grumbled, 'I might have been the first Frenchman in space.'

Before the mechanic could re-enter the building by the side door, Robert had him under interrogation. 'Gustave, he's here?'

The young man shook his head.

'Well, where?'

The mechanic indicated Beaune with his thumb.

'What does that mean?'

'What does it look like?'

There was no change in Robert's expression, but with a slow, sidelong glance at Tom he took three measured steps towards his reluctant informant. He then gripped the front of the young man's green overalls with one meaty fist and, to Tom's astonishment, lifted him three or four inches off the ground. In the same seamless movement he slammed the suspended figure against the workshop wall with a resounding metallic thump.

'My friend,' Robert said in a quiet, menacing voice; 'this is urgent and I am not a patient man. Now, I'm going to ask you one simple question and if you don't give me a sensible answer, before you can say Vanessa Paradis you will be singing soprano. Understood?'

His capacity for manoeuvre somewhat restricted, the mechanic managed a small nod.

'Excellent,' Robert said. 'Here is the question. Where is Gustave?'

'The hospital.' The young man's voice sounded strained.

'Why, hospital?'

'Down here.' The youth pointed to his appendix.

'Appendix?'

The mechanic shook his head. 'That thing where you . . . it's like a big lump,' he said.

'A lump?' Robert was puzzled.

'I think he means a hernia,' Tom said.

'Ah, a hernia.' Robert let the captive down, pointing a forefinger to fix him in place. 'How long ago was this?'

'Ten days, more or less.' Regaining his composure, the mechanic straightened the front of his overalls.

'So he wasn't here when my wife – the Englishwoman – called for her 2CV?' Tom said.

'I just told you, he hasn't been here for ten days,' the mechanic said, his defiance returning in the face of the lesser threat.

The greater threat glared at him. 'The Englishwoman who called, had you seen her before?'

'No. My wife was having a baby the day the car came in. And I've only been here a month myself.'

'So who was minding the place that day?'

'A cousin of Gustave – Albert. He helps out from time to time.'

'What was she wearing, the Englishwoman? Do you remember?' Tom said.

The mechanic shrugged and compressed his lips. 'I didn't pay much attention. White jeans I think.'

Robert looked at Tom, who thought for a second and nodded.

'This Albert; where can we find him?' Robert said.

'There's a number somewhere, inside.'

From the dingy office, Robert telephoned Albert, while the relieved mechanic went back to work on a dusty Peugeot with its cylinder block plucked out and suspended by chains. Reasserting his independence, he switched on the radio, loud. Albert remembered the Englishwoman well. She had been warm and vivacious, he said, just as Gustave had once described her. The husband was a lucky man. She had asked how long the repair would take and Albert had replied that the 2CV would be ready in a couple of days. Whereupon the woman had thanked him and, declining his offer of a lift, had said she didn't want to trouble him and would take the bus back to St Luc.

Emerging from the office, Robert crossed to the workbench where the radio stood and switched it off. The mechanic looked up, willing the cylinder block to crash down on the stocky intruder.

'One more thing, my friend,' Robert said. 'How did she pay – the Englishwoman?'

The mechanic straightened, trying to re-focus his memory. 'I don't think she did pay. No she didn't. She said it was an account job.'

'Whose account?' Tom said.

'How the hell do I know?' Aware of the risks, the young man was nevertheless close to breaking point. 'You think I remember the name of every customer? You want the name, look in the invoice book.'

Robert's expression would have made a drug baron blanch, let alone a gangling garage hand. But Tom restrained him with a cautionary glance and returned to the office to check. A moment later he reappeared and nodded.

' "Account of Mrs Bellman," ' he said.

When Tom and Robert arrived back at the Walkers' château, the mood was calm but sombre. They were shown into the same drawing room as before by a fresh-faced nineteen-year-old from St Luc, Jean-Marie. Robert complimented him on his long black apron, saying he looked so smart it made his eyes water, and the boy beamed.

Madeleine Walker was sitting on the yellow silk sofa. Her face, as she turned to register the visitors, was drawn. Rising from her side, William Walker shook hands with both men, inviting them to take a seat.

'Thank you for coming, gentlemen,' he said. 'There's been a development.'

'They called?' Tom said.

Walker nodded. 'Approximately fifteen minutes ago,' he said.

'Did you ask them whether . . . ? About Helen?' Tom knew the enquiry sounded selfish, preceding any concern for Julia, but he had been unable to restrain himself.

'I did, of course. The man was noncommittal. He didn't say yes but, significantly, he didn't say no.'

'Well, that's very encouraging,' Robert said, his natural

ebullience ignited by the smallest spark. 'If the answer was no, that's what they would have said. It's obvious.'

'What did he say exactly?' Tom pressed.

'Well, first off I assured him his reply would make absolutely no difference to my dealings with him. I appealed as far as I could to his humanitarian instincts . . .'

'What humanitarian instincts has a pig got?' Robert interrupted.

' . . . And then I simply asked was there another woman with Julia, an Englishwoman? For a moment he said nothing. He seemed like it was the one question he hadn't expected. Must have gone quiet for a good four or five seconds. Now whatever we have here, we don't have a glib professional, primed with all the appropriate responses. Clearly we need to be cautious but I would tend to agree with Robert. If the answer had been no, there couldn't be any point in his not saying so.'

Cheered by the interpretation, Tom held his reaction in check. This had to be dealt with a step at a time. He would allow himself no euphoria until he knew beyond doubt that Helen was safe. 'I'm sorry,' he said. 'What did he say about Julia? It's just that I've been so . . . you know, anxious.'

'Don't apologise,' Madeleine said. 'It's natural.'

'I asked him again for proof of life – for both women of course – and he said they were taking care of it,' Walker went on; 'whatever that's supposed to mean. But again he didn't demur at the "both women". Then he said Julia's fine, and they want the ten million francs the day after tomorrow. I told them that was impossible; that I don't have that sort of cash liquid.'

'Did they say where they want the money?' Robert said.

'I said we'd better discuss that when I've raised it.'

'How long's that likely to take?' Tom said, frustrated by Walker's apparent willingness to slow the pace of the transaction.

'Problem is today's Friday,' Walker said. 'Monday at the earliest, and probably Tuesday.'

To Tom, the prospect of the intervening three days was agonising.

'I'm sorry, Tom,' Walker said, noting his anxiety and using his Christian name for the first time. 'I just have no way of doing this thing faster. Believe me, I want Julia back more than I've ever wanted anything. But we also have to recognise that with a little more time we have a better chance of flushing these bastards out.'

'If we had the police they could trace the calls,' Tom said.

'He's probably not on long enough, is he?' Robert said.

Walker shook his head. 'They may be amateurs but they've seen movies,' he said. 'Besides, he said they have a gun and they know how to use it. He said they've never had money anyway, so they've nothing to lose. The first sign of the police . . .' Walker took a cassette out of his pocket, which he handed to Robert. 'I had my secretary, Françoise, make a copy of the recording for you. It's all there. They're calling again tomorrow. He rang off before I could ask him what time.'

'I'm so sorry, gentlemen, we never offered you any refreshment.' Madeleine looked from one to the other.

'No, thank you,' Tom said. 'We ought to get on.'

'Anything?' Walker asked.

'Not yet,' Robert said. 'There's a lot of ground to cover, but we'll find them. That's certain.'

'I don't doubt it,' Walker said.

'Meanwhile,' Robert went on, 'so we're never out of touch, we need mobile telephones.'

'It's taken care of,' Walker said. 'Jean-Marie will let you have them on the way out.'

In the afternoon Madeleine Walker told her husband she needed to be alone for a while. Leaving the courtyard in her white

Mercedes convertible, she drove up to the crossroads and pulled onto the verge, undecided. Should she turn left for Bligny and Beaune, or right – for comfort . . . and for guilt? On impulse she turned right, cutting across country until she struck the old Paris road, where she headed for Chagny. She felt bad about leaving William at a time like this, but if she had stayed she could have done little to alleviate his concern. William was not a man to be stroked and soothed. Self-sufficient, master of his emotions, he was not susceptible to mere blandishments, even if, under these stressful circumstances, she had any to offer. He loved her, she thought, though not as much as his first wife Kate, Julia's mother, who had drowned in a tragic accident off Catalina. That had been a consuming love, one for which he would have been prepared to make almost any sacrifice. This love was more measured, more reasoned – except in bed. Though considerate in other ways, William was an urgent, often insistent lover, who needed to possess her but failed to make her feel wanted as well as desired. It was rare now that his love-making satisfied her, and even on those occasions imagination had become her friend.

Passing the château of La Rochepôt, so romantic with its witch's-hat turrets in the maroon and gold of Burgundy, Madeleine reflected that her life was caught in a balance between two voids. She felt somehow unnecessary. If William were to lose her he would mourn for a few months perhaps, and then with an act of will would make other arrangements. Unable to bear children, Madeleine had established an almost sisterly relationship with Julia. But William's daughter was an independent spirit too. Madeleine admired her marvellous confidence; her ability always to take a positive line. Unless the kidnappers were vile and vicious enough to carry out their threat with the gun, Julia would survive this ordeal, and there was nothing Madeleine could do to help her.

This feeling of being a spectator rather than a player had

been forgotten while Madeleine planned the Shakespearean performances with Helen Bellman. Here at last was a worthwhile enterprise for which she was indispensable. She had revelled in the detailed organisation as well as in the company of a warm, bright woman. Their enthusiastic co-operation had reminded her of her student days at the Sorbonne, when the things of the moment were all-absorbing. But now this cherished project too was in jeopardy. In a curious way, Madeleine felt more concern for Helen than for her stepdaughter. Though the Englishwoman was a realist with more than her share of determination, she also had the vulnerability of the generous heart.

At the sign for St Aubin, Madeleine turned left and drove up through the village. Dominating the stone houses was the oldest church in Burgundy, whose irregular spire looked as though it were hewn from rock. Where the road skirted the lower slopes of vines, Madeleine parked in a small yard. Apart from a cat sleeping in a cardboard box, there was no sign of life. For a moment she considered backing out again and returning to Bessey. That was where her duty lay. But was there not also a duty to herself, to her own self-esteem; her need to be needed?

Getting out of the car she walked down past the old pots of geraniums ranged in haphazard display, towards the large double doors, one of which was open. Looking inside, breathing in the familiar, musty smell of the cellar, she called: 'Camille!' There was no response. On impulse Madeleine went down the steps beside the building and opened the gate that led to the church, where she knew Camille sometimes went. Apart from the birds and the occasional cock-crow, there were few sounds in the village. The people of St Aubin were either out in the vineyards or cooking the midday meal; an unchanging pattern of life in the Côte d'Or. And this place of worship, both demanding and forgiving, had witnessed the growing and the dying back, the pleasures and the sorrows of this small community for a thousand years.

Standing in the nave, close to the slabs inset with iron rings which covered the entrance to the crypt, Madeleine called again: 'Camille! Camille!'

This time there was a reply. From high above a voice answered: 'It's me, your guardian angel. I saw you coming. It's a miracle!'

Madeleine smiled.

'Come up,' the voice invited her. 'Don't be afraid, my child.'

Madeleine mounted the stone steps which spiralled up from the base of the tower, emerging onto a dusty, insecure wooden platform, with a rickety ladder leading to the next stage. 'Is it safe?' she called up.

'Of course,' the voice said. 'It's the stairway to heaven.'

Watched by a phalanx of full-size plaster saints in attitudes of redundant piety, Madeleine tested her weight on the first rung and, emboldened, climbed to yet another, narrower floor, constricted by the tapering of the steeple. 'How much further?' she said, feeling more light-hearted than she had for days.

'One more, my darling,' the voice said. 'And then you get your reward.'

As she emerged onto the last level, Madeleine saw Camille Charbonneaux with the sun behind him like an aura. Though not a handsome man, for that illuminated instant he was beautiful. Walking forward, he held out his strong brown arm to help her up the last step. Rising to him, she could see the veins in his hands swollen with the effort; could smell his sweat and the wine on his breath, and see the dust in the creases round his eyes. Without saying anything, she kissed him and, before he could embrace her, stepped over to an unglazed aperture which looked out beyond the steep pantiled roof to the hills ranked with vines. She could sense him, more than hear him; his warmth, his energy.

'I came here when I was a child,' he said. 'Down there, I climbed on the roof. I was the king of St Aubin.'

'You were reckless. It's dangerous.'

'Kings don't know danger. For them the rules are different.'

Madeleine thought of her husband's story about Louis XVI.

'Look,' Camille went on, 'I want to show you something.' He took her hand and led her to the bells which were suspended over the square opening in the platform. Round the edge of the largest was writing in a mediaeval script. Leaning forward, Madeleine could make out the word 'Charbonneaux'; Camille's name. She tightened her grip in his. Putting his other arm round her waist, he drew her close. Releasing herself, she turned, ran her fingertips across the sweat of his brow, and licked them. She could feel his hand in the small of her back, tracing the parted fullness of her under the cool linen dress. Moulding her body to him, she wanted to lose herself for a few blessed moments; to abandon what was expected of her and be what she desired. As he kissed her, cupping the weight of her breast in the mysterious, infinite grace of its arc from the ribcage, she gave herself to what she knew was not a solution, but an irresistible source of consolation.

She found herself wishing they could make love, there, in the light of the sun and under the protection of the bells, but at once felt as apprehensive as a child. Had this profanity compounded her sin? Had she brought down a curse upon all of them – William, Camille, herself – perhaps even Julia? 'Will we be punished?' she said.

'Only if it's all lies.'

'If what is?'

'If God isn't love after all.'

This silenced her doubts for a moment. As she distanced herself from him, she talked of Julia and the crisis at home. She hadn't meant to, but the need to unburden herself was overwhelming. Helen Bellman's disappearance, the kidnappers' demands, the warning not to involve the police, the drafting in of Robert Ryaux – she told Camille everything without emotion; her account absorbed in the stones like countless other confessions in the church's patient millennium.

When she had finished, Camille questioned her on details, fascinated by this extraordinary development. What did the kidnappers sound like? Were they locals, did she think? How did they want the money? Did her husband intend to get it? Where was it to be left? When Madeleine had answered as best she could, and Camille had soothed her fears, assuring her that all would be well, they descended from the bell-tower. He led the way down the ladders, delighting in lifting her like a dancer before she reached the floor.

Though she was anxious now about returning home, he persuaded her to join him in the cellar. There, in the soundless calm that matched the peace of the church, they ate a fresh, crusty baguette with ripe Epoisses cheese Camille had brought from the house, and drank a glass of the cool, lean red wine that had grown on these hills the year before. She watched him throw his head back and laugh at something his mother had said, the ligaments in his neck taut under the sheen of his flesh. In the tower he had spoken of love as though it were salvation. Was what she felt for him love? At this moment, as he made her promise to return tomorrow, his eyes shining, she decided there was no other name for it; while a small voice warned that it had no power to redeem her.

CHAPTER FOUR

After the visit to the Walkers' château, Tom and Robert had resumed their systematic search of the countryside. Heading north-east from Bligny along the valley of the Ouche, where for much of the way the river ran parallel with the Canal de Bourgogne, they had explored as many possibilities as time allowed, but without success. Though he knew the chances of finding anything were remote, Tom recognised the importance of active involvement. Nothing could be worse or less constructive than sitting at home, waiting for the half-dreaded telephone call. Besides, as Robert kept reminding him, on investigations you made your own luck. The harder you searched, the more questions you asked, the greater your chances of stumbling on some tiny clue that might begin the unravelling process. Robert recalled famous cases where a single human hair, or a fibre of clothing, had provided the key. He also assured Tom that if the missing car were found by anyone else and reported to the gendarmes, the official search would begin regardless of the kidnappers' warnings.

As they drove between watermeadows grazed by creamy Charolais cattle, Tom wanted to ask Robert about specific cases. They had never discussed his friend's career in detail, and he was intrigued to know more about the methods he had used. 'How long were you a detective, Robert?' he said.

'I wasn't,' Robert said, without hesitation.

Tom felt a hollowness not unmingled with panic. 'How do you mean, you weren't?' he said, trying, without conviction, to sound casual.

'Exactly what I say. I wasn't.'

'Just let's be clear about this,' Tom said; 'you're saying you were not a detective?'

'Correct. England, ten points!' Robert said, parodying the Eurovision Song Contest.

'But . . .' Tom had so much to say, he didn't know where to begin. 'Look Robert, do you want to pull in just for a moment?'

Robert pointed to his watch. 'Time, my friend. We don't have much.'

'To hell with the flaming time; pull in – now!' Angry and alarmed, Tom could sense the blood flushing his face, and felt the need to grip something, hard. As his companion drew off the road with a single, unamused glance, he tried to marshal his sudden anxieties into a coherent list of complaints. 'Now look Robert, my wife . . . Helen . . . she's . . . Oh, God what am I trying to say?'

'Calm yourself, my friend.'

'No, I won't bloody calm myself. Helen's out there somewhere with some . . . some raving lunatic and I'm not allowed to call the police in – but that was kind of all right because I thought you were a detective . . . everybody thought you were. What do you think you're playing at? This is people's lives, man. This is as serious as it gets, and you're pretending to be a detective. It's unbelievable.'

Unaccustomed to enduring this sort of tirade without retaliation, Robert tightened his hold on the steering wheel. 'Am I permitted to say something?' he said.

Uncomfortable with his emotion, Tom nodded.

'First, I have never in my life said I was a detective. Why would I say such a thing when I wasn't? Second, nobody has ever asked me in any case.'

'But everybody assumes you were.'

'Well everybody is stupid,' Robert said. 'That's not my problem.'

'So is Walker stupid? Why didn't you tell him?'

'He asked me to help because he trusts me and he knows I was in the police. We have never discussed the matter.'

'Great!' Tom said. 'You never discussed the matter! Well, if you weren't a detective, what the hell were you then? A dog-handler?' The moment the question was out of his mouth, he knew he'd gone too far. Half-expecting his powerful neighbour to strike him, he watched in trepidation.

Looking as though he might wrench the steering wheel off its stalk, instead Robert opened the door with elaborate gravitas and stepped onto the gravel lay-by. A few metres beyond, at the angle of a walled garden, stood a small circular dovecote converted into a summer-house. In its base was a stout metal-studded door. Advancing on this with measured tread, Robert raised his mighty right fist and pounded several times on the unresponding oak, creating a cavernous boom that filled the gazebo with his rage and reverberated along the wall. Frustration vented, he walked back to the car, re-seated himself and slammed the door. 'Now, you listen to me,' he said, though by now Tom was disinclined to do otherwise. 'You want to know, I'll tell you. I was in Traffic. I had a big, beautiful motorbike and I kept order on the streets. I was very good at this. Everybody knew me. Once, on a cold day, the wife of the President of the Republic – Aunt Yvonne we called her – gave me a glass of coffee laced with cognac. She understood, you see – something you and the others do not understand. The business of the police – all police – is defeating crime and protecting the public. They're all part of the team, including dog-handlers; very much including dog-handlers, as a matter of fact. You obviously know nothing about drugs or explosives.'

Tom was beginning to feel ashamed of his outburst.

'And detectives don't have any magic formula, you know,' Robert went on, his diction precise to keep the lid on his impatience. 'They're certainly not Maigret. They observe, they wade through mountains of boring details, they remember, and most important of all, they persevere. In the end it's what you have in here,' he said, pointing to his temple; 'it's your instincts that count, not what it says on your warrant. Now, I would like to help you, Thomas. You may not deserve it but Helen does. But if you feel you can do better . . .' Robert gestured towards the windscreen, indicating that his passenger was free to go his own way.

After a moment's silence, during which he became more aware of the oppressive heat in the parked car, Tom said in a level voice: 'You know that little bar at Pont d'Ouche? The one run by the Englishwoman? Helen and I once had a lovely Chiroubles there. It was her birthday.'

'Then we'd better check it out; make sure they've got plenty for her next one,' Robert said, starting the engine.

'The bastard must be lying,' Henri was saying, as he and Félix squatted over the two rings of a blue camping hotplate, the lit one bearing a battered pan full of water. On the floor beside them, in the vast room where the Polaroid had been taken, were a Camping Gaz canister, a tin of instant coffee, three chipped enamel mugs and two motorcycle helmets.

'How can a millionaire not have cash? It's lies.'

'It's quite possible,' Félix said, his short experience of estate agency giving him the edge. 'They put it all in property and shares and stuff. It's no good to them sitting in a bank. That's why they're millionaires.'

Though the answer didn't please him, Henri was glad Félix

had known it; Félix who knew so much. 'I suppose,' he conceded. 'But that's going to mean days. It's Friday now. When do you think?'

'If he's on to it now,' Félix said, pouring the boiling water into two mugs, 'which he will be, it'll be early next week.'

'God. Three . . . four more days. I'll go crazy.'

Félix reached out for Henri's hand, resting his on top of it for a moment. 'No, you won't,' he said. 'I won't let you.'

It was gestures like that, signs of warmth and caring, that made Félix so special to Henri. As the young estate agent handed him a mug, he thought with thankfulness of their meeting. It had been at the annual feast of Henri IV in Arnay-le-Duc, everybody sitting at trestle tables in the bare hall with a stage at one end. During the meal, Henri hadn't noticed Félix, but when the dancing began, and Henri preferred not to join in, the stranger had sauntered up to the table and introduced himself. Henri felt awkward on occasions like that, unable to make small-talk. But with Félix it had been different. Henri suspected he'd seen off a bottle or two, but who cared? Here was a man who didn't want to show he was better, or boast about his own adventures with women. Instead he'd asked about Henri's life, and seemed interested in the problems of the farm. Félix was better educated than him, but he still liked talking about the great heron down by the canal, and the stupid tourists who raced through Burgundy without stopping to look; about the things the old people remembered, and foreigners snapping up houses that were falling down.

Together they had watched a local woman with three small daughters – the eldest of them, maybe fourteen, dark and beautiful, with bruises under her eyes. The children were nervous, anxious to please their mother, who was dancing with them, one by one. Faster and faster she whirled them, her whole body alive to the music. Perhaps she was remembering her first dance. When they sat down, exhausted, the daughters happy that she was carefree, the tombola began. Félix noticed how, dressed in second-hand clothes, they seemed a group apart. Unlike everyone else, they had no money for tickets. Walking across, he bought three and presented them to the eldest girl. She took them with a blush, while her mother nodded a thank you without smiling.

Henri had been impressed by Félix's kindness, the sort he himself had never been shown. His childhood had been a dark time. When he was awake, he couldn't bear to think about it. His mother, whom he loved, had died when he was four. He hadn't been told what disease killed her, but he somehow had the idea that she hadn't fallen to an illness; she'd been broken, just like you could break a plough if you were too hard on it, or didn't look after it. This woman, with her kids, reminded him of her. After that, his father, who until then had at least put up with him, began to change. He'd always been a heavy drinker but now it got out of hand. He seemed cheated and resentful. Within two months he'd met Francine, a young shop assistant from Semur-en-Auxois. She was plain, but she had shiny black hair and the kind of figure you joked about in bars. She'd known what she was doing all right. She could turn the old drunk any way she wanted. She even bought Henri the occasional lollipop or a bottle of Orangina, the two-faced bitch. When his father married her, and she moved into the farm, the light went out of Henri's world. Now she didn't have to pretend any more, Francine treated him a lot worse than the beasts. Sometimes he'd get no food for two days at a time. Often, in desperation, he chewed foul-tasting pellets of animal meal. And when he cried she hit him on the ears, making them burn and ache. His unwashed clothes became lousy and his hair stiff with dirt.

Within a year she banned him from the house and made him sleep on straw in a corner of the cowshed. At least there he was warm and, at night, beyond her punishment. And all the while his father, crazy with the woman's body, left him to his misery. In his pain and isolation, Henri stopped speaking. In turn his silence became the spur for more beatings, until his despair led him to try and kill himself by swallowing disinfectant he found in the dairy. When, as a last resort, the doctor was called, Henri heard his stepmother pass it all off as the act of a spoiled brat who couldn't have the toy tractor he wanted. In the doctor's presence Henri was put to bed in the house, but as soon as the car had left the yard, he was wrapped in a sack and taken back to the cowshed.

Meanwhile his father let the farm go downhill. Hay harvested too late was rotted by rain, and malnourished animals died. Bills were thrown on the fire unopened. Creditors who had the cheek to demand their money were shown the end of a pitchfork. This depressing state of affairs drove Francine to look for amusement elsewhere. She found it with a young man who worked at a local abattoir. When Henri's father got wind of the relationship, as was bound to happen in a small community, he locked Francine in the house and, in a rage stoked by *eau de vie*, told her he was on his way to kill her lover. Escaping through the scullery window with his cash-box under her arm, Francine telephoned a warning to the abattoir, met the young man at a prearranged rendezvous, and was never seen in the area again. When he got back to the farm, Henri's father went into the cowshed rigid with anger and, in sight of his small son, put the barrels of his 12-bore to his mouth and pulled the trigger.

Though shown some kindness by the grandparents who gave him shelter until he himself took over the farm, Henri was carrying wounds which could never heal. His thoughts were dark and fearful. He expected the little he had inherited to be snatched away, if he was ever less than vigilant. He put his trust in no one, kept his secret hidden. Until now. Until Félix. They were both outsiders, Henri thought. Both on the bank,

uncomfortable with the mainstream. But something had seen
to it that they found each other, and now he wasn't alone any
more. After the feast at Arnay they'd tried to meet once a
week, soon finding out that they were both mad about motor-
racing. In the Café du Nord, with its tall gilt mirrors and marble
floor, and the sporting trophies behind the bar, they would go
over every detail of grands prix they had seen on television,
the clean speed, the guts of the drivers, the power of the
fantastic engines – things as far from their daily lives as the
old kings at Versailles. Those guys behind the wheel were
unbelievable – no nerves, quick as panthers.

Within a couple of months Henri and Félix were making
big plans. They would visit all the great European circuits
together. Maybe get a luxury mobile home and do it in style.
They would always get there early, go down to the pits, get
the inside track from the mechanics. As time went by they
even fantasised about meeting the drivers themselves; drinking
champagne with them after the race, respected for what they
knew. In this dream, Henri had found hope – and it was the
most precious thing he had ever known. But to make it all real
they would need money; enough money to break out of their
drab lives and be free. This had seemed an insoluble problem
– until brilliant Félix had had an idea.

One evening, after a meal at the Terminus in Arnay when
Julia Walker's name had come up, Félix had put his arm round
Henri's shoulder as they crossed to the car parked by the Shopi
supermarket. It was a simple enough gesture but it had a strange
effect. No one, except his mother, had ever done it to Henri.
He didn't know how to say what he felt, but it made him want
to give. The giving had started ten days later with the unfamiliar
closeness of a first clumsy hug; like two lonely animals feeling
safe in each other's warmth. Although it seemed right, this
closeness made Henri worry. Could he tell his friend everything
– even the part that frightened him, that he was finding it so

hard to control? Would Félix understand his craving to cut out the damage done to him as a kid? To watch the knife go into the rotten flesh and slice out the growth that would otherwise spread and destroy him? To end his stepmother's useless, disgusting life, which seemed able to sprout again like a pruned vine that looked dead. If anybody could understand it was Félix, but Henri couldn't bear the thought of taking any risks with this new friendship. No. He would keep it to himself, what he had to do, until he thought the time was right.

So far everything had gone according to plan. Walker talked more like a boss than a worried parent, but Henri knew he must crack in the end. No father, except maybe his own, could just stand by while his daughter's life was in danger. He might hold things up as long as possible, but when Henri piled on the threats he would soon buckle. Henri had read of cases where the kidnappers had cut off their victims' fingers to send to relatives. That was something he and Félix ought to bear in mind. The thought didn't make him feel squeamish, any more than drowning a kitten. But the Englishwoman was still a problem. He was sorry now that he hadn't taken care of her back at the cottage. She seemed to be in a semi-coma most of the time, now and then babbling in a French accent he couldn't understand, but she still had to be fed and watered. And what was the point? She wasn't worth ten francs to them. Paul said she might be ill. All the better, Henri thought. Maybe she would die anyway and save him the bother.

After he and Félix had finished their hot drink, they discussed when and where to leave the Polaroid for collection by Walker. Since the ransom process couldn't begin until this was in place, it was a matter of urgency. As he pondered the solution, Henri walked over to the fireplace.

'Better in the dark,' he said; 'in case Walker's got the cops on the case, even after what we said.'

'It isn't dark till late – maybe ten,' Félix said. 'We can't wait till then. That's another day gone. No, we do it now, but in a busy place. Where there are plenty of people they'll never notice one more.'

Henri admired his reasoning. When this was all over and they were off and running, this was the kind of smart thinking that would keep them one step ahead of the police.

'I'll take the photo to Châteauneuf,' Félix said. 'By the time I get there the office in Beaune will be shut, so if I'm unlucky enough to see a colleague, which is very unlikely, they won't think it's strange.'

'Are they asking questions, the office?'

'No. Not at all. I'm there part of the day, and when I'm out there's always a good reason. I've taken care of that.'

Using his handkerchief, grey for want of washing, to take the Polaroid from his pocket, Henri handed it to Félix, who held open his own jacket pocket so that his friend could drop it in.

'I've got some plain brown envelopes in the car,' Félix said. 'I bought them specially. I'll put this in one.'

'Take care not to touch it,' Henri interrupted.

'Of course,' Félix smiled his agreement. 'And I'll put it in a little letter box kindly provided by mother nature. I'll also use a public phone when I call Walker.'

Henri grinned at this, enjoying the alliance more and more. When Félix had left, he glanced at himself in the dull mirror; the dark hair short, the eyes deep, the nose broken in a playground brawl by a bully teasing him about his mother's death. One day maybe, when he was quite safe and beyond capture, the police would make some lucky connection and this face would be on the front page – not just here in Burgundy but all over France. They would even read about him in chic cafés on the boulevards of Paris. More important still, his neighbours would see that the farmer they had ignored all these years, the loner whose father had shot himself, had become rich and famous; had escaped the cold and boredom of winters in St Luc, when the arrival of the post van was the big event of the day. Then they would respect his face, the face of a man who had got everything he wanted; everything they all wanted. And with any luck that bitch Francine would see her famous stepson, wherever she was; would see that he had survived her vicious cruelty and would know that now she could never be safe.

Henri wondered which photograph the papers would use, and realised with a stab of disappointment that the most recent had been taken three years ago at the summer fête. His pitted wooden ball had just rattled down the skittle-alley and, as he turned, Véronique's young daughter had snatched a blurred shot, which Véronique had later given to him; not so much because she thought it would please him, he supposed, but because she didn't want it. The snap made him look fat and startled, like a cow caught in the tractor's headlights. Because it was the only picture of him since school he had kept it in a drawer. But now he made a mental note to destroy it and get Félix to take a new one.

Lowering his eyes from the image in the mirror, Henri looked at the broad mantelshelf. The torch was still there, with its band of dirty Elastoplast, but something seemed to be missing. Frowning in his effort to remember, he thought back over the past three days. He knew he had put something else on here the night they brought the women back. That was it! The bracelet from the glove compartment in the 2CV. But how could it have gone missing? Apart from the hostages there were only the three of them in the place – Félix, him and Paul. It was possible Félix had taken a liking to it, he thought, but not very likely. No, it was more the sort of thing Paul would do. He would have seen it, thought it would make an ideal present for some plain, spotty scrubber in Maligny, where he lived, and hoped no one would notice. Well, they had. Angry,

Henri decided to face him with the theft.

He found Paul hunkering down outside the door of the American's cell, whittling a piece of wood, the gun and his flour-sack mask at his feet. As Henri approached, the young man looked up, his eyes red-rimmed with lack of sleep. Henri saw no point in delaying.

'Did you take something from the big room, on the fireplace?'

Paul shook his head.

'Are you sure?'

'Yes, I've taken nothing. Why?'

'You didn't find something there and maybe put it away for somebody . . . a girlfriend?'

'I haven't got one,' Paul said.

'You know what'll happen if you're lying, don't you?' Henri came closer, looming over the hunched figure.

'Shit,' Paul said. 'I've no idea what you're t-t-talking about. Leave me alone.'

Furious, Henri got hold of his greasy hair and yanked him to a standing position. 'Now look, you,' he said, 'you talk to me like that again and I'll give you a few more gaps in that stinking mouth of yours. Understand?' For emphasis he thumped Paul against the rough wall whose jagged edges made the young man wince.

'Listen, Henri,' Paul said, pushing him away, 'I've taken nothing. What is there to take anyway? In this dump? I'll t-t-tell you, I've had enough. It's boring and . . I've had enough, that's all.'

Henri looked down for a moment, wondering what to do next. If he hit Paul, as he was tempted to, there was a danger he would make a run for it. That would be disastrous. He knew so much now there would be no alternative but to track him down and shut him up for good. Though Henri had no qualms about that, it was a last resort. And if they lost Paul they'd have to find a replacement; someone they could trust. Neither Henri nor Félix could afford to spend all the daylight hours here. Henri had the farm to run and Félix had to be seen at Cabinet Lamotte. No. Much better, for the time being at least, to humour this stammering cretin.

'I know it's boring. It's boring for all of us,' Henri said, doing his best to sound patient. 'But think of the money. When you've got that you'll never have to be bored again.'

Under Henri's stare, Paul's sulky expression turned to a small, uncertain grimace that was meant to be a smile.

'That's better,' Henri said. 'Now, one last time, the truth. There was something on the fireplace and now it's gone. Are you going to tell me?'

Paul held his hands out in a final gesture of bafflement. 'There's nothing. I promise you. What was it anyway?'

By now it was clear to Henri that he wasn't lying. 'An old metal bracelet,' he said. 'I found it in the Englishwoman's car.'

Without pausing to think of the implications, Paul said: 'Oh, that! I think she had it on inside – the American.' He indicated the door.

For the first time since the unexpected arrival of the Englishwoman at the cottage, Henri felt as though the kidnap plan was coming unravelled, though he wasn't yet sure why. At the very least it was a surprise development, something that had escaped their control. Why would the Walker woman want to put on someone else's jewellery and, more important, how had she managed it? Pulling Paul's limp mask over his own head with evident distaste, Henri turned the large key and pushed open the heavy door.

Thanks to Félix's intervention Julia Walker was no longer gagged, on the understanding that at the smallest outburst she would once more be silenced. The prisoner was making a brisk circuit of the room as Henri entered. She seemed unaware of him as she paced towards the high window; strong and confident. A typical American, Henri thought. Young and cocky, without the nous to see the danger she was in. She would think, like they all did, that money could buy anything, including freedom. He had seen them in Beaune, rowdy young students bawling at each other, behaving as though the town belonged to them. She must be the same age as Francine had been when she first brought misery to the farm, he thought, swallowing back a surge of nausea; the same way of seeming to own the space she moved in. And as he watched her, an idea formed, like water beginning to trickle through a crack in a rain-barrel; an idea he wouldn't yet be prepared to share, even with Félix.

As Julia reached the corner and turned in profile, she became aware of her visitor. Henri expected her to stop, but she continued her exercise, ignoring him. When at length she drew level, she gave him a defiant glare and paused, as though expecting him to make way.

'My, my, grandmama, what a big, fat, disgusting belly you've got,' she said, in English.

'Speak French,' Henri said, his voice muffled by the sacking, 'or you'll get the gag back.'

'I said "I love the hat". What happened to . . .', just in time she stopped herself revealing that she knew Paul's name, '. . . the other guy? What happened to him?'

'He's outside,' Henri said. 'Turn round and hold your hands out.'

Julia sighed and did as he asked. 'You wait, buster,' she said, again in English. 'You're going to pay for this. Oh boy, are you going to pay!'

Punishing her disobedience, Henri kneed her in the back of the legs, making her buckle and cry out with surprise and frustration. 'I told you,' he said. 'The next time I'll shut your mouth for good.'

With a show of will, Julia forced back her shoulder blades and thrust out her handcuffed hands as far as she could. Henri's revulsion at seeing the bulging veins in her wrists turned to alarm as he noticed the rim of the bracelet showing beneath the cuff of her shirt.

'Where did you get the bracelet?' he said.

'An admirer gave it me.'

'You're lying.'

'Look, with you behind me I get a little nervous, you know what I mean? Could you come round here and talk?'

Taking no notice of the request, Henri went on: 'How did you put it on?'

'The usual way. Pick it up with one hand and hey presto. It's easy when you know how.'

Realising he would have to unlock the handcuffs in order to remove the bangle, Henri reached into his pocket for the small key. As he did so, he saw the newspaper they had used in the Polaroid, lying in the corner by the door, and the last piece of the puzzle fell into place. She must have been wearing the bracelet in the photograph, which was now on its way to Châteauneuf. While he and Félix had been distracted, she must have taken it off the mantelshelf and worn it, unnoticed. Before Félix had replaced the handcuffs, she must have pushed it high under her shirtsleeve. This, Henri realised, could connect her with the missing 2CV, but beyond that he was unable to think. Inserting the key, he undid the handcuffs, forced off the bracelet, hurting Julia's sore wrists, and then secured her again.

Was it worth leaving Paul in charge and trying to stop Félix, he wondered? Should they tear up the original Polaroid and start again? But even if the bracelet was noticed, how much could Walker find out from it, and why should he link it with the Englishwoman anyway? Deciding he was over-reacting, Henri asked one last question. 'Were you wearing this before, when I took the photograph? If you lie to me I'll hurt you again.'

Without hesitation, Julia shook her head. 'No,' she said. 'I put it on afterwards, while you were looking the other way.'

'Why?'

'Why? Because I wanted to.'

When Tom and Robert got the call from Walker on the mobile phone, they had just finished questioning villagers in Bessey-la-Cour. Taking six houses each, and keeping a careful note of whom they interviewed, they had asked whether anyone had seen Helen or Julia on Tuesday, the day of the kidnap. The news of the women's disappearance was now common knowledge and most people were anxious to co-operate. Julia's vitality and humour had endeared her to the younger inhabitants and to the menfolk, though one or two of the older women had been disenchanted when she encouraged their husbands to rock 'n' roll at the summer fête. Helen was less well known in Bessey, though word of her beautiful English-style garden had spread, and many a Sunday detour was made to idle past her long wall and admire the blowsy roses.

Three reported seeing Julia in the morning. One, Madame Triolet, who lived in the tumbledown house with the chickens in the front yard, said Julia had made a point of stopping and asking if there was anything she needed from Arnay. She often did that, Madame Triolet said. Nothing was too much trouble. A young man, Louis, on his way back from buying wine at Monsieur Poillot's in Bligny had seen her filling up with petrol. As he described her back view, bending with the pump in her hand, he grinned. It had been magnificent, he said. Robert told him to curb his rapture and see what else he could remember. But there was nothing. The sightings were all inconsequential, proving only that Julia was still a free agent at two-fifteen, when she had been spotted by old Pochet who saw her coming out of a café in Ste Sabine while he was having lunch at his daughter's.

No one, however, had seen Helen. When Tom described her distinctive car, several people remembered having noticed it on previous occasions but not since the beginning of the week. As he and Robert headed for St Luc and a quick supper before more investigations, Tom felt downcast. It was now four full days since he and Helen had spoken on the telephone; four long, empty days. In all that time no one they questioned had seen her or heard from her. And here they were, a teacher and a traffic cop, pretending to be detectives. Though he understood Walker's reluctance to call in the police and anger the volatile kidnappers, the time was coming when Tom would have to insist. It went without saying that Walker's primary concern was for his daughter. For the tycoon, Helen came second. Well, that wasn't good enough. Tom owed it to Helen to put her first, and he must be allowed to make his own decisions about how best to do it.

As they drove through the fragrant woods Robert was trying to take Tom's mind off his disappointment by making plans for laying in winter stocks of logs. They could borrow Jean's huge old saw, that sounded like half a dozen tanks colliding, and pile the fuel to dry in Tom's barn. Robert described the smell of the fresh sawdust with the relish of a man reliving his greatest meal. Going on to tell stories of old Vauliquet, the wood-merchant, he was interrupted by the discreet tone of the mobile phone. 'You take it,' he said. 'The good God was stingy with me. He only gave me two hands.'

Tom picked up the mobile and pressed a digit. 'Hello.'

'Tom, this is William Walker.' The retired publisher was speaking English.

'Oh, hello. News?'

'News!' Walker confirmed. 'Good news. They just called. Can you head for Châteauneuf right away?'

'Sure. Of course. What is it?'

'Proof of life, finally. It's a photograph they took. Today, they say.'

'Of . . . ?'

'Of Julia, Tom. Look, I'm sorry. You must understand this doesn't mean anything. It does not mean Helen isn't with her.'

'It doesn't mean she is either.'

Robert registered the concern in Tom's face, enquiring with his expression what was the cause. Tom help up a hand to signal that he should wait a moment.

'No, it doesn't mean she is.' The American sounded subdued. 'But I asked again. I said: "Just tell me. Is there another woman with my daughter – an Englishwoman?"'

'What did he say?' Tom hunched forward in concentration.

'He said: "We're talking about your daughter." You see? The guy – and it was a different guy this time – he still isn't saying no. Now you have to ask yourself why on earth wouldn't he? What difference does it make if he simply denies it? But he isn't doing that, Tom.'

Tom made no reply.

'Tom? You still there?'

'Yes. Yes, I was just thinking.'

'A step at a time is all we can do. But you have to have hope.'

'Yes. I know. So, where in Châteauneuf, and what are we looking for?'

Walker passed on the instructions the kidnapper had telephoned from a public box. Tom assured him they would ring as soon as they had the proof in their hands and pressed END on the mobile.

'Don't keep me in suspense,' Robert said. 'Tell me.'

First Tom told him to head for Châteauneuf and then outlined the rest of the conversation. White-knuckled with the urge to make the sluggish saloon go faster, Robert listened in silence.

'It's beginning,' he said when Tom had finished. 'At last it's beginning.'

As they crossed the iron bridge over the canal, a hotel barge was heading towards them from the lock. On deck were several pale-limbed tourists in small Union Jack hats, one of whom had a flask at her white, sandalled feet, and a plastic cup in her hand.

'Look at that,' Robert said. 'They're going through the finest wine country on God's earth and she's drinking tea. Strange people.'

'Built an empire, tea,' Tom said, in mock defence of the realm. 'A noble brew, fit to be auctioned at the Hospices de Beaune.'

'Fit for swilling down the toilet,' Robert muttered.

Ahead of them, dominating the valley, was the romantic château that gave their destination its name. With its mellow walls and steep, tapering roofs, it had both strength and grace. In the field to their right a white horse cropped the grass alongside the Charolais cattle. As they climbed the road that curled round the hill, Tom remembered evenings here with Helen. After a drink in the square, with its handsome chestnut tree and the old water trough, they would stroll up the steep street and look forward to the time when they would live in Burgundy. Often Helen would practise her French on him, throwing her head back and laughing when he pointed out her malapropisms. Would they ever do that again, he caught himself thinking? Yes, he told himself, without question they would, and no half-crazed kidnapper would be allowed to stop them.

Parking the car beyond the ancient houses, Tom and Robert walked back to the vantage point overlooking the A6, the canal, and the breathtaking view beyond. Two lovers were sitting on the low wall, kissing as though they alone inhabited the planet. Sympathetic, Tom was prepared to wait. Robert, however, had other ideas. Approaching them, he tapped the young man on the shoulder and took out an official-looking plastic card.

'Excuse me,' he said; 'police. We have reason to suspect there's a terrorist bomb in the vicinity. I must advise you to leave.'

Taking his time, the young man turned away from the embrace and frowned.

'A bomb! In Châteauneuf! You're joking! You don't look like police.'

'Plain clothes,' Robert said. 'We've had an anonymous tip-off that an Algerian group agitating about the treatment of immigrant workers have placed an explosive device here. On this very spot, as a matter of fact. Now, are you going to co-operate, or would you and your beautiful friend rather be sent home in plastic bags? It's up to you.'

Deciding for him, the girl pulled him to his feet.

'But why here?' her lover asked, as she tugged him away.

'Tourism,' Robert said. 'Think about it. Kill that and . . .' He made an open-handed gesture that intimated limitless catastrophe.

By now the girl had broken into a run, though the young man confined himself to a brisk walk.

'Can I see that card?' Tom said.

'Certainly, Mr Professor,' Robert said, handing him the plastic he had earlier produced with such authority.

' "Municipal Library of Beaune," ' Tom read aloud. ' "Madame Ryaux, Yvonne." '

Robert returned Tom's smile, pointing to his temple. 'Say it as though you believe it and . . .' He shrugged and dropped the corners of his mouth to demonstrate the infinite gullibility of the public.

'Now,' Tom said, taking over, 'the call said to look under the fifth coping stone from the left on this low wall.' Counting them with elaborate care, he took hold of the flat, rectangular piece of granite and found it lifted with ease.

'And there it is,' Robert said.

Lying in a hollow formed in the crumbling cement was a small brown envelope. Tom reached to pick it up, but Robert restrained him.

'No,' he said. 'There may be fingerprints. Wait.' Pulling out a blue handkerchief, he took the envelope between finger and thumb, laying it on the neighbouring stone. Next he produced an old penknife and with surprising delicacy sliced along the top fold, taking care not to touch the paper with his bare hands. Drawing out the Polaroid with the aid of the handkerchief, he glanced behind him to make sure they would be undisturbed, and held it up in the evening light for them both to see.

Realising that this was the closest they had come both to the enemy and to Helen, Tom felt his heart quicken. Could there be something here? Some tiny, trivial, unnoticed sign? There she was, that glorious girl, pale but resolute, with what looked like a patch of blood up by her hairline. Had they hit her or had she fallen, Tom wondered with a clutch of anxiety? It was the cold presence of a violence they were powerless to resist that brought the plight of the women home. Obscuring Julia's body was a newspaper, held top and bottom. Without his reading glasses, which he had left in the car, Tom couldn't make out its date. But behind Julia, visible because the photographer had been at a slight angle to his subject, Tom could make out the faint reflection of the back of her head.

'Good,' Robert said, 'she's alive and she's not seriously hurt.'

'As far as we know.'

'Correct. As far as we know. We need to look at this very carefully; get it enlarged and examine every detail. Courage, Tom. We knew Helen wouldn't be in this. That signifies nothing.' Robert replaced the Polaroid in the envelope and slipped it into his pocket.

Appreciating his attempts at encouragement, Tom walked with him back to the car. On the way to Bessey they would telephone William Walker, tell him the mission had been successful and that they would be with him in twenty-five minutes. It was too late now to have the photograph enlarged; that would have to wait until the morning. Another night of uncertainty, Tom thought. But if the prospect frightened him, how must Helen be feeling?

CHAPTER FIVE

Camille Charbonneaux threw out a handful of grain for the hens at the bottom of the yard. He had been meaning to clear up this corner for years but had never quite got around to it. Now that his father was dead there was no one to do the small domestic chores, and running the vineyard was more than a full-time job. The parcels of land making up the property were dispersed over several parishes and the vines were always in need of attention. Apart from planting, pruning, spraying, weeding, and of course the *vendange*, there was the weather to worry about, the rabbits to control, the insects to discourage; to say nothing of cellaring, bottling, corking, labelling and marketing. The late frosts and hailstorms this year had been a terrible blow. Just when he needed a bumper harvest of good quality, Camille faced a disappointing yield of no great merit.

The vineyard had been in the family for four generations. Until three years ago it had held its own in a small way; sales had been steady to local restaurants, regular buyers at the gate, and the Japanese. But now increasing costs had forced Camille to raise the price of his wine to a level where it was becoming uncompetitive. Foreign buyers told him of the product from the New World – Australia, New Zealand, the United States, even Canada, for heaven's sake – which they said was both excellent and a bargain. Well, if that was what they wanted . . . In Burgundy, wine-making had come with the Romans. The wines from the Côte d'Or were acknowledged by connoisseurs to be the best. If the ignorant bourgeois preferred vinegar from a culture still wet behind the ears, good luck to them. Maybe it was time he sold up and found himself another job. But that was easier said than done. And besides, any potential buyer looking at the books would be far from impressed.

The fact was that Charbonneaux & Son was in deep trouble. Having re-mortgaged the modest estate to keep abreast of his debts, Camille was finding it impossible to meet the payments out of sales. He had thought of various schemes to ease the pressure. At one point he had even considered offering tourists overnight accommodation on their way through from Chagny to the north. But then seven months ago his wife, Marianne, had left him and he had been unable to cope with any additional burden of work. He had begged her to stay, but she said she wouldn't come back until he had made a decision – never to see the American woman again. Camille had promised, and meant what he said, but when Madeleine Walker telephoned, asking him to deliver several cases to the château, he had reasoned it was an order he couldn't afford to refuse. Once there, in William Walker's absence, he had found himself powerless to resist her charm and her beauty. And there was something else besides; she seemed to need him. He didn't understand why – a woman with all that power and privilege – but there it was; he supplied something that was missing in her life – something more than sex, though that was wonderful. Madeleine Walker made whole-hearted love like a woman released; like a woman half her age.

Since Marianne's departure, Camille and Madeleine had met more often. Bored with discretion, Madeleine had become less careful. This made Camille nervous. Though he was not afraid of William Walker, he knew that he was a man of influence, and feared the commercial damage he might do if provoked. No doubt he and his powerful friends could, if they chose, make life very unpleasant for a struggling wine-grower. For this reason Camille urged Madeleine to join him on neutral territory. They would rendezvous at the Roman amphitheatre in Autun, or high in the underpopulated country of the Morvan. For Camille this meant stealing precious time he could and should have put to more productive use, but her body, and her unaccountable dependence on him, had become so compelling that he was unable to get her out of his mind. He would leave her feeling his life would have been incomplete without the moments they had just spent together. The gentle arc of her thigh, the warm swell of her buttocks, the softness of her foot in his hand – these were gifts he had no will to deny. Once he had even noticed the tender, vulnerable flesh of her heel as she knelt to lay out a picnic, and knew he would remember the sight all his life.

And yet, when he asked himself whether this was love, he was filled with doubt. In some ways it was more obsessive. What was love, anyway? You could love a horse, or a wine, or a book. You could love in a comfortable way, content in an undemanding relationship. You could profess to love God, whose very existence was problematical. But this feeling was not comfortable, nor was it mere affection, or faith. This was fierce and addictive and consuming. For this he had sacrificed his marriage, and risked forcing the same outcome on Madeleine; for this he was further endangering his ailing business and had surrendered control of his life.

However, in the last month or so these considerations had become more insistent. The very fact that he was now more aware of the price he was paying meant that the fire might at last be contained – or so he reasoned. Madeleine, after all, could return to her husband when all this was over, assuming he would have her. If Camille neglected his business to the point of no return, there was no one to fall back on. And despite himself, when she had talked of the crisis at the château, a small unformed thought had taken root. Suppose this sudden drama could be turned to his advantage . . . their advantage? Suppose, without hurting anyone, except perhaps Walker and his bank balance, some of the ransom could be diverted? Where was the harm? Walker could afford it, and the kidnappers were unlikely to damage their asset. With one cash injection Camille could pay his bills and resume a normal life. If it were possible to bind Madeleine to him in this scheme, he could offer her a future. After all, the fact that she needed him now suggested that her relationship with her husband was unsatisfactory. She must be staying with Walker out of loyalty, or habit, or fear, but not out of love. If she could be persuaded that this was where her escape, her happiness lay, she might seize the chance. It occurred to Camille that explaining his abrupt change of fortune to the tax authorities might prove difficult but that problem lay a long way down the line. Perhaps he could dispense the money a little at a time. He was sure something could be worked out.

As he walked back up the yard, Madeleine Walker's white Mercedes pulled in at the old blue gate, parking in the shade by the stables, with no longer any attempt at concealment. Though he had asked her to come back, he was surprised. Never predictable, she would visit at will. It was a privilege assumed by the rich. As she leaned up for a kiss before emerging from the car, he thought her prompt return must be an omen. But though he had imagined earlier that he was now beginning to be master of this affair, inhaling the sweet fragrance of her skin and hair dissolved his confidence in an instant.

He told her not to get out, and ran to the cellar, where he picked up two bottles of red wine, a corkscrew, and glasses. Armed with these he sat beside her and directed her to drive up the hill, on the narrow lane that led to the ridge overlooking the village. As she drove, Madeleine told him of the Polaroid brought back from Châteauneuf by Tom and Robert. Eager to know more, Camille questioned her about Julia's condition. She looked well, Madeleine said, apart from what looked like a patch of blood on her head. She was holding yesterday's newspaper. If she was frightened, she didn't show it. She was a strong woman.

On the hard ground, with the church far below them, they set out a tartan rug. While Camille opened the wine, Madeleine sat and watched him.

'I shouldn't be here,' she said.

'There's nothing you can do to help her, at this moment. What will your husband do next?'

'Raise the money. He's already making arrangements.'

Camille considered this new information. 'What, for the whole ten million?'

Madeleine nodded.

'It's a lot of money.' Camille felt self-conscious after such a trite remark. It had been mere camouflage for his thoughts. To what extent dared he take her into his confidence?

'For a life?' she said. 'I don't think so. Wouldn't you pay ten million to save me?'

'You know I would. Everything I have.' He paused. 'Unfortunately that's approximately fifteen francs.'

Camille laughed and Madeleine found his amusement infectious. It was only here that she was able to smile these days, under the huge blue sky, with a man who made her feel twenty again. No, better than she had felt at twenty; more mature and less afraid. When they had drained their glasses, she lay on top of him, feeling the heat of the sun like a balm on her tiredness. Unable to sleep after the arrival of the photograph, she had risen at five to work on plans for the Shakespeare event. She knew Helen would want it to go ahead and was more determined than ever to make it succeed, both as an act of defiance and as a symbol of their friendship and co-operation. But in her work she had been distracted by thoughts of this man, beneath her, this candid, smiling face, the mouth full and too wide, the lips crimson from the wine, the eyes telling her they wanted her. He made no demands, other than physical ones, which she needed no persuading to grant. She leaned down and kissed him, holding his face in her hands and losing herself in the embrace; losing the tensions of her over-controlled existence. As she undid his belt and eased herself on to him, she felt in this joining they were part of the land, like the vines.

Afterwards Camille moved the rug to the shade of a clump of bushes on the ridge, where they lay on their backs, side by side. He reached for her hand. 'Will your husband hand over the money, or will he try to trick them?'

'All he wants is Julia back, naturally. He'll do whatever it takes.'

'And the gendarmes?'

'At the moment they're not involved, but I don't think he can keep them out much longer.'

'When do you think the handover will be?'

'I don't know. He'll delay it as long as possible, without endangering Julia, of course. Maybe Tuesday, Wednesday?'

When they parted a short while later, Madeleine drove off realising he was right when he warned that they shouldn't be seen together. Under the circumstances it would seem strange to anyone who knew them. But he had begged her to meet him again tomorrow at a rendezvous they would arrange later, and she doubted whether she had the strength or the desire to refuse. While she was at the château she was prepared to devote all her care and energy to William and the release of Julia. But she couldn't deny herself these brief, intense moments. Life might never offer them again.

* * *

In St Luc, Tom Bellman hadn't slept at all. Since the meeting at the château, his head had been filled with wild thoughts that swarmed in unpredictable directions, only to rebound when all doors were barred against them. Somewhere, maybe not far from here, maybe a few miles away, a man with a cheap camera had stood in front of Julia Walker yesterday and taken a simple photograph. She was holding a local paper and she looked normal. Had it not been for the blood on her forehead, it might have been a holiday snap. And maybe, just maybe, Helen had been close to her, looking on. Tom had tried to imagine what was in the minds of the kidnappers. They would argue that there was no point in putting Helen in the picture too. They would understand that she had no value as a hostage, and they weren't in the business of making people feel good by sending them reassurance just for the sake of it. So, as everyone kept saying, this proof of Julia's life didn't prove anything about Helen.

Tom had been waiting outside the laser printer's in Arnay half an hour before they opened. Switching on the radio, he had listened to the news, half hoping to hear an announcement about the case, but knowing in his heart that there wouldn't be one. Today, he decided, whatever happened, he must insist that Walker inform the police, and if he refused there was no alternative but for Tom to do it himself. They had tried it Walker's way, and as far as Helen was concerned it was achieving nothing.

While the printer's dealt with the three enlargements Tom ordered, he had gone for a coffee and a croissant at the Café du Nord. It was not that he was hungry. He hadn't felt any desire for food since his arrival. But he knew it was vital to remain strong. Walking across the square in front of the handsome Hôtel de Ville, with its blaze of geraniums, he had imagined Helen coming out of the grocer's, laden with juicy tomatoes, and peaches, and plump muscat grapes, and he had felt sick and dry-mouthed with missing her. Sometimes, when fear and loneliness were in him like this, he thought it must be what people meant by hell; a perpetual state of separation from the loved one. As he entered the cool, high room, he had resolved to ring Daisy that night.

Now, in his kitchen, with the sun streaming in through the double glass doors facing the gallery, he studied the blown-up photograph which he had Blu-Tacked to the rough plaster of the wall. What secrets did this image hold or, come to that, withhold? Little definition had been lost in the enlarging process and the quality was astonishing. What thoughts had been going through Julia's mind, he wondered, as she posed for her captors? What message had she hoped to convey? Her face looked calm, though showing signs of fatigue under the eyes. While her beautiful hair was not groomed, it was still well enough cut to look far from dishevelled. Her mouth was set in a firm line, the jaw taut with determination. And the edge of the newspaper ran in a diagonal across her brown, slender neck. The hands seemed unremarkable. The nails were rimed with dirt, as might be expected, and on one wrist there was a loose bangle, which might be made of silver but was now dull with neglect. Meanwhile, behind Julia was her imprecise image reflected in a mirror which, Tom guessed, dated from the eighteenth century.

He picked up a large magnifying glass which he had also bought in Arnay, and went over for a closer look, glancing at the photograph of Helen and her sister on the dresser. They too were watching him now, willing him to use his powers of observation. What would the gendarmes be looking for if they examined the image, he asked himself? To begin with, in close-up, the newspaper print was now legible. At least he could confirm that the date didn't appear to have been tampered with in any way, and Tom had done enough photography to realise that there was no process-work in the shot. The Polaroid had been taken yesterday, or maybe late the night before last, if one of the kidnappers had access to the newspaper presses, which was doubtful and in any case not worth the trouble. Under the scrutiny of the powerful glass, which distorted the photograph at its edges but held true in the centre, there was a guarded look in those frank, brown eyes. And higher up, Tom thought he could make out some dark, indistinct reflection in the top right-hand corner of the frame, no more than a dense shape that might be damage to the mirror's backing.

He made one last pass with the magnifier from top to bottom of the enlargement, lingering for a moment on the band round Julia's wrist. Now he could see that it had delicate beading at the rim. As he leaned closer, he also noticed that there were dents in the metal, suggesting that it was hollow. The longer he looked, the more a feeling grew in him that he had seen this bracelet before. When he stood back, lowering the glass, the inkling grew into a certainty; a sensation not based on the evidence alone but on a deep-seated impulse that it was there to tell him something. It was telling him that this was Helen's bracelet, a present he had bought her on a weekend break in Norfolk when they had been young and short of cash. Because of the memory, rather than the beauty of the object, it had become her favourite piece, borrowed by Daisy in her early teens and the victim of many a mishap. Familiar and comforting as an old sweater, it had become one of the household gods.

Without taking his eyes off the photograph, Tom sat down, and found himself smiling. Now the weariness he had held at bay all week flooded over him. He remembered the day he had bought the bracelet, in a small shop in Blakeney. They had just one showcase of jewellery, he recalled, shining among the Aran jerseys and the sheepskin gloves. While Helen bought their favourite Dairyland ice-creams from the van on the quayside, overlooking the estuary, he had made an impulsive

choice to surprise her. Impatient while the gift was wrapped
in tissue paper, he had hurried out of the shop to see her coming
up the street holding two huge cornets like frozen torches.
The smile on her face when she saw him was full of joy and
anticipation. As they met, without speaking, he took the ice-
creams from her and handed her the package. Unwrapping it
like a child, she took out the bracelet, and the smile seemed to
grow wider while, at the same time, her eyes filled with tears.
Then she had flung her arms round his neck, and kissed him
hard and long, crushing the cornets between them and laughing.
It was a moment of utter content, followed by a day when the
mood had never broken. That evening, instead of eating at a
pub, they had taken fish and chips along the path that led to
the sea, beside the moored yachts, and sat in the coarse grass
with only the birds for company. This small life, with its easy
pleasures, had been all they wanted. The future they planned
held no great adventures. All they asked of it was that it should
let them stay together. And on Helen's wrist the bracelet
gleamed as though setting the seal on that wish.

But how did Julia come to be wearing it in the photograph,
and what did it mean? In his mounting excitement, Tom tried
to order his thoughts. First, and best, it might be a sign that
Helen and Julia were together, as Walker suspected. What other
possibilities were there? Tom forced himself to face the worst.
Might it have been stolen from Helen? She was apt to leave it
in all sorts of places when she wasn't wearing it. But who
would take something of so little value, and why would Julia
put it on? Unless, for some reason, she had been told to . . . ?
No, it didn't make sense. The most reasonable conclusion was
that Helen had been kidnapped along with Julia, perhaps
because she had happened to see something, and this was either
the kidnappers', or Julia's, way of telling him she was alive.
Now, when he rang Daisy, at least he would have some good
news for her.

Hurrying out to tell Robert, he paused at the front door overlooking the small courtyard. The sun, climbing now, was uninterrupted by clouds. To his right, over towards Lacanche, the orchards were heavy with fruit. Little Georges, the octogenarian father of the village, passed by on the road, leaning on his stick and waving with his free hand. The world was going about its business in the normal way, and Tom thought with satisfaction that it was becoming more normal by the minute. As long as Helen was alive, he could cope with anything. Now it was just a matter of time.

When Tom and Robert reached the château, in buoyant mood, with the enlargements, there was a gendarmerie car parked by the back door. Robert looked at Tom and raised an eyebrow. Let in by Jean-Marie, as they crossed the hall they passed a uniformed gendarme on his way out. William Walker, standing in the doorway of the drawing room, smiled as he motioned to them to join him.

'Gentlemen,' he said; 'am I glad to see you. I have a little good news.'

'That's funny, he does too,' Robert said, indicating Tom.

'Well, it's too early . . .' Tom began to protest.

'I'm telling you, it's good news,' Robert insisted.

'Well, who first?' Walker said.

'You start,' Tom said.

'OK. Well, they found Julia's car. A small step for man . . . but along with the Polaroid, it's a start. At least things are moving, thank God.'

'Where?' Robert said.

'In Beaune. You know that little street by the Hôtel du Centre, with the antique shop on the corner? Well, at the end of that there's a cul-de-sac on a hill by the town wall. It was up there, in an unrestricted parking space.'

'So why did they report it?' Tom asked.

'Fortunately it had been broken into. All they took was the radio. I say fortunately because otherwise it could have been there a couple of weeks before anybody asked questions.'

'So the young man I saw driving it must have been one of the kidnappers?' Robert said.

'Quite possibly,' Walker agreed.

'Did you tell the gendarmes the rest?' Robert said.

Walker shook his head.

'I think it's time,' Robert went on. 'Apart from anything else, holding back information now would be a serious business.'

'I agree, Robert. It's just that he clearly wasn't the right guy to tell. Do you have the time to drive into Beaune? I'll talk to the major right now. As a matter of fact I know him slightly. He has a house in Veilly.'

'We'll all go,' Robert said. 'It's important we know who we're dealing with. But first, my friend here has made a discovery.'

Tom allowed himself a small smile. He must not let himself, or anyone else, build too much on such fragile foundations. Unrolling one of the enlargements, he moved aside a silver ornament and laid it on the sofa table. Walker helped by weighting down the corners with books and a glass paperweight.

'The quality's amazing,' Walker said.

'Does this look familiar to you at all?' Tom said, pointing to the bracelet.

Walker leaned closer, concentrating. 'No,' he said, 'can't say it does. But without being a traitor to my sex here, I have to say that men don't invariably have the keenest eye for these things. I suspect we need my wife for this.' He turned to the wall and pressed a discreet bell. 'Why do you ask, Tom?'

'Because I have a strong feeling it's Helen's. I'm pretty well certain in fact. I gave it her a long time ago.'

Walker straightened and looked at him. 'Well, that's wonderful. You know I had the feeling . . .'

'The thing is,' Tom interrupted, 'I need to try and take this thing a step at a time. I'm not too sure what it means yet.'

'Caution!' Robert said. 'If he won the lottery he'd think they'd given it to the wrong man.'

'I know what you're saying, Tom, and I respect that, but it seems to me we have to regard this as a positive sign,' Walker said.

Tom couldn't suppress a smile in agreement, and at that moment Madeleine Walker appeared.

'There you are, darling,' Walker said. 'Now, we want you to take a good look at this.' He indicated the bracelet. 'Tom had the enlargement made in Arnay. Does anything strike you at all?'

Madeleine studied the blow-up. After a moment she looked up. 'I don't recognise it,' she said. 'It's curious but in the original I didn't pay any attention to it. Julia must have bought it recently, second-hand or something.'

'It's a whole lot better than that,' Walker said.

'I think it's Helen's,' Tom explained. 'She's had it for years.'

To Tom's surprise and slight embarrassment, Madeleine took his hand and pressed it between hers. 'That's marvellous,' she said. 'I'm so happy.'

'Thank you,' Tom said. 'Yes, it's got to be good hasn't it. The thing is how did Julia come to be wearing it?'

'It's a signal,' Robert said with great confidence. 'That's obvious.'

'Women don't usually put on the jewellery of people they hardly know,' Madeleine said. 'I agree with Robert. I think Julia is telling us Helen's with her. It's wonderful news.'

Despite his reluctance to count any chickens, Tom couldn't help but be cheered by this genuine reaction. 'So what do we do now?' he asked.

'First – right now – we report the case to Major Granier. He's not going to be too happy about the delay but he'll understand.'

Attentive, Tom admired the confidence of a man who knew that status would overrule even the most legitimate objections the gendarmes might raise.

'That means the hunt's on. Within an hour they'll have the entire region crawling with cops.'

'But the kidnappers said . . .' Tom began, half pleased and half concerned.

'We have no choice, Tom,' Walker interrupted. 'As Robert says, not to come clean now, or worse, actually to hamper the gendarmes, would be both irresponsible and extremely unhelpful to Julia and Helen.'

Tom nodded, accepting the reality of the situation.

Forty minutes later a large blue Citroën saloon pulled into the Rue des Blanches Fleurs in Beaune. The gendarmerie was in the severe outskirts of the beautiful town. A two-storey rectangular concrete block built in the 1960s, it was painted peach and cream. Why was it, Tom wondered, that surrounded by the examples of rounded, timeless magnificence the mediaeval architects of Beaune had left them, the modern school had thought fit to abandon the graceful curve altogether? Outside the building was a poster for the Foreign Legion, showing a clean-cut young officer wearing the familiar white cap against a desert background. 'Look at life another way,' the slogan invited.

As they passed it, Robert said: 'Sand and camels, that's life? Who are they kidding?'

Despite the seriousness of their mission, both Tom and Walker smiled. Before they had left the château, Walker had given strict instructions for any calls to be put through to his mobile, which Robert took with him into the gendarmerie. Tom, meanwhile, had been entrusted with the Polaroid and the enlargement. As they waited in the bare hall for the gendarme at reception to contact Major Granier, Robert explained to Tom that in France the police operated in towns with more than ten thousand inhabitants, while gendarmes took care of the country. In Beaune there were both, the gendarmerie being a regional headquarters.

Impressed by Walker's arrival in person, Major Granier himself came down to meet them. He was a pale, intense man in his forties, with deep, vertical hollows from cheekbone to jaw. Shaking each of them by the hand, with the nearest he could come to a smile for Walker, he led them up the stairs and into his office in silence. Major Granier's room was as uncompromising as its occupant. On his desk was a single photograph of his wife, a determined, bespectacled woman, with hair permed to within an inch of its life. There were charts on the walls, a map of the area, and a view of low-rent flats with billowing washing. Granier motioned his guests to three metal-framed chairs.

'It's good of you to see us at such short notice, Major. I appreciate it,' Walker began.

Major Granier joined the tips of his fingers in front of his face. 'It was a good time,' he said. 'Burgundy is behaving itself.' It was the first, wry indication that the stern mask might conceal a trace of whimsy. 'Besides, it's not every day that we receive a visit from a press mogul. What can I do for you, Monsieur Walker?'

'I'm afraid I have an admission to make,' Walker said. 'I wouldn't blame you for being very angry.'

By way of reply, Granier raised an eyebrow. Tom and Robert dug in for the storm.

'The car – my daughter's car – that's only part of it.' Unlike his colleagues, Walker showed no sign of nervousness.

Tom had to remind himself that a man who had dealt with world leaders was unlikely to buckle in the presence of a small-town official.

'On Tuesday she was kidnapped, and Tom's wife, Madame Bellman, disappeared.' With great clarity, Walker told Granier everything he knew, not forgetting a single important detail. Throughout he stressed the fact that the kidnappers had issued dire warnings of what would happen should he inform the authorities.

Granier listened without interrupting. When Walker had finished, he sat back a little from his desk and picked up a pencil, tapping alternate ends. 'This is a very serious business,' he said, 'and you have lost us four precious days.'

'Do you have children, Major?' Walker asked.

The major nodded. 'Two.'

'Then you understand there are laws more ancient and more compelling than those passed by parliaments.'

Granier inclined his head, accepting the point. 'May I see the photograph?'

Tom held out the envelope containing the Polaroid and removed the elastic band from the furled enlargement. As he laid out the poster-sized image on the major's desk, he hesitated before weighting down one corner with the portrait of the permed madonna. Seeing his dilemma, the major wagged his forefinger in a small gesture of disapproval and produced a stapler from his desk. His eyes registering every detail, he studied the two versions in silence.

After a few moments, Tom couldn't restrain himself any longer. 'The bracelet she's wearing; I'm sure it belongs to my wife. It was a present, some time ago.'

Granier looked at him. 'You have a photograph of your wife too, monsieur?' he asked.

Tom produced from his inside pocket the smiling snapshot of Helen and her sister, Nancy, surrounded by summer blooms, which he had remembered to take out of its frame. Though they were not twins, there was something about their eyes and their shared *joie de vivre* that made the relationship unmistakable.

While Granier held up the likeness, handling the edges with care, and then placed it beside the others, Tom ran through the enquiries he had made and mentioned Helen's acquaintance with Julia. The major seemed satisfied with his thoroughness. When he had finished, Granier asked simple, searching questions which demonstrated that everything he had been told had been filed away with great precision. He said that violent crime was a rarity in the region – perhaps three or four murders a year – and that these were almost always crimes of passion. He couldn't remember a kidnapping since he had been in Beaune, which suggested that if this was not the work of foreigners, it might well have been carried out by opportunists. That, he said, meant two things; he and his colleagues might get little help from criminal records, but the perpetrators would make mistakes.

Never raising his voice, Granier stamped his authority on the meeting. He explained that he would lead the investigation, reporting to his superior, a Captain, and through him to the Procureur de la République. While the Beaune police would co-operate with the gendarmerie in the city itself, the enquiry proper would be based at a command post on site – perhaps Bligny, manned by twenty or thirty gendarmes, some in plain clothes. In addition, Granier said, a member of a specialist research unit from Dijon would be attached to the team. The first task would be to give Julia's car a thorough examination, and to check the Polaroid for fingerprints, though he doubted whether any would be found. The outline of the operation complete, he looked at Walker. 'And the tape you mentioned, Monsieur Walker? You have it with you?'

Walker produced a cassette from his pocket and handed it over.

'Thank you,' Granier said. 'This may have a lot to tell us. With your permission we will also need to keep a unit stationed at the château of course, and to make arrangements with the telephone system.'

'Absolutely,' Walker said, without hesitation. 'Whatever it takes.'

Heartened by this immediate and dramatic widening of the net, Tom nevertheless felt he must raise the question hovering over the plan. 'But how do you hide an army like that?' he asked.

'You forget, monsieur, that this "army" is made up of individuals, all of whom are trained to be invisible when it's necessary. We work by night as well as by day, you know.'

'Yes,' Walker said, indicating Robert. 'My friend here is familiar with those methods.'

Tom and Robert exchanged a glance.

'I used to be a cat burglar,' Robert said, by way of explanation.

Tom and Walker laughed but Granier confined his mirth to lining up his pencil parallel with the blotter. Rising from his desk he pointed to the photograph of Helen and her sister. 'May I keep this for the time being, with the others?'

Tom felt a moment of panic. He knew it sounded absurd to say so, but it was the only likeness of Helen he had with him in France, and if that were missing, so, in a way he couldn't explain, was the spirit of the house. 'Er, yes . . .' he stumbled; 'yes of course, but . . .'

'Don't be concerned, monsieur,' Granier said, already ahead of him. 'We'll run off prints. I'll have someone drop round the original. Today, probably.'

Tom smiled his gratitude.

Granier told them to inform him of any developments at once, and assured them that although it was the holiday season, and the manpower at his disposal was therefore limited, the enquiry would begin without delay. Without making extravagant promises, he left them with a sense of growing confidence.

* * *

'Gentlemen, I think what's called for is a half-hour of r and r,' Walker said, as they turned out of the gate and headed back the way they had come. 'We have the technology,' he added, glancing at the telephone. 'Let's do it. Robert, you're the man. Where does a fellow take a glass of wine in Beaune?'

Thrusting his arm forward like the leader of a cavalry charge, Robert said: 'Follow me.'

'It's market day. It'll be murder,' Tom said.

'We're not going to the sixteenth arrondissement of Paris,' Robert said. 'In Dédé's bar, market day or no market day, it's the same.'

Having parked with difficulty, directed by Robert who knew all the back doubles, they entered the cool shade of the Café Claudette. Dédé, the proprietor, had his back to them, talking to an old market trader in a faded denim jacket. Robert greeted his friend and introduced Tom and Walker, mentioning that the latter was American and lived at the château in Bessey.

'And meet my friend the Marquis of Coquelicot,' Dédé said, indicating the noble cut of the market trader's court dress. 'He drops in here regularly for three dozen oysters and a bottle of Puligny Montrachet.'

The old man's fit of giggles could only be arrested with a glass of Ricard, on the house.

'What will you take, messieurs?' Dédé asked Tom and Walker.

'For me, a *canon*,' Walker said, without hesitation.

Now it was Dédé's turn to laugh. 'What's this? A cheap red wine for the owner of a château! My God, no wonder you're the richest country in the world.'

Walker smiled.

'Me too,' Tom said, with a grin. 'But with me it's because we're no longer rich.'

Dédé thought about this as he poured three glasses. 'Ah,

no,' he said. 'It's the same everywhere. Soon it will be poverty for us all.'

'Well, at your prices it certainly won't be poverty for you, you old robber,' Robert said. 'I've heard you lend money to the Société Générale.'

'Gentlemen,' Walker said, holding up his glass in a toast. 'Julia and Helen.'

Before drinking, Robert whispered in Dédé's ear, whereupon the proprietor's manner changed as he too raised his small glass of Pernod. 'I'll join you in that with all my heart,' he said, motioning them to a table. 'You have things to discuss. The house is yours.'

Acknowledging his generous response Walker, Tom and Robert sat at a Formica-topped table in the corner.

'Well,' Tom said, 'where does that leave us?'

'Where we were before,' Robert said.

'Granier was impressive, I thought,' Walker said.

'Of course, he sounds impressive,' Robert said, unimpressed. 'But those gendarmes . . .' He opened the palms of his hands.

'There speaks a policeman,' Walker said, smiling at Tom. 'The French police have a healthy disregard for their country cousins.'

'But what you said before, Monsieur Walker, is still true. The way to find Julia and Helen is the way of the fox,' Robert said.

'What way is that, exactly?' Tom said, frowning.

'He's the colour of the countryside in autumn,' Robert said by way of explanation. 'He keeps to the hedgerows. His eyes are sharp. He doesn't travel in noisy cars with "gendarme" scribbled all over them.'

Walker nodded, enjoying the metaphor. 'But if we're to carry on making our own enquiries,' he said, 'we must make an absolute condition. Everything we discover independently, and I mean everything, must be passed to Granier and his team.

We can't have this thing firing in two directions at once.'

'I agree,' Tom said.

'Fine,' Robert said. 'It's fine with me. Dédé, the same again,' he called to his friend. 'And this time, no short measures.'

As Dédé replied with a shrug of mock disdain, the mobile telephone rang.

Robert held it to his ear. 'Yes. Hello. Speak to me.' From his expression the others could see that he was having difficulty hearing the caller. 'A moment,' Robert bellowed into the mouthpiece and, kicking back his chair, went to the doorway. 'Yes, hello. Louder please.' At last the message, whatever it was, became clear and Robert motioned to Walker to join him, fast. 'It's them,' Robert mouthed.

As Walker took the telephone, Tom feared that the kidnappers had somehow spotted their visit to the gendarmerie. Perhaps they had followed them all the way? In which case the optimism of a few minutes ago had been misplaced. Meanwhile Dédé and the market trader had become aware of the real-life drama unfolding at the Café Claudette.

'. . . Yes, we have it,' Walker was saying, tense as he held a hand to his free ear, dulling the noise of the busy town. 'And physically she's well, you say. Now . . . no, I insist, you listen to me for a moment. Hello . . . now, before we go any further with this thing I want to know about the second woman, the Englishwoman. Until you give me this information we have no deal. Do you understand me? No, I can't hear you. Repeat that please. Hello . . . Hello . . . Goddammit!' Frustrated at the loss of the signal, Walker looked ready to throw the mobile on the ground.

Tom, who had been keyed up to receive news of some sort, now felt more anxious than before.

'I'm so sorry, Tom. It was just total shash. Couldn't make out a thing. That's why we need someone permanently by the phone back home,' Walker said. 'Françoise, my secretary, gave them the number OK but then the system falls apart. With a unit from the gendarmerie on the spot, they'll monitor everything. Whether we like it or not, gentlemen, we can't do this without them. Let's go to it.' He plucked a fifty-franc note from his wallet.

'That's too much, monsieur,' Dédé said.

'Next time we come to your excellent establishment,' Walker said, sounding determined, 'we'll trouble you for champagne. Please set it against that.'

CHAPTER SIX

In the evenings, Julia Walker was more aware of the sound of crickets. Often, too, she could distinguish the monotonous chant of frogs, which must mean there was water nearby – a pond perhaps, or even a lake. Wherever they were, they established a slender link with a world outside this featureless cell. She dreamed of sitting on the terrace she planned to build at the cottage, drinking wine with friends and listening to the incessant dialogue of the land; millions of creatures voicing messages of fear, parenthood, warning, attraction. And in the midst of this energy, this urgency, here she was with only mosquitoes for company.

She was tired now. The confidence which had carried her through the first three days of the ordeal had begun to leak away. Despite her strength, doubt had started to nag at her determination. Though she was hungry, she had no appetite for the stale bread and milk which had become her habitual diet. On a couple of occasions the regime had varied. Twice Paul had brought her cold garlic sausage, and last night he had appeared with a banana and a small piece of cheese. Julia had the feeling that his heart wasn't in it. He seemed like a reluctant recruit to this ramshackle operation. She had the impression that he was a little afraid of Black Helmet, though so far she had been unable to open him up on the subject. Black Helmet was also the one she feared most. There was something about his obvious distaste for contact that made her feel uneasy. Whereas with Paul and Blue Helmet there was a small sense of humanity hidden beneath the surface, in his case there was none. He had the cold separateness of a misfit. She sensed that if he chose, he could be pitiless, and the longer she remained his prisoner, the greater the likelihood of that happening.

She tried to imagine what her father and stepmother would be doing about her disappearance. Blue Helmet had told her that they had received the photograph, and for a few hours this news had given her heart. At least now they knew she was alive. But why had nothing happened? Why didn't they just pay up and get this thing over with? She supposed the kidnappers had asked for a realistic sum, but maybe she was wrong. Perhaps their demand had been too great even for her father to meet. And what had they done with her little Peugeot? Surely the police would have no trouble tracing that, unless it had been dumped somewhere outside the region?

When she found herself lapsing into unhelpful speculation like this, Julia tried to divert her thoughts elsewhere; memories, plans, people. More and more she thought of her late mother, missing her as much now as she had on that terrible day. At the same time she knew this cruel uncertainty would have made her unhappy. When her father remarried, she had at first found him hard to forgive. Madeleine – chic, cool Madeleine – had been so different. The shock had been made worse by Julia's suspicion that her father's relationship with Madeleine had begun before her mother died. Though she had never dared confront him with this, her intuition told her she was right. Now that she was isolated and fearful, fantasies wove themselves around a possible plot between her father and Madeleine to treat her plight as something less than a priority.

No sooner had these insidious thoughts surfaced than she dismissed them as ludicrous.

And what of the other woman, whom no one mentioned? How was it that she never heard a sound from her, or a reference of any sort? She supposed it was possible that the second victim was being kept in another part of the building. That was a simple enough explanation. But it was also conceivable that she was dead; sacrificed because she was of no financial value. Julia felt she couldn't let the matter rest without doing her utmost to discover the truth, even if it meant a hunger strike. Yes, that was it. She would refuse food until they told her. Giving up dry bread would in any case be no great hardship. And while they failed to answer, they would have to watch their valuable asset grow weaker by the day.

Julia felt heartened by this decision; somehow it gave her imprisonment a purpose. And it was not long before she had a chance to put her plan into effect. A few minutes later the door opened and Black Helmet came in, carrying the brown plastic tray. As he approached, Julia could see that on it was not the usual chunk of baguette but a piece of ham with a sliced tomato beside it. How cruel of fate, she thought, to bring her an appetising meal just when she had vowed to refuse all food.

Black Helmet laid it on the floor close to her foot. 'Special for Saturday night,' he explained.

'What?' Forcing him to repeat sentences made indistinct by the mask was one of her few satisfactions.

'Eat it,' he said.

'I don't want it.'

'Don't be stupid. Eat it.'

'No. I don't want it.'

Black Helmet squatted in front of her, bulky and menacing. She could smell his sour sweat and see the small, hard eyes behind the greasy film of the visor.

'If you don't, I'll make you.'

'Oh, really? How will you do that?'

'I know how to make animals eat.'

Julia registered this, the first information he had so far revealed about himself. 'How do you know?'

'I know. That's all. Now . . .' He held the tray in front of her unflinching face, and with the other hand picked up the fork, 'eat it.'

'On one condition,' Julia said.

'We make the conditions.'

'The what?' she said, playing the infuriating game again.

'The conditions,' he shouted, his eyes widening; 'We make them, not you.'

'Well this one I make, so you'd better listen for a change. I want to know what happened to the other woman. I saw another woman at the house. If you don't tell me, or if you've harmed her, I will not eat. And if I don't eat, I will become weak and I will die. And then you have nothing to sell, and the charge will be murder. It's up to you.'

Black Helmet was silent for a moment, before replacing the tray on the ground. 'She got away,' he said at last. 'She escaped.'

'Ah, so you admit there was somebody. And you let her get away?' Julia sounded incredulous.

Black Helmet nodded.

'I don't believe you.'

Black Helmet stood up. From her sitting position, Julia glared at him, daring him to do something.

'Two grown guys and a small woman! I don't think so. Who was she anyway?'

Black Helmet shrugged. Then, seeming to realise he was out of his depth, he turned and left the room, locking the door behind him.

Julia analysed the exchange. Two things seemed clear. There

had been a second woman and she had not escaped. Therefore she was either dead, or a prisoner, like herself. Meanwhile the tray with the ham sat taunting Julia. After days of tasteless scraps it was like a dream of banquets – game decked out with its feathers; roast suckling pig with an apple in its mouth; poached salmon laid on a salver with fine scales of cucumber. It was easy to decide on a hunger strike, but when confronted with the means of ending it, the appetite was almost passionate, panting to be fed. Nudging the tray with her foot, Julia pushed it to the corner of the room where it would be out of her eyeline.

Enjoying the freedom of her arms, the kidnappers' zeal for handcuffing her having waned, she held them out to her side and made small circles, feeling the stiffness in her shoulders. She imagined being on a beach with a curving line of coconut palms and the silhouette of a crude wooden pier in the distance. As she crossed the white sand to the water, she felt new-born, lithe, warmed by the sun after the fear of hurricanes; free. A few yards out, in the reef, the most beautiful sight in the world awaited her; better than Venice, or the Himalayas, or the Grand Canyon. She only had to break the surface of the water with her head and there, renewed every time she marvelled at it, would be an indescribable kaleidoscope of swift, inspired, intense colour, impossible to reproduce anywhere else in life.

Sustained by the fantasy, Julia thought again of the other woman and resolved once more to go on the offensive. For the sake of her fellow human being, as well as herself, she must manipulate the kidnappers with her own value to them. But first, with Black Helmet gone, her eye was drawn to the newspaper she had held in the photograph. It still lay in the angle of the wall behind the door. She supposed the old trick they always tried in comics was a fiction, but with nothing else to occupy her she might as well try it. After all, what was there to lose? Opening up the paper, she pushed it far enough under the door to catch the key, should it be co-operative enough to oblige, the way it did in stories. Next she searched the ground for something slender to use as a prod, and found a piece of wire which had broken off the length used to bind her legs. Twisting this to give it more rigidity, she paused for a moment to listen. Since there had been no reaction to the paper, she inserted the probe into the keyhole. What were you supposed to do now, she wondered? Bank robbers in films would turn knobs on the doors of safes for mere seconds before the correct combination offered itself like magic. In her place they would poke around for a few moments and the obedient key would no doubt describe a neat triple somersault on to the patient page.

But reality, it seemed, wasn't familiar with the movies. However she angled the wire, with gentle coaxing and mumbled prayers to an imagined patron saint of escapers, the key failed to budge. Julia tried sliding the wire in at the very top of the aperture, holding it with both hands to keep it level. Then she switched to the left, edging it in so that it might catch the side of the key and dislodge it. When that too was unsuccessful, she tried the other side, her tongue out and her brow breaking into a sweat with concentration and the will to make it work. On the underside of the keyhole, she attempted to worm the wire in below the key, pushing up the tip at the last moment to ease it out. Tired now, but still determined, she decided to stick to the task until her hands were unable to hold the wire any longer; until she was too weary to lift her arms. It appeared that, for once, there was no guard on the other side, and this might never happen again. She would try every imaginable position, in every imaginable order, until either she or the lock surrendered.

For once Julia was glad they had taken her watch. Measuring time always made the work seem more desperate. As she manipulated the wire, she tried to divert her thoughts to other things; to the attic she had shared with Charles just round the corner from the Buci market on the Left Bank; to the curious florist's shop built in the angle of the giant wooden props holding up a tall building; to the morning when Charles, frightened by her expectations, checked out while she was still asleep. Gone like a half-smoked Gauloise rolled in maize paper. They went out quicker. Creep. Julia found herself laughing and crying at the same time. She imagined the tears making lines in the dirt on her face. When she had finished this she must spit on her handkerchief and try for a makeshift wash. 'Preserve your mystery,' she heard a small voice say, and she smiled at the memory. Annie, her schoolfriend; Annie Caplan. Whenever, as kids, one saw the other in an inelegant situation – taking a pee behind the bushes on a picnic, or falling off a bicycle, legs sprawling, knickers showing – the cry would go up from the witness: 'Preserve your mystery!' The trick was to do it in the voice of Mrs Carnoustie, the starchy old matron who taught them math. Where was Annie now she needed her, Julia wondered? Married with two kids in Connecticut? Telling her daughter to preserve her mystery?

The attempt was beginning to look hopeless. Throughout, there had not been the slightest sign of encouraging movement. She had tried every angle, perhaps twenty, thirty times, and the key seemed immovable. Just ten more, she thought. Whenever she paused now there was a pain in her shoulders so sharp that it made her grimace. Once more to the left; not too fast – just a gentle introduction to let the wire sneak through the mechanism and lie up against the key on the far side. No, damn it! Solid, as though the thing were welded in place. Try down the middle now; hold it straight and level and just go right to the heart of it. Believe it will fall; believe it like you've never believed anything; tell it to drop; coax it out with promises of . . . To Julia's astonishment there was a sudden jiggle at the end of the probe; a definite change in the status quo. Something, somewhere had moved with a tiny realignment. Here, at last, was the right track. The goddammed lock was yielding to treatment. The wire was working its magic, like it did in the comics! Well, not quite. In those you blinked and hey presto, Jack was free! Here, now, it had taken how long? Maybe half an hour? Maybe more. But it was working. To make quite sure she hadn't imagined it, with great care Julia once more put pressure on the wire and felt the thrill of another small movement. This was the best moment since her kidnap; a change in her circumstances due to her own action.

She took a deep breath to steady herself, and eased the wire in further, feeling a distinct give in the resistance that had so far defied her; further and further, a fraction of an inch at a time, until there was a dull impact on the other side of the door and the probe had gone all the way through. Julia wanted to shout, scream, do a wild dance round the hard, disapproving room. Time for that later. Preserve your mystery, she thought, and laughed to herself. Better take advantage of this success fast, before the slobs came back on parade. Kneeling, she peered through the generous gap under the door. Sure enough there, on the newspaper, was a fat old key. Now it all seemed simple. Just draw back the paper, unlock the door . . . and then what? And then run like the wind, anywhere, out of this place, into the warm evening, and home, and a bath . . . But what about the other woman? Yes, first she must search for her. She must be in this building somewhere. Keeping her anywhere else would mean a ridiculous waste of manpower.

Julia took the edge of the paper and drew it towards her, half-fearing that the key would be too large to come through the gap. But no; here it was, at this moment the most precious metal on earth. As she rose, she threw the paper back into the corner. Her heart seemed to have dislodged itself and was now beating in her throat. Her palms felt moist, and the pain in her upper arms was insistent. Holding the key as though it were fragile, she brought it to the mouth of the keyhole. This was it then; five more seconds and she would no longer be a prisoner. In it goes, and then a simple turn clockwise and ... To her consternation, though the key was a snug fit, it failed to turn. Maybe it was one of those maddening locks which would only yield when the key was half-out, she reasoned. Nauseous now with hunger and disappointment, she tried withdrawing the key a fraction more at each attempt. Perhaps it turned the other way, she thought. A single pressure, however, showed her otherwise. Nothing she did – no adjustment of the shaft, no angling, no delicate re-positioning made any difference. From this side of the door, key and lock were not compatible.

For the first time Julia wanted to sit down and howl. Fate had played with her, offering her freedom with one hand and snatching it away with the other. Now she was back where she started. Worse off in fact, because when Black Helmet found out what had happened he was capable of anything. Though she tried to reassure herself that it was not in his interests to damage his investment, even she was far from convinced by the argument. On current form he was not a man who made cool, logical assessments. All the evidence suggested that he was a sadistic thug whose mood might swing if he were crossed, and devastate his half-baked plans.

As, sick at heart, she wondered what to do, she thought she heard muffled voices. God! What now? If it was Blue Helmet and Paul, she might stand a chance of talking her way out of this. Though she had no idea what she might say, she suspected that they at least wouldn't harm her. But if one of them was Black Helmet, or if word reached him ... With a sudden effort of will, she slipped the key back under the door and retreated to the far wall, under the window. The position was unlikely to fool anyone but it gave her a small measure of security. It was her station, near to the natural light, just as she had read that fighting bulls had favourite areas of the ring where they would choose to stand, and die.

The voices grew louder, and then were silent. Julia imagined the sluggish mechanisms of the kidnappers' brains registering the change of scene and weighing up the possibilities. Light-headed, she reviewed the range of excuses she might use. A freak wind, a ghost, woodworm, someone trying to break in? The hell with it, she thought. She would tell them the truth and take the consequences. Better do some exercises before they bound her hand and foot again. As she jogged on the spot, eyeing the ham and tomato that looked more appetising than ever, she heard a rattle and saw the door begin to open. Keep moving, she thought. At all costs, keep moving. Compliance would provoke them; a prisoner doing aerobics might further confuse their already addled minds. Despite herself, when she saw the colour of the helmet entering her cell, she couldn't force her feet to go through the motions any longer. Panting, she took a step backwards and steadied herself against the wall.

The pudgy, unwholesome figure, his blue T-shirt stained under the arms, his trainers scuffed and grimed, advanced, seeming to grow larger and more menacing. Once again, she sensed the violence in him; a sullen, suppressed rage, not just at her but at everything. In other circumstances she might feel pity, Julia thought. But what she felt now was the nearest she had ever come to terror. Stopping in front of her he did not, as she had half-expected, raise a fist to hit her. Instead, after a pause during which her mouth dried out and she found herself holding her breath, he began to speak. Behind him, the door was open perhaps a foot. If she could dodge his grasp, she might sprint across and escape, assuming that his companion was no longer there. But something about the murmured words, which as yet made no sense, transfixed her with a dreadful certainty of horror. As she concentrated, focusing on the indistinct movements of the mouth beyond the Perspex, she began to pick up words and phrases. Soon, by straining to the limit of her attention, she found herself drawn into a narrative more sinister than any she had ever imagined.

As Black Helmet spoke in a mesmeric undertone, the room seemed to darken. He was telling a story in the third person, with few pauses, as though it had been rehearsed many times, or had become as much a part of him as bone or sinew. The central figure was a boy whose much-loved mother died when he was small. Never changing its pitch, the unemotional voice described the misery of the child's life as though it were reading from an unremarkable manual. ' . . . Some nights he was so cold he thought he would die, lying in the shit from the animals, and too frightened to get closer to them for warmth. The hunger was like a rat eating him. Sometimes there were scraps of potato peelings or cattle feed, but often they would make him puke in the dark. The only good thing was while he was there they couldn't thrash him, his filthy stepmother and his father. They were screwing like pigs in the house, under the hot blankets. Him, he couldn't run away. The cowshed door was locked from the outside. All he could do was wait for the morning to come, and another day in hell . . .' Unmoving – unseeing, even – he went on as though entering a trance. 'Work started again with the light. In some ways he was glad of it. There was ice on the trough. He could see his own breath. The spiders' webs shone. He put sacking on his hands but they got cut and the cuts wouldn't heal. Dirt got in them. He felt sick when he looked at the yellow pus that came out. When he saw the woman walking across the yard, he wanted to . . . he wanted . . .'

The account had lost its momentum. Something terrible in the memory had come back to haunt Black Helmet, taking him back to the scene of his subject's degradation. By now, however, Julia understood that the third person was Black Helmet himself. This was his own childhood he was describing. Torn for the moment between apprehension and pity, she could do nothing but wait for him to continue, knowing that at any moment the grief might overwhelm him, casting his damaged mind adrift.

'. . . She stood there, with her hands on her fat hips, and she laughed at him. Laughed at the dirt on him, the state of him. She called him a dog, a mongrel. She said he wasn't fit to be alive. Soon he'd be dead, she said. Good riddance. On the midden with the shit from the cows. He wanted to stop her . . . with a sickle, or a scythe. Slice that fat flesh, for his mother's sake. She was in the churchyard, by the wall, next to the old cottage that nobody lives in now. When he went in there, he could talk to her. And she told him. She told him. Do it, she said. Do it. Do it . . .'

Still the voice was monotonous, holding itself at one remove from the events it described. Why was he telling her this, Julia wondered? Why was he sharing this painful secret with her? He knew she couldn't be trusted, so why? No sooner had the question raised itself than she knew the answer. He could only take this risk if he could be sure of her silence. And the only way to achieve that . . . Perhaps he had already given up hope of getting the ransom. Perhaps he had decided, in his despair, that his sole satisfaction now would lie in an act of vengeance. Julia felt more vulnerable and afraid than at any time in her captivity. And still Black Helmet probed deeper into his mind's wound.

'. . . He was fourteen. She was older. Sixteen. She looked at him like . . . She had cow's eyes. She said she wanted it, fancied him. One night they went down to the common; over towards Arnay. It was red right across there. All red on the hills. He followed her. They didn't talk. He didn't know what she wanted to do to him. There was a wild cat there, watching. And you could hear the crickets and the bullfrogs . . .'

Julia couldn't avoid her change of expression. For the first time, carried away by the memory, he had made an unconscious slip and dropped the pretence of the third person. Now she knew for sure the true danger she was in. She wanted to scream, but it was hopeless. Worse, with him in this disturbed state it might trigger a violent reaction. She had no option but to listen to an account she must never be allowed to repeat.

'. . . undid his trousers. The red sky behind her. Hands . . . hard hands . . . hurting . . . hurting him, and she started to laugh. Said he was deformed. Not like the others, she said. Plenty of them. Laughing . . . ugly . . . On top, laughing. That big red face, and the red, and the red, and the red . . . She was on him, and the knife was in her. Do it. Do it. Do it. And the red, and the red, and the red . . .'

Unable to bear it any longer, Julia put her hands to her ears and started to moan, trying to drown the dreadful sound. Moving her head from side to side, she made a tuneless keening, howling out the horror of this quiet evil. When she could no longer see his lips moving, she stopped, and the tears came. She despised herself for breaking down in front of him, but relief that the hateful account had ended, at least for the moment, had overcome her will. Now she was sure that here before her was a killer; a man driven by terrors to avenge his mother's death with more blood. Perhaps he had murdered more than once, this pathetic psychopath. Perhaps, in her, he was beginning to see another victim, to be sacrificed to his only precious memory.

As she tried to contain her sobbing, Julia looked up to see Blue Helmet entering the room, with Paul hanging back at the door, his whole posture proclaiming anxiety as he inclined his head under the absurd flour-bag. There was urgency in Blue Helmet's movements as he crossed the floor. Either he had something important to tell his colleague or this development had taken him by surprise. Standing beside Black Helmet, his body tense, he asked what was going on. There was no reply. Blue Helmet glanced at Julia, full of concern. She sensed that half of him wanted to comfort her. But from Black Helmet there was silence. It was almost as though he was exhausted by forcing himself to re-live the experience. Julia thought it must be something like a fit, whose occurrence he could not predict, and whose terrible intensity drained him.

Instead of answering Blue Helmet, Black Helmet gave Julia a curious, compelling stare, more like a plea than a threat. At the same time he raised an index finger to his mask. What did that signify, she wondered? Was it a nervous, involuntary gesture or was he asking her to keep his secret? Before she could be sure, he turned and left the room. Blue Helmet tried to tell him something as he went but there was no reaction. As soon as he was gone, Paul took a few steps towards her, looking comical and inadequate. She knew he wanted to say something but couldn't in the presence of his friend. Instead it was Blue Helmet who spoke.

'Are you all right?'

Julia nodded.

'What happened?'

Calm again now, Julia realised that as far as she was concerned, two things had happened. First Black Helmet had revealed himself to a stranger; had uncovered information which, if it were true (and of that she had no doubt), could condemn him. She also had the strong impression that it was unknown to Blue Helmet who, in his restrained way, seemed the dominant partner in this relationship. And second, confronted with her distress, both Blue Helmet and Paul had shown unmistakable signs of sympathy. Julia's instincts told her that these two shifts in the balance had altered the situation in a fundamental way. What she had to do in the hours ahead was decide how to use her new knowledge. If she blurted out Black Helmet's story she risked both the disbelief of Blue Helmet and the homicidal rage of the confessor. No; for the moment, caution was the safest policy.

'I've had enough,' she said by way of explanation. 'I want to go home.'

'Me too,' a muffled voice said from the middle of the room.

'Shut up,' Blue Helmet said, turning. 'Who asked you?'

Paul shrugged.

'Why don't you eat?' Blue Helmet asked Julia.

'You know why. I told your friend. He is your friend, isn't he?'

Blue Helmet hesitated for a moment, torn between wholehearted assent and the need for discretion. In the end he settled for being noncommittal. 'If you don't eat . . .'

'Precisely. So you'd better tell me now. What happened to the other woman? I want to know where she is, how she is, who she is.' Julia paused. 'We could keep it just between us.' She let this sink in for a moment. 'Your friend doesn't need to know you told me. Where's the harm? Then I eat. Then you get your money. Simple.'

Blue Helmet seemed tempted, but then changed his mind. 'It's none of your business,' he said.

'Of course it's my business. That's a human being we're talking about, not some lump of meat. I mean what I say. I will not eat until I know these things. I will grow weak and I will die. And I don't have to tell you what that makes you.'

Paul came two steps closer, attempting a silent prompt. Half-turning to acknowledge him, Blue Helmet said:

'She's all right.'

At this, Paul registered agitation.

'He doesn't seem to think so,' Julia said.

'She's all right,' Blue Helmet repeated.

'Well, is she here? In this building?'

Blue Helmet didn't reply, but Paul made a slight nod. Julia knew this was an answer she could trust.

'OK. So who is she?'

There was a slight shrug of Paul's shoulders, as Blue Helmet said: 'It's nothing to do with you. Now, eat.' He went and picked up the tray, returning with it held high. Julia ignored it.

'Is she French, German, Italian . . . ?'

Again, a slight shrug from Paul.

'We don't know,' Blue Helmet said.

'What do you mean, you don't know? Does she speak French?'

'There's something you must do,' Blue Helmet said, brushing aside the question. 'Your father wants to hear your voice.'

This abrupt change of direction stopped Julia's enquiry in its tracks. 'When was this? When did he say this?'

'A few moments ago. He says he'll do nothing until he hears your voice.'

Julia paused to take this in. How bizarre the situation was. Her father's voice had been present in this godforsaken hole; his living voice, but detached from his living being. It seemed surreal, like something at a seance. And this sound in the ether had summoned her from perhaps a mere few miles away; both a connection and a failure to connect. Nevertheless the contact was a big boost. Knowing her father's request must be a form of ultimatum, she decided to use it as a bargaining counter. 'When is this to be?' she said.

'When we choose.' Blue Helmet tried to sound cool; in command. 'Perhaps tomorrow.'

'I see. Well, here's the situation. You tell me about the other woman and I will gladly talk to my father. No information, no conversation. You understand?'

Putting down the tray, Blue Helmet considered the demand. 'There's nothing else to say,' he said.

'Of course there's something else to say, you . . .' Switching from French to English, she added 'moron'. 'Who is she? What is she? What nationality?'

'She doesn't speak,' Blue Helmet said, while Paul mimed being hit on the head.

'Why? Have you harmed her? If you've harmed her I'll . . .'

Before she could finish, Blue Helmet shook his head.

'It's not us. She doesn't speak. That's all.' He turned away, ready to leave the room.

'It's not enough. And one more thing,' Julia said, suspecting that he had told her the truth and would reveal no more for the moment. 'Your friend . . .'

Blue Helmet stopped, without looking back.

'I think maybe he needs a doctor. You know, for his head. He's been saying some strange things. Frightening things. Things the authorities might like to hear.'

Though there was no visible reaction, Julia could tell by the tension in his body and the way Paul looked at him that the statement had struck home. As Blue Helmet resumed his exit, followed by Paul, she added:

'Here, I think you've forgotten something.'

Born to obedience, Paul came back and picked up the tray, pausing only to look in her direction for a moment.

CHAPTER SEVEN

Comfortable in the old deck chair, Tom listened to the night sounds. Somehow even these seemed more gossipy in France, nature sharing the common need to express itself. Opening his eyes, he watched Monique take chicken off the barbecue. Her short Parisian haircut made her look younger than her thirty-six years. Helen and Tom had known her and her sister Zazie ever since their arrival in Burgundy. Tom had bumped into her in Beaune market and sent her basket of oranges bowling over the cobblestones. Instead of being impatient, she had seen the humour of his clumsiness and accepted his apology. Together they picked up the fruit, helped by Helen, who introduced herself. By way of reparation, Tom offered to buy Monique a drink and they had all sat at a pavement table in the Place Carnot, enjoying large kirs in brandy balloons, and laughing.

Monique had lived in Paris, working at a small gallery in the Rue Jacob. Married for nine years, she had a six-year-old son, Leo. Her husband, Guy, had been an accountant with a bright career ahead of him. The future looked assured. But one evening, Monique had returned to their apartment in the Rue du Bac, after picking up Leo from school, to find a note on the kitchen table. In it Guy explained that he was desolate but there was no point in trying to hide the truth any longer. He was in love with another woman and felt the only honest thing to do was to let Monique continue her life without him. He would, of course, make the necessary financial arrangements, and knew she would find it in her generous heart to grant him access to Leo, whom he professed to adore more than his very existence. Telling the story, Tom remembered, Monique had described her reaction to this seismic shock. Instead of bursting into tears or hurling herself off the balcony, she had held her lighter to the note and used it as a spill to light her Boyard. She had then poured herself a large scotch and taken Leo to a movie.

The change in her circumstances didn't strike home until she reached Burgundy, where she and Zazie had been born. Putting distance between herself and the event had made her realise that things would never be the same again. Once this had sunk in she made an impossible pact with herself never to look back. The blow to her confidence was considerable, but her warm instinct for making the most of the moment pulled her through. Friends, and Zazie, had become more important than ever, and Burgundy itself had proved a great healer. With financial help from her father, she had opened a gallery in Beaune, mixing the best work of students with that of interesting young established artists, all at affordable prices. Though she complained of having to please the tourists in order to survive, the venture had proved a modest success, and Monique's life had settled into a new pattern. Leo too, though given a hard time at first for being a hated Parisian, had thrived in the country, loving the freedom and the open roads to adventure.

Tom and Helen had developed an easy, trusting relationship with Monique – a friendship which had created its own codes and references. Helen and Monique enjoyed scouring junk shops together, returning with obscure objects they persuaded themselves were indispensable. Helen always promised herself she would take some home to Bury and sell them at unimaginable profits, but somehow the great commercial coup never happened. The fact was that they looked better here, where they belonged. With Tom, Monique was fond and teasing, almost as though he were an elder brother. Knowing of his interest in the region, she would sometimes bring him small gifts; an old street plan of Dijon; a paperweight showing the magnificent twin towers of Tournus from across the river; and on one occasion a large tome on heraldry, with several missing pages.

As Monique transferred pieces of cooked chicken to a plate on the adjacent table, her sister Zazie emerged from the house with a bottle of red wine. Seven years older than Monique, she was plump and bustling. She had also been married once, to Gabriel, a man who manufactured mattresses. There had been the inevitable jokes in the family about making your bed and lying on it. But poor Gabriel had died at the age of twenty-nine in a tragic accident on the A6. Hurrying home after a business trip to Lyons, he had collided with other vehicles in thick fog. Zazie had never re-married and, though she longed for children, remained childless. When Monique and Leo had arrived, and decided to stay, she had been overjoyed. God, she felt, had found a way of compensating her.

As Zazie passed Tom's chair she topped up his glass. 'There,' she said. 'Finally it's almost ready, Tom. Blame Monique for the delay. These Parisians have no sense of time.'

'Hah!' Monique pretended outrage. 'There speaks the woman who took two hours to buy a hat this morning. It's true. We had to wake up the stall-holder to pay him.'

'Lies,' Zazie said. 'It was you saying they didn't suit me. And you were probably right.'

The chicken was brought to the round table under the tree

and the three of them sat eating, wrapped in the warm evening. Towards the wall bordering the road, a glow-worm generated a green halo. Bats had taken over from the swallows, and the owls called. The crickets were discreet but insistent, and the frogs from the nearby ponds contributed an occasional solo. It was the first time Tom had felt anything resembling relaxation since the nightmare had begun. In this garden with good friends, persuading himself that Helen was alive and would soon be free, there seemed to be hope. He must cling to that at all costs, and build on it. He must will her release by believing it.

'This sounds ridiculous I know,' he said, 'but I feel a bit guilty. It's so pleasant.'

'If you're miserable, it won't bring Helen home any quicker,' Zazie consoled him.

'You have to be positive, Tom,' Monique added. 'Helen will be. She'll be counting the hours; planning the things she has to do when she gets home. Her head will be full of lists. She loves lists.' She put her hand on his arm and smiled encouragement.

'You're right of course,' he said. 'There's no point in moping. Tomorrow Mr Walker is talking to Julia. They're putting her on the phone. We should find out more.'

'That's marvellous,' Monique said. 'That's real progress. How's Robert?'

'He's a tower of strength, that man. Every day when we're not elsewhere he goes round the village, house to house, asking if anyone's seen anything strange going on. We both do.'

'And?' Zazie said.

'So far nothing, but it'll come.'

'That's for certain,' Monique reassured him.

As she spoke, the peace was disturbed by the sound of backfiring from the direction of the front door. Through the open house a rich baritone rang out, singing a country song in heavy patois. Looking round they saw a small, wiry, dishevelled figure wearing an old straw hat approaching, performing an unsteady jig. In one raised hand was a yellow cigarette, and in the other an empty wine bottle. Zazie rose to greet him.

'Roland! You look like a satyr.'

'Come here, cabbage,' Roland said, stretching out his arms. 'Come here. Let me hold you, my little chicken.'

Declining the invitation, Zazie stood her ground.

'No, you come here,' she said, taking his hand and kissing him four times on alternate cheeks, while he released the bottle and tried to squeeze her buttocks. 'Now, behave yourself and sit down, like a good boy.'

Gesturing a vague greeting at Tom and Monique, Roland Viggars identified a spare deck chair and, with an elaborate show of positioning, like a pilot making a tricky approach, sat in it. As he made contact with the canvas there was a ripping sound and the faded fabric gave way, depositing him on the ground, with his knees over the leading edge of the frame. At the same time the hat had fallen over his eyes, leaving him sightless and confused. Making exaggerated flailing movements with his hands, he cried out: 'Help! My eyes! I've fallen down a well. I'm blind. Help!'

Laughing with the others, Tom rose to heave him upright, realigning his hat and dusting him down.

'My God,' Roland said. 'That was a very nasty experience. It was touch and go there for a moment. I could see hell, you know. Feel the ferocious heat and see the licking flames. See Satan himself beckoning me into the furnace. Worst of all, the bars were shut. That's what hell is, I suspect. North Wales on a Sunday.'

Baffled by the allusion, Monique brought him another, rigid chair from the terrace and placed it at a safe distance from her. 'There,' she said. 'Park yourself on that. Where's Mary?'

'Madame Viggars . . .' Roland began, and then interrupted

himself, '. . . look, I suppose there's no chance of a glass of something, is there at all?'

Zazie poured the wine and handed it to him. 'I was only waiting for you to be vertical,' she said.

'*Tchin, tchin*,' Roland said, draining the glass in a single gulp and holding it out for more. 'Probably the smallest glasses in the world, the French,' he said. 'They give you *marc de Bourgogne* in a glass so small it is actually invisible to the human eye.' Accepting another drink, he went on: 'No, Madame Viggars has taken it upon herself to establish a faith-healing salon in Lacanche. There is much laying-on of hands in an atmosphere of mutual reverence. At least, that's what she tells me. For myself I have little doubt that were one to peer through the lace curtains and gaze upon this august assembly, one's vision would be assaulted by scenes of unbridled debauchery. The laying-on of hands indeed! But who am I to deny her these unsophisticated pleasures; I who have drunk deep of life's . . . life's . . .' To no one's astonishment, Roland had slumped asleep in the middle of a sentence, his cigarette threatening to set fire to his already nicotine-stained fingers.

Monique leaned across and removed it from his slack grasp. 'All this talk of escapades and he looks as innocent as a child,' she said.

'He spends his life with puppets,' Zazie said. 'What else could he be?'

'He's a free man,' Tom said, 'probably the only one I know.'

A few minutes later, Roland woke himself up with a grunt, spilling the remains of the second glass over his threadbare cotton trousers. Pushing back his hat, and concentrating on the purple stain, he observed: 'Africa. See? Almost perfect. Must be an omen. Malawi. Now there's paradise. Village by the lake. Off to market with the fish, bulging in panniers either side of an old Rudge bicycle. A game with the smooth stones

under the trees. Give a show in the evenings in return for food.'
He held out his glass for a re-fill. 'Off to Lausanne tomorrow.
In Switzerland there's still respect for an artist. Boring buggers,
but respectful. Cheers!' Savouring the wine, Roland looked
into the darkness beyond the trees. Turning back to Tom, he
gazed into his eyes for a moment. 'I'd do anything for her,
you know; for Helen. Truly I would. You only have to say the
word, my dear fellow.'

Tom was touched by the sudden reference to reality, but
before he could say anything in reply, Roland was off again,
following wherever his fancy led.

'There was a man kissing parking meters in Beaune this
afternoon. Embracing them passionately. Can you imagine a
sterner mistress? Entering her with a two-franc piece? There's
what we've done to ourselves. There's how it ends; not with a
bang, but a wanker.'

Monique looked at Tom with a smile and a raised eyebrow.
While the puppeteer embroidered and reminisced, Tom wished
he could talk to her alone; walk down towards the grey wooden
cross at the edge of the village and share his fears and
uncertainties. There was no one else to whom he could
unburden himself with complete honesty, except Frank and
Daisy, and it was too late to ring his daughter now. He must
do that first thing in the morning. Would she forgive him, he
wondered, for not having said anything before now? Looking
at Roland, recounting with relish an escapade in Rabat, he
envied for a moment the old man's capacity for ignoring the
mundane.

The following morning Félix was woken by distant church
bells. As a child he had liked the potent magic of Sunday Mass.
He had found the priest a romantic figure, like a sorcerer, to
be feared and respected. Before he was old enough to take
communion he would go to the altar rail with his mother and

feel the priest's hand on his head, conferring a blessing. Back at home, near the railway station, he would drape one of his mother's shawls round his shoulders and hold up a vase, in imitation, mumbling half-remembered incantations. The act gave him a sense of secret power, called to his aid whenever he encountered insoluble problems. In his teens the magic had waned for a while but, finding a lack in his life, he had returned to the church with a renewed sense of almost passionate commitment. His was not a conventional faith but rather an emotional dependence on the sensual experience of worship. When he knelt in the darkened nave, he felt secure, loved in an unmessy way; though it was a public building, he felt it was something to which he belonged, and would always belong.

In a smaller sense he had hoped the same would be true of Henri. He had wanted their relationship to be one of utter mutual trust, and for a while that had seemed possible. But ever since the kidnap, things had been different. Though so far their plan had worked, Henri had begun to change. Instead of rejoicing in their success he had become more and more moody and reserved. In spite of the fact that the Walker woman was their ticket to escape, Henri seemed to resent her. Sometimes he talked as though he loathed her, though why this should be Félix had no idea. Julia was arrogant and demanding but that wasn't surprising in a pampered, frightened young woman. In any case, soon she and the other woman would be off their hands and he and Henri would be lying on a beach, drinking champagne. So why the agitation? And what had the American meant when she had mentioned Henri saying strange things? At first Félix had dismissed the allegation as an attempt to worry him; to drive a wedge between himself and his partner. But the more he thought about it, the more he began to wonder whether something had happened to upset Henri; something he had chosen to hide?

Félix unzipped his sleeping-bag on the folding bed, and

swung his legs over the side. He would go to Mass this evening, and pray that the affair would end well and that Henri would be restored to normal. Beside him on the stone floor, the other sleeping bag lay open. Henri must have got up earlier. Félix fantasised about him bringing fresh coffee with warm croissants and orange juice. Instead, at that moment, Henri pushed open the heavy door and emerged empty-handed. When he sat on his own camp bed, Félix joined him, feeling his warmth.

'Are you OK?' Félix asked.

'Yes. Why?'

'It's just that the American . . .'

Henri turned his head with a look part surprise, part apprehension.

'She said something about you saying strange things,' Félix went on. 'Things the authorities might like to hear, she said.'

Henri looked at his feet. 'She'd say anything,' he said.

'It seems a peculiar thing for her to make up.'

'Are you saying you don't believe me?'

'Take it easy, Henri. I'm just saying if there's something you want to tell me . . . We don't have secrets from each other.'

Henri thought for a moment, staring at the wall. 'We all have secrets we can't tell anybody,' he said.

Concerned by the tone of his friend's voice, Félix got up to face him, sinking to his haunches in front of the brooding figure. 'You're very unhappy, aren't you?' he said.

'You can't be happy suddenly, just like that.'

'Of course. I understand. But everything's going to be fine. The girl talks to her father today. We make the arrangements for the money. We disappear. It's simple.'

With a careful, tender gesture Félix held his big, calloused hands. They were dirty, the nails grimed and uneven. Before Henri had met Félix they had never been held by another human being. Now, their tension was released. Félix saw tears forming in Henri's eyes; tears of gratitude, disappointment, fear, unaccustomed affection? Leaning forward, Félix embraced him, feeling the heavy head on his shoulder.

'Sometimes I get lost,' Henri said. 'After, I don't know where I've been.'

'Did that happen with the girl?'

'I don't know.'

'Well, whatever. It's OK. Look, I'll tell you what. Why don't we get Paul in and go and have a magnificent lunch? Get washed round at your house. Put on a clean T-shirt and go down to the Terminus. Maybe eat under the trees, with the tourists. Do us good. What do you say?'

Henri said nothing. Félix smiled encouragement, urging him to his feet.

'What if they see us?' Henri said.

'What if they do? They've seen us plenty of times before. If they didn't see us they might start to ask questions. Mmmm? I'll go and call Paul.'

As Félix left the room, Henri felt himself once more in the grip of his lonely terror. 'Do it', a remote echo kept repeating far away in the margins of his mind. Henri clenched his jaw and made tight fists, fighting the instruction. When this voice had called in the past, it had soon blown away, like chaff. But this time it had gone on the whole sleepless night and still it wouldn't stop. Maybe the only way to end it was to do what it said; cut it like a kale-stalk with one quick act. Not now, but when the money was safe. One woman or the other; it didn't matter which, as long as the price was paid, like before. And then he would be free, at last. But what, he wondered, would Félix's reaction be? He'd be worried at first, but Félix would understand. It might even be possible to do it without him knowing; fast and clean. Henri would give it some thought.

In St Aubin, at eleven o'clock, the heat was like a glass dome over the village, paralysing the life it enclosed. Even the dogs couldn't rouse themselves to bark. Madeleine Walker and Camille were sitting on barrels, taking refuge in the cool of the cellar. Slipping off her sandal, Madeleine rested her foot on his dusty boot, feeling the warm, dry leather beneath her sole. Why was it that in everything he did she had such a compelling sense of his body? Even here, relaxed in his work clothes, the sensuality of his presence drew her to touch him. 'Hold out your hand,' she said.

'Can't.'

'Hold it out!'

He obeyed. Madeleine traced the swollen veins from the knuckles to the wrist and then held the hand to her breast.

'I want to be with you,' Camille said.

'You are.'

'All the time.'

'Not possible. You know that.'

'Of course it's possible. It's only necessary to want it enough.'

'Well, I don't want it enough.'

'What do you want?'

Madeleine removed his hand. 'I want things the way they are,' she said.

'And me?'

'Oh, you. I'm just an amusement for you.'

Camille shook his head. 'I'm in love with you,' he said.

'I don't want love. It's too complicated.'

'It sounds as though it's me who's the amusement for you.' He paused. 'Do you love your husband?'

'In a way.'

' "In a way",' Camille mimicked her. 'There's only one way.'

'There are many. It's something you'll never understand.'

'Then perhaps you love me . . . in a way.' Leaning over, Camille kissed her.

She felt the tenderness that would become insistence; a lover hungry for her. As she held his face in her hands, she closed her eyes, shedding everything that was not present. He held her tighter, willing her to rise. She wanted him now, but not here. Instead she pulled away, and led him towards the doors of the barn.

'In the house,' she said.

They made love in the neglected bedroom, with the shutters drawn. There was dust on the furniture, and the two prints on the wall were crooked. Camille's clothes were heaped on a bedside chair. The wardrobe door was ajar, revealing one tweed jacket and a number of wire coathangers. The reflected sun painted geometrical patterns on the ceiling as Madeleine felt the heat and the urgency of him in the kind shade. Now they lay beside each other, sweating. Leaning over, he licked her body from the navel in a line between her breasts to the hollow in her throat, where drops had gathered, savouring her and wanting to remember the taste. In turn she reached for a glass of chilled white wine and held it to his lips. As he drank, she stretched up and took a sip herself. Beads of moisture ran down the part-frosted glass. She held it to her forehead. Satisfied, Camille laid the side of his face on the swell of her sex, looking up at her.

'You've said nothing about your stepdaughter,' he said.

'Don't.'

'Why?'

'I feel so guilty. Content, but guilty.'

'If the poor girl isn't at home, there's no more you can do there than here. And you can do a lot here.' He smiled.

'When it's over . . .' She had meant, in a half-hearted way, to say that when it was over, seeing him might be more difficult for a time, but the words had not wanted to form.

'When it's over, come away with me.'

She looked into his frank eyes. Was that what she wanted,

after all? If he were ever to leave without her, could she bear it? 'I've told you, it's not possible. Especially then. Julia will need me.'

Camille raised his head. 'I need you, for God's sake. I need you so much I can't sleep at night. This body of yours keeps me awake. I try to shut it out but I can't. I want to eat you, be in you, see you naked all day, everywhere, doing ordinary things . . .'

'That's the fantasy of a small boy.'

'It's what I feel. It drives me mad.'

'Good.' She leaned down, making him stretch up to reach her lips. 'Now I have to go.'

She swung her legs over the side of the bed and stood with her back to him. His eyes traced the gentle curve of her hips from the full buttocks to the slender waist, and the fine shallow valley of her spine where, higher, the small vertebrae were visible under the taut, shining skin. Her short hair was a startling gold against the sculpted surface. Camille stirred himself and clasped her from behind, feeling her vulnerable warmth against his chest and her belly under his hands. With a gentle but emphatic movement she eased away from him and walked to the bathroom.

In her brief absence, Camille lit a cigarette and lay propped up by pillows. His need for her was overwhelming, but it had become indivisible from a desire to involve her in a scheme which, he believed, would free them both. Despite her protestations of loyalty to her husband, he felt sure that her greater priority, if only she could be brought to recognise it, was to be with him. Who else could give her the utter, timeless pleasure they had just enjoyed? Madeleine had committed her entire being to the act of lovemaking, without reserve. He knew it had never been like this for her, just as he had never known anything to match it. She would think hard before she abandoned that.

Returning, dressed, she held the rail at the end of the bed, smiling. 'What about this?' she said. 'The vineyard?'

'What do you mean?'

'You talk about leaving. What about this?'

'Oh, I don't know. Get rid of it. Sell it. Get an agent to sort it out. I don't care.'

'And money? In the meantime?'

'I have a bank. I have a cheque book.'

As she lifted her soft black bag from a chair, her thigh was tight against the short, cream skirt, and his mouth was dry with wanting her again. 'So you've been thinking about it?' he said.

'Oh, no, not really. I just . . .'

'You're a liar. Come here.'

When she moved he could see the golden hairs on her legs, like a young girl's.

'What if there's no money in your bank?' she said, teasing.

'Then I borrow some, until the sale.' He paused. 'Or . . . I find another way.'

She sat beside him on the bed, the fragrance of her scent making him feel for a moment like taking her with aggression.

'What other way?' she said, twining her fingers through his.

'I'll think of something. Who knows? Turn the hillside into a golf course. Maybe I'll strike oil.' He laughed.

She turned and kissed him.

'When do you get Julia back do you think?' he said, changing the subject with apparent casualness. 'When's the handover?'

'They've promised to put her on the line today. Then we make arrangements. I hope to God it won't be long. Maybe a couple of days. Poor child.'

'It's strange,' he said. 'I've only seen her once but I can't stop thinking about her.'

Madeleine rose to go.

'Please tell me what happens. I want to know,' Camille said. 'Ring me and tell me. Promise?'

'Promise,' she said. 'The gendarmes are on the case now. We expect things to move fast.'

As she moved her fingers in a token wave, Camille seemed subdued.

'Darling, good morning.'

'Morning.'

Tom had been dreading the call ever since his arrival. He had delayed breaking the news about Helen to Daisy, in the hope that something good would happen to make it unnecessary. But nothing had. Now, as he sat in the kitchen looking at the enlarged image of Julia Walker on the wall, he knew Daisy would be hurt by his leaving it so late. 'I'm in St Luc,' he said.

'All right for some.'

'I came on Thursday.'

'Oh, right. What's it like?'

'Lovely earlier, now it's wet. There's big raindrops plopping in the cat's bowl.'

'How's my little Puss?'

'Thin, like always when we've been away. A couple of meals a day she'll soon be two stone again. You know what . . .'
He was about to say: 'what mum's like' but stopped himself in time.

'Mum OK?' Daisy said, as though reading his mind. 'Into Monsieur Shekspair is she?'

'Darling . . .' This was it. Get it over with. Just be straight, Tom thought. 'Darling, something a bit weird's happened.' He tried to keep his voice even and reassuring. 'I got a call at home on Wednesday from Robert. He said mum hadn't been around for a while.'

'What's weird about that? She's probably legged it at last with that swarthy lover of hers from Grasse.'

'No seriously. I got a bit concerned so I came over. And she still hasn't turned up.'

'Well . . . there's always a rational explanation for these things. She might have . . .' It was clear that Daisy could think of nothing she might have done for that length of time, without being in touch.

'I've tried everything; hospitals, police, friends, you name it.'

'Are you sure, Dad? Maybe she told you about a trip or something and you just forgot. You know what you're like. The end of term and everything.'

'The thing is, the Walkers' daughter . . . you know, the Walkers from Bessey?'

'Miss California?'

'She went missing too, about the same time. Darling, she's been kidnapped.'

'She's what?'

'The kidnappers want ten million francs.'

'Oh God, Dad.' Daisy sounded frightened and bewildered.

'I know, love. Here, of all places. They think mum might be with her. Don't ask me why they'd want to take mum because I've asked the same question hundreds of times. I don't care, as long as she's all right.'

'But they hardly knew each other, did they?'

'Not well, no. They'd met a few times. But that doesn't mean they couldn't be in the same place at the same time, I suppose.'

'Oh, Dad . . . I'll come over. I'll get the train today.'

'Darling, honestly there's nothing you can do. I'm sorry I've left it so late but I promise I'll ring every day now. You've got your job and everything. It's going to be fine. I'm absolutely certain of that.'

'What do the police say?'

'They're on the case. Seems a good guy, the boss man; Major Granier. The kidnappers are supposed to be calling again today. They're going to let Julia talk to her father.'

'Poor him. Poor everybody. Dad, I'd rather be there, I honestly would. I'll get the . . .'

'I know you would, love, but we'd just sit here looking anxious together. You're better off just thinking of us and the minute anything happens I'll be on the phone. I promise. Robert's being fantastic. Just the best friend you could imagine. No fuss. Just gets on with it.'

'Bless him. Give him a big kiss from me.'

'Will do. You haven't been in touch with Frank, have you?'

'You're joking. Last card I had he was in some dump in Mexico with a lot of consonants.'

'If he rings, put him in touch won't you?'

'Of course. Oh, Dad . . .' Daisy sounded on the verge of tears.

'Chin up love. We'll beat the bastards. Then we'll all have a good laugh about it. Take care of yourself.'

'Listen, don't forget – the second you hear, day or night . . .'

'You bet. 'Bye love.'

When Tom put the telephone down he found his hand was shaking. Taking a bottle of calvados from the dresser, he poured himself a small glass and downed it in one. Calmer, after a few moments, he looked for the hundredth time at the blow-up on the wall. It seemed so unreal, like a photograph in a magazine. A young woman, maybe only a few miles from St Luc, staring at a stranger with a camera; familiar, and yet as remote as though she inhabited another time or another planet. The bracelet seemed clearer now; a precious symbol of hope. With a deliberate effort, Tom took his eyes off Julia and scanned the periphery of the picture. Up in the top right-hand corner he was drawn again to the vague shape darker than the rest of the background; perhaps a stain on the mirror behind Julia? He stood up and moved closer. Now he could see that it was not a stain but an incomplete pattern, reflected in the glass. In reality it must therefore be high on the wall in front of Julia. Why hadn't he paid more attention to it before, he wondered? But then, why should he? After all, what difference did it make – an insignificant detail in an unidentifiable space? Nevertheless, he must take a closer look with the magnifying glass.

Before he could do it there and then, he was interrupted by the unmistakable sound of his neighbour entering the house. Framed in the doorway, Robert was wearing a sleeveless green fishing waistcoat and a small, jaunty hat with a feather in the band. Through the crook of his arm was suspended a double-barrelled shotgun.

'Mr Professor,' he said; 'a small calva and then you're coming with me.'

Tom poured a glass and handed it to him, topping up his own at the same time. 'I've just noticed something,' he said; 'on the photograph here.'

'No time for that now,' Robert said, draining the calvados. 'Come, my friend. I've made a discovery.'

'What?'

'Patience.'

Tom followed him with a smile. It was evident that under the bluff exterior Robert was in a state of high excitement. Stowing the shotgun in the back of the old Renault, he drove out of the courtyard with the air of a man on a mission. A beat out of synchronisation, the windscreen wipers mocked his air of determined efficiency.

'I told you, Thomas,' he said, as they negotiated the mini-roundabout on the wrong side and headed for Bligny; 'just because you put a man in a uniform it doesn't make him an investigator. It's something you have to feel, like an artist. You have to use your nose; your instincts. Have you ever watched a retriever? They might not know how to take a statement but they do know how to follow a trail. Mmmm? The senses! To hell with the képi and the white gloves; it's the senses that count.' Gesticulating as he made his point, he took his eyes off the road. Neglected by its helmsman, the Renault veered into the path of an oncoming saloon whose two ramrod occupants were a living portrait of rectitude, like pale burghers in a painting by a Dutch master. Alarmed at the sudden invasion of their territory, they honked and glared.

'What dramas!' Robert said, correcting the aberration. 'That was Roussel, the undertaker from Arnay. If we'd killed him there'd have been no one to bury us.'

'There'd have been no one to bury him either,' Tom said.

'That's true,' Robert laughed.

'There's an English painter who had a dead man stuffed,' Tom said. 'And then he stood him on a rug in front of the fire.'

'Good idea. I think that's what's happened with this government. They've been stuffed and sat in the Assembly. I've heard geese talk more sense.'

'Where are we going?' Tom said.

'I was hunting this morning, before the rain. It's not the season, but the birds and the rabbits don't know that. Dédé came over from Beaune. Paf! Paf! And then . . . Well, like I say, patience.'

'Any luck?'

'Not much. We almost had a wild boar but he was too quick for us. Now that would have been something. We could have roasted him on a spit in the garden. At night, so the mayor didn't get to hear of it. What a feast!' Relishing the thought, Robert swung left in Bligny to take the road into the hills.

'Will they have set up the command post yet?' Tom said.

'I imagine so. Because it's holiday time though, they may have to draft people in from other forces. They know that when the press get hold of this the spotlight will be on them. It's another reason they'll want to do well. Show Paris how good they are.'

'I hadn't thought about the press.'

'Why think about vermin?' Robert shaped his hand into a pistol and fired. 'Paf! That's what you do to vermin. They'd rather tell lies than the truth.'

'They might be useful, though. Put pressure on the kidnappers.'

'Pressure can go both ways,' Robert said. 'It can make people panic.'

The old Renault complained as they climbed, and Robert cajoled it with obscure endearments. 'Come on my little cabbage,' he said; 'take courage for Papa. Come on my pretty little mare.'

As though responding, the car took heart and, cresting a rise, charged down the reverse slope into Chaudenay-le-Château with renewed vigour.

'Not far now,' Robert said.

Half a kilometre further on, with the château guarding the bluff to their left, Robert slowed down by a dense wood and guided the Renault off the road. The smell of the wet leaves was fresh and pungent as they nosed down a narrow, overhung track.

'Before this morning,' Robert said, 'I don't think anyone had been down here for a long time. Except once.'

Tom longed to ask him what he meant but sensed that the answer would soon be revealed. Sure enough, fifty metres down, as the neglected green tunnel curved to its right, he glimpsed a colour low on the other side which had not been mixed by nature. It was an unmistakable maroon, and Tom knew it at once. As they drew closer it became clear that Helen's car had left the track and lurched down an embankment, coming to rest against a stout old tree. Tom felt both elated and sick. The maroon and cream 2CV was as familiar as Helen's hat or gardening gloves, and here it lay – helpless. The familiar fleur-de-lys on the driver's door wasn't visible from this angle, but Tom noted that the number plate was missing. As he got out of the Renault, Robert watched his reactions.

Tom took three unsteady steps down the bank and tried to open the passenger door, but it was jammed. Pulling harder, he managed at last to free it. Like the house, it seemed unnatural without Helen. Over the years its idiosyncratic charm had become a reflection of hers. But now, without her, it was just an anonymous shell. He reached over with difficulty and looked in the glove compartment. There, as always, was the map of Paris – more a souvenir than a practical guide, since after their first experience of the whirlpool round the Arc de Triomphe they had decided never again. Beside it were the boiled sweets dusted with icing sugar. Tom held the tin for a moment, reminded of how Helen would offer them as she drove, telling him not to be greedy with the red ones. He took off the lid and held them out. 'I'm sure there used to be more stuff in here,' he said, indicating the glove compartment.

'Careful what you handle, Mr Professor. There might be prints.' Despite the warning, Robert accepted a sweet. 'What sort of things?'

'Oh, you know, just all sorts. Bits and pieces that never got thrown away. Now there's just these – the map, a pencil; hardly anything.'

Robert shrugged, sucking his boiled sweet, offering no theory.

'Well found,' Tom said, beaming. 'This is real progress.'

Robert smiled. 'The moment I spotted it,' he said, 'I knew this was the beginning. Now we will win, I'm sure of it.'

Examining as much of the car as they could see, they tried to piece together what might have happened.

'She can't have been driving at the time,' Tom said.

'Why?'

'The driver's seat, look. It's too far back. That's adjusted for someone with longer legs.'

'It might have been forced back by the impact.'

'Well, the other one wasn't. Anyway, the impact wasn't that great. There's not that much damage to the front.'

'No plates. No licence.'

'Fingerprints maybe, as you say. We'll ring Walker and the command post. He'll have their number by now.'

'They'll have wiped them mostly,' Robert said. 'Even amateurs would do that.'

'You never know. Maybe they missed something – in the dark. Presumably they came up here at night and just pushed it off the road. It was their bad luck that the great bloodhound sniffed out the trail.'

Robert was pleased by the reference, twitching his nose. 'I came through the wood there,' he said, pointing to the trees behind him. 'Dédé was lower down, probably blowing the brains out of an ant. Suddenly I saw this maroon colour, beyond the track. I knew it at once.'

'I'd like to take these with me,' Tom said, holding the map and the tin of sweets. 'Something of Helen's. Do you think the cops would mind?'

'It's not a question of minding. It's just that we might be moving useful evidence, and that's bad for us. Better leave them and get back to the château. We can call Walker from the car.'

'I can't tell you how relieved I am,' Tom said as they reversed up to the road. 'It just feels like it's all possible now.'

'But of course. I told you so all along, my friend.' Bursting into a country song about a gullible girl and an old goat of a farmer, Robert reached into his pocket and produced a pewter flask half-bound with leather, worn to a deep shine. 'There,' he said. 'Drink. Who needs the gendarmes, mmmm? This is the team that gets the results. It's cognac. The good stuff.'

Tom accepted the offer and took a small swig. 'All the same, we should ring them from here,' he said. 'They may want us to stay and answer questions.' He punched William Walker's number on the mobile. Jean-Marie answered, agreeing to tell his employer that Tom and Robert were on their way, and passing on the number of enquiry headquarters. Tom tapped it out and was surprised at the lack of response. A second attempt met with the same result.

'What did I tell you?' Robert said. 'Not even an answerphone. Imbeciles!'

After a second refresher from the flask, they made their way back to the château. En route, Robert asked Tom to join him and Yvonne for a late lunch in Arnay, as a celebration. She had complained that it was a ridiculous waste of money, but Robert had insisted. Feeling positive and hopeful, Tom accepted.

Parking in the courtyard of the château, they saw a blue van and an unmarked car which bore the featureless air of officialdom. Walker himself met them at the door and escorted them back to the drawing room, shaking them both by the hand.

'Very well done gentlemen,' he said. 'This is marvellous news.'

'It was Robert,' Tom said. 'I'm just the assistant round here.'

Robert pulled a self-deprecating face, but then said: 'That's true,' and all three men laughed.

In the long, elegant room overlooking the formal gardens Walker offered them both a drink. Tom asked for a scotch and Robert said he would have the same. As Walker poured from the cut-glass decanters he seemed buoyant.

'It doesn't do to tempt fate,' he said, 'but I just have a feeling, gentlemen, that we've turned the corner. The cars are both found; today, God willing, I talk to Julia; and early next week . . .' He handed them the heavy tumblers, and raised his own. 'Cheers. Here's to the end of this terrible business. Sit, please.'

Robert sank into a chair, but more accustomed to a wooden, upright back, looked rigid. Tom, however, hadn't felt so relaxed since his traumatic arrival.

'What I'd like when it's all behind us is for you gentlemen to bring your wives over here and we'll have one hell of a party,' Walker said. 'We'll get a band, a marquee. I hear you're a mean dancer, Robert. They say Fred Astaire has nothing on you.'

Robert turned down the corners of his mouth in a characteristic, non-committal expression. 'I just put one foot in front of the other.'

'Rubbish,' Tom said. 'He spins like a top.'

'It was the way to get the girls,' Robert said. 'That's all. No woman can resist a dancer. If they liked bakers I would have learned to make bread.'

'Me, I never did get the hang of it,' Walker said. 'Maybe you'll give me a lesson sometime. Anyhow, consider yourselves invited. This one may last several days.'

'Did they say a time when they'd ring?' Tom said.

Walker shook his head. 'They're never that organised. It's all random. But you saw the van outside. There's a couple of guys in there ready for the call. Every so often they come up for air. They've listened to the tapes, over and over. Tomorrow they've got an expert from Dijon coming. They had to pull him back from the Côte d'Azur. He's supposed to be the hot-shot on voices – accents and so on.'

'There's no need for an expert,' Robert said. 'They'll be locals. I'm sure of it.'

'They might live locally but they could come from somewhere else. Like old Vauliquet, from the Midi,' Tom said.

'Perhaps,' Robert conceded. 'But you don't catch a wolf

with computers. And you don't catch a wolf if you don't work Sunday mornings.'

'Give them a break, Robert,' Walker said. 'They're having some difficulty raising a team, with the holidays and all. But I rang Granier in person with your news. They'll probably want you to go up to the car with them I would imagine.'

'Sure. Any time,' Robert said.

'Look, won't you gentlemen stay and have some lunch? You're most welcome.'

'Thanks but we're taking Robert's wife out to Arnay.'

'Madame the General,' Robert said. 'She has kindly agreed to be entertained.'

Walker himself escorted them across the hall. 'The minute they ring, I'll be in touch,' he said. 'And rest assured, Tom, I'll ask about Helen. They know we can't do business until we get an answer on her. Courage, gentlemen. We're on our way.'

Fifteen minutes later the Renault pulled up outside Robert's door, the horn sounding an uncertain blast which tailed off to little more than a moan. Within seconds, Yvonne had appeared at the door; a robust woman of medium height, with a stern face that concealed both warmth and humour. Wearing a cotton print dress with smart cream shoes, she looked brisk and purposeful. Tom opened the door, intending to vacate the passenger seat, but Yvonne would have none of it.

'No, no, thank you,' she said. 'I'll go in the back. That way I can keep my eye on him.'

'Listen,' Robert said. 'This is the woman I adore and still she doesn't trust me.'

The N6 was busy with lunchtime traffic, and Parisians heading south.

'Look at them,' Robert said. 'From a town with millions they go to a beach with millions. It's insane.'

'It's what they want,' Yvonne said. 'What's it got to do with you?'

'I pay the taxes here, they don't. That's what it's got to do with me. Let them go and foul up somebody else's roads.'

'I'm glad about the car,' Yvonne said to Tom, changing the subject when she saw signs of Robert overheating.

'It's great isn't it?' Tom said. 'Like Mr Walker said, I feel we're on our way at last.'

Robert put the heel of his hand on the horn and kept it there as an overtaking car towing a caravan took up more than its fair share of the road. 'Hooligans! Terrorists!' he roared, waving his fist, as the unrepentant driver stared him out.

Across the road from the Terminus cars were parked almost as far down as the disused station. Tom had often thought that the handsome, neglected building, which had once witnessed Arnay's comings and goings, would make a wonderful house. Beyond it the route of the railway track was overgrown now, and there was an air of abandonment, as though the town had turned its back on the whole idea of travel by train. Robert cursed fate for making him search for a parking space and settled for half a gap between a British car and one of the hated caravans. Making no attempt to do more than wedge in the hindquarters of the Renault, he left the bonnet well proud of the otherwise neat ranks and slammed the door to register his protest.

'He's in a mood now,' Yvonne said, as she and Tom followed several paces behind. 'But in a moment he'll see an old friend and the sun will come out again. You watch. Children!'

Sure enough, as they approached the Terminus a red-faced figure in a flat cap emerged and held up both arms in greeting. 'Robert, my friend, I didn't see you in church this morning.'

'No,' Robert said. 'This morning I left the frogs in the font all for you. How goes it, my friend?' After passing the time of day, Robert turned to see what had happened to Tom and Yvonne, signalling, as she had predicted, the end of the brief squall.

The bar was crowded. Farmers in their Sunday best, with weather-beaten faces and gaps in their teeth, were engaged in animated conversation. Interspersed with them, groups of young men and women laughed and flirted. Presiding over the hubbub, the serene *patronne* behind the counter served her customers with calm, good-humoured efficiency.

As he and his party made their way through to the restaurant on the other side of the passage, Robert exchanged raucous greetings with several acquaintances. In the long room, loud with families, the waiter showed them to a corner table near the window, with a view of the entire assembly. Robert joked with him and sat down with the air of a man restored. A number of faces beamed in his direction and he acknowledged them all with a wave, or a bellowed pleasantry.

'Right,' he said to Tom and Yvonne, rubbing his hands. 'An aperitif, I think, and then the full works.'

While Robert ordered the drinks, and Yvonne studied the menu, Tom looked round the tables, struck, as always, by the remarkable contrast with Anglo-Saxon reserve. In France it was plain that the guests took real joy in being there together, whereas often in Britain it felt as though they had been forced to sit down by a whipper-in, and couldn't wait to return to the womb of their precious privacy. Long tables of ten bubbled and grinned like friends deprived of each other's company for decades. Children mimicked the adults and rolled their eyes. Young couples held hands and laughed, while here and there a grave, envious bourgeois tried to turn on silent charm for a woman nearby who seemed more desirable than his chill wife.

Tom recognised some faces from St Luc, or mornings at the market, petrol pump attendants, or people who had served him in shops. There was the butcher with the enormous wart on his nose, often seen at the back of the shop in his bloodied apron while his dark, handsome daughter dispensed liver and kidneys to her discerning customers. Two tables away sat the builder who had broken his leg in a fall from a roof, animated now as he told stories of his clients' unreasonable demands. And in the far corner, below a triangular shelf bearing a stuffed, snarling fox, Tom saw a face he knew from walks round the village with Helen. Sitting with a thin, pale, intense-looking young man was the farmer from St Luc who was said to be a loner. His powerful shoulders hunched, he looked ill at ease in unfamiliar surroundings. While his companion talked, the farmer seemed restless, in contrast to the relaxed mood of the room. From time to time he would take a deep gulp of his red wine, appearing to drink more for the effect of the alcohol than its savour. Tom remembered that whenever he and Helen passed the property in the evening, with its grey, empty cowsheds, they wondered how one man could cope there on his own. Judging by the untidy yard and the farmhouse in urgent need of paint and repair, the task had proved too much for him. There was gossip about him in St Luc – something about an unhappy childhood – but for the most part people preferred not to discuss him at all. Despite the fact that he belonged there, he was considered an oddity best left to his own devices. Trying to recall his name, Tom leaned across to Robert and pointed out the couple under the fox.

'Gazin,' Robert said, answering his question. 'Henri Gazin. He's a mean mongrel. Let's not spoil a delicious lunch.' Raising his glass he proposed a toast. 'To Helen's return,' he said. 'This week, without doubt.'

CHAPTER EIGHT

William Walker did not think of himself as a nervous man. At college, where he had been a promising lightweight boxer, and in the navy, he had known moments of apprehension, but nothing amounting to deep or long-lived anxiety. Since childhood in small-town Montana, where his father had been a teacher, he had been conscious of an ability to cope with situations. At first, girls had made him a little wary, it was true, and the occasional bully like Ollie Svenson had made him unsure what his next move should be, but that was about the limit of it. His confidence derived not from smugness but from an innate ability to assess risk. If, when you took a cool look at the threat, it was unlikely to do lasting damage, then what was the point in fearing it, he had reasoned? Later he had learned that there were creatures who harmed others for pleasure, but that they were avoidable.

Now, however, at twenty minutes past four on a Sunday afternoon, in the security of his own comfortable home, William Walker was nervous. Thirty-five minutes ago the kidnappers had called to say that within the hour they would put Julia on the line. The one who spoke had sounded slurred, and that was part of the reason for Walker's uncertainty. Sober, the kidnappers had seemed slow but not illogical. With a few drinks inside them they were a cause for very real concern. Even the most rational individuals could be transformed by alcohol. Besides which, no one could assess an enemy whose motives were unknown and whose moves were invisible.

Walker had tried to telephone Tom and Robert but their mobile number had been unobtainable, and neither was at home. They must have forgotten to switch on when they went to lunch. In a selfish sense he was relieved. This was an encounter he needed to handle on his own. He knew the conversation would be brief because the kidnappers wouldn't want its source traced, so it was vital to make the most of the few precious seconds. To that end it was important neither to be distracted nor emotional. Instead he must somehow ask questions which allowed Julia to answer without putting herself in greater danger. The kidnappers would be close to her, breathing cheap red wine. At the first hint of complicity they would slam the telephone down and the process would revert to square one.

As Walker paced the room, trying to clarify his line of questioning, Madeleine joined him. There was a radiance about her lately, an air of wellbeing. Her brightness at this difficult time was a solace and an inspiration. As she approached, he opened his arms and embraced her. Feeling her body against his, he wanted to be out of here and losing himself in her, shedding the tensions of the past few days. Would that please her, he wondered? For some time now he had sensed that she was making love at one remove, as though watching herself. It was not that she was unenthusiastic or unwilling, but there was a certain spontaneity lacking; a certain underlying self-consciousness. Unsurprising perhaps, under the circumstances. Though not bound to Julia by blood, Madeleine loved her and was as concerned about her safety as he was. Yes, that was it of course. How stupid and male of him ever to have overlooked the obvious answer. When this dreadful thing was behind them he would take her away, with Julia. Should he surprise them, and choose the destination himself? Somewhere exciting, exotic? Or somewhere familiar, after his daughter's ordeal? Doubtless she would be exhausted, and perhaps she would suffer a delayed reaction to the trauma. Better to be close to good nursing and psychiatric counselling. Maybe just Switzerland then; the three of them in a small hotel by a lake, walking, and laughing again; and in the warm nights he would encourage Madeleine to relax and give her whole self, like she had when they first met.

As she poured herself a glass of mineral water, he noticed that her hand was unsteady.

'When?' she said.

'Soon,' Walker reassured her. 'The hour's almost up.'

'I wonder how she'll sound?'

'Try not to wonder.'

'I can't. She's so vulnerable. She must be terrified.'

Walker took her hand. 'These guys may be stupid and misguided but they've no reason to harm Julia. And she's not a child. She's resilient. She'll want them to see they can't beat her.'

'I know. But when the moment comes . . .' Removing her hand, Madeleine sat down. For a moment she was isolated in her thoughts. Then, looking up, she said: 'Do you love me, William?'

Surprised by the abruptness of the question, Walker sat beside her. 'Madeleine . . .'

'No; I want you to answer me.'

'Don't you know that I do?'

She leaned back and looked at him as though after a long absence. 'You never say it. Hardly ever.'

'Now darling, that's not . . .' He was interrupted by the white telephone on the table at his side. Turning away, he picked up the receiver and held it between himself and Madeleine, who moved closer to listen. 'William Walker,' he said, his attempt to sound calm not altogether convincing.

'Papa!'

Despite his strongest intentions, Walker had to fight back the emotions at the sound of Julia speaking in French, no doubt at the demand of her captors. 'My darling, this is wonderful. How are they treating you?'

'Could be worse I suppose. How are you and Madeleine?'

'Just fine darling, but terribly concerned. Now listen, we'll only have a few seconds. We'll have you out of there within the week, I absolutely promise – if we have to raid every building in Burgundy. Do you know how far you travelled?'

There was a brief pause. 'College age maybe. It's like a big . . .' The remainder of the sentence was muffled.

Walker assumed that one of the kidnappers had become suspicious and had put his hand over Julia's mouth.

'. . . Can't say much,' she went on, and then added an apparent *non sequitur*: '. . . Xanadu.'

Puzzled, Walker let it pass. 'Darling, is there another woman there? Was she kidnapped with you? Just say yes or no and OK if she's OK.'

'Yes, more or less OK.'

'More or less?'

'Not talking . . . separate. Bad luck. The wrong place at the wrong . . .'

Again she must have been gagged. When she went on, her voice seemed more forced. 'Please get the money, Dad. For God's sake get the . . .'

The line went dead. Unwilling to accept the fact, Walker still held the receiver. 'Hello! Hello! Darling . . . ?' After a few moments he bowed to the inevitable and hung up. 'Poor kid,' he said. 'She won't have gotten much comfort from that.'

'You did what you could,' Madeleine said. 'Julia will

understand. What did she mean, "Xanadu"?'

' "In Xanadu did Kubla Khan a stately pleasure dome decree." Before that she said it was big. So I guess she means like William Randolph Hearst's folly.'

'A château perhaps? And what's this "college age"?'

'I guess it's just code for maybe eighteen, nineteen kilometres. But distance can be very hard to judge, especially under stress. She sounded quite different at the end, didn't you think? Kind of desperate.'

'Yes, of course desperate. She's very brave but she's very frightened. She sees nothing happening and she asks herself a lot of questions.'

'What did you make of what she said about the other woman? "The wrong place at the wrong time?"'

'She obviously isn't speaking for some reason. Perhaps she isn't able to. And they're not together. Poor Helen. She must just have fallen into this thing. It's so cruel.' Unable to hold back her tears any longer, Madeleine leaned her head against his shoulder and sobbed.

Putting his arm round her, Walker held her close, ignorant of the full extent of her confusion and unhappiness.

'It's going to be fine,' he said. 'But it's strange how powerless this sudden, terrible thing has made us. It's taught me a lesson. After this we'll be closer, you and me and Julia. That way this suffering won't have been wasted.'

'What do you know about suffering?' Madeleine said, pulling away from him and getting to her feet. 'Already your neat little mind is organising all of this as though it was a flower bed. The world is in chaos, William. People are in pain all their lives. Babies are slaughtered before their mother's eyes. What lesson does that teach you? Mmmm? How do you fit that into your tidy little jigsaw? Your daughter's out there with dangerous men. They might do anything. She's terrified. You just don't want to believe it. You just think you have to pay the money and it solves everything. We'll all be happy ever after. But this isn't Disneyland. It's real. Like Auschwitz was real. Like Sarajevo. They don't go away. They change things forever.'

As Madeleine left the room, Walker, shaken by this sudden attack, rose and crossed to the window. Beyond the enclave of the formal garden, the hills and woods looked serene, oblivious. Never in Julia's life had he heard that note of doubt and need in her voice. But then, until now, she had never known hardship or threat. Emotional disappointments and minor injuries had been the extent of her suffering, as far as he knew. Now it was different. Now she was forced to accept that only an outside agency could save her. Walker realised that Madeleine had been right. In his heart, or rather his head, he had made assumptions based on past experience. He had presumed that if he remained rational, unemotional, and made the money available, the problem would be solved with a minimum of lasting damage. After all, these were the techniques he had adopted in business with notable success. But this was not business. This was an exercise where the variables were infinite, and he was aware for the first time that it might indeed leave all three of them altered.

In Madeleine herself the process appeared to have begun already. What had prompted her outburst? The tension of the telephone call? Anxiety about Julia and Helen? Her own memories? Or was there something else? The harsh words had seemed almost prepared, as though they had been banked, ready for withdrawal. Had this evident resentment been building for some time, or was he imagining difficulties where none existed? Madeleine was upset; too upset to confront with these questions. When it was all over, and Julia was safe, he would ask his wife what she had meant. By then, her nerves restored, she might even be unable to recall the incident. Convincing himself that this was the probable outcome, Walker left the room to compare notes with the listeners in the blue van.

On their way back from Arnay, Tom and Robert had received a call from William Walker. When they heard of the brief conversation with the kidnappers, they dropped Yvonne at the Ryaux' house and drove at once to the château. Listening to the tape in the surveillance van, Tom was moved, his mood of euphoria shattered. Julia had perhaps been only a few yards away from Helen when she spoke. If Helen had raised her voice during the call, she might even have been heard in the background. It was unbearable. She might be only twenty kilometres away and yet she was so remote. The questions multiplied. What place had she been in at the wrong time? And what had Julia meant by 'more or less OK' and 'not talking . . . separate'? Did that suggest she'd seen Helen? Why make a point of saying she wasn't talking if they weren't together? And why the hell hadn't Walker mentioned Helen by name? Why hadn't he just said: 'Is Helen Bellman with you', for God's sake? Angry, Tom had asked Walker this and he had explained that using names might have alerted the kidnappers and made them abort the call. Tom could see some sense in that but still felt it would have been a chance worth taking. This was where, unable to negotiate himself, he was at a big disadvantage. Walker's first, natural concern would always be for his daughter.

Robert had tried to calm Tom on their way home, suggesting that they make a slow tour of the surrounding villages. For days now, he said, he had been looking for small signs; for any unusual activity, any comings and goings which were in any way out of the ordinary. Still in turmoil, Tom had declined, saying he needed to be alone for a while. Setting him down at his door, Robert had promised to let him know as soon as the gendarmes rang about identifying Helen's car.

In the old wicker chair, under the greengage tree, Tom tried to get a grip on his emotions. Just as he had begun to take a firm, positive line through the crisis, this sudden revelation had rocked him off balance. But still, there was no point in gloom, he told himself. It was a destructive indulgence that helped no one. The point, the only point, worth considering was that Helen was alive and close. He hated to think of her alone, denied even Julia's company, but he knew she would find a way of coping. More than likely she would devise arrangements for future, greater Shakespearean festivals; decorate her prison in her imagination; write a memoir of the experience in her head. When she was released, he thought, the press would turn her into a heroine, both here and at home, and she'd loathe it; but even that ordeal she would handle with grace and humour. Anyway, the next time the kidnappers called (assuming the gendarmes hadn't already found them) they would make arrangements to pick up the ransom and the whole terrible business would be over. Should he take Helen away for a while, to help her recuperate? Would she need to spend some time under medical supervision? No point in speculating. Bring her home first and then see how she felt. He suspected she would like nothing more than to get on with her life in the house she loved.

Tom looked at the trees and shrubs they had planted. Once, in a bar in Bligny, a complete stranger had asked them where they lived. When they said St Luc his eyes lit up and he asked them if they knew the Englishwoman's garden? Whereupon Tom introduced the presiding genius, and the stranger was delighted. Without them being aware of the fact, Helen's creation had become a local landmark.

The thin white cat from the farm next door stalked through the grass and rubbed up against Tom's hand, asking to be fed. She followed him as he went into the kitchen, poured milk into a shallow enamel soup plate, and laid it on the ground in the shade next to the lilac. He watched her as she rippled the white surface with her busy tongue. Deciding to try and concentrate on a book, he turned back to the house. As he passed through on his way to the passage where the bookshelves were, next to the main room, he found himself drawn once again to the photograph of Julia, focusing on the dark patch in the top right-hand corner. Though fuzzy at the edges through enlargement, it seemed nevertheless to represent a definite shape rather than a random blot. Loosening the Blu-Tack at the corners of the poster with care, he took it off the wall and laid it on the table. With the magnifying glass, he peered at the denser section in close-up. Hadn't he read somewhere that these days even satellite photographs could be blown up to reveal an ear of corn? Must be an exaggeration, but they could do incredible things. What he needed was a computer enhancement, and that shouldn't be hard to arrange.

At that moment the telephone rang in the sitting room. Tom went through to answer it. A weary-sounding officer at the Bligny command post was asking if it would be convenient for him to come and make formal identification of the 2CV? It struck Tom as he replaced the receiver that Granier's men were not the sort to let an investigation spoil a good lunch.

After talking to her father, Julia Walker had lain on the floor and tried to sleep, but it had proved impossible. The dialogue replayed itself over and over in her head. Black Helmet putting his filthy, sweaty handkerchief over her mouth whenever Blue Helmet became suspicious of what she was saying had destroyed her train of thought. She had planned to convey as much information as she could in what she knew would be a short conversation, but the interruptions had made her emotional. Above all she was unhappy about the pleading at the end. She had sounded weak and helpless, and that would upset her father and Madeleine. He would be doing his best in any case to end this thing and here was a hysterical daughter unable to take the strain. Julia beat her fist on the door in frustration. Would they be able to make out anything from the call, she wondered? She thought they'd understand 'college age', but even if her estimate had been right, an eighteen-kilometre radius from Bessey would still represent an enormous area. And what about 'Xanadu'? Her father would of course pick up on the Hearst connection but would he realise what she meant? Was he getting help now from experts? The kidnappers had threatened dire reprisals if the police were brought in but William Walker had access to other agencies. To perk up her spirits Julia imagined lean, suited men with bulging armpits, who looked a lot like Clint Eastwood, combing the countryside with cold, relentless zeal. How was Clint's French, she wondered? When she translated 'make my day' it didn't sound quite the same.

Black Helmet had seemed drunk. The smell of his sweat had always been sour and overpowering but as he held the mobile telephone to her ear she had been nauseated by the stench of wine, even through the mask. When he ended the exchange by pressing the red button, he told her that the phone was hers, taken from the Peugeot. Black Helmet thought this was hilarious, throwing back his helmeted head. She had noticed that when he put his handkerchief over her mouth he had held his hand cupped, to minimise the risk of contact. For some reason this revolting misfit feared the touch of flesh; at least of hers. Why would that be? The traumas of his childhood, she supposed. Whatever it was, fear and loathing made a volatile mixture. From now on she would be in greater danger than at any time since her capture.

Contact with the outside world had made loneliness harder to bear. Her father had promised rescue within the week, but that had just been to make her feel good. In any case even that would mean several more days of boredom and uncertainty, with the added possibility that Black Helmet would lose control and take out his problems on her. Sitting down, her back against the uneven wall, on impulse Julia hatched a rudimentary plan. What was there to lose by trying to get out of here, she asked herself? Supposing they caught her in the act, the one thing her kidnappers couldn't afford to do was harm her. On the other hand, now that her father had proof that she was alive, perhaps that was no longer a priority. Black Helmet and his pathetic henchmen could arrange to pick up the money and disappear before anyone realised what had happened to the victim. No, her father would insist on seeing her first, she thought, reassuring herself. That was how it worked. It was like those handovers you saw in old movies where spies in long raincoats were released to their own people at Checkpoint Charlie. You made sure the goods were undamaged and then you did the deal.

The only remaining question was the big one. How to get away? At least the options were uncomplicated. That was to say, there weren't any. The single route was via the big, heavy door which was opened at irregular intervals by unsympathetic gaolers. At least, two were unsympathetic. It was just possible that the third, Paul, concealed a trace of humanity under his flour-bag mask. If, poised beside the entrance, she waited for him to come into the room, there might just be a chance of using the element of surprise and pushing past him. She felt an atom of remorse, targeting the one person who had shown her any consideration, but dismissed it at once. If he had cared that much he could have let her go anyway.

Making her mind up to act coloured several minutes with hope and euphoria; a sense of doing something at last, rather than being the passive object of action. But during the immeasurable time that followed, the mood began to evaporate. The energy Julia needed for an explosive spring was impossible to sustain. It would have to be coaxed again when the moment presented itself. At least now that her hands and feet were left unbound, thanks to the inertia of her captors, she had freedom of movement. In an effort to prepare herself for the great leap forward, she raised her arms and started to circle them from the shoulder. Next she put her hands on her hips and twisted from the waist, feeling unused muscles complaining. After so many days unwashed she was aware of her own body smell.

Fantasising, she imagined herself in the cottage on an evening when the sun was still warm on the pantiles, and the pigeons in the orchard sounded softer than flutes. Lying in the old turquoise bath with the big, brass taps, which she had spotted in a reclamation yard in Beaune, she reached for a glass of Meursault with a cool bloom disguising its fine, delicate promise. With a slow movement of her fragrant, brown arm, to prolong the anticipation, she brought it closer over the foaming ocean of the bath. Closing her eyes, she held the glass to her lips, allowing the miraculous light golden liquid to trickle into her mouth and seduce her with its two thousand years of savour. It was an experience that could not be improved upon; as absolute in its perfection as a spider's web. Wine bores might flounder for clumsy comparisons, but there was none. It was incomparable, and even the dream of it transported Julia from the fetid prison that had been her world for far too long.

The prospect of returning to the neglected, overgrown haven filled her with determination once again. She would survive, she told herself; she would defeat these shambling half-wits. One day she would look back at this unhappy time and feel stronger for having come through it. Who else knew about the incident, she wondered? Could the press have got hold of the story, since her father was still a public figure? When she got out, might there be flashing bulbs and hacks asking dumb questions? What a ghastly thought. That would be exchanging one kind of prison for another. As long as she lived people would point her out as the woman who was kidnapped. She would have to start running again, away from the place she'd been so happy to find. No, she was damned if she would do that. Whatever happened, however much of a freak they tried to make her, she would cross those old flagstones and shut the door on all the voyeurs. In time they'd find another nine-day wonder to stare at.

The conversation with her father had revived Julia's worry about the other woman. What kind of state must she be in by now, without medical attention? If she wasn't talking, maybe she wasn't eating either? How long could you go without food?

Weeks, she supposed, but if you were hurt too there must be a limit to your endurance. That was another reason why she owed it to both of them to try and make something happen. By now her guards had become more relaxed, casual even. They would leave the door ajar as they brought her the tray, assuming in their male arrogance that even if she did bolt, they would be strong and fast enough to head her off. And today they seemed even less alert than usual. Wine had made Black Helmet in particular swagger with phoney confidence. Even so, he might still be the trickiest of the three to outwit. His animal strength might be too much even for her best shot. She just had to hope and pray that the next man through the door was one of the other two.

Where should she position herself, she wondered? If she stood to the right, she'd be spotted at once and there'd be no gap to squeeze through. If she hid on the other side, in the angle of the wall, whoever came in, seeing no one, would guess at once where she was and there would be no way past them. Opting for the first alternative, she crouched on her haunches beside the leading edge of the door. Here at least she would have the advantage of surprise. For a split second, used to seeing her across the room, the gaoler's eye wouldn't adjust to the unfamiliar angle. If she sprang with enough power, she might catch him off balance and force herself beyond his grasp before he realised what was happening.

After a while the position became agonising and she rose to relieve her aching knees. Returning to the squat, she tried to while away the limitless waiting by taking a mental stroll through the clock-level galleries of the Musée d'Orsay. Only the French, she thought, would have the creative *chutzpah* to convert a railway station into a temple of high art, and make the building as brilliant as any of the works it housed. Standing before Van Gogh's bedroom, with its sturdy chair, itself as rich in character as a portrait, she marvelled at the truth of the painter's vision. He had understood and loved these objects just like a master carpenter must love the grain of his wood. More, even. He had given the bed and the chair the imprint of the lives that had been lived on and around them. They weren't mere furniture. They were as particular and honest as a human hand. Beyond, she stopped in front of Bonnard's cat. The impossible arch of its back never failed to make her laugh, and yet she laughed knowing that by sure exaggeration the painter had found the exact, spontaneous nature of the animal.

Even in memory, the feast of colours could be too rich. Turning aside, she sat at a table in the café dominated by the huge station clock. Sipping a cappuccino, she revelled in being alone. Much as she loved the company of friends, the only way to absorb the gift of this place was without distraction. To hear its music you had to empty your mind of clutter. Like wine, in the end it was impossible to discuss without sounding pretentious. Best just to surrender and let it glow in the head, inextinguishable.

Julia had no idea how long she had been lost in the daydream when she heard a faint sound outside the door. Since all the kidnappers wore filthy trainers, they never gave much notice of their approach. But soon there was the familiar clunk of the large key in the lock. Despite the days of confinement, she felt a pump of adrenalin that made her feel as fit for action as at any more auspicious moment in her life. Making her hands into fists, she psyched herself into a taut coil, with an energy that she felt could not fail. For what seemed like minutes, but might well have been a mere thirty seconds, nothing more happened. Could whoever it was have changed his mind? Would he think better of it and grind the key back the other way? Please God, no. Please make it open. Make it open now. Wide. Good and wide. Make a gap big enough to just slip through and . . .

God obliged. Dry on its hinges, the door opened, revealing the side of a plastic tray bearing a paper cup and a plate with something yellow heaped on it. Julia felt as though her pulse rate had doubled. By the feet and jeans she knew this was Blue Helmet – slight, quiet, an unlikely partner for his psychotic friend. The scuffed trainers advanced another pace before pausing, and in that hiatus Julia guessed what was going through Blue Helmet's mind. Knowing it was now or never, since the helmet hampered his downward line of sight, she rose and twisted in a single, exhilarating movement. Feeling his lean hip as she barged past him, she found herself in a stone corridor which stretched away to her right, with a cavernous arch leading off it perhaps ten metres away. Behind her she could hear the clatter of the tray and Blue Helmet's muffled oath. He would pad after her now, but with a head-start like this she knew no one would ever catch her. This was a heaven-sent break – a chance she was meant to seize. She felt like yelling with joy. The marvellous liberation of just being free of that hard, boring, unrelenting cell; the sense of going somewhere, getting nearer, exploding out of this dump, beating these bastards.

At the arch leading off the passage, Julia turned her head to check on her pursuer. Four or five metres behind her, he looked top-heavy; comical, even. If luck was on her side, he should never be able to close that gap. In fact she knew she could increase the distance between them, but that depended on being sure of her route. Swerving to her left she entered a darker tunnel which seemed to widen into a larger, lighter space at the end – a space in which she could see the bottom steps of a stone stairway. Once up that she expected to be on the ground floor and within a door's width of the welcoming night. To breathe that warm air, unfouled by the sour stench of her own sweat; to smell the night smells and hear the crickets, without walls. She forced herself to accelerate, once more glancing behind her at the straining figure with the swollen head of an insect. Blue Helmet was yelling something, but breathlessness and the mask made his message unintelligible.

As she emerged into the flagstoned chamber at the base of the flight of steps, Julia had time to register a door on either side. On the floor next to the right-hand one was a plastic bottle half-full of water. Could this be where the other woman was kept? She longed to knock and at least offer encouragement, but realised that such a gesture would jeopardise her own chance of escape. Compromising, she shouted: 'Hey. Hello there! We're out of here. Very soon. Promise. Courage, my friend!' Even as she reached the bottom step of what seemed a long, steep climb, Julia tried to stay alert to a possible reply – but there was none. Maybe if she called again? 'Hi! You in there. I'm coming back and get you out. Don't give up!' Her words bounced back off the dense walls and mocked her, accompanied by more swallowed anger from her frustrated pursuer, who must by now be cursing his disguise.

Despite the ache in her joints, stiffened by cool nights on the hard floor and the lack of exercise, Julia bounded up the staircase two steps at a time. Would it be possible to keep her promise and go back, she wondered? If . . . no, *when* she made it out of this place, she could lead a small army back to it and drag these animals out of their stinking hole. If the water had been provided for the woman, then at least she was still alive, and between them the Walkers would see that she got the best medical attention in Burgundy. They would have so much to talk about; so much in common, though they had never met, Julia thought. Looking up, to her disappointment she could now make out another door at the top of the steps. What if it was locked? Then she would have no alternative but to turn and fight. With the advantage of height, she would kick with all her power and send the skinny creep sprawling backwards until he lay in a heap at the bottom, like a dead fly. Much better if it was unlocked, though. Better if it co-operated and opened like a dream, with a friendly key on the outside which, with a deft twist, would turn the tables and leave Blue Helmet a prisoner in his own dungeon. No, that was fantasy. Don't expect the impossible. Take every obstacle as it comes. But above all win, win, win!

In the event the door did respond, but not in the obliging manner of a dream. It opened inwards, so that Julia had to waste a precious moment stepping back to give it clearance and slamming it closed, since no inviting key revealed itself. Turning, Julia found herself in what seemed to be the vaulted ante-chamber to a larger room. Through yet another doorway in the corner, she could make out the far wall of this further area and judged it to be some thirty metres away. With no option but to head for it, she prayed that it might contain the last door that would lead out of the maze. Buoyed by hope, she launched herself on what she wanted to believe was the last lap of this first phase. After that, in open country and at night, there would be places to hide, telephones, passing motorists, people eager to help. Another few seconds of maximum effort and she could put this bad dream behind her for ever.

As she crossed the threshold into the room beyond the ante-chamber, she heard Blue Helmet negotiating the door at the head of the flight of stairs, cursing its awkwardness. Her lead increased, Julia drove herself harder with images of sprinters in her head, breasting Olympic tapes with heads flung back and arms outstretched. Something about the huge chamber seemed familiar. Glancing round she saw the old mirror over the broad stone mantelpiece, recognising it as the place where she had posed for the Polaroid. That seemed like weeks ago. How strange to have taken so long to travel such a short distance. The shadows were gathering now and little else was noticeable, except what looked like two slender camping-beds with sleeping-bags on them, under the window. The beds were aligned together, with no gap between them, as though for lovers or nervous children. At the time the detail seemed insignificant to Julia, but later she would analyse it and wonder what it meant. Meanwhile she could smell the fragrance of the warm evening air through the unglazed windows, and couldn't hold back a smile of anticipation.

The huge door leading out of this still, eerie chamber was ajar. With Blue Helmet panting some way behind her, she slipped through the gap without pausing to close it. Here at last was the entrance hall, with its monumental stone staircase. In an intuitive moment it struck Julia again that, while the building was of château-like proportions, it didn't give an overall impression of great age. Steps, for instance, were not worn lower in the middle than at the sides, as they were at, say, Châteauneuf. The flagstones, while otherwise authentic enough, didn't somehow give the impression of having lain there four hundred years. Perhaps some *nouveau riche* had replaced them to impress the neighbours, as though re-tiling a bathroom. Anyway, who cared? Just a few steps and it would all be over; all the loneliness, the uncertainty, the fear. Out there, ten metres away, was the normal world that held the antidote. Even if Blue Helmet did catch her now, and she knew that he would not, the sheer energy of her anger and determination would defeat him.

Julia was high on excitement as she headed for the massive double doors which must be the last remaining barrier. Taking both hands to the enormous black handle, she gripped and turned. To her horror there was no movement. Trying again, this time with more concentration, she realised that handle and opening mechanism had become disengaged, either through repeated use or deliberate sabotage. One more swift wrench and, with a sinking heart, she must divert to another route. But which? When the door failed to respond a third time, in the moment before Blue Helmet caught her up, she assessed the alternatives. The stairs couldn't be a sensible means of escape, since once she was on the first floor there would be the added problem of reaching the ground. No, whatever happened she must stay on this level.

Set in the wall to her right was yet another door leading, she supposed, to what had once been some sort of drawing room, and there were two more in the dark recesses at either side of the staircase. It seemed obvious that the only route to the outside world from the drawing room would be via a window which, even if it were broken, might be hard to open. On the other hand, there must be at least one back door to the building, so her best chance lay with the shadowy exits behind the broad steps, which reared up like something out of a Forties movie.

Blue Helmet's breathing had become harsh with the unaccustomed effort. As Julia changed course, he was within three or four metres of her, still yelling that her attempt was doomed. Half-turning to check the threat, she sprinted across the hall to the left-hand rear door which, she thought, might lead to a wing, rather than the main body of the house. To her intense relief it opened, and she found herself in a long passage lit only by a window at its distant end. Even this light was feeble since the window was opaque with years of neglect, and Julia had to charge into virtual darkness until her eyes adjusted. Here it was cooler than in the rest of the building. The air was musty; unwholesome. It reminded Julia of a deserted house she had once explored with a friend, Ellie, while holidaying with her family in Maine. Local legend had it that a woman had hanged herself there. Deceived by her husband, and in despair, she had tied a light flex round a meat hook in the cellar ceiling and kicked herself off from a chair. Her body hadn't been found for four days. Julia and Ellie had dared each other to go down to the scene of the tragedy. In the event Ellie had chickened out, but with Julia it was a matter of pride. Nauseous with fear, she had made her watery legs descend the steps and cross to the very spot under the rusty hook where that poor woman had ended her precious life. The smell there had been the same; the smell of being ignored, redundant, unloved. Her fear conquered, Julia had felt calm. She had said a prayer for the woman, knowing as she did so that this would never happen to her. That was the woman's gift, she sensed; to let her know that she must never despair.

As her eyes grew accustomed to the gloom, Julia could pick out a number of doorways on either side. To enter one that led into a small airless room would be fatal. Then she would have no option but to turn and fight. Maybe she should do that anyway? Blue Helmet's breathing was laboured now. She sensed that if she turned and ran straight at him with all her strength, he might be surprised and winded enough to let her past. But where would she go from there? Since the front door was ruled out as an escape route, she would be forced to re-trace her steps, thereby risking an encounter with Paul or Black Helmet. No, the time to confront Blue Helmet was when her back was to the wall for the last time. If the door she chose led her to a dead end, then she was prepared to summon all the ferocity that was in her and inflict as much damage as she could on her pursuer. If she had a weapon, could she kill him, she wondered? While she couldn't imagine willing his death, she was determined enough to disable him as an obstacle to her freedom. And in any event, she promised herself she would tear off the preposterous mask, without which he would be more vulnerable. For a moment she imagined him as a snail deprived of its shell; a soft, unstructured creature, powerless without its protection.

Now there were only three doorways remaining on the right before the window. It was possible of course that none led anywhere. They might all be disused storerooms. Strange to think that once the passage had seen the bustle of uniformed servants, scurrying to pamper the owners of this curious mansion. Julia tried to think herself into their patterns. Which door would they have taken as they carried the trays bearing silver domes? Her intuition told her to swerve into the second entrance from the end. Sure enough the handle turned and Julia burst in, backing up against the heavy door to slam it shut. The report echoed round what seemed to be a large, high-ceilinged space, with a huge unglazed window facing an outside wall. From the passage Julia heard Blue Helmet stop, his gasping for breath close and unmuffled. She guessed he had removed his stifling mask while deciding on his next step. Now, for the first time, she held the initiative, though as far as she could see there was no other way out of the room. As Blue Helmet began a rhythmic hammering on the dense oak, she reached across and felt the substantial shaft of the key. She had been right to trust her instincts. She might be making yet another prison for herself, but at least it was one where she controlled the right of entry. As she felt movement in the handle from Blue Helmet's side, she turned the key and made his efforts impotent. Glancing up, she saw a thick, black bolt. When she shot that home, it would take a tank to prise her out of there.

'You can't win. You'll starve, stupid woman. Get this door open or they'll find you dead,' Blue Helmet shouted.

'On the contrary,' Julia said. 'You guys have lost control of your only asset, and the entire French police force is chasing your tail. I'd say the chances are you'll end up dead, wouldn't you?'

CHAPTER NINE

The following day Tom woke at six. In the large bedroom, with its balcony bearing pots of geraniums, he propped himself up on the pillows and listened to the morning sounds of the village. Even these, which needed no interpretation, couldn't be mistaken for England. The pigeons, the cockerels, the tractors, and above all the recorded church bells had a different timbre. In the courtyard he could also hear the chink of glass. This would be Robert, an early riser, soaking his wine bottles in the trough. He would leave them there for twenty-four hours before replenishing stocks at Monsieur Poillot's in Bligny. Some would be reserved for the *eau de vie* made every year from the plums in his orchard. This would be dispensed by Yvonne in tiny, decorated glasses, with a sugar lump nestling in the clear liquid.

Tom thought how lucky he was to have such a resourceful ally. Without Robert, the past few days would have been unbearable. Their joint investigations might not yet have borne much fruit, but Tom's active involvement in the partnership – the very fact of making a positive effort to glean information, however unscientific – had been of enormous value. Alone, Tom would have lacked any sense of direction. Paralysed with uncertainty, he would have been reluctant to leave the house for fear of missing an important telephone call. And besides, all the evidence so far had been discovered not by the professionals but by Tom and Robert themselves. Despite the gendarmes' sophisticated methods, it wasn't they who had found Helen's car but the persistent tracker who lived next door. It was true the force had come across Julia's Peugeot in Beaune, but no doubt that had been reported by a traffic warden.

Tom's first job today would be to see if he could get the poster enlarged; or at least, the part of it that intrigued him. As soon as businesses were open he would head for Beaune or Dijon and find out who was prepared to computer-enhance it for him. He supposed the gendarmes would have access to the technology, but as yet his reasons for wanting to clarify the image were too vague to describe. Better to do his own spadework first, and then present them with something to go on. If nothing came to light, he wouldn't have wasted their time.

In an automatic gesture, he reached out and laid his hand on the pillow where Helen's head would rest. In summer she would sleep without a nightdress, her tanned arm free of the sheets. As she moulded herself to him, she would luxuriate in this first half-hour of the day, talking of things to be done. He would enjoy padding down the stairs to make the coffee for her, the first to open the back door and breathe the green air of the garden. After the aromatic beans were ground, the daily grind they called it, he would walk out in his bare feet and dressing gown while the percolator started its boil. As he inspected the flowers and shrubs, their surrounding earth still stained with the watering of the night before, Puss, the white cat, would skitter across the browning grass, thirsty after a night's hunting in the fields. Returning to the house he would pour her milk into the enamel bowl and take the coffee up to Helen, with perhaps a peach or a nectarine. Fresh croissants would come later, with another cup of coffee under the trees. In this simple routine they both found contentment. No amount of money could have improved it; no added ingredient could have made it more satisfying.

Tom withdrew his arm, wondering whether he would ever know those moments again. And where was Helen now, at this moment? Was she thinking the same thoughts, holding on to memories to keep her hope alive? Tom found that if he let himself slip into deep anxiety, an ever-present temptation, it would gnaw at him like an ulcer and almost deprive him of the will to act. Somehow he must try to lay it aside and concentrate all his energy on going forward. Throwing off the sheet, he walked over to the balcony. The hills beyond Arnay looked blueish, as they did on fine days. Somewhere in that landscape, whose tallest features were church spires and water-castles, as the locals called their water-towers, Helen waited to be claimed. By this time next week, Tom thought, the whole hellish thing would be in the past. Lying in bed, making love with the tenderness of those who thought they might never hold each other again, they would resolve on a fresh start, determined never to take anything for granted.

Aroused by the sweet anticipation, Tom slipped on a pair of jeans and a T-shirt and headed downstairs, taking care to avoid the seventh step, which creaked. The house smelt tangy with woodsmoke. When he opened the shutters it was like dipping his toes in a warm tide. Putting on the percolator, he fed Puss before opening the front door and greeting his neighbour, still bent over the trough and presenting a broad backside. 'From here you look like a prize pumpkin,' Tom called.

'That's prime Burgundian beef,' Robert replied without troubling to straighten. 'The housewives of Arnay dream of meat like this.'

'You slept well?'

'Always, my friend. It's the army. In Algeria we slept anywhere. On decks, floors, by the roadside . . . Seldom in beds.'

'Coffee?'

'Of course.' Robert doused the last of the bottles and followed Tom into the kitchen. 'Well, Mr Professor,' he said, once settled with a mug at the table, 'very soon Helen will be home and you will be a hero of the press and the tele. St Luc will be on the map. The first time in ten years.'

'God forbid.' Tom drank a mouthful of coffee. 'What happened then?'

'It was horrible; a horrible reason to be famous. A young girl was murdered, over towards Lacanche; stabbed to death. She was only sixteen. Stéphane. Her mother never recovered. She's in a mental institution.'

'Nobody's ever told me this before.'

'It's not a memory we want to keep fresh. Naturally it's better to forget it.'

'Did they find whoever . . . ?'

Robert shook his head. 'No. They questioned many people but . . . nothing positive. We had our suspicions, of course, but they aren't enough. It might have been a stranger. The countryside is empty now that farming doesn't pay any more. In the night, who's going to see?'

'Which family was it?'

'The Lachaux. They lived in the small house behind the churchyard. After the tragedy Pierre moved to Carcassonne to be with his son. He drives back to see his wife once a month.'

'That's a terrible thing. Hard to believe somehow. It's so calm here.'

Robert shrugged and gestured towards the garden. 'It's calm out there, but here,' he pointed to his forehead, 'it can be something else.'

'These people you were suspicious about – was it anybody we know?'

'Well, yes, we know them. There was Alain. He likes young women. It's no secret. He sees what goes on from that tall tractor of his. But I never believed it myself. He wouldn't do a thing like that. Then there was Monsieur Petitjean, the businessman from Orleans. He only spends a few weeks a year here – in the new house near the water-castle. But he was able to prove he was in Morocco at the time of the murder. Naturally he was very upset. There were others too. But the girl is dead, and no one was punished.'

Pouring more coffee, Tom described his plans for the poster. Robert nodded approval.

'Anything,' he said. 'Any thread might unravel the whole story. Last night I thought I was on to something. Catherine told me that Pennec, the labourer who built his own house on the Lacanche road, was driving out at night a lot. At strange hours. So last night I followed him. Not easy, my friend, with the moon floodlighting the place like the stadium at Auxerre. I had to wait until his car was round a bend before I put on a spurt. All the way to Ste Sabine he led me, where they've restored that little château, and then down towards the canal. Some of the time I had no lights on. Once I almost ran into the ditch. At one point a barn owl flew parallel with my window, as though he was guiding me. Anyway, finally Pennec pulled up at a small house. Funny, I thought. Doesn't look the sort of place where a kidnapper would keep his hostages. What are they doing, sitting in the front room watching Mickey?'

Tom smiled at the fanciful idea.

'So I pulled up where Pennec couldn't see me and crept round to the back of the house, through the gardens. It was all going well until I stepped on a cat and . . . waaaaaaaaarrrr!' Robert imitated the animal's squeal of pain. 'Suddenly lights go on and I have to make myself small. Lying low for a few moments, like a terrorist, I crawl across to the house. Pennec enters and, with caution, I raise my head. My God, what a sight!'

Enthralled by the narrative so far, Tom had not the remotest idea of what might follow.

'The curtains were open just so much . . .' Robert held his forefingers close together, '. . . and through the gap I could see a large woman with grey hair drawing Pennec by the lapels of his jacket towards the kitchen table.' Relishing his own story, Robert began to smile. 'The woman was wearing a purple dressing gown – something she must keep in her bottom drawer for special occasions. The dressing gown fell open and Pennec was gazing upon his beloved like a cow before a hypnotist. I promise you, his eyes were out like lollipops. When they reached the table she slipped off his belt with some difficulty – Pennec was holding his belly in to try and look slim – and undid his flies. Whereupon Pennec's trousers fell to the ground like the flag at sunset and there he was, standing in his clean underwear, obviously selected with something more important than kidnap in mind. Now madame reclines on the table, inviting her visitor to do likewise and, revealing a backside as white as a Charolais bull, he endeavours to concentrate on the task in hand. Heaving himself on to the dish of the day, he is on the point of making madame's dream come true when – crack! A leg of the old table buckles under the pressure and a great avalanche of flesh starts to slide towards the floor . . .'

By now Robert was guffawing so loud he couldn't continue for a moment.

'What then?' Tom said.

'Then I beat a retreat and left them to their passion. But I want you to know, Mr Professor, that we are ruling Pennec out of our enquiries.'

At nine-fifteen, having telephoned Daisy with as cheerful a report as he could manage, Tom headed for Dijon. The directory listed a large number of computer retail houses but the one that looked most imposing, in a bold box, was the Computer Store in the Rue Musette. Tom knew the street well. When he and Helen visited the huge indoor market on Saturday mornings, they would often spare ten minutes to walk in the cathedral's cool nave. Today he would do the same, and say a prayer for Helen's release.

Beyond the A6 the road was fast; dual-carriageway into the city itself. Passing under the railway bridge, where they often saw the elegant TGV on its route to Paris, he headed for the underground car park in the small square not far from the mustard shop. Having found a space in the third level, he took the rolled poster off the back seat and rode the lift to the ground floor. The sun in the square was already hot as he passed the baker's where he and Helen often bought walnut bread, and the fishmonger's displaying oysters in wooden boxes. Soon parallel with the handsome market building, he kept an eye out now for the Computer Store. At the second-hand bookstall, he paused to talk to the earnest young man who shared his love of films, and from whom he had bought a book on Jean Vigo during the Easter holidays. After their brief chat, the young man pointed out the Store, which Tom now saw was only a few doors away on the other side of the road.

The façade – smoked glass with severe, stainless steel edging – gave little away. Even the name itself was in discreet, stylish silver lettering. Opening the door, Tom could see a small number of computers and accessories in understated display on shelves, and a groomed blonde woman sitting at a large space-age desk. Behind her was a corridor with doors leading off it. The atmosphere was almost religious in its reverent stillness; a temple of technology, where a raised voice would seem a sacrilege.

Tom found himself making his enquiry in an undertone. 'I have an image I want enhanced. A photograph.' He indicated the rolled poster.

'Are you interested in buying something?' The woman was packaged with the same attention to unfrivolous design as the merchandise she represented. The cut of her jacket, the gold earrings against the smoothness of her neck, the neat gloss of her nails, all proclaimed care and cost lavished on cold perfection.

Tom did a rapid assessment. If his answer was no, this might be the end of the line. Why should anyone waste their time showing him something for nothing? 'Yes,' he lied. 'I might very well be.'

'Then down the corridor on the right is a lift. Go to the second floor and turn left.'

The lift was as silent as its surroundings, impersonal as a surgical instrument. On the second floor it gave a small sigh and the doors parted to reveal yet another corridor, this one carpeted in dark blue, its walls displaying framed photographs of new computer models, like mechanical Playmates of the Month. 'Miss August,' Tom mused, 'the fabulous MS29300 oblique 36. Chic and ambitious, Miss August has her sights firmly set on becoming the even more sensational MS29300 oblique 37.' Turning left, as he had been instructed, he pressed a discreet button beside a steel door. For a few moments there was no response. Tom imagined he was being scrutinised by some device so sophisticated that it might even expose the fillings in his teeth. He began to feel chilled by the place, and longed to escape to a scruffy bar for a couple of glasses of raw red wine. If this was the future, he thought, it didn't work. Not for a human being anyway. Fine for microchips. Maybe they would inherit the earth.

When the dull click of a well-made mechanism interrupted his reverie, he gave the door a tentative push. It opened onto a large room furnished with metal shelves from floor to ceiling. Stacks projected from the walls, giving it the appearance of a library. Instead of books, however, the shelves held cardboard boxes whose contents were announced on the sides in letters and numerals so meaningless to Tom that they might have been written in Linear B. This then was the Holy of Holies; the Oracle; the source of all wisdom. Here you could tap a million plastic keys and communicate with Ulan Bator, or solve mathematical conundrums of unimaginable complexity, or design cities. Marvellous though the possibilities were, they made the thought of that cheap red wine seem ever more tantalising.

To Tom's left was what appeared to be a counter, with no sign of anyone in attendance. It occurred to him that if he was embarrassed into buying anything, it could prove a disastrous expense as well as a useless acquisition. Familiar with these machines only at a basic word-processing level, he might as well sit and contemplate a nuclear power station as hope to master the intricacies of computer-speak. 'Hello,' he said, in a voice expressing more doubt than enquiry.

'Hi.'

To Tom's surprise the response was immediate, and in English, with an unmistakable North American accent. From a couple of stacks down the line the owner of the voice was made flesh; a young, slim, tousled figure, wearing tortoiseshell glasses, advanced with a small smile.

'Oh, hello,' Tom said, thrown by the sudden appearance of normality. 'You speak English.' Stating the obvious, he felt foolish.

'Sure,' the man said. 'Richard O'Brien. What can I do for you?'

Tom wondered for a moment whether to pretend he was in the market for a piece of equipment, as he had suggested downstairs, but realised that apart from anything else he lacked the vocabulary to bluff. No nouns in his non-technological experience matched the awesome, streamlined knowledge-boxes. And this was not the sort of shop where you could point and say: 'I'll take one of those.' No. The young man seemed amenable enough. Better to tell the truth and hope for the best.

At least the fact that both kidnap victim and expert were from the same part of the world seemed a good omen; except that Tom would have to be careful about how much he said. 'The thing is,' he began, 'it's a slightly unusual request.'

'Good,' O'Brien said. 'The unusualler the better.' He smiled at his own invented word. 'You can tell I didn't major in English.'

'Can I lay this out somewhere?' Tom said, indicating the photograph.

'Right here.' O'Brien led the way between the stacks nearest the door.

At the end was a work-surface bearing a grey monitor, what looked like a loudspeaker, a large, lidded, rectangular box bearing the words Hewlett Packard Scan Jet, and a small piece of moulded plastic with a semi-circular protuberance in the middle, which Tom recognised as a mouse. Removing the elastic band, he laid out the poster. O'Brien helped him by securing the corners with small cardboard boxes which he took from a shelf.

'Wow,' he said; 'she in movies? She ought to be.'

'No. No, she's not in movies. To be honest with you I can't really tell you very much about her.'

O'Brien seemed a little uneasy. Tom had the feeling he was wondering whether this was some kind of weirdo he was dealing with.

'I know that sounds strange,' Tom said, 'but it's a question of her safety. I can only ask you to trust me. Soon the whole thing will come out anyway. We might be able to help it come out sooner rather than later.'

Reassured, though none the wiser, O'Brien appeared to accept this garbled explanation. 'OK,' he said. 'Shoot.'

'This was originally a Polaroid,' Tom went on. 'I had it blown up.'

'Mmm. Didn't do a bad job.'

As O'Brien smoothed the paper with his hand, Tom noticed

he was wearing a large, yellow, plastic watch, fulfilling a multiplicity of functions with a pleasing playfulness.

'What I want to know more about,' Tom said, pointing to the dark patch in the top right-hand corner, 'is this bit here. The more I look at it, the more I seem to think it isn't just a shadow or a vague blob. It seems to have a shape that's half-familiar, but I can't make it out.'

'Could I cut this?' O'Brien said.

'Cut it?'

'The scanner won't take the whole thing. If we could just cut out the section we want . . .'

'Oh, yes, of course.'

Taking a pair of scissors from a drawer, O'Brien cut a neat rectangle out of the poster and placed it under the lid of the Scan Jet.

'How come you're here?' Tom said.

'Oh, I'm just a hired hand. I'm only here for the summer.'

'Can you get a job just like that? I thought they were having a hard time?'

'Painful admissions department. You can if your dad runs the company. We're looking at blatant nepotism here.'

Tom smiled, fascinated by the baffling symbols which now filled the screen of the monitor. Manipulating the mouse, O'Brien explained that it helped him select and control the options he needed. Meanwhile a horizontal bar of light on the scanner was working its way across the image with painstaking slowness, advancing a millimetre and then retiring again in a repetitive search for visual information. O'Brien explained that he was starting with a resolution of six hundred dots per inch, but that they could go higher if necessary.

Now the core of the dark image was displayed on the screen and Tom felt the stirrings of excitement, conscious that they were entering territory intended to remain hidden. But with this technology there could be no secrets. Probing with pitiless insistence, it would penetrate the most profound concealments. At higher resolution still, the screen was filled with what looked like coloured sugar crystals, each one analysed into its infinitesimal pigments. As O'Brien panned across them, searching for a meaning, Tom realised he was holding his breath, while, like a recalcitrant child, his heartbeat refused to lie down. He felt, as he had felt all along, that in some unexplained way this obscure part of an obscure scene had something particular to say. Now the message, whatever it was, could hide no longer. The Scan Jet was removing the layers of veils to expose . . . what?

As absorbed as Tom, O'Brien was zooming in, limiting the area under scrutiny. As he did so, he let out a sudden puff of breath.

'What?' Tom said, sensitive to any signal.

'Not sure. But something.' Using a thin, broken white line O'Brien began to draw round the centre of the exposed mass. Broad at the top and tapering to a point, the outline was convincing. O'Brien had not contrived it but had confined an area somehow denser than the rest.

'Looks like a heart, maybe,' he said.

And in that moment Tom knew. Taking a deep breath – the release of unconscious tension – he felt a certainty which had been hovering out of reach since his first sight of the poster. This image of a frank young girl had at last given up a fragment of its hidden clue.

'No,' he said; 'it's not a heart. It's a shield. A heraldic shield. Must be in stone up high on the wall. In the shadows.'

'It's the right shape OK, but what makes you so sure?'

'See these?' Tom said, pointing to three identical, ill-defined stripes on the right-hand side of the contained area. 'They're chevrons. They're a device used in heraldry. For days it's been like something I knew but couldn't put a name to. You know that feeling?'

O'Brien nodded.

'The question is, what's on the left-hand side?' Tom said. 'I can't make that out at all.'

Once again O'Brien began to trace a shape with the broken white line, defining something that seemed several shades darker than the surrounding pigmentation. 'Looks like something stretched; kind of reaching,' he said.

Tom doubted that he had ever concentrated harder in his life. His entire focus was on the tiny mosaic of dots, like atoms given substance by a microscope. 'Well, I think that's exactly what it is,' he said. 'Funny how, when something's confirmed, its parts start to make sense, when before they were just chaos. It's a heraldic animal of some sort, standing on its hind legs. They had all sorts of strange creatures. Some they just made up – like enfields. You don't see many of them in pet shops.'

O'Brien laughed. 'You an expert?' he said.

'No. But I will be if I have to,' Tom said.

'Maybe I shouldn't ask, but where does this get you exactly?'

'Not all that far, but in this whole thing it's the first small breakthrough. I really wish I could tell you more, but for the moment . . .'

'No problem,' O'Brien said. 'None of my business. Glad we were able to help.'

'You've been great, thanks. She's American by the way.'

'Right. Even better.'

'Could you do me one more small favour?'

'Sure.'

'Could you let me have a copy of this – with the bits outlined? I'd be very happy to pay.'

'Forget it. Have it on me. If one copy's going to break this company, the stockholders better head for the hills.'

Impatient with the car for its sluggishness, Tom drove back to St Luc, glancing from time to time at the blow-up on the back seat as though it were a coveted painting, long saved for and now, at last, acquired. As he cruised on the motorway, he struggled to control a feeling of euphoria. Despite his attempts to hold it in check, however, he still had the curious sensation that fate had meant him to interpret the sign in the shadows. Though it defied reason, if that were true it must be intended to lead him on. What was the point of a premonition if it turned out to be a dead end? Unless of course fate – whatever that might be – was partial to a practical joke. In any case Robert, four-square and unfanciful, would snort at the notion. Detection, he often stressed, with the supreme confidence of one who until now had never indulged in any, was a matter of endless, patient checking. If you persisted long enough, the facts themselves must solve the case. The more Tom thought about the proposition, the more he realised it had to be true, of course. But at the same time there must be room for instinct. Perhaps, he reflected, the fragment of poster would prove to be the turning point – where supposition was converted into reality.

Back at the house, he laid the image on the kitchen table, weighting the corners with the old water glasses Helen had found in Chagny. Next he took from the shelf in the main room the large book on French heraldry given to him by Monique. Though the spine was split and the edges were foxed, the colours of its illustrations, veiled by sheets of flimsy paper, still had a surprising freshness. Tom loved it because the blazons were not mere badges of rank. They told an unchanging story in a bold, simple language governed by strict rules. In fact they were not badges of rank at all. Until the beginning of the nineteenth century, according to the little he had read, the use of coats of arms had never been the exclusive preserve of the aristocracy; anyone could have them as long as they didn't choose someone else's. Ignoring their democratic nature, the French Revolution outlawed them and, though later restored, they never regained their former significance.

Sitting at the table Tom opened the book, the origins of whose symbols lay a thousand years ago when helmets so obscured warriors' faces that they painted identifying emblems on their shields. Only seven colours were allowed, he had learned: yellow, white, red, black, blue, green and violet-grey. Yellow and white (*or* and *argent*) belonged to one group, while the rest (*gueules, sable, azur, sinople* and *pourpre*) belonged to another. The rules stated that two colours from the same group must not be placed next to (or on top of) each other. Turning the pages with care, Tom found this sense of order and continuity satisfying; something small that had survived intact over centuries of turmoil. Referring to the blow-up, he hoped to match the chevrons and the vague, stretching shape with an existing pattern. Half-way through, he came across a device which for a moment looked similar, but on closer examination the mythical beast on the left-hand side was facing the wrong way. While other designs resembled in small details the one uncovered by the computer, none was its twin.

Too much to expect success first time, Tom thought. He remembered reading that at the end of the seventeenth century, Louis XIV had commissioned a census of all coats of arms in the kingdom, with the intention of taxing them. For obvious reasons many people had been reluctant to register and, ten years later, the scheme had been abandoned. But by then the list in the unpublished Armorial Général ran to more than twelve thousand names. Somewhere there must be records of all of them. Even if it meant going to the Bibliothèque Nationale, where the original manuscript was kept, Tom was determined to check every one. Once he knew the provenance of the emblem, identifying the building that housed it must be easier. The plan, however, was far from watertight. The device which was so zealous of its secret might be among the unregistered ones, or it could have been established after the census closed for lack of interest.

Rising from the table, he heard a car draw up in the courtyard. By the time he reached the main room, Monique was already at the front door. Full of energy and the optimism of a bright morning, she kissed him twice on each cheek.

'You look a little less sad this morning,' she said. 'Has something happened? Something good?'

'Come and have a look at this,' Tom said, leading her by the arm to the kitchen. 'I've got a feeling I'm on to something but I'm not sure what.' Showing her first the poster and then the enhanced image, he explained how he and the helpful American had detached and analysed the section bearing the obscure device.

'Yes, I recognise Helen's bracelet now,' Monique said. 'And this young woman – Julia – looks strong and determined.' She covered Tom's hand with both of hers, giving him a reassuring look. 'Very soon, Tom; normality again. When Helen's back I want to have a party. A big party. With music and dancing. We'll get Roland to bring the puppets. He won't need any persuading for Helen. He's devoted to her.'

Tom smiled. 'I know. But there's a long way to go, Monique. This lovely book you gave me makes me realise that. Matching this . . .', he pointed to the outlined shield, '. . . with an existing coat of arms might take ages.'

'But that's only part of the search don't forget. The gendarmes will be making progress too. And Robert, of course.'

'I've got much more faith in him than I have in them. If they're making progress they're keeping extremely quiet about it.'

'It's probably better that way. They won't want the kidnappers to know what's happening.'

'That's true,' Tom conceded.

'And on this,' Monique indicated the pattern of dots

contained by a broken line, 'I've got a friend who might be helpful. She teaches history in Beaune. Thérèse. Shall I give her a ring?'

'Absolutely. Maybe we can see her together?'

CHAPTER TEN

Henri Gazin still couldn't bring himself to speak to Félix. How stupid he'd been. This man he trusted and admired had let the woman out of her cell and into a part of the building they hadn't even been to. For all they knew she might be able to reach the roof from there, and that meant she'd be out of their control. One careless moment and all the planning and the hoping were worth nothing. Félix, the brain, had failed with something so simple, and Henri felt betrayed. At first he had been so angry that he struck his fist against the stone wall four, five times, to stop himself punching his friend. When the knuckles started to bleed Félix wanted to bathe them, but Henri pulled back. His hands still bore the scars of earlier self-inflicted wounds and he knew peace of mind was the only thing that could heal him. That had begun to seem possible when the kidnap went so well. He and Félix had been within perhaps two days of having everything they wanted – money, freedom, the pleasure of knowing they'd won. Now it was all in the balance because the big certainty had gone. While they'd held the key to the Walker woman's prison, they were in charge. Now, short of breaking her door down, they had handed her the advantage.

It was all part of a pattern, Henri thought. However untrustworthy men were, they had their feet on the ground, like horses. Women blew about like the leaves on the walnut tree. There was no knowing what they thought. They cared about nothing but themselves, and that made them cruel. Because of that his mission seemed all the more urgent. He could see the common land again, and feel the painful hands, and hear the hard, taunting voice telling him he wasn't a man. He could feel the weight on him, and the thrusting – the blade going in at the same time, and the sound she made. And the red . . . Then, as she died, the spasms and shudders that made him afraid, and the body without any movement on the dry earth. He had given her that peace. It was a favour he brought; and then had brought again when the voice begged for action. Doing what had to be done, he had buried his slut of a stepmother. But since then he had begun to realise that unless he kept the thing fresh, she wouldn't stay quiet. She would be the undead he had read about once in a comic; coming to life when it was dark, or at the new moon. He knew now that he had to give the American woman the same favour. She hadn't kept the simple rules and she must be punished. And for her that would be a release. With this knowledge he felt as wise as Félix. Wiser. He would never have let the snake escape. He would have stopped it there and then, with one blow. Just as long as there was no need to touch her. Something heavy, like a car jack; hard and fast, so she wouldn't know anything about it.

That was how he would have done it. Still would. Now they had proved to Walker his daughter was still alive it didn't matter what happened to her. What was the point of letting her live to cause trouble; blow the whistle on him and Félix? Made no sense. He kicked himself for not seeing it sooner. Get rid of her and the gendarmes would have nothing to go on; no evidence whatsoever, once the car jack was at the bottom of the reservoir. It meant sorting the Englishwoman out as well of course, but he'd wanted to do that right from the start. The double deal would buy him time; would mean there was no need to do this again for years; maybe not ever.

But how was he going to tell Félix all this; Félix with his kind streak? Better not tell him at all. Better to get on with it; contact Walker, promise to deliver, do what had to be done at the last minute without Félix even realising, and pick up the money. Henri smiled at his simple scheme. It made him the boss of the team. From now on he could call the race plan. He would be the big man in the pits with the baseball cap, giving the orders to his squad of mechanics. He would say when his champion should come in for a tyre-change, and the tactics for the last laps. In his head he was getting what he'd always wanted: a place where they looked at you with respect.

The only thing was, his thoughts were running quicker than Formula One. From being a slow thinker he felt he had fireworks in his head. There were flashes and sparks, most of them gone before he could grasp what they meant. He would reach for an idea to try and pin it down but it would sputter out in the dark. Then dozens more would come and go the same way. For a time it was exciting, but soon he was feeling drained. Was this just a passing thing, or would it always be like this? Why had it happened now? The questions buzzed like wasps and flew at the backs of his eyes, trying to get out. Sit down, he thought. Be calm. Sinking to the floor in the vast hallway, he put his head in his hands, his knuckles raw from his own fury.

Seeing his rage subside, Félix approached from the foot of the stairs. He held out his hand as a gesture of reconciliation and said: 'All right now?'

Not ready to forgive, Henri looked up with a frown.

'Look,' Félix said. 'It's not that bad. I've checked the rooms either side of the one she's in and I've been out in the overgrown courtyard under her window. There's no way out. She couldn't have got on to the roof or any of those things you were worried about. Honestly. She's just as much a prisoner now as she was before.'

'She's got the key,' Henri said, as though explaining to a child.

'But Paul's on the door with a big stick. What's the problem? As long as we keep someone posted it's situation normal. You mustn't get worked up, Henri. It's bad for you. It's not very good for me either.' Smiling, he sat down beside his friend. 'I told you. I just couldn't help it. She slithered out in a split second. It could have happened to any of us. Even you.'

Henri rested his head against the wall with sudden weariness. 'We have to be quick now,' he said. 'We'll call Walker today. Arrange the pick-up for as soon as we can. This place is making me mad.' He raised both his hands, rubbing his forehead until the flesh reddened. 'I get like this sometimes.'

'Like what, exactly?'

'I can feel these faces in my head. Not just see them, but feel them there. They move like things underwater. Sometimes I go cold and sweat at the same time. They say things.'

'What things?' Félix felt the prickle of alarm.

'I don't know exactly. It's like murmuring. Well, I do know but it's not because of what their words say. It's because I know what's behind them; what they mean. When it happens I feel sick and for a minute I'm not in the same place as I was before. But it's necessary. I know that.'

Reaching over, Félix took one of Henri's injured hands in his. It looked as pathetic as a shot rabbit, the blood congealing on the swelling knuckles. Henri's face was bleached of colour now, and moisture beaded his brow. His eyes were fixed on a flagstone at his feet and his upper body started to rock backwards and forwards. At the same time he made a low moaning sound, over and over; the sound of someone being shown a sight of such horror that it made him cry for pity and release.

'What do you mean, "necessary",' Félix said. 'What do you mean you know it's "necessary"?'

There was no reply. The question had failed to reach Henri. Never before in their brief relationship had Félix known this sensation. At this moment the man beside him, so close and yet so isolated, was a complete stranger. His hand might have been the paw of a dead dog for all the sense of shared warmth between them. But what was the meaning of Henri's nightmares? Had he been unhinged by the disappointment of Julia's temporary escape; by the anger that had torn through him? Was this why he had always been so friendless; so apart? Was Félix the last to learn a dreadful secret already well-known to everyone else? Anyway, whatever the roots of his irrational behaviour, this whole thing would soon be over. Then Félix would take Henri to places where the sun could heal him. It was just the cruelty and unhappiness of his past, Félix reasoned. All that would wash away as soon as the South could soothe him; the scent of wild thyme on the hills and no sound louder than crickets and skylarks.

Meanwhile Henri had a point, Félix conceded. It was now a week since the kidnap and all the gains had been on Walker's side. Proof of life had been provided, the girl had talked to her father, and still there wasn't a sou to show for it. Félix had no doubt that despite their warnings, by now Walker would have contacted the gendarmes so that, while he played for time, the net was beginning to tighten. Julia's car would have been found. No clues there; Félix had been careful to wipe the steering wheel and any other surface he might have touched. He doubted whether the Englishwoman's 2CV had been discovered yet; its hiding place was so remote. And the old cottage would reveal nothing. Would it? Thinking the unthinkable for the first time, Félix wondered whether forensic science might somehow pick up a trace the kidnappers had overlooked; a single hair, perhaps, or a tiny drop of blood? But then what was there to lead the investigators to the property in the first place? Sensing his opportunity, he had made sure from the start that his dealings with Julia had been one-to-one. His colleagues at Cabinet Lamotte knew nothing of the transaction. And Julia had told him that she preferred to keep it between them too, until the deal was done and the cottage was hers.

Nevertheless, the longer the business dragged on, the greater the danger of unpleasant surprises. And the greater the danger that Henri's unpredictable temperament might crack under the strain. Paul too was showing unmistakable signs of disillusion. Enticed by the promise of fifty thousand francs he had appeared motivated for a short while, but the excitement had soon worn off and Félix could see that boredom had taken its place. Only fear of Henri kept him here. Félix even suspected that Paul had taken a liking to his prisoner. No doubt it was the closest the inadequate, lonely kid would ever come to a beautiful woman. Whenever she was talked about in his presence, Paul would clam up, refusing to join in speculation about her personal wealth or her love life. Teased about her fancying him, he had blushed and stammered. Yes, Paul would have to be watched. It was no longer safe to leave him in sole charge.

The Englishwoman too worried Félix. She had eaten nothing since the day of the kidnap. Neither had she said anything intelligible. Whenever he went to check on her she looked like someone in a trance. Her face was white and her hands shook. Twice when he had tried to make her stand, her legs had buckled and she had sunk once more to the ground. By now she must be growing weak, and despite himself he felt sorry for her. Only a terrible coincidence had landed her in this. What if there was a sudden deterioration and she died? Then the charge would be murder. But regardless of that, Félix didn't want it to happen. She was a kind-looking woman who had done nothing wrong. She reminded him of his aunt in Nolay; the deep laugh-lines beside her eyes, and the gentleness. At the same time he realised that her safety would be his responsibility. When the moment came to move out and hand over the American, he would have to watch Henri like a sparrowhawk. Otherwise he feared that, in the grip of his demons, the powerful farmer might dispose of the other poor woman. Félix had already talked him out of it once, at the cottage. In the flurry of a sudden evacuation he would have to be twice as vigilant; all the more so since the Englishwoman was separated from the Walker girl.

Félix looked at his companion. At last Henri was calm, his head sunk on his chest.

'I'm going to check on Paul,' Félix said. 'Afterwards, we'll make a telephone call.'

For Julia, the exhilaration of the night before had worn off. Since first light she had accepted the fact that she had exchanged one cell for another. True, this one had a small, bare ante-chamber but it still offered no possibility of escape. The large, unglazed window yawned a wide invitation but the fall to the courtyard was a good ten metres, and if she were insane enough to jump she would land on a jagged heap of masonry. Since, in any case, the rectangular space had no exit that she could see, the prognosis was far from encouraging. And yet, when she forced herself to be rational, she had to concede that there were some grounds for optimism. Her father had sounded confident and determined; she did hold the key to her own captivity; and everyone concerned, including the moronic kidnappers, must by now be longing for this thing to end. At all costs she must hang on. Telling herself over and over that she had survived the worst, she was filled with a sudden passion for freedom; she felt she would hug it with all her strength, make love to it, devour it; above all, never again take it for granted.

Meanwhile her prison continued to puzzle her. The masonry piled in the yard below, though long ago overgrown with weeds and saplings, didn't look ancient. The huge mossy blocks showed no sign of wear, other than the discoloration caused by weather. Julia doubted whether they had lain there more than a hundred years. And since they hadn't fallen from a precarious battlement, why had they been unused for so long? Had the guy who built the place run out of money? Or died? Or decided his ego was satisfied? In any event the redundant stones argued that there must be an entrance to the courtyard, invisible from Julia's window.

Moving to the door she called: 'Hello. Who's there?'

As she expected, there was no reply.

'Come on, for God's sake. What have you got to lose by talking? We all want the same thing, remember? It's OK with me if you get the money. And you're going to get it very soon, so we may as well talk. You can't still be mad at me. I didn't get very far, did I? Come on, who is that?'

After a moment a voice said: 'Me.'

'Which "me"? Paul, is that you?'

'Yes.'

'I'm really glad about that. Do you know something? You're the only human being in this dump. Those other apes, they've got something badly wrong with them, you know that? They've got something wrong in the head. When the gendarmes catch them, they're in big trouble because they're obviously mad. But you'll be OK because you're not. You're perfectly sane. You can say they forced you into it. I know that's the way it was. And I'll back you up. I'll tell the gendarmes I saw the way the others treated you. I'll tell them you're the only one who cared; who showed any pity.' Julia paused for the thought to register. 'What did they promise you, those types? Mmmm?

I mean there's no point in hiding it now. I know they offered you money because you're much too nice a person to do it for any other reason. Yes? What did they say they'd give you? If you like I'll promise never to tell anybody. It'll just be between us. Just you and me.' Julia held her breath.

'Fifty thousand f-f-francs.' Paul's mutter was just audible.

'Fifty thousand francs! God. Do you know how much they're asking for me? Do you have any idea?'

'Two hundred and fifty thousand. They said they're getting more than me because they planned the thing.'

Julia laughed. 'I'll say they're getting more than you. Do you want me to tell you how much they're really asking?'

'How do I know you're t-t-telling the truth?'

'Why would I lie? What difference does it make to me? Now listen carefully, Paul. This is the real figure, I swear to you. Your friends are asking probably millions. You got that? Millions. And you're getting a pathetic fifty thousand.'

There was silence from the other side of the door.

Leaning closer Julia went on: 'They lied to you, Paul. They deceived you. You can't trust them.'

'I don't believe you.'

'OK. Ring my father and ask him. If you slip me a piece of paper under the door I'll give you his number. You go to a phone. You ring him and ask him. You don't have to say who you are. He'll tell you what I've just told you. Millions. Believe me, they lied.' Julia felt that the improvised proposal was less than inviting. Nevertheless, it had the desired effect.

'Shit,' Paul said.

'It's not a nice feeling, is it, when your friends betray you? You think you know them. You think they care about you a little bit, then they turn round and kick you in the balls. I know how it feels, believe me. I know how much it hurts.'

'Shut up.'

Julia could tell by the anger in his voice that her words had hit the spot. 'OK. Sure. I know you want time to think about this. But let me just say one more thing. I have money too, you know. Lots. And when I tell you things you can believe them. I promise you I will never lie to you. I have too much to lose. If you help me . . . if you help me against the men who've betrayed you, I'll give you a hundred thousand francs. That's twice what they're promising. And let's face it, what's their promise worth? Mmm? They've cheated you already. Who's to say they won't cheat you again? Use you 'til the pay-off and then vanish without giving you a thing? Can you honestly guarantee that won't happen? Can you really trust them on that?'

Once again Julia knew by the silence that Paul was weighing up the alternatives.

'And you,' he said, at length. 'Why should you give me the money once you're f-f-free?' He sighed. 'Anyway,' he went on, 'I'm sick of the whole thing. It's boring.'

'I know how you feel,' Julia said. 'You think it's boring out there, you should try it in here. Listen Paul, about the money. I can afford it. I won't even miss it. Think about it. Keeping my promise is very easy for me. I can put it in cash wherever you like. I give you my word. What we could do is I could write my father a note, explaining the situation, and he could have an advance left in cash somewhere for you to collect. Is that a good idea? And the rest the minute I'm out of here.'

'They aren't my friends,' Paul said. 'They're just a couple of stupid queers.'

'Look, I'm not even talking about you having to do anything. The way it goes is you simply aren't there for a while. We pick a time when the other guys – the ones who betrayed you – are busy elsewhere, and you simply . . . well, it doesn't matter what. You simply go to the toilet; anything, just so that I can slip out and it's not your fault. I mean, come on – they can't object to you going to the toilet. The only other thing is, I need to know which outside door you use. It's so simple. And for that, a hundred thousand. It's worth thinking about isn't it, Paul? Wouldn't you say? Just think what you could do with that money.' Julia wondered whether the figure was high enough; whether she should have doubled it, but something told her the higher she went, the less likely she was to be believed.

There was no sound from the passage. At least Paul hadn't dismissed the offer out of hand.

'They'd kill me,' he said at last.

'Who would? Which one?'

'Henri. He'd kill me.'

'The thick-set guy?'

'Yes.'

A name! At last a name. So the psychopath in the black helmet with the personal hygiene problem was Henri. Julia almost wished she hadn't found out. The sheer ordinariness of it, the mundane safeness of it, somehow made him seem less monstrous. It was easier to hate the unnamed. And the hatred was important. It was the dynamo that powered her resistance.

'Look, think about it,' she said. 'What's he got to gain by a pointless killing? Listen, here's my idea. I write the note, in French if you like, so you know exactly what I'm saying. No tricks. Right? Next time you have a period off you go to some place we'll arrange – doesn't matter what – say a litter bin, or a tree or something – you pick up the advance, what shall we say, fifteen thousand, and with it there'll be a note saying you can have the balance anywhere you like as soon as I'm free. You come back here. When the coast's clear you tell me where there's an open door and you simply take a short break. Hell, if you prefer you can just run for it.' A thought occurred to her. 'I take it they come from this part of the world, your so-called friends?'

Paul murmured: 'Mmmm.'

'OK. Well, they find me gone, they're not going to hang

around and comb the countryside for you. They're going to head for the hills. That's if they get that far. I suspect the gendarmes will pick them up before they've gone fifty metres. There, that's your problem solved . . . Tell you what. We don't even have to tell the cops you were in this thing at all. If Henri and the other guy . . . what's his name . . .?'

This time, perhaps fearful that he had already revealed too much, Paul wasn't biting.

'If they try to make out you were in on this thing I can just deny it. What evidence is there? Just a piece of paper with some writing, and paper burns at four hundred and fifty-one degrees Fahrenheit.' Even as she said this, Julia wondered whether it was a promise she could keep. If he stuck to his side of the bargain, would she be able to join his companions in betraying him? And if she did, would that make her as despicable as them? Moral dilemmas would have to wait, she thought. For now the absolute priority was survival. 'Just don't put the cash in your bank account,' she went on.

'I haven't got one,' Paul said, more in a tone of resignation than resentment.

'Better still,' Julia said. 'They're never going to trace used notes. Then you just keep a low profile for a while and pretty soon the whole thing will be forgotten. And the men who claimed to be your friends will be looking at a lot of years in gaol.' Exhausted by the effort of conjuring a plan which, until she lent it conviction, had been a vague swarm of thoughts, Julia leaned her forehead against the door, willing Paul to accept. Squeezing her eyes shut, she remembered snatches of a prayer she and her Catholic mother had often said when she was a child: '. . . Hail our life, our sweetness and our hope . . . to thee do we cry, poor . . .' Poor what? The wispy memory was out of reach. '. . . Children of Eve . . .' That was it, ' . . . to thee do we cry poor banished children of Eve . . .' It sounded like a ragged orphan in a Victorian oleograph.

Had the plan been too complicated for Paul to follow? The question was whether greed would overcome fear. Would he have the strength to defy Henri for the sake of the money? And having collected the deposit, would he still come back for more? Julia gambled that the prospect of another eighty-five thousand francs would prove irresistible. 'You don't have to make your mind up now, of course,' she reassured him. 'Take your time, Paul. Think it over. But look at it this way. How often do you win the lottery in a lifetime? How often do you get handed a hundred thousand just for turning your head away?' That ought to do it, but how long would it be before the unoiled machinery of Paul's brain got to grips with the proposition? In a way, perhaps, she had been wrong to give him time. Better to urge a spontaneous decision. Ah well, what the hell. The thing was done. 'Tell you what,' she said. 'I'm terrifically hungry. Any chance of a fresh croissant and a nice cup of coffee?'

'You're to have nothing. It's for trying to escape.'

Was it Julia's imagination or did Paul sound almost apologetic? To pass the time and subdue the craving in her stomach, she decided to make two hundred circuits of the room. As she began, in a determined way, to cover the ground, two thoughts were uppermost, beside the burning issue of which way Paul would jump: one was the realisation that a single blast from a shotgun could shatter her refuge at any moment, and the other was concern for the woman in the basement. In the fever of hatching her scheme she had forgotten to involve her fellow prisoner in the deal. If Paul took the bait she would work on that. She suspected that once he had found ways of spending the money in his head, handing over an extra key would not be a problem.

Since Monique's gallery in Beaune was closed on Mondays, she said she had all the time in the world. Leo, her small son, was out for the day with Zazie. The pair had gone fishing from a boat on the reservoir. For Zazie, this was the ultimate sacrifice. The sport bored her, the water terrified her, and the heat was intense. Sheltering under a large straw hat and a faded parasol, she would look like a Renoir, never for an instant spoiling Leo's enjoyment by showing her discomfort. After these trips, however, she would arrive home tense with the effort and throw herself into cooking for its therapeutic release.

Sitting in the shade of the awning at the café in the Place Carnot, Monique described her sister with affection. Beside Tom's cup, furled tight, was the computer enhancement of the shield. As he listened his hand fidgeted with the elastic band. Tourists streamed past, in search of the picturesque, looking driven and unlovely. The sightseeing seemed to give them little pleasure. It was an item on a check-list, a photo-opportunity, a duty done. At a level to which they never raised their eyes, the elegant windows in the steep roofs looked over their heads to the more pleasing prospect of the town walls.

A middle-aged woman with a slight limp detached herself from the oncoming horde and headed for the table. Monique rose with a smile to greet her. Kissing her twice on each cheek, she introduced Thérèse to Tom. The formalities over, Monique ordered Thérèse a cappuccino and left Tom to explain. Confining himself to the puzzle of the shield, he tried to convey a sense of urgency without being too specific about the circumstances. As far as he knew he was still forbidden to discuss the case. Opening the computer enhancement with care, he turned it for Thérèse to see, and outlined the shield with his forefinger. She took her glasses from her handbag and peered at the pattern of dots, nodding at Tom's explanation. When she had studied the image for a few moments, she removed the glasses and settled back a little in her chair.

'It's very interesting,' she said. 'Amazing, the technology. But I am a history teacher, monsieur . . .'

'Tom. Please call me Tom.'

Thérèse inclined her head to acknowledge the courtesy. 'I told Monique on the telephone, give me dates, wars, the seeds of the Revolution – no problem. But this . . .', she indicated the paper with her pale hand, 'this is a foreign country to me. You need a specialist.'

At that moment the smiling young waiter approached with her coffee. It was clear that she was a regular and that he had great respect for her, which made Tom wonder whether he was a former pupil of hers.

Taking a sip, she went on: 'But all is not lost. It occurred to me after I had spoken to Monique that I have a friend, a former colleague actually, who knows this subject. I rang him and told him about you. He's content to see you any time. After this if you like.'

Encouraged, Tom said that would be perfect. When Thérèse had finished her cappuccino, he left coins on the saucer with the bill and followed her and Monique past the flower bed surrounding the statue of Gustave Monge, with its air of tranquillity and order. He and Helen had often crossed this sunny square to treat themselves at Bouché, the miraculous pâtisserie on the corner. There they would order a blackcurrant and almond tart, or a *tarte tatin*, relishing it all the more for knowing it was bespoke. The manageress presided with the gravity and professionalism of a hospital matron, her obliging manner concealing a will of concrete.

Pressing a labelled bell beside an old, nondescript door, Thérèse ushered them into a courtyard that might have been painted by Monet. The wistaria, thicker than a liner's hawser, had such a sure grip on the walls that it seemed to reinforce them. Geraniums on the sills of windows shuttered against the heat were as startling in their assertive display as tropical fish. It was impossible to look at them and not feel a surge of hope. And the white metal bench in the corner, under the mulberry tree, seemed shaped more by time than the craftsman's hammer.

'His mother died,' Thérèse said. 'He was very sad, naturally, but now he's the master of all this. Lucky Alain.'

Alain Quignard answered their knock. He was tall and slim, with an unhurried, fastidious air. Tom guessed he was in his early sixties, but thanks to a life free from stress he could have passed for ten years younger. After kissing Thérèse, welcoming Monique and shaking hands with Tom, he showed them into the library which led off the panelled hall. For a moment Tom thought how enviable other people's lives could seem. This donnish existence in a privileged setting appeared at first glance the height of cultured wellbeing. But that was only one way of seeing it. Who knew anything? Perhaps this was no more than a lonely old man trapped in a web of his mother's spinning; perhaps he cried in the night for a more vivid existence which he could never know.

When they were seated at the oval mahogany table, surrounded by hundreds of volumes – some bound in leather, others in cloth of faded rose and turquoise – Tom once again produced the pattern of dots with its slender outline. Without over-stressing his slight acquaintance with heraldry, he mentioned his theory about the chevrons and the heraldic beast. Quignard listened, holding the edges of the paper with his long hands which had a slight shine on them, as though buffed by contact with a million pages. Turning, he opened a drawer in the bookcase behind him and took out a rectangular magnifying glass with an ivory handle. Then once again he concentrated on the image, frowning more the longer he scrutinised.

'It's curious,' he said at last. 'It's familiar and yet it's not familiar. So difficult to make out the creature on the left. One feels great dignity there, great vigour, but not very much precision.' When he smiled at Tom the alteration in his expression was confined to his mouth. The eyes were reluctant to trust. 'A moment.' As he said this he held up a forefinger and rose to face the shelves. 'Somewhere here lies the answer,' he said with outspread arms. 'But where?'

As Quignard began to search, Tom looked at Monique, daunted by the size of the task. Even if they found the needle in the haystack, what then? At best it might direct him to a family, but the chances of them still living in the building that housed the shield were remote. They might have sold it generations ago. Seeming to read his thoughts, Monique reached out and touched his arm.

'Courage,' she said.

'The life of a scholar,' Thérèse said, echoing Tom's earlier thought; 'it's enviable.'

Quignard gave a small shrug. 'It's tranquil,' he said. 'No thunderclaps. Ah! There it is.' With this he eased out a tall leather-bound volume and brought it to the table. 'The stories in here,' he said, running his hand over the broad surface. 'True stories. Stories of chivalry, ambition, alliances, conquest, bourgeois aspiration . . . Completely fascinating. And so economical. All told in pictures, so that even the ignorant may understand.'

Tom was beginning to dislike Quignard, with his pedant's self-absorption and his evident assumption of superiority. But that was unimportant. All that mattered was his usefulness. If it meant getting closer to Helen, Tom told himself that he would have dealt with a child-molester. Talking of whom, he thought, looking at Quignard. No. Stop it. Just listen to what the mandarin has to say.

Sitting down again, Quignard turned the pages separated by sheets of flimsy paper as though they were silk. Tom could see that the colour plates were even brighter than those in the book Monique had given him. As he progressed, Quignard reached for a blank sheet from the table drawer, and, folding first, tore it into three equal strips which he placed at intervals throughout the large volume. The ceremony complete, he turned the book round and gave it a measured push towards Tom.

'There,' he said. 'Three possibilities. Perhaps you would care to turn to the first. The de Franchevilles. A very old family. They had a son who was disgraced in the Great War. Perhaps by then the blood had thinned.'

'How "disgraced"?' Tom asked.

'He was a coward. He ran away from the guns. His commanding officer shot him in the field.' Quignard was matter-of-fact, as though his sympathies lay with neither party. 'Their home was close to Nolay. I don't know whether it still stands or whether they survive. Next,' he went on, moving Tom along, 'the Chenonceaux. Money from Canada. Trade.' He pronounced the last word as though he were saying 'pornography'. 'They have a very small château at St Martin. I heard they're restoring it. Probably using a great deal of coloured marble.'

Quignard arched an eyebrow for Thérèse's benefit. Responding to his expectation, she smiled at his discernment and wit. Monique, meanwhile, gave Tom an amused glance.

'And finally,' Quignard said, as though rounding off a well-rehearsed lecture to illiterates, 'the Musset-Contini. Part Italian, as the name implies, and wholly insignificant. They have a pleasant house here in Beaune. They are winemakers, though their wines lack distinction. I believe they have a cellar where the tourists purchase the uninspired fruits of their endeavour.' This time he reserved the full weight of his disdain for the word 'tourists'. 'And that's all,' he went on. 'Beyond those I think there is nothing more I can suggest.'

'Well, that's been extremely helpful,' Tom said, swallowing his distaste. 'Do you think I might borrow this book? So that if I do find something I can compare it?'

Without hesitation, Quignard shook his head. 'Out of the question, I'm afraid. It's very valuable. One has a duty to books like this. You may look at it for as long as you wish of course but . . . No. That is not possible.'

Unable to restrain herself, Monique began: 'But his wife . . . !'

Now it was Tom's turn to lay a hand on her arm. 'Don't worry, Monique,' he said. 'I'll make sketches. After all, we mustn't neglect our duty to books.' He hoped Quignard had caught the irony, but not to such an extent that he would withdraw all co-operation. Taking a pencil from his pocket, Tom made rapid drawings of all three coats of arms. Each featured a design bearing a strong resemblance to the shape in the enhancement. Asking again for the present whereabouts of the Chenonceaux, the family tainted by trade, Tom pushed the book back towards Quignard. 'And are you in here?' he added.

'My mother's family is represented, of course.' As Quignard rose to end the interview, it was clear that he was disinclined to reveal more.

Tom suppressed an urge to say something outrageous, like: 'So your father, the collaborator – his lot aren't there then?' Instead he thanked Quignard for his help and walked with Thérèse and Monique back to the street.

There Thérèse took her leave and Tom and Monique strolled the short distance to the car.

'What do you think?' Monique said.

'I think I wouldn't like to be stranded on a desert island with Quignard. But I'm very glad we met. This coat of arms thing, it might be a complete waste of time, but at the moment it's all I've got. People have all sorts of things in their houses that don't belong to them. I know that. But I've just got a funny feeling about it.'

'Then let's start now. Which one first?'

'Look Monique, can you really spare the time for this? I feel I'm . . .'

'Don't be silly. Even if I had something wildly important to do, I would find time for this. And I haven't. So *avanti*. Which one?'

'Well, if the Musset-Continis are here in Beaune we'd better start with them. And if their wine's as bad as Quignard says, let's hope they don't offer us a drink.'

Monique laughed and linked her arm in his. 'Good,' she said. 'We'll ask the wine merchant in the square where to find them.'

While Monique made enquiries at the shop that sold expensive burgundies and souvenir corkscrews of ornate design, Tom telephoned Robert to check that there were no new developments. Robert reported that Major Granier was due to visit Walker during the afternoon, and that Walker expected to have the money ready the following morning. Things were moving towards a conclusion, he said, and he, Robert, was following up a lead which he would tell Tom about later. When Tom relayed all this to Monique as they walked past the Hôtel du Centre, she said the end was in sight.

'Oh God, I hope so,' Tom said. 'I can't stop thinking about what's happening to her. The nights are the worst.'

'She's stronger than you think, Tom.'

'No, I know she's strong. In many ways she's probably coping with it much better than I would. Or am, come to that. But she must be afraid all the same. Maybe hungry. Maybe hurt. God, how I loathe the bastards. If I get near them I'll . . .'

Monique took hold of his hand, interlacing her fingers in his.

'You've been incredibly kind,' he said. 'I'm very lucky.'

'I love Helen,' she said. 'And when Guy and I broke up I think I only survived because of friends . . . and Leo and Zazie of course.'

'Do you still miss him?'

'No. Yes. His body. I miss that. Does that embarrass you?'

'No.'

'He was a very unselfish lover. It was the only unselfish thing about him. The problem was he was unselfish with many women. So in the end he was selfish in that too.' Monique laughed. 'How complicated we are.'

Set back from the street behind a tall wrought-iron fence, the house of the Musset-Continis was handsome and substantial. Formal flower beds, the raked drive and the fresh paintwork on doors and ivy-framed windows spoke of civic pride, conservatism, and little imagination. Perhaps that was the clue to their pedestrian products, Tom thought. Looking up he was aware of a security camera monitoring them, and hoped it couldn't read his mind. Moments later there was a discreet click and, taking her cue, Monique pushed the gate open.

'I hope they never invite Roland here,' she said as they walked up the drive. 'It would bring out the worst in him.'

Tom smiled, imagining the puppeteer hanging from an Audubon tapestry and singing lewd songs to shock the solid burghers. 'I'm not sure it doesn't bring out the worst in me,' he said.

They mounted the steps to the gleaming front door, pressed the bell, and waited, expecting to be met by a uniformed servant with a face as lugubrious as a turkey. Instead they were confronted by a round-bellied figure in early middle age with amused eyes and a tan which gave notice of having been acquired at considerable expense. He wore a monogrammed white shirt and dark blue trousers; a living portrait of confident bonhomie. Beaming in at once on Monique, he gave her a dazzling smile and asked what he could do for them. Even while Tom replied, the proprietor, if that was who he was, ran his frank brown eyes over her features. Careful not to deter him for the moment, Monique gave him a look which was cool without being confrontational.

Their urbane host introduced himself as Antoine de Musset-Contini, and showed them into his drawing room. Photographs in silver frames appeared to occupy almost every polished surface. Musset-Contini with President Mitterrand; with Catherine Deneuve; with Yves Montand, Charles Aznavour, Serge Blanco, Alain Prost and dozens of others Tom didn't recognise. The grand piano groaned under the weight of celebrities, all of whom (if Quignard was right) must have gritted their teeth when asked to endorse Musset-Contini's wines. But Tom had an inkling that, if challenged to describe their quality, this genial character would have made no bones about them, and opened an excellent bottle of Puligny-Montrachet.

Offered a seat, Monique disappointed Musset-Contini by choosing a single damask-covered armchair, rather than the sofa. Undeterred, he stood close to her, with his back to the marble fireplace, and gave her a brief history of the house. Tom could see that, in spite of herself, she was charmed by him. It seemed clumsy to intervene, but time was short and there was so much at stake. Removing the elastic band from the computer enhancement, he waited for a pause.

'I'm sorry to trouble you,' he said, 'but believe me this is very urgent. Does this mean anything to you? I know it's a little difficult to make out but an expert we consulted thought it resembled the arms of your family. We think it must be on a ceiling, or high on the wall of a house somewhere.'

Taking the picture, Musset-Contini studied it for a short while before shaking his head. 'No,' he said. 'I have a strange feeling I've seen it before but . . .', he shrugged and dropped the corners of his mouth; 'I regret, no, it's not ours. And the period of the house, you see, we don't have this feature. Not here or in Paris. No, I'm sorry.' He handed the paper back to Tom while turning once more to Monique. 'May I offer you an aperitif while you're here? It would give me great pleasure.'

Smiling, Monique declined and rose from the chair. With a small shrug of regret, Musset-Contini escorted them to the front door.

'You must do me the honour of visiting again, madame,' he said. 'You live here, in Beaune?'

'No,' Monique said. 'I'm only here for a very short time.'

'Pity.' Musset-Contini seemed reluctant to shut the door. 'Such a pity.'

'You have an ardent admirer,' Tom said, as they headed back to the car. 'I wonder where Madame Musset-Contini is?'

'The Côte d'Azur, probably, chaperoning her daughters. There was a photograph of them on the mantelpiece – between Jean-Marie Le Pen and Johnny Halliday. Such distinguished company.' Monique laughed. 'Men! They're so obvious.'

'And women?'

'Women? Oh, they're so prone to generalisations!'

The second port of call, the intimate château of the Chenonceaux, with its dry moat, set on a hill overlooking orchards and an idyllic panorama on every side, proved no more rewarding that the first. The young son of the house, about to play tennis, had shown them the largest rooms, but none bore any relation to the computer image. Neither, when compared with it, did the family crest.

As they set out for Nolay, and the seat of the de Franchevilles, Tom was beginning to feel that his hunch had been a delusion – something he wanted to believe. Nolay's mediaeval market building, with its intricate pattern of beams, was the coolest outdoor spot Tom and Monique had so far encountered. Pausing under its shade, they asked two passers-by the whereabouts of the property. One, an old woman, gave them a blank stare and the other answered in Dutch. At last, after wandering the empty streets for twenty minutes, they came across a sensible-looking figure wearing a straw hat, yellow with age, and wire-framed glasses. This turned out to be a retired geophysicist whose hobby was the history of the town. Delighted to be asked a pertinent question, he was able to tell them at some length that though the de Franchevilles had indeed been local landowners, the line had died out sometime in the nineteen-twenties. Not many years after the unfortunate business of the son, he said. Soon after that their home, a modest château with pointed turrets tiled in the yellow and maroon of Burgundy, had burned to the ground. Thanking him, and following his directions to the melancholy spot, Tom and Monique confirmed that if any piece of masonry did remain bearing the heraldic beast and the chevrons, it was buried under tons of grass-encrusted stone.

On the way back to St Luc, Tom reminded Monique that two people, Quignard and Musset-Contini, had both said the coat of arms looked somehow familiar. How could that be, he wondered? Monique had no explanation but asked whether it might be in the public domain? The arms, perhaps of a *département*, or a large town? A design which might be exposed to regular view; of which one might have subliminal awareness. As he considered the possibility, Tom remained quiet. Time was short, and for the moment the quest had led them nowhere. Finding it impossible to sit and wait for the handover, he felt he had to keep the investigation alive for the sake of his own sanity. Any new knowledge represented progress of a sort. And besides, who knew whether the kidnappers could be trusted to keep their side of the deal? If the gendarmes made even the smallest mistake when it came to the exchange, Helen might still be at risk. No, to have her safe beside him again he would follow any lead, however discouraging the odds.

CHAPTER ELEVEN

Monique dropped Tom in St Luc before picking up Leo and Zazie at the reservoir. Promising to ring her as soon as he heard anything, and accepting an invitation to supper the following evening, Tom gave her a hug and opened the door of the house. After her companionship it seemed emptier than ever, waiting for Helen to animate it. The flowers she had arranged on the mantelpiece were drooping, but he was reluctant to throw them out. Mindful of the need to be occupied, he remembered Robert's mention of a development and determined to follow it up. The sun had left the courtyard now, and the swallows were showing off. With sublime confidence the pair that lived in the barn negotiated the hole in the door without seeming to position themselves, or deviate. One smooth, powered swoop and they glided in with graceful certainty.

As Tom walked the few metres to Robert's house, he heard a car horn on the road leading from the church and looked up to see the ex-policeman approaching. Swerving on to the patch of grass in front of his house, where he and Yvonne often entertained in the evenings, Robert got out of the car and slammed the door.

'Idiots,' he said. 'They've got night-sticks for brains.'

'What?' Tom was baffled.

'Granier's bloodhounds. Morons. The great man has just been to the château. Monsieur Walker asked him what he had found out and do you know what he said? Imbecile.'

Tom shook his head.

'Granier said: "We're almost sure they come from the region." "Almost sure!" My God. This is what their expert from Dijon is telling them. Expert my arse. What are they getting paid for this astonishing information? Of course they're from the region. My cockerel could have told them that.'

Robert's cockerel, scratching for grain beside the gate opening onto the field, declined to confirm the claim.

'Sit down, Mr Professor,' Robert said, motioning Tom to a chair at the white plastic dining table. 'It's fatiguing, all this stupidity.' With a surreptitious glance towards the house, he held a finger to his lips and went over to the lean-to behind his toolshed, where he stretched up to a shelf and moved a large, rusty tin to reveal a bottle of red wine and two small water glasses. Concealing them, and walking with exaggerated stealth, he sat beside Tom and poured them both a drink. 'Health,' he said, raising his glass. 'Yours and Helen's, my friend.'

Tom returned the toast. 'What else is happening over there? Have the kidnappers been in touch yet?'

'Not yet. Everyone's standing by. It won't be long now. Monsieur Walker will call the moment he hears anything.'

'Do you think they know the gendarmes are on to it?'

'It depends. This is a small community. If they have any day-to-day contact, they must know.'

'What do you think they'll do?' Tom felt an ulcer of anxiety high in his stomach.

'Think about it. There's nothing they can do. It was all a bluff in the first place. They knew the gendarmes would be involved. Of course they did.' Robert re-filled the glasses.

'There is something they can do.' Tom's expression made his meaning plain.

'Oh no. Absolutely not. Why would they add that to the list of charges? For what? Risk a lifetime in gaol – for nothing? They aren't angry with their prisoners. Often they even like them. No. That makes absolutely no sense. Now they've come this far they'll believe they're cleverer than the gendarmes.'

'According to you they probably are.'

'Listen, my friend, even the gendarmes can't screw up when they're surrounding a position in strength. This story can only have one ending, and we'll be celebrating it very soon.' He drained his wine in a single swallow, as though initiating the party. 'And you? Did you have any luck with the teacher?'

Tom told him of his fruitless enquiries with Monique, mentioning the fact that Musset-Contini had fallen in love with her.

'Who hasn't?' Robert said. 'She's magnificent.' There was a dreamy look in his eyes as he filled their glasses for the third time. 'It's a tragedy that she hasn't got a man – a partner.'

'I don't think she wants one. Not on a permanent basis.'

Robert took a deep gulp. 'Ah, youth,' he sighed, 'but afterwards comes loneliness . . . Enough,' he said, following a maudlin pause. 'Goodbye, sadness.'

'You said you had something to tell me,' Tom said.

'Well, don't get excited but you know I've been asking a lot of questions. I pester people. Make them try to remember. Make them use their eyes. Well, old Crotet, you know, the bent old fellow who lives on the Veilly road, the one who gave you a bowling lesson at the fête last year? Well, he told me something. He said that loner from the farm, Gazin, he said two or three times he's looked out of his window in the night and he's seen Gazin returning home, or driving away. This is one or two o'clock in the morning. Now, perhaps

Monsieur Gazin also has a rendezvous on a kitchen table.' He laughed, reminding Tom of his abortive vigil at Ste Sabine. 'Perhaps, but I don't think so. This is not a romantic type. This is a type who prefers his own company, if you know what I mean.'

Tom nodded.

'His mother died when he was young. She was a good woman. After that, his father went to pieces,' Robert went on. 'Took up with a slut. When she did a vanishing act with all his money, he shot himself.'

'Sad story,' Tom said. 'So what are we saying about Gazin?'

'We're saying it pays to watch anyone we have any suspicions about. Ninety-nine per cent will turn out to be angels. There is one who will not. Tonight, I watch.'

'Shouldn't we tell Granier about this? Walker was keen that we should.'

'There's nothing to tell. I go to Granier and say a farmer's going out at night, he'll have me fitted with a jacket that does up at the back. No. Believe me. When I've checked it out, if there's anything interesting, that will be the time to tell Granier.'

'I'll come with you,' Tom said.

'Good. Meanwhile, you eat with us. You look as pale as Crotet's cat.'

All afternoon Félix had been trying to persuade Henri to agree to a plan. Since they both knew that matters must now be brought to a head, there was no point in delay. But Henri was proving difficult and Félix found it impossible to read his mood. At one moment he seemed lucid, at the next distant and suspicious. At first Henri had argued that they should blast the door off Julia's hiding place and put her back where she was before. When Félix had stressed the danger of injuring, or even killing her, and thereby wrecking the entire operation, Henri had seemed unconcerned. Félix found this sudden shift of mood alarming. What had been the point of the past week if they were to throw it all away now? In any case, he hated violence. Even when Julia had escaped and made a fool of him, he couldn't have brought himself to do her serious injury. For him she had always been a means to an end, but Henri seemed to be losing sight of that. And Paul too was showing signs of having had enough. With two less than wholehearted accomplices, Félix felt isolated.

Perhaps he should cut his losses and just leave? Who would the gendarmes believe then? Him, and the Cabinet Lamotte witnesses who could testify that he had made regular appearances there, or Henri and Paul who found it hard to express themselves at the best of times? Julia couldn't make a positive identification because of the helmet. But even if he could bluff his way through, it was a defeatist idea. And besides, if he left, who could guarantee the safety of the women? More important still, who would care for poor Henri? Whatever pain and confusion his friend was going through was no fault of his own. It was what life had done to him. No, Félix thought, there was nothing for it but to hold this shambles together. For everyone's sake he must be firm. As things stood the crime he'd committed hadn't hurt anyone, apart from cuts and bruises. Walker could afford to part with the money, and when it was all over no one would be any the worse for it.

Félix had pondered these thoughts while he paced the hallway. Henri had disappeared half an hour ago, saying he needed to be alone for a while. Now, knowing that Paul was stationed at Julia's door, Félix went to reassure Henri and enthuse him with his resolution. Calling his friend's name, he entered the large chamber where he had chased Julia, but there was no sign. The ante-room was also empty. Pushing open the door to the cellars, he spoke louder this time, his voice echoing in the stone passages. Since there was still no reply, he was about to move on when he heard what sounded like a muffled whimper from the bottom of the steps. If this was Henri, what was he doing in the dark? Returning to the chamber where Julia had posed for the Polaroid, Félix took a torch from beside his sleeping-bag and hurried back to the cellar entrance. The beam picked out the edges of the steps and glimpses of the walls. At the bottom of the steps, he kept as still as he could, listening for a repeat of the sound. Since there was none, he directed the torch to his left and made a slow pass along that side of the passage. Half-way down, near the junction with the corridor which had contained Julia's first cell, a door was ajar. With sudden apprehension, Félix forced himself to be positive and walked towards it. As he drew closer, he heard the whimper again, sounding like a frightened child. He pushed open the door of the windowless cavity, his brain reviewing the awful possibilities. When the torch beam had reached the far corner without discovery, he let it travel along the remaining wall.

It was now that he could smell the overpowering, sour sweat, and something just as acrid but more ominous. The lowered torch revealed at last what the darkness had been hiding. Squatting on his haunches behind the door was Henri. His head was down, half obscured by his folded arms. Beside him was an open bottle with only a few centimetres of colourless liquid left in the bottom. By its pungency Félix recognised it as *eau de vie*, and anger banished his fear. From the moment they had embarked on this plan, he and Henri had both agreed that clear heads were essential. Alcohol was banned inside the building. On Saturday, when he had discovered Paul with a can of beer while on duty, Henri had wrenched it from him and hurled it out of a window, threatening to hit him if he ever did it again. And now Henri was so drunk he couldn't speak. What had brought this on, Félix wondered?

'Get up,' he said, determined to show no pity.

Henri raised his head with difficulty, though his eyes remained at knee-level.

'Get up you stupid animal.' Félix got hold of Henri's arm and tried to pull him to his feet.

With a vigorous, uncoordinated effort, Henri began to rise but lost his balance and hit his head as he fell back against the wall.

'I don't believe this,' Félix said. 'Now, when we have to act, you're useless. Well, understand this, Henri. I'm doing this my way now. If you don't like it, that's tough. I'm going to telephone Walker right now and I'm going to make the final arrangements. I'm going to fix the handover for as soon as possible. With a half-wit and a drunk for companions, I have no choice. How could you, you . . . ? Oh, shit.'

Leaving Henri once more in the dark, Félix raced up the cellar steps two at a time. Anger had fired him with adrenalin and he felt charged enough to see this thing through without any help. In many ways Henri's condition made it easier. In the end it was best to make decisions alone. That was the way it had worked so far. But it did mean delaying the handover until Henri was sober enough to help. As he entered the large chamber where the sleeping-bags were, ready to telephone Walker at once on the mobile stolen from Julia's car, Félix was astonished to see Paul sauntering in from the hallway. It was clear that the reluctant guard – hands in pockets, truculence furrowed across his features – had more than a casual conversation in mind.

'What do you think you're doing here?' Félix said.

'Why not? Where's she going to go?' Paul's voice was quiet but showed no sign of nervousness.

This new note of defiance was a bad sign, Félix thought. But what, apart from frustration, had changed his attitude? 'Well, OK for a moment,' he said, trying to avoid confrontation. 'What's the problem?'

'You think I'm an idiot,' Paul said. 'I do more work than anybody else, and for what?' He took a hand out of his pocket to demonstrate the emptiness of the palm.

For a moment Félix almost pitied him. From his childhood, in hand-me-down clothes, he had been a victim; first of a mother too preoccupied with hardship to show affection, and later of bullies who took advantage of his mildness. Félix had first noticed him at the feast of Henri IV in Arnay le Duc, sitting in a family group but seeming alone. When the idea for the kidnap had taken root, he had cultivated Paul, judging him to be needful and trustworthy. Until now there had been no reason to revise his assessment. 'What's happened to make you say this?' he said.

'Tell me again what you're getting,' Paul said, ignoring the question.

It was unheard of for Paul to query instructions, Félix thought. Someone must have been talking, shaking his already fragile confidence. And there was only one possible candidate. How clever of her to try and drive a wedge between them. But in the end Paul would trust the people he knew; Félix was confident of that. However, there was no point in altering the figure, since that would be an admission of deception. 'The same as we were getting when I first told you,' he said. 'Two hundred and fifty thousand. Nothing has changed. You get fifty. It's very simple. Naturally she'll say something different. That's easy for her. She'll say anything to be free. So it's up to you. Either you believe someone you know, or you believe a complete stranger who's so desperate she'll make up any lie. But I tell you this. If you leave her unguarded I can give you nothing. That's fair isn't it? I do my job, you do yours, and we all go home happy.'

'I'm fed up,' Paul said. 'It never ends, just sitting in a dark passage. We live like rats.'

'That's true. But there's an important difference. Very soon these rats will be out of here with exactly what they wanted. You see this?' he went on, holding up the mobile. 'When you go back to your post I'm phoning Walker with this to make the final arrangements. We don't even have to pay for the call. Think of the money, Paul. The things you can do, the places you can go.' But even as he spoke it occurred to him that Paul would have no idea where to go, on his own. The thought might even panic him. 'We haven't really discussed it, have we?' Félix said. 'Where will you head for?'

Paul frowned, confused by conflicting versions of the reward, and by the unfamiliar prospect of choice. 'I don't know,' he said. 'Maybe Autun. I've got a cousin there.'

'But that's only a few kilometres away,' Félix said.

'They have a Roman spectacle in summer,' Paul said. 'I like that. Chariots, and gladiators, and everything.'

It was a close horizon, Félix thought, and perhaps all the better for that. The further afield Paul travelled, the less happy and the more conspicuous he would become. But even in Autun, if for any reason he were questioned, or if he let slip details of the kidnap in casual conversation, he might still prove a liability. Félix cursed himself for not giving the matter more thought. What would happen when Paul's money ran out? Fifty thousand francs wouldn't last long. What would be his incentive then for keeping their secret? Thinking on his feet, he approached his dejected accomplice and put an arm round his shoulder. 'I know it's hard,' he said. 'And I know she's probably making all sorts of promises, but listen to me. I will give you what I said, and if you want to come with us when it's over, you can. I can't promise you Roman spectacles, but you won't be alone.'

Paul looked at him and relaxed his frown. It was clear that this pleased him more than the thought of money. 'But what about Henri?' he said. 'What will he say?'

'He'll say what I tell him to,' Félix said. 'At the moment

he's too pissed to speak at all. No, it'll be the three of us. Trust me. The Three Musketeers. Now, get back to that woman, there's a good fellow, and don't be deceived by what she says.'

When Paul had returned to the passage, convinced at least for the moment, Félix had felt a sting of conscience. Had he meant what he said? Could he imagine standing trackside at Monaco with Paul in tow? One companion too drunk to stand and the other incapable of doing anything on his own? It was not the vision of freedom he'd had in mind when they started. But neither was this the time for doubts. Whatever happened, when he steered this affair to a successful end, all the more satisfying for knowing he'd done the lion's share himself, it would release him to take more realistic stock of his circumstances. Picking up the mobile, he pressed the eight digits that would set the final process in motion.

William Walker took the call in his study, knowing that it was being recorded in the courtyard by the gendarmes in the blue van. From the best of motives, and without in any way wanting to jeopardise Julia's safety, Granier had tried to persuade him to play for time. The major had, for instance, urged him to avoid a handover during the hours of darkness. But Walker was weary and anxious. Whatever it took, he wanted his daughter home. Concerned also by the effect the crisis was having on Madeleine, and always conscious of Tom Bellman's fears for Helen, he felt a greater weight of responsibility than any he had experienced in his professional life. If he mishandled this there could be no forgiveness; no explanatory speech to stockholders; no press handout to guide opinion. Though still confident of his ability to free the hostages unharmed, he had never felt so alone. As he picked up the white receiver, he concentrated on a photograph of Julia in a silver frame. All that energy, that glorious vitality, caged and endangered. How dared they, the bastards?

'Monsieur Walker?' The voice sounded flat and muffled.
'Yes.'

'I know this is being recorded so I'll make it short. Tracing
it won't help. It's a mobile that belongs to someone else. No
more excuses. No more delays. Tomorrow night, eleven p.m.
The cemetery behind the church up the hill at Bligny. Not the
one in front, the one behind. Just inside the gate on the left-
hand side is a large grey gravestone with the name Gagnepain
in gold letters.' He spelled it out. 'Have the money there in a
tied plastic bag. A strong bin-liner will do. The spot is exposed.
The least sign of your friends and you get nothing. But our
patience is exhausted and your daughter will no longer be safe.
You understand?'

'I understand. And the Englishwoman? I can't let this go
forward without her.'

The question was ignored. 'Once we have the money your
daughter will immediately be released within a short distance
of your home.'

'How do I know . . . ?' Walker began.

The caller interrupted him. 'This is your only chance. You
know she's alive. You know we have no further use for her. If
you attempt to play tricks you must take the consequences.
Can you live with that, Monsieur Walker?'

'Look, can we make it earlier? I'll do exactly as you say,
but why wait . . . ?' As Walker had expected, the line had gone
dead, cutting off his enquiry. Leaning back in his chair he
realised for the first time that his body had begun to ache with
the tension of craning forward. He reached for the tumbler of
bourbon beside him and took a deep draught, reviewing the
conversation. There was no reason to believe they didn't mean
what they said. They wanted the money and they didn't want
to be responsible for their prisoners any longer. But how would
Granier's men fit into this? How would they remain
inconspicuous and yet close enough to the cemetery to make

their arrests? If the kidnappers saw them, how would panic affect their actions? Unlike the problems he had faced in business, these would not fall into in-trays, ready for logical and systematic sorting. This was a game of chess where the other player's pieces were hidden.

First things first. He must tell Madeleine, Tom, and Robert, and confer with the gendarmes. At least the waiting was over. The cash was already in his safe, drawn that day from a bank in Dijon and driven back under escort. As he walked down the polished passage towards the hall, he saw Madeleine emerging from the drawing room, her eyes expectant. Quickening his step, he held out his arms and embraced her. Not since the death of his first wife had William Walker felt so close to tears.

Twenty minutes later Walker was breaking the news to Tom and Robert. After listening to the tape in the van, they both accepted whiskies as they sat in the drawing room. Madeleine smiled with anticipation and Walker was euphoric beneath his customary restraint but, with Tom's approval, Robert counselled caution.

'It's great news of course,' he said. 'But you know, it's like a plane coming in to land. They say it's the most dangerous part. Me, when I fly I prefer not to believe it, but it's true.'

'You're absolutely right, Robert,' Walker said, 'it can still go wrong but we're getting awfully close to the end of this ghastly thing. And they're still plainly not denying there are two of them. It's moving the right way.'

'If only Granier wasn't involved, I'd be happier,' Robert said.

'That's a bit harsh,' Tom said.

'No, it's just that without his men this thing is clean. We put the money by the gravestone, Mademoiselle Walker and Helen are released. There it is. But Granier complicates the arrangement.'

'But they can't be allowed to go free,' Madeleine said. 'This is a terrible thing they've done.'

'I know, of course,' Robert said. 'I'm just saying without them the business is simple. It depends what is more important. Getting back the people you love or bringing these animals to justice.'

In its straightforwardness his argument was undeniable.

'It's too late in any case,' Walker said. 'The gendarmes are involved now and we must accept it. I have to say Granier's team haven't made very significant progress but then they haven't had much time. We have to believe they'll do this thing professionally.' Reaching for the decanter, he topped up Robert's glass, though Tom declined. 'The main thing is,' Walker went on, 'God willing this will be the last night Julia and Helen have to spend . . .' unsure how to complete the sentence, he looked to the window and the late evening; ' . . . have to spend out there.' Despite his natural confidence, his voice betrayed an edge of uncertainty.

Tom understood. The desire – the need, even – to believe in a happy outcome now was overwhelming, but there remained the dreadful fact that nothing was known. Their faith was pinned on an indistinct telephone call from a man whose mental stability must be in question, and a gendarmerie unaccustomed to dealing with cases like this. Perhaps, in their amateur way, he and Robert really were the hostages' best hope. But what could they achieve before tomorrow night? Nothing by sitting here anyway, encouraging though it had been to share Walker's moment of optimism.

Tom got up. Seeing him, Robert downed his whisky at a gulp and followed suit.

'Thank you,' Tom said.

Walker took him by the hand. 'I think you've borne this with extraordinary courage, Tom.'

Tom smiled. 'It's not what I'm feeling.'

'Well, I suspect it's something most of us have to pretend. But that's enough, after all.' Walker turned to Robert. 'I've a feeling it's not a pretence with you though, Robert.'

Robert shrugged. 'Me, I get up in the morning, I do what has to be done. Right now, Mr Professor and I have a little call to make. Isn't that so, my friend?'

Tom nodded. 'It's nothing concrete yet,' he explained to Walker, 'but we're still following up one or two things. We'll let you know the second we have anything.'

'And I'll be in touch in the morning,' Walker said. 'Try to get some sleep. It's going to be a big day.'

As Robert drove Tom towards the turning for Veilly, on a road where it was rare to see a car after nine o'clock in the evening, he talked of the way things had been in his childhood. Then there were two bars in St Luc, and the school had been full of children. Now there were only fourteen pupils, and if the number dropped much lower there was talk of closure. The population was ageing. Farms were empty, leaving much of the land unworked. The Dutch came to view them, and the Germans. That was where the money was. But what kind of Burgundy would it be in another twenty years, he mused?

Tom knew the distraction was for his benefit, a kind attempt to take his mind off the latest development. Though it failed in that, he let Robert ramble on while his thoughts rearranged the likely events of the following day in endless combinations. In a way Robert had been right of course. Granier's people were the rogue element which could still upset the barter. Tom wondered whether Helen would have any inkling that the end was in sight, but supposed that the kidnappers would reveal nothing until the last minute. Either way, he knew he wouldn't be able to sleep that night. However harebrained Robert's scheme, it was far better to be occupied than lying awake in the large bedroom, aching for Helen to be beside him again.

'. . . A collection of gîtes owned by foreigners, and a few

ruins nobody wants; that's the future,' Robert was saying. Taking his hands off the wheel, he opened his arms wide. 'It's hard to imagine the young not loving this pretty corner of the world, but in the end you can't blame them. It's obviously more fun in Dijon, or Chalons, or Auxerre. If I was their age now I'd probably feel the same. I can't see myself courting a grandmother! I mean, I always liked a little experience in a woman but . . .' His attention drifted back from the romantic shortcomings of modern village life to the matter in hand. 'Good,' he said. 'It's clouding up. Soon it will be nice and dark. This is one night when we don't want a bright moon.'

Turning into the Veilly road, he pointed out a small house with a barn set back behind a sloping grass verge. 'Now that's where your little bowling instructor lives,' he said. 'The one who's spotted Gazin coming and going.'

'How would he know his car?' Tom said.

'Listen. When you're over seventy in this part of the world, you know everything. You know when the woman who delivers the letters changes her stockings for winter. You know when old Bettine has her niece visiting because she orders two croissants with her *pain de campagne*. You know René is going to visit his mistress because he's flattened his hair at the front with water. Everything. It's all there is.' He paused. 'So, Gazin uses this road in the early hours. When he's coming home, he's coming home. That's evident enough. But where's he going when he's travelling in this direction? That's the question, Mr Professor. It could be anywhere. Or he might even be doing it to deliberately mislead. No. On second thoughts, not possible. Gazin couldn't be that clever. Anyway, since we have no answer, I propose a visit.'

Without warning, Robert braked hard, backed into a farm gateway, and headed back for the road to St Luc. On the way his dim yellow headlights picked out an owl sitting on a post beyond the tunnel of trees at the edge of the village. 'He knows,'

Robert said. 'He knows it all; but even professors don't speak owl.'

Branching to the right past a wall crowned with geraniums, he charged on with infectious abandon. Tom had the impression that if he were confronted with a spindly bridge over a vertiginous chasm, he would gun the tired engine and set the old car at it without the least hesitation. As they passed, ducks dozing under a walnut tree ignored the urgent intruder.

Moments later, Robert pulled off the road and doused the lights. 'From here we walk,' he said.

Easing through a gap in the hedge, he led Tom across a field. Ahead stood a farmhouse with no lights showing, flanked by barns or cowsheds on two sides of a yard. In daylight, Tom had often thought it looked neglected. Now, without benefit of sun, it seemed cold and secretive.

'Where's this getting us, Robert?' Tom said.

'Maybe nowhere. Maybe we learn something.'

'And maybe somebody blasts us with a shotgun. There are laws against trespass in France, I take it?'

Robert patted his pocket. 'I have the law here,' he said.

'What are you talking about?'

Robert handed him a revolver. 'I carried one every day for so long, I felt naked without it. It's just a little insurance.'

As he felt the unfamiliar weight of the weapon, its metal warm from contact with Robert's body, Tom was horrified. 'But this is mad. Is it loaded?' As soon as he said it he realised how absurd the question was.

'Well, it's not a water pistol, I assure you.'

'But do you use it? Have you used it since . . . ?'

'You mean do I go round the place killing people? No, I try not to do that. Calm yourself, Mr Professor. But it's very effective against crows and rooks.'

'But would you? I mean, if you had to?' Tom handed the weapon back.

'Oh, to protect my family, or to free Helen? Yes, of course. Without hesitation. Listen to me. While you've been teaching in your warm classroom, I've been out on the streets, my friend. There they don't hold their hand up when they want to ask a question. The world is as it is, not the way we want it to be. You can either be prepared, or you can trust in people's good nature. Me, I prefer to be prepared. That's all. I leave the theories to the intellectuals.'

Hampered by a sense of order, Tom found himself wanting to tell Robert that was all very fine, but if everyone went around armed, life would be intolerable. There was no point, however. The former policeman had taken his stand based on irrefutable logic and nothing would change him, except perhaps arrest for possession of a firearm, and maybe not even that. Besides, Tom had to admit to himself that in a crisis such as this, a trusted ally with a gun was preferable to one who relied on the art of gentle persuasion.

The farmhouse, at right angles to the yard, had a large wooden door in the end nearest to them at first floor level, where perhaps in Gazin's father's day the hay would have been stored. The building appeared to have two front doors facing a long stretch of overgrown garden. One section might once have been let to a labourer, Tom thought. Leading from the yard, a short flight of stone steps connected with the back door. As Robert approached this entrance, followed by Tom, a sudden growl alerted them to the presence of a dog whose tone did not presage a warm welcome. Moments later its hostility became plainer still as it began to bark in a rasping bass.

'Shit,' Robert whispered.

'Sounds big,' Tom said.

'Let it bark. If Gazin's out, there's no one to come running.'

'And if he's in?'

'If he's in, you'll have to break the British record for the hundred metres.' Robert chuckled. 'You stay here while I check the outbuildings.'

Tom tried to control what he told himself was irrational fear of a tethered pet, while, with the help of a small torch, his shadowy companion crossed the yard and peered into the barn. Satisfied, Robert rejoined him.

'No car. Just the old tractor,' he said. 'Try the door.'

Startled to find himself pitched into a break-in with apparent ease, Tom took hold of the handle and gave it a gentle turn, but there was no response. 'He's hardly going to leave his back door open is he?' he said.

Robert was already padding down the steps and round the corner towards the garden. Feeling a little foolish, Tom followed, inhaling the strong smell of cattle and glad to be putting distance between himself and the enraged dog. Even if they succeeded in entering the house, what was Robert hoping to find, he wondered? And what if Gazin came back while they were inside? As he turned the corner, conscious again of the bullfrogs in the nearby ponds, he heard a small crack and saw Robert intent on forcing a window beside the further of the two doors. The former policeman leaned towards him and mimed a double-handed lift, as though inviting help in mounting a horse. Facing the window again, whose shutters had at some time been removed from their hinges in the wall, Robert waited with one foot raised like a hoof. Tom cupped his hands and took the strain, feeling Robert's bulk ease itself over the sill, nudging apart the glazed panels with his powerful head and shoulders. In search of an object to give him a similar purchase, Tom found what appeared to be an upturned zinc tub at the base of the wall which, though no doubt rusty, gave him enough support at its rim to lift him into the opening.

Once inside, he watched as the small beam from Robert's torch picked out the shabby details of a damp, unfurnished room. The faded paper was peeling off the walls and stains spread for a metre or so up from the stone floor. Tom guessed that these flags had been laid on the bare earth, as they had at his house, and that in wet winters the water seeped up, marking its progress like a tide. Even on this warm night, the dark space was cool. In the grate, under the grey granite mantelpiece, a pile of caked ash and yellowing paper was the only sign that it had ever been otherwise.

Its bark muffled by the thickness of the walls, the dog still complained as Tom and Robert emerged into the gloomy hallway off which, through an open door the colour of nicotine, they could make out the stone sink of a kitchen, with a single tap protruding above. Here there was a sour, stagnant smell, like water in a rain barrel mingled with wine turned to vinegar. On the central table were a dirty plate, a greasy glass, a half-empty container of margarine, and an unlabelled, green, litre bottle. Registering these details, Robert held the torch under his chin like a child at Halloween, and grimaced. As he turned the beam back to the wall, it came to rest on a low, heavy, unpolished sideboard with two drawers. The first made a slight metallic chink as he opened it and ran his hand over knives and forks. When he shut it again, he froze for a moment at the sound of a car approaching from the direction of Charmoy. Robert clicked off the torch, and Tom could feel his blood pump while they waited to hear whether the vehicle turned into the yard. After a hiatus it went on its way towards Maligny, prompting Robert to let out his breath with the exaggerated desperation of a pearl-diver released from the deep.

Tom gestured to him that since they had found nothing, they should leave. Robert nodded agreement, but as Tom made for the door, with a desultory tug Robert pulled open the remaining drawer and directed the torch at the contents. They were a jumble of bills, vouchers, several shotgun cartridges, a screwdriver, two batteries, an old wooden-handled penknife, a dog-eared seed catalogue; the typical detritus of a disorganised farmer who lived alone. Robert was about to close the drawer when a small rectangular cardboard box at the back caught his eye.

'Are you coming?' Tom whispered.

'One moment.' As Robert reached for the box, he noticed that the dog had stopped barking. No doubt the container would be full of paper clips, or perhaps it was empty. Resting the torch on the surface of the sideboard, he took off the lid in the light of the beam. Inside, to his surprise, a woman's curved tortoiseshell comb lay with its back arched upwards. Robert's first thought was that it must have belonged to Henri Gazin's mother; a sentimental memory of someone he had cared about. But when he looked closer he thought he could see a name scratched in the curved surface. He leaned forward, holding the torch over the box. The uneven, childish letters spelled 'Stéphane'. In that instant Robert recalled stark headlines and a shocked village unable to understand. And he knew at once that far from being a loving souvenir, the comb was a gruesome trophy.

'Come on, Robert,' Tom urged from the doorway. 'There's nothing here.'

'No,' Robert said, slipping the box into his pocket and shutting the drawer. 'No, nothing. Let's go.'

CHAPTER TWELVE

Even after what had appeared to him an uneventful raid, Tom had been unable to sleep. Excited, fearful, doubtful, he had wanted to call Daisy in London when he got back from Gazin's house, but realised it was unfair to ring her so late. Besides, chances were she would have been out enjoying herself. Tom was glad of that. While she would be full of concern for her mother, it was far better for her to be occupied. In the end he had gone down to the sitting room and tried to make a note of the day's sequence of events in an attempt to see if any pattern presented itself. When none did, he found himself wandering through the downstairs rooms earthing himself to the things that were Helen's – the straw hat, a pair of black canvas slippers, the small fork with the bent prong she used in the garden, the bottles in the bathroom, her red toothbrush. For some reason this affected him most of all. Holding it, he could see her in the mornings, calm, enjoying a ritual of small tasks, eyes alive with plans for the day. Reluctant to leave the memory behind, he put the toothbrush in the pocket of his dressing gown.

Aimless now, he went into the kitchen and boiled the kettle to make instant coffee. He knew it was the least practical drink if he wanted to sleep, but that was unimportant. Sitting at the table while he waited, he concentrated again on the emblem at the top right-hand corner of the poster, and on its enlargement which the helpful American had made for him in Dijon. Once more he was struck by the fact that two independent observers had thought they recognised it, though neither knew why. Perhaps now, in any case, it was too late for the information to be useful. Nevertheless it still seemed curious that his strong intuition had proved misguided. As he poured the hot water over the granules, he noticed a small sketch pad alongside paperback cookery books on the top shelf of the dresser. Helen had fantasised about compiling her own, with recipes gathered from the old people she met as they browsed the region. Tom took down the pad and turned the pages. They bore Helen's pencil sketches and watercolours of the garden – amateur, but loose and bright. Tucked among them was a caricature of Tom by Frank, drawn when he was a child, sulking after some discovered misdemeanour. It showed Tom with a neck so wreathed in double chins that it looked like a blacksmith's bellows. Tom smiled. Perhaps it was just as well that Frank was incommunicado. It was bad enough that Daisy had to share the uncertainty.

The teenage years had not been easy. Having a father who was a teacher was an unfair burden on any son. But in a paradoxical way, Frank's travels were bringing him and Tom closer by revealing to both how much they missed each other. Tom lingered on almost every page. Though less accurate than photographs, in their directness and simplicity the drawings were far more eloquent. However crude, they were the interpretations of a singular mind, a way of seeing that said as much about the artist as it did about the subjects. In the end the drawings *were* Helen. Towards the back of the book, Tom came across a childish watercolour that emphasised this self-revelation more than any other. Beneath a beaming yellow disc, green-stemmed and fringed with white, Helen had written, in pencil: 'Daisy – the eye of the day.'

Mounting the stairs once more, Tom had taken the sketchbook to bed with him. Around four o'clock he had fallen into a fitful sleep, only to wake at six when Robert's cockerel had begun his querulous fanfare. His first urge was to see the cemetery where the handover was to take place. There was nothing he could do to ease the process, but he needed to place it in his imagination. If he went early enough there would be no danger of obstructing the work of the gendarmes. Whatever happened, today he wanted to fill every moment. Mere speculation would be an agony. For that reason he hoped Helen was unaware of the latest developments. For her, even another day's boredom would be kinder than unbearable anticipation.

Plunging his head into a basin of cold water, Tom switched on Radio 4. He and Helen found staying in touch with events at home a comfort and a pleasure. But distance lent a measure of disenchantment. It somehow shrank the issues discussed with such earnestness, putting them into perspective. Viewed from Burgundy, the preoccupations of the minister interviewed on the 'Today' programme, so significant to a domestic audience, seemed over-emphatic. Britain's officials still spoke as though theirs were the weightiest voices in the international debate; as if they, and they alone, had been entrusted with eternal certainties. A bit like the cockerel, across the courtyard, Tom thought; all feathers and pouter chest. Viewed from elsewhere, would the same seem true of the French, the Germans, the Italians, and the rest? He supposed that, like flags, it came with the territory. And yet, by committing themselves to the club, the others showed more convincing confidence.

The sun was in the yard as he opened the barn doors and took out the car. When he drew level with Robert's house, tractors were already on their way to the fields. Tom slowed, wondering whether to invite Robert along, but decided it was unfair to wake Yvonne. Just as he was about to pull on to the road, the ex-policeman appeared, no doubt alerted by the sound of the engine. Miming the jabbing thumb of a hitch-hiker, Robert opened the passenger door and climbed in.

'Good day. Where?' was all he said.

'I just thought I'd take a look at the cemetery. I know there's nothing we can do, but I'm curious.'

'No problem. Let's go. You can drop me in the town on the way back.'

'An assignation?' Tom teased.

'Oh yes, of course. It's Sophia Loren. She always waits for me at the bus-stop on Tuesdays. It's a long way from Rome, but what can I do? She insists.'

The steep, narrow road from the market place to the parish church in Bligny, flanked by stone-built houses, was the oldest in the town. Splashed with geraniums, it led to a high, handsome view of the valley, with white cattle cropping the misty fields opposite, and the bright River Ouche still little more than a stream, so close to its source at Lusigny. Fronted by a small square, the church was sturdy and irregular. The substantial spire looked like a pencil sharpened with a kitchen knife. Inside the wall, to the right of the gate, was the smaller cemetery, where families vied with each other for the splendour of their marble slabs. Discoloured by the weather, crucifixes stared up at the sun, and photographs of loved ones peered with dead eyes through protective layers of plastic. Everywhere, bunches of artificial flowers looked self-conscious beside the green magnificence of the surrounding hillsides.

Walking to the larger cemetery, behind the church, among the dedications to Roussel, Nourry, Ruffoni, Besnard, and dozens more, Robert at once pointed out the Gagnepain grave where the money was to be left. He added that there was easy access across the fields, beyond the wall, where a white horse cropped the dew-sodden grass. Beside the cemetery gate was a three-storey building where marksmen might be stationed, front and back, while facing the entrance was a tall house which looked as if it had once been part of the mediaeval castle that had enclosed the site. Though this too was a useful vantage point, Robert said that the kidnappers would have little difficulty in identifying sniper-positions and in avoiding their lines of fire under cover of darkness. In that sense the spot was well chosen. This assessment did not disturb Tom. As Robert had told Walker the night before, the overwhelming priority for him was the safety of the hostages. If, without risk to Helen and Julia, the kidnappers could be arrested, all well and good. But that objective came a long way second.

'Will they let us be here?' Tom asked.

'How can they stop us? Are they going to shoot us?'

'I thought they might want us out of the way.'

'This is your wife, Tom. It's not their wife. We tell them where you will be. They don't tell us. Now, if you'll drop me in the square, it's time for Sophia.'

As Tom delivered his passenger outside the Hôtel de Ville, he wondered what was the real purpose of Robert's errand, but assumed it was an unavoidable chore which for some reason his friend preferred not to discuss. Arranging to rendezvous in St Luc at ten o'clock, they went their separate ways.

Madeleine Walker had slept well for the first time in a week. Her insomnia had been traceable not to a single cause but to many. Foremost among them were her fears for Julia and Helen. Though powerless to help them, she had been unable to stop herself imagining their ordeal – the loneliness, the uncertainty, the threat of violence, the vulnerability to sexual abuse, the thought of dying far from the comfort of those they cared for – terrors echoed in the news headlines every day. Magnified by the kidnap, they had haunted her day and night. Allied to them was the feeling of guilt and betrayal sown by her relationship with Camille. And yet that very relationship had made the anxiety more bearable. In those intense, surrendered moments with him she had been able to fasten the shutters against reality. Meanwhile, unable to discuss with her husband either the depth of her concern for the prisoners, based on a woman's perspective, or the desires of her body, she felt isolated and dishonest.

At a practical level she was also worried about the performances of *A Midsummer Night's Dream*. Plans were so far advanced now, with posters and tickets printed, seating specialists, electricians, carpenters, and stewards organised, that cancellation would be a major disappointment, not least for the drama group from Bury St Edmunds. And Madeleine knew that, if she returned to find that all their work had been wasted, Helen's sense of let-down would be the greatest of all. But now, at last, the most pressing problem was about to be resolved. With Julia and Helen home, Madeleine could confront her own emotional dilemma with greater clarity. Perhaps, when the crisis was over, her need for Camille would diminish.

This morning, however, as she turned off the N6 for St Aubin, buoyed by last night's news and seven hours uninterrupted sleep, she was excited by the prospect of seeing her lover again. Since there was already a car in the yard, she parked by the wall at the base of the upper slopes. Crossing the road, she caught Camille's broad smile over the shoulder of a tourist who had stopped to buy wine. Camille was explaining with charm and patience that the early frosts followed by a wet August had made this a difficult year, but he invited the potential buyer, a burly Englishman with silver-grey hair and a ruddy complexion, to try his *premier cru* red, bottled two years ago. Camille said he had been told by a regular customer that it bore the unmistakable 'pawprint' of a Charbonneaux.

Madeleine thought he sounded like a small boy complimented

on his homework. She wanted to stand between him and his customer, put her arms round his neck, kiss him, and tell him at once about Julia and Helen. Discretion won, however, as she felt it did too often in her life, and she accepted his chaste kisses of welcome as though she were a visiting cousin. The Englishman stammered a greeting, and the ruddy complexion deepened to the colour of a fresh-bottled beaujolais.

It said much for Camille's dedication to his craft that he spent another twenty minutes on his buyer, and was rewarded with a sale of a mere two cases. Or perhaps, Madeleine reflected, it was a sign less of his devotion to viticulture than of his impracticality. In any event, frustrated by the slow progress of the sale, she lit a Gauloise and walked down to the church. Looking up at the ancient spire, she remembered every detail of the golden afternoon when she had joined Camille in the belfry. Whatever happened, nothing could erase that memory, just as nothing could bring the moment back. She put out her cigarette and entered the nave. Beside the narrow stairway she had climbed that day, a flagstone had been moved to one side, revealing an illuminated subterranean space. Intrigued, she descended the four steps of a makeshift wooden ladder and, bending almost double, found herself in what seemed to be a man-made cave, or crypt. Edging forward, she put her head through a crude arch and saw a sight which at once banished warm thoughts of lovemaking. In the small, rounded chamber facing her, skulls and other nameless bones in neat ranks lined the walls in mute witness. Transfixed, Madeleine took in the details of hollow sockets and obscene cavities no longer masked in the comfort of flesh. Here they were, the lovers, the haters, the makers, the users, the pious, the venal; piled at last in a common heap; all ugly and brutish in death. If they had ever known grace, it had not survived them. And if their souls were beautiful, as they had been taught, they must have been fashioned by some other hand.

'Customers,' a voice said. 'All customers whose Eurocheques bounced!'

Startled, Madeleine looked over her shoulder to see Camille beaming from the edge of the aperture.

'Come out of there,' he said. 'Come and meet the man who's just become richer by twelve hundred francs. Imagine that! Now I can buy you dinner at Lamelloise.'

'You're a little behind the times. Twelve hundred francs will hardly buy you two bottles of wine at Lamelloise. However, I accept!' Relieved to have her sombre mood broken, Madeleine took his outstretched hand and rose from the underworld. 'Now, get me out of here,' she said. 'This place makes you feel the dead hate us.'

In Camille's small kitchen, neat and featureless, Madeleine held his hand in both of hers, drawing strength from it. 'What frightens me,' she said, 'is ending up there, in that crypt, and never having been complete. What were they, those people? Just fragments. What did they learn? What did they contribute? What did they ever do that was fulfilling? Was there ever a part of themselves that they explored for all it was worth? That they exhausted?'

'Their hearts. They exhausted them.'

'But that's exactly what I mean. Did they really? If you exhausted your heart, you wouldn't mind a bit ending up among them. But people don't. They're too frightened. They use their hearts as though they were small accounts at the Crédit Agricole. They draw on them a little at a time. They're misers with their hearts. And then they die, and their hearts rot and stink, and are eaten by rats. Unused. One careful owner. Wasted.'

Camille unbuttoned his shirt. His chest was lean and brown, the breastbone protruding and the ribs plain to see. 'Have mine,' he said. 'Take it before it rots and stinks.'

Madeleine leaned forward and put her hand on his breast,

feeling his warmth. 'You don't eat enough,' she said. 'There's barely enough flesh to cover your poor heart.'

He put the tips of her fingers to his mouth, parting his lips.

'Listen,' she went on, 'I've been dying to tell you but you were so wrapped up in your little customer.'

Camille concentrated as she described the latest arrangements with the kidnappers. At intervals he stopped her, asking her to repeat a detail or to supply additional information. 'Well, that's wonderful,' he said, when she had finished. 'At last. Those poor women.'

'When Julia's home, William might want to go away for a while. Julia might want it.'

'And you?' Camille frowned with anxiety.

'In this case it doesn't matter what I want.'

'But you talked about those people in the church; dying without giving their whole hearts.'

'Then for the moment I'll give mine to Julia. And some for Helen Bellman.'

'And what about me?'

'They need it more. And William. For now.'

Camille got up and walked to the window. The church bells were tolling ten o'clock. 'In the end this is just a game for you isn't it?' he said, his voice flat and almost accepting. 'It's a thing for rainy days.'

Madeleine stood behind him and put her arms round his waist. 'I don't know what it is,' she said. 'Sometimes it's as necessary as eating. Why can't it just be simple, like that? Something we take pleasure in when we need it?'

Camille turned. 'Fragments. A little bit here and a little bit there. I want more than that.'

'I told you; for now there is no more. These people have been through a terrible ordeal. And I love them. Surely you understand that? Maybe after . . .'

Holding out his hands, he framed her face with them, looking into her eyes as though for confirmation. When she turned her head to kiss his palm, he did not react.

In need of physical work to distract him, Tom was weeding Helen's rock garden. Made of stones excavated from the floor of the cowshed when it was converted to a kitchen, the asymmetrical outcrop, planted with mosses and fleshy-leaved alpine flowers, looked more like a natural feature than a planned arrangement. Studded with fossils of shell-fish, the rocks showed that the area had once formed the ocean bed, a timeless provenance that gave Tom great pleasure. The bindweed however, with which they were also well stocked, gave him none. He cursed as he tugged, failing always to coax out the deep, insidious roots. But Helen would be glad he'd made an effort. If there were no sign of activity in the garden, he knew she would accuse him of moping – an indulgence she couldn't abide.

As he worked, visited from time to time by inquisitive lizards, he worried away at the puzzle of the coat of arms. Something in him still refused to acknowledge that it was a red herring. Despite the discouraging results of his enquiries, a small voice nagged away, vague but unrelenting. But where to look? Quignard, the pedantic authority, had been quite clear about the possibilities and none had yielded anything. If the symbol in the picture had its origins outside the region – outside the country, even – it might take months to trace. And even then it could prove to be nothing more than some interior designer's whimsy.

For half an hour Tom managed to lose himself in exertion and speculation. But as the day grew warmer and time seemed to be slowing down, he began to wonder how he could survive the next thirteen hours without losing control. Even now he could sense himself at the edge of a precipice. It would only take an unexpected development to push him over. When that happened, he thought, it would strike him like a fever. His body seemed on the verge of violent spasm, like when he'd eaten a bad oyster. Then he had lain for hours like a victim of the palsy, cold with sweat, and for some reason counting numberless legions of Chinese soldiers. But now there would be no one to sit at his bedside and reassure him. He must hang on, for Helen's sake. He must be ready to devote all his energy to her, whatever her condition. How would she be, he wondered? Hungry, hurt, exhausted? Could there be permanent damage, even to such a strong constitution? God forbid. Quick, think of something else. Dig. Exhaust yourself, he thought. But when he tried with the fork to penetrate the flower bed near their favourite seat in the sun, the baked earth rejected the effort as futile.

Tackle the breeze blocks then, left in a pile at the roadside by Laurent the builder. There must be a couple of hundred of them. Get the wheelbarrow and cart them, six at a time, to the barn. That should take an hour at least. They were an eyesore anyway. Helen had been nagging him to do the job for ages. Yes, that was it. Start now. Focus on that and nothing else. Clinging to the urge, Tom took hold of the wheelbarrow and trundled it across the garden, relieved to be doing something positive.

As he passed the back door, the telephone rang. Half running into the house, he fought to stay calm, still imagining the breeze blocks under cover in neat stacks. 'Hello,' he said, conscious that he sounded both breathless and uncertain.

'Daddy.'

'Daisy! How are you, darling?'

'Dad . . .' Daisy broke down.

Tom felt his fists tightening. Her tears were too much for him. 'Don't, love. It's going to be . . .' He swallowed hard. 'Mum's going to be fine. She's . . . We've just had some terrific news . . .' As though himself convinced by the process of trying to convince his daughter, he grew more confident. 'It's tonight, love. The handover's at eleven o'clock. I wanted to delay ringing you so you wouldn't have a horrible day, waiting. But it's not long now.'

'It's in the papers, Dad. All about Julia Walker. The kidnapped heiress, and stuff. But it doesn't mention . . .' Again she broke down.

'I wonder where they got that? Someone must have . . . I suppose it was inevitable sooner or later. They're bound to concentrate on Julia, love. It doesn't make any difference.'

'When did they say all this?'

'A phone call last night.'

'Is he really paying them all that money, Julia's father? It says it's over a million pounds.'

'I think he'd willingly pay more.'

'Did they mention mum? Actually mention her, by name?'

Tom was faced with a rapid decision. Should he lie? Say yes? Would that be the simplest, kindest way? But he found himself unable to do it. 'Not actually by name. They probably don't know it anyway. But they've never denied there was a second woman involved. It's obvious really. Walker's quite convinced.'

'Are you?'

'I am now. I wasn't sure at first but . . . yes, I am now.'

'I want to be there, Dad. I'm coming.'

'Look Daise, maybe it's better if we just see how she is, first . . .'

'I'm coming. I'll get the first train to Paris and then the TGV down to Beaune. If there isn't one, I'll take the one that stops. I'll give you a ring from the station. If you're out doing something I'll get a cab. I've already phoned my boss at home.'

Tom saw no point in trying to dissuade her further. She was as anxious and fearful as him, and she had a right to be there. Besides, it would be wonderful to have her with him, and Helen would be thrilled to see her. 'I can't promise you much in the way of grub,' he said. 'Might manage an omelette.'

'Don't be daft. I'm on my way.'

His excitement at Daisy's imminent arrival, added to the prospect of a reunion with Helen overwhelmed him. After putting down the telephone he sat on the threadbare sofa in front of the stone fireplace, and in spite of his resolve, the tears came. Leaning forward, his hands to his head, and conscious of looking absurd, he was powerless to stop the relief of emotion that he knew to be premature. His body needed to let go for a few moments as much as it needed sleep. But that would come later. Meanwhile all the tension of the last eight days burst out now, unable to withstand the pressure. Grateful that he was alone, he surrendered to it, and when, two or three minutes later, the convulsions subsided, he felt a momentary peace. As he blew his nose with an exaggerated blast, to hide the slight embarrassment he felt even in private, he looked up to see a familiar shadow behind the pitted glass panels of the front door. Fate had been benevolent with its timing, he thought, as Robert knocked and waited to be invited in. Knowing that his neighbour would prefer to sit on an upright chair in the kitchen, Tom opened the door and led him through.

'It's going to be hotter than the Sahara,' Robert said. 'And the night will be fine. That's good for us.'

'Any news?'

'I paid a call on Granier's men. They were interested in our friend Gazin. Very interested.'

'What, that he's away at night?'

'Yes.' Robert answered as though there were more he could add. 'And they'll keep the farmhouse under surveillance. Which we can do anyway. Big deal.'

'Well, it all helps. I just had a call from my daughter. She's coming over. She says the story's in the English press.'

'Yes, of course. It was in the French press too, yesterday,

but I saw no point in worrying you with it.'

Tom frowned. 'I'm not a child, Robert. I need to be worried with it. What did it say?'

'Oh, just a simple little story. Mademoiselle Walker has been kidnapped. She is beautiful. Her father is a very important man, et cetera, et cetera. The gendarmes are hot on the trail . . .' Robert laughed. 'So I think we know where the story came from, don't you? Hot on the trail, my backside.'

'But what if the kidnappers see it? They specifically said not to call the cops.'

'It makes no difference now. They have to go through with it or the whole thing has been for nothing. Anyway,' Robert went on, changing the subject, 'it's good that your daughter's coming. Now you'll have a great welcoming committee.'

There was no reply.

'I said, Mr Professor, now you'll have a great . . .' Looking round to check why there was still no response, Robert saw Tom intent on studying a black packet containing ground coffee. 'Is it the winning lottery ticket he's studying with such devotion? No, it's two hundred and fifty grammes of coffee!' Robert teased. 'What's so fascinating?'

Tom handed him the packet. 'What do you see? Tell me what you see.'

Robert read the bold wording. ' "*Chapeau Rouge . . . Café Moulu . . . Goût Généreux*", and there's the hat of a . . . what do you call them? The bossmen priests.'

'Cardinals. It's a cardinal's red hat.'

'Well . . . ?' Robert shrugged.

Tom turned the back of the packet to face him. 'Here. There's something else,' he said. 'A coat of arms. Maybe the manufacturer's. Maybe the cardinal's, whoever he was.'

'So?'

'I've just had a thought.' Tom pointed to the poster on the wall and the computer enlargement tacked beside it. 'Suppose, for a moment, that what we're looking for isn't old money at all but new money. Suppose this coat of arms in the kidnappers' photograph isn't ancient but modern. And the building likewise. A monument to commerce, rather than bloodlines. Not a coffee manufacturer perhaps, but somebody like that.'

Robert was unimpressed. 'But it's obvious from the photograph the building is old. The state of the mirror . . . everything.'

'Is it? Why is it so obvious? You mean to tell me you can't have old things in a new house? How do you think the antique dealers in Beaune make their money?'

Robert shrugged. 'Even if it's possible, which I doubt, what are you going to do about it?'

'Look. In England, successful businessmen sometimes used to build things called follies. Sort of fake castles with towers and battlements. Just like the real thing. To tell the world how important they were.'

'Ah, in England,' Robert said, as though referring with some sympathy to a brain-damaged cousin.

'Come on,' Tom laughed. 'You're just as bad. I've seen bourgeois houses here that look like mini-Versailles. Anyway, it's a thought, that's all. I just can't get it out of my head that this badge, this emblem, has been trying to tell me something all along.'

Robert drummed his fingers on the table. 'Well, you never know,' he said, in a tone which implied you always know. Then, with a rapid change of subject: 'When did you last eat, Mr Professor?'

'Last night sometime. Can't remember now. I haven't got much appetite.'

'We'll go for lunch to Chez Lucotte.'

'But we can't. What if . . . ?'

'Of course we can. We have the mobile. Plus Chez Lucotte has a phone. We'll be as close to Bligny there as we are here.

No problem. I'll pick you up at midday.'

Tom walked him to the door. As he opened it, a car containing two uniformed gendarmes passed the end of the courtyard on the Charmoy road.

'Oh, that's great,' he said. 'Now everybody knows. What are they doing up here?'

'Just a routine patrol, I expect,' Robert said. 'I'll see you shortly.'

What on earth would a routine patrol in broad daylight reveal, Tom wondered, as he shut the door?

Since exchanging one cell for another to which she held the key, Julia Walker had alternated between elation and growing fear. On the one hand she liked the feeling of greater space, the ample light through the large windows – though this made sleep more elusive than ever – and the illusion that she enjoyed a small degree of control over her own destiny. On the other, she knew that her possession of the key must be infuriating to her gaolers, and that their anger and frustration might result in violence. For this reason she avoided standing or sitting where she might be vulnerable from the door. At least if she restricted herself to the wall which bounded the long, dark corridor, she would not be susceptible to a shotgun blast through the thick oak. But the irony was that this restriction meant less freedom of movement than before. In an attempt to stay supple, she had improvised a number of on-the-spot exercises, though her energy was soon exhausted. Since her escape bid she had been starved, by way of punishment. The hunger itself was not yet unbearable, but the thoughts of food, the images of laden tables crisp with white napery, and leaning bottles nesting in ice-buckets, were driving her mad. She tried to divert her mind to more practical matters: the addresses and telephone numbers of friends; the geography of the sixth *arrondissement* of Paris; the layout, room by room, of the glorious basement at the

Marmottan, with its calming Monets and the Gauguin flowers the colour of blood. She strained to recall in detail the stories of books and films, and even to write a mental diary of her imprisonment, but all the while the cruel fragrance of chicken, and garlic, and fresh bread taunted her. She sang the few songs she remembered over and over again, looping her hair round her finger, as she had when she was a child. On one occasion she found herself sucking her thumb and, with mild surprise, taking comfort from it.

Paul had not responded to her efforts to bribe him. At the time the plan had seemed promising. Perhaps light-headedness had unbalanced her judgement. Perhaps he was more afraid of his friends than eager for money. Either way she wondered how much longer she could survive the uncertainty and the loneliness. She had read of hostages who spent years in solitary confinement, but doubted whether she had the strength. She supposed they must somehow blindfold hope. She still expected every day to be her last in this place, and so every day ended in disappointment. No human spirit could endure that bruising pattern for long. But without hope, what was there to stiffen the will?

With the passing days she had found herself thinking less and less about the other woman. It wasn't a matter of callousness. It was just that being alone focused attention on self-preservation. Julia supposed it was inevitable. But now that she did spare her fellow prisoner a thought, she wondered what sort of state she was in? If only they had been together, how much easier it would have been. Easier for the kidnappers too, come to that. So why had they separated them? Because they didn't want them to meet, or because their plans for each were different? Plans! It was hard to believe these morons had any. But just suppose they did, and they aimed to release her for the ransom, what did they have in mind for the other woman? They wouldn't kill her, would they? Did they have it in them? Threats, yes, and pain, but murder? Henri might, she thought. But why keep a prisoner all this time before ending her life? Unless they were undecided and then, at the last moment . . . ?

No. Better not to think about it. Bend the knees, arms out to the side, circle the hands. God, her legs ached. And the stench of sweat. How would it smell to other people if it disgusted her. She thought of Antoine, a little surprised that he had not been more on her mind. That was because, even in her present condition, he was liable to treat her with less absolute seriousness than he treated himself. Antoine wanted to be a writer. Furthermore Antoine wanted to look like a writer, whatever writers looked like. It was not that he affected floppy silk bows, like Baudelaire, or curious carnations. It was more the long, soft hair parted in the middle and a facial expression that affected to look beyond the speaker. The eyes of a visionary. Except that so far the visionary had only managed to publish two short stories, not uninfluenced by Alice Munro, and a brief article about Alphonse Daudet in an obscure literary magazine. Having said that, Antoine could be charming, amusing, and stylish. And he was rather beautiful, there was no point in denying that. But he was young beyond his twenty-eight years, and as for coping with a situation like this, still less riding to the rescue, forget it. His romantic view of himself would encourage him to be involved, if he could, but somewhat at the level of a fictional hero. Practicality would be out of the question. Confronted with Julia in her present state – filthy, smelly, dependent, afraid – he would go through the motions of consolation but he would not be altogether comfortable. Julia was fond of Antoine. She loved his company, both in bed and at the café, though that too was a bone of contention. Antoine thought that in the publicity-obsessed late twentieth century, writers should drink at the Deux Magots, ignoring the fact that he couldn't afford it, and was not yet Jean-Paul

Sartre. Julia, preferring student bars, found it pretentious. Still, despite his many absurdities, she did very much want to be with him again, but as for having him around in the immediate aftermath of this shabby crisis, no way. Reality would burst his soap bubble. He would care all right, when he heard the news. He would care a lot. But she knew there would be something about the caring that involved him in the misfortune as much as her; that lent him the opera cloak of tragedy to wear. He would begin to see it in words. Julia wished in a way that there was someone more mature waiting; someone who could hold her as she stood, and put the fear of God into these bastards, but she knew that was as romantic an ambition as Antoine's.

As she rose from the crouching position, unable to bear the pain any longer, there was a thump at the door.

'Open!'

Julia recognised the voice as Blue Helmet's. 'Why?' she said.

'Listen, open the door and I'll tell you.'

'How do I know you won't shoot me?'

'Think about it. What have we got if I shoot you?'

'That all sounds very rational but you guys aren't, are you? Rational people don't go round kidnapping innocent women. How do I know your friend isn't with you; the one with the personal hygiene problem? He's definitely not rational.'

'I spoke to your father this morning. It's all arranged. Now let me in and I'll explain.'

Trying to unlock the door without facing it proved difficult and uncomfortable. Julia reached across with her right hand and strained to twist the key back in her direction, but it was impossible to get enough purchase on it.

'Just open it.' Blue Helmet was growing impatient.

Julia crouched, in the belief that she was presenting a smaller target, and, feeling foolish, positioned herself in front of the door and reached up. As the large key yielded, she withdrew it from the lock, took three short steps to her left, and once again raised herself to her full height, with her back to the wall.

The door opened and the slight figure of Blue Helmet appeared, unarmed, shutting the door behind him and leaning against it. 'Where's the key?' he said.

Julia indicated a point between her breasts. 'Right here.'

'This wasn't a very clever move.' Blue Helmet looked round the room. 'You were better off where you were.'

'At least I have a view. And I have a key.'

'How long do you think it would take me to get it off you, if I wanted?'

'I don't know. We'll see.'

'You must be hungry.'

'I'm slimming.'

'Don't slim too much. Your father will say we starved you.'

'You did. What are these so-called arrangements?'

'Tonight at eleven o'clock we will collect the money and you will go home. So now there's no need to bribe Paul.'

Julia was noncommittal, noting Blue Helmet's carelessness in using his friend's name. 'Exactly how do I go home?' she said.

'We'll drop you close to the château. From there you'll have to walk. You can still walk, can't you?'

'What about the other woman?'

'Her too.'

'How do I know you'll keep your side of the deal?'

'I'm not a murderer, mademoiselle.'

'Maybe not, but what about Henri?'

With a sudden movement Blue Helmet swivelled to face her. 'Who's Henri?' he said, after a pause.

'Come on. Quit the games. Henri's the spooky guy from *Cold Comfort Farm*.'

'Where?'

'It's a book. Don't worry about it. But Henri could murder all right. He as good as told me so. You know that, but still you're in business with him. You're not safe either, you know. Once he gets his hands on the money who knows what he'll do? Maybe he'll decide cutting it three ways isn't a very appealing idea any more. It happens. Think about it.'

'Shut up.'

'OK. But don't say I didn't warn you. Look, if we're going out together, could I see the other woman now? I mean, what's the difference?'

'No.'

'Food, then. Could I eat something?'

'First give me the key.'

'No.'

'Give it to me.'

'No.'

Blue Helmet took a step towards her, his body tense with anger. Julia retreated a step.

'Last time we fought you came off worst, remember? One kick in the balls and the French resistance collapsed. I warn you, I've been practising.' She started to circle in front of him so that once again she could face the door. Keeping her distance, she measured a slow kick.

Blue Helmet made a clumsy grab for her foot but failed by centimetres. Again he took a step forward.

'Come on,' Julia said, taunting him. 'Come on. I'm only a soft little woman. Surely you can beat a little soft woman.' If she could only draw him far enough she might outflank him and reach the door first. 'Or you could leave. You could just turn and walk away. An honourable draw, let's call it.'

'Shut up,' he said, advancing another metre towards her. 'Give me the key and you can have all the food you want.'

'I've suddenly lost my appetite. Besides, I told you, I'm on a diet.'

With a wild lurch, Blue Helmet reached out to try and rip her shirt, almost losing his balance as his weight was thrown forward. Evading him with ease, Julia jinked and sprang for the door. Turning the handle, she pulled it open with a sense of elation, but was halted where she stood. Framed against the darkness of the passage was Henri, grotesque in the black helmet. Cradled in his right arm was the shotgun. Raising it with a slow, deliberate movement, and supporting it with his left hand, he pointed the barrels at her mouth.

CHAPTER THIRTEEN

During lunch at Chez Lucotte, feeling excited and a little guilty, Tom found it impossible to relax. Anonymous, beside the canal at Vandenesse, the small, unpretentious restaurant was a great favourite with travellers. Its smiling welcome, the simple excellence of the food, and the modest prices, made it the ideal refuge from work and worry. And yet, as he clinked glasses with Robert in a toast, and drank the robust red wine, Tom was distracted. Try as he might not to imagine what Helen was feeling now, assuming she knew what was about to happen, he couldn't draw a curtain across her face. Her shining eyes, the smell of her hair, the warmth of her hands, were as real and present as the table.

Without a false note, Robert did his best to hold Tom's attention and keep his mind where it would come to least harm, sometimes breaking off to answer a ribald taunt from an acquaintance, of whom there seemed to be several. Robert talked of the iniquity of the French electricity billing system, where consumers were required to pay in advance, on estimates. It was, he said, an outrage. As he warmed to his subject, his voice rose and his face flushed, as though he were a tenor in mid-aria. Soon the subject of his tirade became almost incidental, as the eloquence of his arguments took on a life of its own. By the time he came to his final recommendation – that the people should rise up, assert their democratic rights, refuse to pay – his passion alone would have swayed any audience, whatever message they had come to hear. In recognition of this, three fellow diners joined in ironic applause. Thanking them, and urging them to 'Vote Ryaux' in his imaginary campaign, Robert drained his glass at a gulp and re-filled both his and Tom's from the carafe. Then, realising that Tom's interest in the French electricity board couldn't be expected to match that of a native, he set off on a new tack. As his veal and potatoes were delivered by an indulgent waitress who treated him like a wayward elder brother, Robert cautioned Tom that it was only safe to eat meat in responsible restaurants such as this. Supermarkets were selling kangaroo, giraffe, anything they could lay their hands on, he claimed, and some farmers were injecting their cows with so many chemicals the milk was burning holes in buckets. That was why he favoured the butcher in Arnay; because he slaughtered his own beasts. Well, that and the fact that his daughter was a goddess. And prompted by this vision of the ultimate woman in white, he was off on yet another vivid fantasy, pausing only to swallow, and enthuse over the veal.

Borne along by Robert's exuberance, and cheered just enough by the wine, Tom began to feel calmer. The cheese arrived. Here there was no question of the waitress shaving mean slices and laying them with communion reverence on a side plate. Five large, creamy cheeses were presented, two of them intact, and diners were free to finish all if they chose. This would be the place to celebrate with Helen when it was all over, Tom thought. No fuss, no falseness; just the pleasure of eating well-cooked food in an atmosphere of mutual enjoyment. But that would not be for a few days, he supposed. First, whatever injuries the last week had inflicted – whether mental or physical – would need time to heal.

'Is there anything useful we can do this afternoon?' he said.

'Sleep,' Robert said.

'You're joking!'

'No. I'm serious. Tonight you'll need all your strength. You handle these things better when you're rested.'

'I couldn't. I'm too excited.'

'Pity.'

'Where should I be, do you think Robert? To meet Helen?'

'If they're being released together near the château, they'll head there first.'

'But what if she tries to get home and I'm not there?'

'It's three kilometres. She wouldn't do that. Not at night. She'd go with Julia to the château and ring you from there.'

'How about you?'

'I'll be at the cemetery. I don't trust Granier's gang. They're quite capable of arresting each other.'

'I don't think you'll be very welcome.'

'I wasn't thinking of asking for a formal invitation.'

When Julia had found herself staring into the dark eyes of the shotgun, she had thought for a moment that this was the end. With Blue Helmet crowding her from behind and Henri pushing the cold metal hard against her mouth, she had seen an image of herself as a child again, in the bare room in Maine where the sad woman had ended her life. It was a sense of abject surrender, of having exhausted all hope. But when Henri made her open her mouth, and she felt the steel against her teeth, and Blue Helmet made a sudden grab with rough hands to take the key, her rebelliousness had redoubled, and she struggled with all her remaining strength. Bringing up her knee she had tried to inflict the same pain on Henri as she had on his partner at the cottage, but he bent back from the waist and avoided the blow. Next she jabbed her elbow into Blue

Helmet's stomach and had the satisfaction of hearing him grunt as she hit the target. But something about Henri's breathing made her pause. It seemed laboured. And still he forced the gun into her face. Heaving herself back against Blue Helmet with all the power she had left, Julia at last pulled free of the obscene weapon, at the same time plunging to her right and heading for the fireplace. Standing with her back to it, she tried to control her breathing and the shaking in her legs and arms.

'Look you idiots,' she shouted, tightening her fists to keep the anger strong, 'you're just making things worse for yourselves. Can't you think at all? All you have to do is wait a few hours and it's done. What's the point of this? Mmm?' Then, in English, she added: 'Goddamn morons. God how I hate you. Hear? I *hate* you.'

Without warning, by way of reply, Henri jerked the shotgun so that it was aimed at the windows, raised it to his shoulder and pulled the trigger. The noise of the report was unbearable. Both Julia and Blue Helmet turned away from the blast in an automatic effort to escape it. The sudden, terrifying brutality made Julia tremble worse than before. She hugged herself, trapping her hands under her armpits to keep them still. Was it all about to end here, among strangers? Was this lunatic going to turn the gun on her next and, with a tiny movement of his finger, obliterate everything? She wondered how it might feel. Would her body be aware of the terrible violence, or would blackness be instantaneous? Would she ever be found? And if it was so simple to stop her life, what had been the point of living it?

Henri turned and faced her, the muzzle of the gun wavering a little but pointed in her direction. Blue Helmet looked on as though paralysed. Julia glanced towards the door in the hope that Paul might make a sudden appearance and, with foolish humanity, disarm his colleague. Instead Henri's knuckles whitened as he took a firmer grip, his head angled to line up the shot.

'Stop this!' Julia shouted at Blue Helmet. 'I told you, if he can do this to me he's perfectly capable of doing it to you. This is murder. For nothing. For absolutely nothing at all. It's the act of a madman. Please. Whatever you're getting from my father I'll get you more. It's not a problem. But this way . . . if he . . . you're just looking at all of your life in gaol. For *nothing*.' With this last appeal the tears of frustration came, and her head sank on to her chest. In a strange way she felt almost ready; exhausted, humiliated, with nowhere to run. Let it happen. Let anything happen. There was nothing to be gained from trying to reason with these deadheads. Might as well talk to a hyena. No more begging. Get it over. And hope the police blow the bastards away.

The long moment grew longer. What would end it? An infinitesimal click and then a shattering oblivion? Would there be colours, at least? Perhaps a sense of peace, or that moment people described when they hovered between life and death? There was no sound in the room, except Henri's breathing. He must be prolonging his pleasure, jerking off maybe at the thought of his power. How could there be any honour in dying, Julia thought, when the executioner was fit for a padded cell? She tried to count the seconds. How long had it been now? A minute and a half, perhaps? And one, two, three, four . . . Pretty soon the artificial calm of surrender would give way again to a new determination, and a new fear. She couldn't remain stooped for much longer. Since the *coup de grâce* had been so long in coming, she would have to satisfy her curiosity. Raising her eyes without moving her head, she saw Henri's filthy trainers a few metres away, and imagined the gun being lowered to cover her position. But something else intruded on her line of vision. It was another pair of trainers closing in from the direction of the door. As they took up a position close to the first pair, the tone of Henri's breathing changed and Julia heard what she thought was a sob, held back until it became a desperate, choked sound. Too intrigued now for caution, she raised her head and witnessed an extraordinary scene. Blue Helmet had his arms round Henri's neck. Henri's head rested on his shoulder, and the gun was trapped, vertical, between them, with the barrels pointing at the ground. With gentle pressure, Blue Helmet then led Henri, who seemed distraught, to the door, shutting it behind them and locking it.

Her legs unsteady, Julia walked to the window and looked out at the overgrown courtyard. She heard bees and thought she could taste honey. Holding out her hands, she let them feel the warmth of the sun. A lizard scuttering across the stone windowsill paused to stare in her direction, and never had she felt more glad to be alive.

Tom had occupied the afternoon by putting two coats of white emulsion on the bathroom. He'd been promising Helen he would do the job for ages and this was the perfect opportunity. The work was therapeutic. Listening to Radio 4 as he sweated, and splattered his face and arms with paint, for two hours he was able to keep his deepest anxieties at bay. Nothing could drive out thoughts of having Helen home, but the ache was containable. When he had finished, he went out of the room and came back again, putting on the light to see his work as Helen would see it. In the corner he noticed a patch that looked streaky. With a full brush he leaned over the bath and gave it several more vigorous passes. Soon he would reward himself with an early Talisker, but first he cleaned the brush under the kitchen tap and put it on the old barrel in the garden to dry. The two wooden chairs in the shelter of the wall, where he and Helen would sit and talk on sunny evenings, reminded him of Daisy's imminent arrival. In the passage, he slipped out of his painting clothes and switched on the hot tap in the bath, waiting for the water level to rise until it would cover him.

Later, cool in jeans and clean shirt, he savoured the whisky and thought of the night last week when this whole awful thing had begun. Since then he had not known a single moment without the tension of fear and concern. Whatever happened, when it was over, he and Helen must do the things they had always planned. The only positive aspect of this horrible business was that it had taught him never again to take anything for granted; never again to put off a pleasure they dreamed of, assuming they had enough money. A moment no longer than a heartbeat could turn the world upside down. In future, he thought, they must be more alive to new experiences.

As he was about to re-fill his glass, Monique appeared from the gate leading to the Charmoy road. Against the parched grass, under the old apple tree whiskered with grey moss, she looked vital and excited. They exchanged kisses of greeting and, in response to Tom's offer of an aperitif, she asked for a spritzer. Motioning her to the other chair, he went to fix the drink.

'I met Roland,' she said, when he came back and handed her the glass. 'In Arnay. He was just coming out of the Café du Nord.' She raised her thumb and little finger, miming Roland's tryst with a bottle. 'He was singing a little song, from one of his shows I expect. The Arnaytois didn't know what to make of him. A pretty young girl smiled and blushed though, and that made him very happy.' She laughed. '*Le chanson de Roland!*' She raised her glass and said in English: 'Cheers Tom.'

Tom returned the toast.

'He said he was coming here, to see you,' Monique went on. Then, after a pause: 'You must be very tired.'

'No, funnily enough. Not now, I'm not. I have been. Can't sleep somehow. But now it's getting to the end, and Daisy coming and everything, I feel great.' He looked at his glass.

'You've been marvellous, Monique. I can't tell you how much difference it's made, having friends. Without you and Robert and everybody I'd have been hopeless.'

'Nonsense. You're stronger than you think, Tom.'

Tom shook his head. 'I've just about held on, if you want to know the truth. Just about. There were times when I was right on the edge, staring down at this . . . this black hole, thinking if I fell in that would be it. Disintegration into tiny particles.' He looked from his glass to her and broke into a smile. 'One way of losing weight, I suppose.'

As Monique laughed, a green van appeared, coughing, from the direction of the N6.

'There he is,' she pointed. 'Don Quixote!'

The van pulled up by the wall, making a final lunge forward after the engine had been switched off, as Roland neglected to engage neutral. Despite the fact that Tom and Monique both heard the driver's door open and shut, no one appeared. When a minute or so had passed and there was still no sign of the visitor, they exchanged a look of baffled amusement and both rose at once to investigate. Before they had gone five paces, they heard a shrill woman's voice wailing close behind them.

'Help! Help me! I'm on my way to the Negresco and I'm lost.'

Tom and Monique turned to find Roland, a handkerchief tied round his face like a headscarf, brow furrowed with distress.

'Why the Negresco?' Monique said. 'You're hundreds of kilometres from Nice.' As she spoke she untied Roland's handkerchief and handed it back to him with an affectionate smile. 'Silly woman.'

'The Negresco serves the best Negronis in the world,' Roland said. 'They're worth travelling hundreds of kilometres for.'

'Will a scotch do?' Tom said. 'Can't run to a Negroni, I'm afraid.'

'A scotch would be most agreeable.'

As Tom went back to the kitchen, Roland followed him. In an instant the puppeteer's mood seemed to have changed to one of unaffected concern.

'Monique told me about tonight. I'm so glad for you, Tom.'

'Thanks. It's not quite over yet though.'

'It must have been torture.'

'It hasn't been too good. Still, nearly there.' Tom himself was aware of the ludicrous understatement but felt he didn't know Roland well enough to go into greater emotional detail. 'Malt OK?' he said, indicating the duty-free litre of Talisker.

There was no reply. Looking up to check on the whereabouts of his unpredictable guest, Tom saw him gazing in rapt attention at the poster of Julia Walker and the blow-up of the coat of arms.

'Where did this come from?' Roland said.

'That's an enlargement of the photograph the kidnappers sent the girl's father. I don't know whether you can make it out but the bracelet she's wearing belongs to Helen. That's what gave us the idea they were together. Julia must have done it as a kind of sign.'

'What about this other one? What made you blow that up?' There was no trace now of the clown in Roland's concentration.

'It's just a feeling I've had all along about that blob in the top right-hand corner of the big picture. I took it to Dijon and this American bloke very kindly did a computer enhancement for me. They're fantastic, those machines. Then I tried to check it against known coats of arms in the region but I came up with nothing. A couple of people said it looked familiar, but apart from that . . . '

'What do you think it is, that curious creature?'

Tom handed him a glass of whisky. 'One of those mythical

beasts, I suppose. An enfield or something.'

'Thank you. Got a bit of paper and a pencil?'

Tom pushed them towards him as Monique came in from the garden and stood listening at the doorway, glass in hand.

With a practised eye, Roland made a rapid sketch from the blow-up, its line sure and bold. When he'd finished, he held it up to check the accuracy and then laid it on the work surface. 'It's not an enfield, it's a common or garden horse,' he said; 'rearing on its hind legs, look; front feet aloft, like the Lone Ranger's Silver. There's nothing heraldic about this fellow.'

'What makes you so sure?' Tom said.

'I do know my horses, Tom. The Second Law of Thermodynamics is a bit hazy, but nags, I know. Believe me, this is a horse in absolutely classic mode. No question.'

'So that might mean it's not old at all, the coat of arms? They didn't go in for anything as ordinary as a horse, did they?' Tom was excited to have an earlier suspicion endorsed.

'Far too practical,' Roland said.

'But how can this help us now?' Monique said, looking at her watch. 'In four hours Helen will be free, thank God. What time's Daisy arriving?'

'She couldn't say. As soon as she can get here.' A thought occurred to Tom. 'You couldn't do something for me could you, Monique?'

'Tell me.'

'I want to be there when . . . '

'And you'd like me to be here in case Daisy comes while you're out.'

'Do you think you could? What about Leo?'

'I'll look after Leo. He tells me wonderful stories,' Roland said.

Monique smiled. 'That's very kind, Roland, but Zazie will be there. No, really Tom, that's very easy.'

* * *

At the château in Bessey, William Walker was soaking in a bath. It was the only room in the enormous building where he could achieve any degree of calm. Even a lifetime of high pressure deals and crises had not prepared him for this. This had been a situation where the big decisions were taken out of his hands; where the other side had no face and no concept of human decency. It was more akin to war then any experience in his professional life, except that, in their skirmishes so far, only the enemy had been armed. For once Walker had known something of how it felt to be the underdog, and it was not a comfortable sensation. Though he resolved to learn from this and not to leave his family so vulnerable again, he knew that in truth there were times – would always be times – when chaos got the better of order. That at least was a salutary lesson. With what sudden ease his elaborate security, the best that money could buy, had been brushed aside. But at this moment, when his daughter was about to be restored to him, nothing else mattered. He had never been so taut with anticipation. It was intoxicating; even dangerous, perhaps, because it might distort his judgement. Nevertheless it prickled in his nerve-ends, as pervasive and undeniable as it had been in his teens.

Reaching for his cut-glass tumbler of bourbon from the space by the taps, he was surprised to hear a discreet knock on the door. Strange. The household knew there were to be no interruptions while he bathed. 'Yes,' he said, in a voice that did not encourage further exchange.

'It's me.' The voice was Madeleine's.

'Darling?'

'Can I come in?'

'Just a moment.' Walker got out of the water, wrapped a towel round his waist and let his wife in, locking the door behind her. 'This is rare.' He sat on the side of the bath. 'Something happened?'

Madeleine still stood by the door, looking a little hesitant. 'Nothing. Nothing at all.'

'What then?'

'I don't want to be alone. It's idiotic.'

He held out his hand for hers. 'No, it's not.'

Madeleine advanced two steps and gave it to him, as though unsure.

'It's good,' Walker said.

'Get back into your bath. You'll get cold.' Madeleine pulled forward an old, cork-topped stool and sat down.

Walker slipped off the towel and stepped back into the deep bath.

'This waiting . . . ' Madeleine said.

'It's an agony. But think what it must be like for Julia.'

'I can't. I've tried. I'd rather have gone through it for her.'

'What makes you say that?'

'Just that I'd rather it had been me than her.'

Walker looked at her over his shoulder. 'That sounds unhappy.'

'I am for them . . . Julia and Helen.'

'Of course. And for you?'

'Sometimes.'

'About what?'

'Myself. Things.'

'Us? I hope not.'

Madeleine picked up the scented soap and began to rub his back.

'Us?' Walker repeated.

'No,' Madeleine said in a quiet voice.

'You would tell me?'

'Yes.'

'Promise?'

'Yes.' Putting down the soap, Madeleine caressed his shoulder with her hand, brown against his paler skin.

Walker leaned back his head. Madeleine bent forward and slipped both arms round his neck, holding him against her. Then she rose and, unbuttoning her silk shirt, laid it on the stool. When she was naked, she stood and looked at him, her arms by her sides, her eyes unsmiling. He took her hand again and, turning to face him, she stepped into the water, confident only of his desire for her.

'I've missed you,' he said.

Offered an official car by Granier, Tom had thanked the major but said that he preferred to travel with Robert. By the time they left the house at five past ten, Daisy had still not arrived.

'She'll be so worried,' Tom said to Monique. 'She won't know what's going on.'

'She'll understand,' Monique insisted. 'She'll know you'll contact us the moment you have any news. Go, Tom. You can't be in two places at once. Go where you're needed most.'

In Robert's car, Tom was still undecided about where to station himself.

'I told you, you must be at the château,' Robert said. 'There's absolutely nothing you can do at the cemetery.'

'That's what Granier said.'

'Well, for once he's got it right. They'll have medical facilities at the château and everything . . . ' Realising that this might sound tactless, Robert back-tracked. 'They probably won't need them, but . . . And then, after the pick-up, I'll come straight over too. Courage, Mr Professor. It's almost over.'

'We've got nearly an hour to wait. Maybe we should have left later.'

'Don't worry about it.'

On the way to the château they passed gendarmes mounted on motorbikes and in parked cars. It was clear that every approach to Bessey was well covered.

'But surely the kidnappers won't come within a kilometre

of these people,' Tom said. 'They're so obvious.'

'Very soon they won't be. These guys are classed as soldiers, don't forget. They'll pull back and blend into the night. If there's one thing a gendarme's good at, it's pretending to be a tree. Come to that, most of them don't have to pretend.' Robert chuckled.

As they pulled into the well-lit courtyard of the château, there were half a dozen vehicles, including the Citroën ambulance predicted by Robert. Everywhere figures, uniformed and plain clothes, went about the business of co-ordinating the operation.

'I hadn't realised it would be so big,' Tom said. 'All these people.'

'It's probably the biggest operation most of them will ever see,' Robert said. 'The kidnappers have got no chance.'

Reassured, Tom got out of the car and, giving Robert a thumbs-up, entered the building. Here too there was a flurry of activity. Breaking away from talking to two officers, Walker greeted Tom, linking an arm through his and ushering him into the study.

'Can I get you anything, Tom?' he said.

'No thanks. I want a clear head.'

'It's felt like a lifetime, hasn't it?'

'Two. It's been bloody awful.'

'These guys appear to be on the ball. They've got marksmen surrounding the cemetery. There's a net around the whole area. I have to say, I'm impressed.'

'Robert isn't.'

'Ah well, the cops like to think they're just country cousins. It's all nonsense of course. They do a fine job.'

'Is the money in place?'

'It will be in . . . ' Walker consulted his watch. ' . . . It's ten eighteen now. It'll be there in twenty-two minutes precisely. Any earlier and they said some nightbird who had nothing to do with this might stumble into the graveyard and find himself ten million francs richer. I wanted to drive it myself but Granier said no. So a guy in plain clothes is making the drop. No funny business. He just dumps it and gets out. I told them I don't want to be smart. We just want them safe and sound, is all.'

Happy that time was passing, and that Walker shared his priorities, Tom told him about Roland's theory.

'Well, if it helps, great,' Walker said. 'It'll be fascinating to know where these swine holed out.'

When the door opened, Julia couldn't help smiling, even though Blue Helmet was holding a piece of wire.

'What time is it?' she said.

'Ten twenty-three.'

What a marvellous feeling, Julia thought. Just over half an hour and this nightmare would end. Home, and her father, and Madeleine; a bath, a bed . . . a fresh apple, for heaven's sake, and the dog snuffling her hand – plain things even the poorest took for granted. Peace, freedom, air to breathe. And the cottage. How would she feel about it after this? Worry about that later. Right now, keep calm to the end. Hold the happiness in check, just until she could smell the sweet night around her.

Walking towards Blue Helmet, she held out her hands in willing surrender. 'Does it have to be the wire?' she said.

'It's all there is,' Blue Helmet said. 'I won't make it too tight.' His tone was kinder than before.

'You must be happy?'

Blue Helmet didn't react but made a circle with his forefinger, signifying that she should turn round.

'What will you do with the money? Have you thought?' To her amazement Julia found that, at this moment, she felt no malice towards him. It was almost as though, now the ordeal was over and both of them were about to get what they wanted, there was a form of bond between them; an intense experience shared and survived.

Having bound her hands without hurting her, Blue Helmet touched her elbow to make her turn back to him.

'I think your friend's going to need some care,' she said, looking at his eyes through the visor. 'I really do.'

Blue Helmet remained silent but didn't turn away. Then, with apparent reluctance, he took out of his pocket a piece of white cotton ripped from a sheet. 'I have to do this,' he said. 'It's the only way.' With some care he gagged her, raising her hair to tie the knot at the nape of her neck.

Julia felt she wanted to say more. Now that he was ceasing to be a threat, she longed to know about him. What had made him do something which, even from the little she knew of him, seemed untypical? Who was this fellow human being who, even in this dreadful place, had shown signs of pity? Most important of all, how was the other woman? But the questions remained unasked, except by her eyes. Moments later they too were blinded with another piece of material.

As they crossed the threshold of the room, Julia could sense a change of atmosphere. The passage was cooler. What an age it seemed since she had run down here, desperate for an open door leading to the light. She had failed in that, but at least for a short time she had known the satisfaction of a small independence. Now, walking in the other direction, to her surprise she felt a mixture of elation and apprehension. Until her final release she was leaving the familiar and entering the unknown. She felt no fear of Blue Helmet, but between here and the château who knew how Henri might react? Who knew how humiliated he had felt when she witnessed his breakdown? In the stress of the handover, would Blue Helmet have the time and the energy to restrain him?

It was Henri's voice she heard as, by the change of acoustic, she judged that they had emerged into the large entrance hall.

She was also aware of another presence, though whether this was Paul or the woman she couldn't tell.

'Let's go,' Henri said, his voice flat and edgy.

Instead of being taken through the huge front door, Julia felt Blue Helmet, rougher now as though to please Henri, pulling her towards the chamber where she had been photographed. The footsteps of whoever the fourth person was were so light as to be inaudible. If it wasn't a female, Paul must be barefoot. Julia imagined the old mirror over the fireplace and wished she could see the intriguing image reflected in it. If only it could re-play its memory, that mirror could tell the police the whole story.

Again, by the change of tone, Julia guessed they must be in the small ante-chamber containing the door to the cellar, and the prison from which she had escaped. Crossing that, they went through another entrance and all at once she could feel the warm night air on her face. Six stone steps, down which whoever was in front appeared to stumble, and there was gravel underfoot. Now she thought she could make out the distinct footsteps of four people. Please let it be Blue Helmet or Paul who drives us, she thought. Please not the psychopath.

'See you at the rendezvous,' Blue Helmet said. 'Good luck.'

Julia felt herself being passed from one to another, and she could tell by the vicious prod in the ribs from her new guide that her prayer had gone unheard. This was Henri all right. If she hadn't known by the sense of violence, she would have recognised him by the overpowering, sour smell that made her nauseous. Next she heard metal doors opening, and at the same time she could feel another presence beside her – a slight, softer figure who must be the other woman. So she was alive, and capable at least of standing. Julia felt moved by her warmth. The tears pricked her eyes under the blindfold. It was almost like confirmation that a legendary figure existed – some brave heart who had undertaken a terrible journey and come through weak but unbroken. Julia longed to reach out to touch and comfort her. Unable to do that with her hands, she moved closer until their bodies made contact at the hip. As she did so, the other woman seemed to lose her strength and fall to her knees. Julia felt her head against her leg, like a sign that she too wanted to maintain their closeness.

'Shit,' Henri said. 'She's weaker than a calf. I told you . . . '

'Never mind that now,' Blue Helmet said. 'Just get her in.'

'Get up,' Henri said. 'Get your backside into the van or I'm going without you. Get up and feel for the edge. Well move your hands, you stupid cow.'

Julia wished she could give the woman some support. It was heartbreaking to hear Henri treat her like this. In sympathy, Julia too sank to her knees. 'If you can just do this,' she said, 'it'll all be over. We're on our way home. Have they told you?' Her voice was muffled. She had no idea whether the woman would understand.

'Shut your gob,' Henri said, prodding Julia again. 'Get in, you. We don't need any more of your bullshit.'

Blue Helmet must have helped to manhandle the other woman into the van because moments later she and Julia were lying beside each other on a bare metal floor. Julia manoeuvred herself so close that she could hear her light breathing. Turning her head and stretching as far as she could, she laid it on the other woman's slender shoulder, nuzzling her neck like an animal. In response, the other woman's head seemed to fall to its left with exhaustion, rather than by volition, and the two drew silent solace from the contact. But the hardness of the floor and the bumpiness of the ride made it difficult to remain like that for long. Every time Henri took a sharp bend, both bodies slid across to one side, their arms made sore by the grit on the surface. Julia no longer minded the pain and discomfort for her own sake, but the state of her companion began to alarm her. The woman seemed almost inert, as though she were conscious but unable to function. What had they done to her to make her like this, Julia wondered? Had she been tortured? If so, why, when she had only been captured by accident? Or maybe that was the reason – the fact that they didn't need her? The pigs! Now her momentary fellow-feelings for Blue Helmet haunted her like a betrayal.

Over the harsh noise of the engine, Julia tried to listen for anything that might provide clues to their route, but there was nothing. That alone suggested they were on country roads but, apart from ruling out the motorway, the intuition was useless. Once she heard Henri speak on his mobile telephone, but was unable to pick up any of the conversation. The caller must be Blue Helmet, or Paul, Julia presumed, on their way to pick up the ransom money. She made repeated counts from one to sixty, numbering the completed minutes with her fingers. Eight so far, plus perhaps another five before she had started. How far did a van go over winding roads in thirteen minutes? Something like seven kilometres, maybe? No, less. Five or six. Not much, but five or six closer to a glorious release she could almost taste. And however serious the condition of her travelling companion, once they were free she would have the best possible medical attention. Julia wanted to nurse her herself since, though apart, they had in a sense been through so much together. She supposed she wouldn't be allowed to, but at least she could visit often and they could compare notes. Then, one day soon, they would laugh at some of the things that had happened to them, and that would be the beginning of their cure.

At Bligny there were clouds across the moon. Robert had driven in from the top road and left the car up a dirt track, beyond the gendarmes' cordon. On foot he had then taken to the sloping woods and meadows above the town and made his way to a vantage point overlooking the cemetery. Twice he had stopped and telephoned the château, to keep Tom informed of his progress. Taking advantage of plentiful cover, in copses and folds in the ground, and drawing with some relish on his army experience, he stooped and crawled to within thirty metres of the spot where the money awaited collection. Once, in the lee of a dry stone wall, he had spotted a gendarme taking up his position, but apart from that he congratulated himself on an uneventful approach.

Angling his watch with the luminous numerals, he saw that the time was ten-fifty. Tom would be anxious to know what was happening, but Robert didn't dare ring him from here. Another ten minutes and he could tell him the whole story. Including the part that Tom knew nothing about. Unbelievable. All those years and no one realising. The kidnappers would be in contact with each other, Robert assumed, so the women wouldn't be released until the ransom was picked up and counted. Walker had made it clear that he wanted no heroics, so Robert supposed the gendarmes would let it all happen and then, at a discreet distance, give chase. That way, after the rendezvous, they could round up everyone involved.

Just as he was considering this probable outcome, yellow headlights approached fast down the top road and a car swung into the gravelled forecourt of the cemetery at speed, skidding as it braked. The door opened and a figure emerged. Bending double, the driver ran to the open gate and for a moment was lost from sight. In that same instant a second car approached down the hill, this one at a more cautious pace. As it began its turn into the forecourt, the first figure emerged from the cemetery clutching what must be the bag full of money. At this the second car reversed with an urgent screech and headed back up the hill twice as fast as it had descended, pursued at a considerable distance by a slow-reacting gendarmes' car, whose driver couldn't have expected this development. Pandemonium followed. A powerful light on a building opposite the church was switched on and the figure with the money was illuminated like an escaper in no-man's-land. Transfixed, he didn't know whether to attempt a getaway by car, or a retreat on foot across the fields. In the event his mind was made up for him within five seconds by the emergence into the light of three gendarmes carrying guns. Dropping his black bag, the man had no option but to raise his hands.

'What did I say?' Robert muttered to himself, still stunned by the suddenness of the disaster. 'Unbelievable! Absolutely unbelievable! They couldn't organise a game of *pétanque*.' What the hell had gone wrong? How could such a simple operation have turned into a rout in a matter of seconds? Hadn't he told Walker they'd be better off on their own? But how could there have been two cars? Somehow the handover had become public knowledge. That was what happened when there were too many cooks in the kitchen. What should he do now? No point in staying here, that was obvious. Realising that the gendarmes would tell him nothing, indeed as yet they would *know* nothing, Robert decided to drive back to the château. Better to tell Tom in person than break the news over the telephone. In any case, Tom might already have heard that things hadn't gone according to plan. What would he be thinking, poor man? Then again, maybe the gendarmes who had taken off so late in pursuit of the second car had managed to catch up? Maybe. On the whole, Robert decided not to put his money on it.

CHAPTER FOURTEEN

Granier himself briefed Walker, Madeleine, Tom and Robert on what had happened. It had been an unprecedented misfortune, he said. The gendarmes had supposed, as was reasonable, that the first car belonged to the kidnappers. Only when the second appeared, moments later, had it become clear that there was an unknown factor in the equation. By then the retreating kidnappers had got a head start and, after a brief chase through the night, had managed to elude their pursuers. As soon as they realised something was wrong, they would have telephoned their accomplices driving the women and told them to abort. Turning round well short of their dropping-point, they would have had little difficulty in escaping over minor country roads and tracks. There were indications, Granier said, that these people knew the area well.

In Walker's study the tension was palpable. Tom found the failure hard to comprehend. After all the concern and the waiting and the unbearable expectancy, this was more than he could deal with. To be robbed of release at the last moment by a chance in a million seemed a refinement of cruelty. Having rung the house before it happened and spoken to a tired but elated Daisy, who had been expecting to see her mother before midnight, he wondered how he was going to tell her. And what would happen next? The kidnappers might assume the debacle was a put-up job and grow desperate. Don't even think about it, he told himself.

Sensing what was in his mind, Walker said: 'We've come too far now, Tom. Just hang on. I'll make it tomorrow even if I have to double the money – whatever – I don't care. They'll call any minute, you can bet on it.'

As he finished speaking, the telephone rang. Even Madeleine, who had her head in her hands, looked up.

Lifting the receiver, in a voice as level as he could command, Walker said: 'Yes. This is William Walker. Yes. Yes, of course.' There was an edge of disappointment as he handed it to Granier. 'It's for you, Major.'

'Hello,' Granier said. For perhaps thirty seconds he listened, adding nothing. Then, with a final 'thank you', he hung up. Turning to his anxious audience, he looked grave. 'That was my adjutant,' he said. 'Already we know who the intruder was. I don't think his name would mean anything to you.'

'Try us,' Robert said, still angry at the failure and familiar with the art of evasion.

'He comes from some thirty kilometres away,' Granier said with a slight shrug. 'Apparently his name is Charbonneaux.'

Despite herself, Madeleine was open-mouthed.

'Are you OK, darling?' Walker said. 'Let me get you something.'

'No, really, I'm fine. It's just the shock. All this . . . ' She rose. 'I think I'll go to my room. I'm sorry.'

Walker got up to escort her but she told him he must stay. They would talk later, she said. As she left the room, Walker sat down again. 'What on earth got into the guy?' he said. 'How could he possibly know?'

'At the moment we have no idea,' Granier said.

'He was told. That's obvious,' Robert said.

'Of course it's obvious, monsieur,' Granier said with a cold stare. 'Perhaps you can tell us who by? Is that obvious too?'

'He'll tell you himself,' Robert said, ignoring the sarcasm; 'if you handle him right. It's just a matter of time.'

'Thank you for the tip.' Granier looked drawn.

'I still can't believe you let them get away,' Tom said, shaking his head.

'You can cover every eventuality and still . . . '

'But you didn't cover every eventuality. They got away right under your nose. Now Julia and my wife are in very great danger.'

Walker put a restraining hand on Tom's arm. 'This is a terrible blow, Major,' he said, looking at Granier. 'Hopes were very high. Of course you understand that.'

'Of course,' Granier said. 'I regret it very much. But now we must be positive and face the facts.'

'What do you think they'll do?' Tom said.

Granier thought before he answered. 'Initially I think they'll be thrown into confusion . . . ' he began.

'They're not the only ones,' Robert muttered.

' . . . but when they've given it some thought I believe they'll try again,' the major went on. 'They've taken a lot of risks for that money. They're not going to give up now. I must ask you to be patient a little longer. I know how hard it must be.'

'I wonder if you do,' Tom said.

'We haven't been idle you know, Monsieur Bellman,' Granier said, his voice sympathetic. 'We have people under close surveillance. We've put more man hours into this hunt than any other operation for some considerable time.'

Robert gave Granier an enquiring look, not unmingled with anxiety.

Noticing this, Tom said: 'Can you tell us who?'

Granier returned Robert's glance. 'I think perhaps better not for the moment.'

When Granier had rejoined his team, Tom and Robert sat with Walker for another forty-five minutes. Despite Granier's attempts at reassurance and Walker's pragmatism, Tom was in turmoil. Who knew how near Helen and Julia had been to the château when their driver had got the panic call to turn back? A few hundred metres perhaps? A stone's throw. And yet it might as well have been a hundred miles. Now they must wait for another telephone call from these bastards, if it ever came. Yet again the kidnappers were being allowed to call the tune.

After examining the incident from every angle, Walker suggested that Tom and Robert should go home. He would call the moment he heard anything. Thanking him, they returned to the car, finding themselves unable to look at the gendarmes' vehicles parked in the courtyard. The road to St Luc was moonlit now, and deserted.

'Poor Helen,' Tom said as they passed the public wash-house beside the church.

'She's strong. She'll wait another day.'

'It's wondering what's happening all the time. It gnaws at you.'

'What's happening is that we've had a setback, but we're getting there. Tomorrow will be the end. Just a few hours. They're doing their best.'

'Do you really think that?'

'It's painful to say it, but yes. I give them a hard time to keep them on their toes, but they're not a bad bunch. Not as good as they think, but not bad.' Robert chuckled.

'Why's Granier being so cagey about these suspects?'

There was no hesitation. 'After tonight, he probably wants to be extra sure before he says anything he might regret.'

Robert dropped Tom at his door. Tom could see Daisy and Monique talking on the sofa. When they heard the engine they both rose.

'What am I going to tell Daisy?' Tom said.

'Give her a hug and tell her the truth. I'll see you in the morning, early, unless Walker rings first.'

'Thanks Robert. Goodnight.'

By the time Tom reached the door, Daisy had snatched it open, arms wide and eyes full of expectation. When she saw that her father was alone, however, her face fell.

'Where's Mum? Have they taken her to hospital? Where is she? Can we go?'

Tom hugged her and held her tight. Behind her, Monique seemed to understand already that the news wasn't good.

'Darling,' Tom began, 'I'm sorry, there's been a slight delay.'

'What? What happened?'

'It didn't quite go the way it was meant to. These things are very delicate. Mum's fine but we'll have to wait just a little bit longer.'

Daisy pulled away. 'Dad, for heaven's sake don't talk in code. It's me, remember? Not some school kid. I don't want to be protected, I want you to tell me the truth. What's going on?'

'It was insane. Somebody, some total stranger turned up and grabbed the money just before the kidnappers arrived. The gendarmes got him but the kidnappers got away.'

'On no. That's terrible. Who on earth was he?'

'They've no idea. A bloke called Charbonneaux. How he cottoned on nobody knows. It's a farce.'

Tom kissed Monique in belated greeting. 'I'm sorry,' he said. 'I was a lot longer than I said.'

'It's not important,' she said. 'I'm so sorry to hear . . . Look, you two have things to talk about. I'll go. You know where I am when you need me. The minute you hear anything, please call me. It doesn't matter what the time is.'

'Thanks, Monique.'

When Monique had left, Tom and Daisy sat close on the sofa. He put his arm round her shoulders and she leaned across with her head on his chest, crying.

'How could it happen to someone like mum? I just don't understand. She's so good.'

'I've been asking myself that a lot. It must have been a random thing, love. Sheer, cruel bad luck. Poor mum must have somehow got herself in the wrong place at the wrong time.'

'What do they think's going to happen now?'

'They seem pretty confident,' Tom lied. 'They reckon it'll be tomorrow.'

'How can they be so sure the kidnappers won't . . . ?'

Horrified by the awful possibility she had raised, Daisy was overcome. Tom tried hard to improvise words of comfort, though not convinced himself.

'No, it's going to be fine love, honestly. The kidnappers aren't about to give up the prize just because of a cock-up. What they want's the money. They don't care about anything else. It's a transaction; a horrible, twisted one, but for them that's what it is.' He paused, remembering Daisy's long day. 'Let me get you something to eat. A drink? What would you like?'

Daisy shook her head and blew her nose. Bending over, she picked up a carrier bag from the floor. Inside was a square, white, cardboard box tied with rose-coloured ribbon. 'Looks a bit pathetic now doesn't it?'

'What is it?'

Daisy undid the bow on the top and lifted the lid, revealing a cake. Piped in blue on the white icing were the words: 'Welcome home, Mum,' with three neat kisses underneath.

'It's lovely,' Tom said. 'She'll love that.'

During the desperate drive back through the winding lanes,

with the lights of cars he imagined to be gendarmes appearing at intervals, Henri had tried to contact Félix again on the mobile but it was hopeless. In some spots the signal was too weak, at others Félix was engaged, trying to call him, and anyway it was impossible to control the van at that speed with one hand off the wheel. In the end he had abandoned the attempt and concentrated on giving any pursuers the slip. It hadn't taken long. No one knew this part of the country as well as he did. He sped down back doubles and farm tracks that weren't even on the road map. Sometimes, when the moon emerged from behind clouds, he switched off his lights. That must drive the *flics* mad, he thought with pleasure. Now you see him, now you don't.

Fuelled with anger and frustration, and never pausing to ask why the gendarmes should be chasing him, he found the drive exhilarating. Fancying himself the star of a Grand Prix team, Ferrari, or Williams Renault, he held the wheel at arms' length, spacing his hands like the professionals did. Raising the visor of his helmet for better visibility, he could sense the moment when he had shaken off his challengers for good, and punched the air as though he were first past the chequered flag. But this was not a Ferrari or a Williams Renault, he reminded himself. This was a van. He had beaten all that smart-arse technology in a van! It was the proudest moment of his life.

Once the van was out of sight, however, in the neglected stable block of the château, which he had hoped never to see again, his mood changed. One call from Félix, sounding panicky at the cemetery, and the whole plan had been destroyed. All the boredom, pussyfooting around these stupid women, the nights on the bony camp-bed, the day that never came, the photograph, the phone calls to the stupid American, and what were they left with? Nothing in their hands but the callouses of labourers, the same as when they started. Whoever got the

money must be laughing his head off. Who could that freak
have been anyway? A friend of Félix's maybe? Had Félix just
used him all along and then set him up at the last minute? Was
Félix on his way now to the Côte d'Azur with that cretin Paul
and the other one who'd snatched the ransom for them? He
should have travelled with Félix himself, let Paul drive the
women in the van. Bad move. Big mistake.

I'll do it now, Henri thought. Before . . . Before what? If
Félix was not coming back it wasn't before anything. It was
after. After the whole thing had turned into a shambles. At
least he'd have the satisfaction of knowing that the other side
– the rich, soft side – had lost. Better not do it out here though.
The blast of a shotgun might be noticed at night. Pity you
couldn't get a silencer for them. Then he could just do it in the
back of the van and drive the bodies to the reservoir. Weigh
them down with stones, dump them in and head for . . . He
couldn't think. Somewhere. But not in this. Have to steal
another one. One that couldn't be recognised. No problem.
Take a tourist's from outside the Hostellerie at Ste Sabine;
something decent – an Audi, say, or a nice BMW; change the
plates and hit the A6 going south. Easy.

Better get the women inside first. Drag them down the steps
to the cellars, then a couple of shots that nobody would hear
and they wouldn't be found for months; years, maybe. Where
was the shotgun, though? Had he taken it or had it been in
Félix's car? How strange. He couldn't remember. Maybe it
was still in the building. Opening the rear doors of the van he
grabbed the leg of the American's jeans and tried to pull her
out. Sitting upright, she kicked with all her strength. The other
woman lay beside her, taking no part. Finding his view and
manoeuvrability restricted by the helmet, Henri decided to take
it off. What difference did it make now? Even if they hadn't
been blindfolded, they'd never see him again anyway. Standing
back for a moment, he raised his hands to his head, looking

forward to freedom of movement and the air on his face. As he did so, the American burst out of the van and started running towards the entrance to the stable-yard. For direction, her guesswork was good. Throwing his helmet to the ground, Henri chased her, cursing the fact that nothing was easy. As he ran, gaining on her a little, the familiar feeling returned. Like a bucket of paint thrown against a whitewashed wall, the red stain was spreading in his head, this red that was as rich and bright as a cow's afterbirth in the snow. It was so vivid that he narrowed his eyes against the intensity. And as it spilled down the spaces of his mind, the voice came back; the voice that told him it was time. Even without the helmet he felt hotter now. If he could put his hand on his forehead it would be burning, he thought. It made him stronger too. Now he knew he would catch this nothing, this rag, in a few strides. When he did he would do it, do it, do it, do it, do it . . . The words repeated themselves over and over, louder with every step. Now she was two metres away. All the time it was getting easier. He could run for miles, he thought, and never have to stop. Reaching out, he took hold of her shirt and, catching her off balance, used his momentum to push her to the ground. She fell hard, but at once tried to scramble to her feet. Before she could rise, he picked up a large stone and drew back his arm to finish it. Do it, do it, do it, do it, the voice roared, and the red had coated all the walls of his skull. Arm raised, fingers tight on the stone – while her hands clawed at him, then covered her head. DO IT!

It was as though he was outside himself, watching. The blow seemed to fall in slow motion. The stone didn't seem heavy any longer. It moved through the air in an easy arc, somehow catching a brilliant light as it dropped. Now it was like a moon rock he had once seen in the local paper. He could make out every hollow of it, like miniature mountains and valleys, bathed in that eerie, yellow glare. He was fascinated by it. It was the most marvellous thing he'd ever seen. Looking up he saw two brighter lights, growing larger and ending up very close to his face. But these lights were so near he could feel their heat. This hadn't happened the other times. This was new, and it felt good. Now there were moths in the beams, homing in on them from the darkness and flying against something hard that seemed to be the source of the light. And there was a voice. At first he couldn't make out what it was saying, but then he realised it was repeating the same word. It was calling his name; loud, louder, from above and beyond the beam. He knew this could not be a friend. He knew that when this happened, this voice in his head, and the colour of blood, nobody should see. It was a secret thing, to be done in darkness. So when a hand, not the American's, appeared in the light and seemed to want to push him backwards, he knew what he must do.

Tightening his grip on the stone, he lifted it fast and hard, aiming at a point higher than the hand. He felt it make contact with something and heard what sounded like a grunt of pain. When he drew back the stone and looked at it, there was a blotch of red on the surface. And then a body fell, and lay in the light of the beam.

At once Henri recognised the face. It was Félix. His eyelids were flickering and there was white froth round his mouth. So he had come back, after all, Henri thought. His friend hadn't let him down. But what was he doing on the ground? Why was his skin so white, and how could there be blood in his eyes? Putting down the stone, Henri leaned over and listened. Félix's breath sounded strange. It wasn't regular and it wasn't very loud. Must be a stupid joke, Henri thought. Trying to frighten him, pretending he was hurt. This was great though. Back together again. They'd been right into the net and escaped like crafty trout. Now they could put the price up – do anything they wanted.

The feeling in Henri's head was changing. The red had gone and he was beginning to see things in a different way. He no longer felt hot, and he realised that the beams were headlights. He also became aware that Félix's breathing wasn't even irregular. It had stopped. If Félix was playing a trick, this had gone far enough. Putting his hand on his friend's brow, Henri was puzzled. It seemed cool for such a warm night, and the blood from his eyes had made lines down his cheeks. Henri took out his handkerchief and wiped them, but that made a bigger stain on the pale skin. Better get him inside. Let him rest for a while. Clean him up with some bottled water.

Then Henri remembered the women. What was he going to do about them? Looking round, he saw the American trying to get to her feet. With her hands tied behind her back it was proving difficult. She seemed unsteady, swaying a little as she rested on her knees, gathering the energy to stand. She held her head to one side, as though she had earache, and when she straightened for a moment Henri could see that there was a big red patch on her neck and jaw. Even though the gag had slipped a little, she was silent, except for a slight moan as she raised one knee. Should he deal with her first, Henri wondered? Then Félix. Or Félix first and then her? But if he did it that way round she'd be off, out of the gate. So there was no option. Anyway, two minutes and he could have her inside again and be back out. Where the hell was Paul? If he was here the whole thing would be simple. He'd been in the car with Félix, hadn't he, or had Henri imagined that? No, no question. Looking up, Henri saw now that Paul was standing by the passenger door of the car, staring at him.

'Don't stand there like a dumb heifer,' he said, 'come and give me a hand.'

Paul said nothing and made no move.

'Are you deaf? Get over here or you'll feel my fist, right?'

Registering this, Paul took two steps.

'Now,' Henri said, pointing to the American, 'get her locked up again as fast as you can, back where she was in the first place, down below.' He paused, as an earlier doubt struck him. 'Who's got the gun?'

'It's in the boot,' Paul said, his thumb indicating the rear of the car.

'And put those lights off.'

Paul obeyed. Out of the beam, Félix's body looked even more still.

'You've killed him,' Paul said. 'You have, you've killed him.'

'Don't be stupid. He'll be all right when I get him indoors.'

'That stone you hit him with, or whatever it was . . . I'm t-t-telling you, he's dead.'

'What do you know about it? You know nothing about anything. Get the American in and then come back for the other.' Henri aimed a kick at Paul but failed to connect.

Paul helped Julia to her feet. For a moment she struggled and tried to break away, but she seemed unequal to the effort.

'If you make any trouble,' Henri said to her, 'he'll finish you.'

Still defiant, Julia said through her gag: 'What happened? You guys screwed up?'

'Shut your mouth,' Henri said, adding, to Paul: 'Get her out of here.'

As Paul took a grip on her arm and half-dragged her towards the château, Henri bent over and, putting his arms under Félix's neck and the back of his knees, lifted him like a new-born calf. Unsupported, Félix's head fell back, and his eyes were fixed on the stars.

'We'll have you right in no time,' Henri said, surprised at the lightness of his burden. 'A good sleep and in the morning you'll be good as new. We'll screw them for more now. Now they've done this to you. We'll make them pay until there's nothing left. Then you'll have the sun on your back. We can lie in it and drink all day if we want. Just lie there, and maybe shoot a couple of rabbits for dinner. Get some dry brushwood and make a fire. Put them on a spit. There's rosemary growing wild down there. Just lay some on them as they cook, that's all you have to do. It's what my mother used to do. She *was* a cook . . . ' As he talked, Henri could smell the fire and the rosemary, and taste the juices of the rabbit, and he knew, by Félix's silence, that his friend was enjoying them too.

By the time Paul had manhandled her down to the cellar, Julia was in such pain from the blow to her jaw that even though the situation was desperate, she had little strength left for resistance. When she heard Paul push open a door, however, she somehow summoned the will.

'I'm not going in.'

Paul made a clumsy attempt to force her by putting his arms round her waist and pulling.

'Get your hands off me.' Julia squirmed and strained until, more than anything, she embarrassed him into letting go.

'He t-t-told me to . . . '

'I heard him. He told you to finish me. Do it then. Go ahead. But just do one little thing for me first. Let me see you. It's not much to ask. Take off this blindfold. You can't let me die blind. If you do that for me I won't fight.'

Paul considered the proposition for a moment and then, with nervous fingers, untied the knot behind her head. Her gag, meanwhile, had slackened further, making her more intelligible.

'OK. Now, go ahead. Kill me.' Drained of every emotion by the disappointments of the night, and the throbbing of her jaw, Julia looked at him without fear. It was the first time she had seen him unmasked. He had the round, unformed face of a child. His eyes were troubled to the point of panic and his short hair tufted at tangents. At once she knew that he could not harm her unless he feared for his own life.

'What are you doing in this mess, Paul? You don't want to be here any more than I do. You want to be out with your girl. You have got a girl, haven't you?'

Paul turned away, appearing to scrutinise the stonework.

'I'm sorry. That's none of my business. Anyhow, before you kill me . . . How will you do it, by the way? Do you plan to strangle me, so that my tongue lolls out, like you see in the movies?' Though her mouth was half-obscured, she mimed the grotesque after-effects. 'Or shoot me? All that blood. Ugh! All over the floor? Probably get some on your shoes, your jeans? It's terrible stuff to get off. And those awful dreams afterwards. Nightmares. Wounds spurting, and screams, and everything. Or what else is there? Hit me to death, maybe? Get a stone like your friend and whack, whack, whack until something breaks. Could take a long time. Such a messy business. Cut my throat maybe, hack your way through gristle? But you don't have a knife, do you? Unless I've missed something, those seem to be the options. But before you go ahead, would you tell me one thing? Please? Makes no difference because after you've killed me I won't be around to make trouble.'

'What?' Paul said, in a voice that acknowledged the absurdity of his predicament.

'What happened? What went wrong back there?'

'Somebody got to the cemetery before us. Félix was brilliant. He got us out of it brilliantly.'

So that was the last unknown name, Julia thought. Paul, Henri and Félix. How innocuous they sounded. Quiet and serious. 'I heard you tell your friend he'd killed him out there. Is that right?' she said.

'I don't know. You'd better get in there. He'll be down in a minute.'

'How about you leave the door unlocked?'

'I can't. He'll check.'

'I'm not expecting you to do this for nothing, you know. Like I said before, it's very easy for me to arrange money for you, lots of it. I absolutely promise you it'll be where I say it will. No strings. You should have taken my offer before. You'd be out of here by now, where you want to be, instead of in this dump with a madman. Well, let's face it, he is isn't he? Henri kills people. He's a murderer. He's murdered his best friend. Why wouldn't he murder you? Then he keeps all the money. Think about it.' She paused. 'Two hundred thousand francs. How does that sound? All in used notes. Left wherever you want it.'

'I can't spend it if I'm dead,' Paul said. 'If he gets angry he'll shoot me.'

'But he needs you. Can't you see that? He can't do this thing on his own.'

'He needed Félix.'

As he spoke, Henri appeared out of the gloom; one arm round the waist of the other prisoner who, blindfolded and gagged, seemed unable to stand without support, and the other cradling the shotgun.

'I told you,' Henri said, raising the weapon with some difficulty to take aim.

Giving Julia a look in which pity and terror were mingled, Paul made a silent request for her co-operation.

With a small nod, she whispered: 'Only if you untie my hands.'

As she turned, he followed her a short way into the cell and managed to untie the cloth binding, disguising his movements as a series of prods. He then shut the door and locked it.

For a long time after hearing the dreadful revelation in her husband's study, Madeleine Walker had lain on the bed without drawing the curtains. Tonight, and for some nights past, she wished she had a bedroom to herself, a private place where there was no need for pretence. Soon William would be here, gentle and solicitous, making no demands, but unable to restrain questions. And what would her answers be? Though she had long been adept at diverting his attention, she feared that this time emotion might catch her unawares and make her explanations sound hollow. Her lover. The word was so much more beautiful than husband, or partner. Lover was a word poets used. It sounded like a caress. But her lover, whose caress she could feel now, in the night, had poisoned every moment they had shared, for money. The times they had lain in each others' arms, ignoring any other reality. The recklessness of giving, without shame or reserve. The uncomplicated, selfish joy of it, in the intimacy of guilt postponed. The feel of the soft skin over the muscles of his arm, the veins erect; the scar on his knee where he had gashed it as a child. Had he planned this from the start? Could what she knew now change what they'd had before; make it valueless? Could the joy be removed by hindsight? Exhausted by the day, she had no energy to pursue the thought.

But even if nothing could taint the actual pleasure stolen, there was no denying the brutal fact that her unwitting frankness had supplied the fuel for Camille's betrayal. And what had that done to Julia and Helen? Beside their fate, her sensibilities were unimportant. For them the events of the night must have been the ultimate agony. One moment freedom had been within their grasp, and the next it had been snatched away again. Madeleine had little doubt that, as a result, they would now be in even greater danger. And, in the most direct way imaginable, it was her fault. If anything happened to them, the blame would lie with her for the rest of her life. That would be a burden almost impossible to bear.

As she reached for the bottle of sleeping pills in her bedside drawer, Walker came into the room, shutting the door behind him.

'How're you feeling?' he said, sitting on the edge of the bed and holding her hand.

'It's all so terrible.' She remembered his tenderness earlier, in the bathroom, and realised that she wanted – needed – to tell him the truth.

'All we can do is pray,' he said.

Madeleine sat up, studying his face before she spoke. 'I want to tell you something. It's difficult . . . painful for both of us.'

'Maybe you don't have to.'

'What do you mean?'

Walker looked down at her hand. 'For some time now I've known that things were different. That you were preoccupied. At first I thought it was Shakespeare, but then I realised even Shakespeare doesn't make your eyes shine. Not before the performance, anyhow.'

'Is that all?'

'What more is there? Naming names? I'm not very interested in that.'

Madeleine withdrew her hand in irrational anger. 'What are you interested in?'

'I love you and I couldn't bear to lose you. I also love Julia and I want her back. That's what interests me.'

'You won't love me when I tell you. I don't love myself. I hate myself.' She resolved to have done with it here and now. Whether it was wise or foolish, there was no holding back. 'The man who ruined everything, the one who arrived at the cemetery – Charbonneaux, Camille Charbonneaux.'

'Him?' Walker's tone was both hurt and dumbfounded.

Madeleine nodded.

'And *you* told him?' The emphasis was quiet but insistent.

'Not like you mean. I talked, of course. I thought he was interested for Julia's sake so I talked. In that way I told him.'

Walker got up and crossed to the window. Looking out he said: 'Who is he?'

'Nobody in particular. A wine-grower. Not very successful.'

'Young? Old?'

'Thirty-six.'

'A little young for you, isn't he? Do you love him?'

There was no reply. Walker swung round, his tone no longer subdued. 'It's not a complicated question. Do you love him?'

'It's the most complicated question.'

'Don't play fucking word games with me. I want an answer. You owe me that. Do you love him?'

'Sometimes, in a way. That's why I trusted him. It was very, very stupid. I hate what he's done.'

Walker turned back to the window, unable to comfort her.

CHAPTER FIFTEEN

Daisy, her eyelids swollen from crying, was already sitting at the kitchen table when Tom came down again at five-thirty.

'Daise,' he said, bending to hug her. 'Have you not slept at all?'

'Not much. You?'

'Maybe an hour or two. I don't want to be asleep.'

'What are we going to do? They don't seem to have anything to go on. After all this time.'

'They'll have the registration number of the car they saw driving away from the cemetery for a start.'

'They could be false plates. Almost certainly will be.'

'They say they've got people under surveillance.'

'Well they would, wouldn't they? That's what they always say.'

Tom straightened up and poured himself a cup of coffee. 'Yesterday a friend of mine – Roland – came up with something about that.' He indicated the blow-up of the coat of arms. 'I had it done from the Polaroid the kidnappers sent. Roland reckoned it's not a heraldic beast at all. He says it's a horse.'

'Dad, for God's sake.' Angry, Daisy rose from her chair

and walked towards the open French windows. 'What's that got to do with anything?'

'I'm sorry, love. I know it seems trivial . . . '

'Too true. This is . . . this is the worst thing that's ever happened, Dad. We've got to do something. There's no time for being fanciful.'

Tom stood behind her and put his hands round her waist. 'I know. Do you want some toast? Bread or something? We've got honey and stuff.'

Daisy shook her head. 'I feel sick. Queasy. It's just nerves.'

Releasing her, Tom reached over and picked up Roland's drawing. 'The thing is, I've had this strange feeling about that crest right from the start. I can't really say why. I went and saw an expert. He had a few ideas but nothing came up. Then the minute old Roly saw it he spotted something I'd missed.'

Daisy turned and studied the sketch. 'Have you told the police?'

'No. Actually it's the gendarmes on this case. What could I say? "Look, Inspector, I've got this funny feeling?" He'd tell me to keep taking the tablets. Then Roly didn't see it till last night, and what with everything else it went out of my mind.'

'We'd better tell them now. Then at least we'll have done it. Just say it's probably nothing but it's something you've noticed. I suppose stranger things have happened.'

'OK. Do you want to come down to Bligny with me? Bit early but presumably there'll be somebody there.'

Daisy nodded. 'Is there anything else we can do to chase it up? I'd rather be doing something than nothing.'

'Well this chap in Beaune, an ex-teacher, Quignard, he's supposed to be an expert on families in the region – posh families, anyway. He might be worth asking. It's like pulling teeth, but what the hell.'

Daisy got up, her energy returning with the prospect of action. 'Let's do it. Bligny first, then on to Beaune.'

'Quignard's not going to like being woken up this early.'

'Tough,' Daisy said.

As they swung on to the Bligny road in the early morning sun, Tom told her what a magnificent ally Robert had been; how he had given his time and his total commitment.

'He's a good man,' Daisy said. 'We owe him a lot.'

At the incident room in the Hôtel de Ville, facing the main square where the Wednesday market was held, there were several weary faces. Gendarmes, male and female, uniformed and in plain clothes, had the anxious, haunted look of the sleepless. Explaining who they were, Tom and Daisy were treated with deference and taken to a trestle table in the far corner of the room, where a uniformed officer with a brush-cut, Adjutant Bouillot, was typing at a computer keyboard. As they were introduced he looked up and rose, holding out his hand first to Daisy and then to her father. His eyes, frank and alert, despite the shadows of long night hours, fixed on each in turn as he invited them to sit down.

'Major Granier told me he saw you last night,' he said to Tom, settling back in his seat. 'It was a catastrophe.'

Tom was encouraged by his frankness.

'But since then we have made considerable progress,' Bouillot went on.

'May we know what?' Daisy said.

'If you don't mind, just for the moment I think it's best if that information remains with us.' The look Bouillot gave her was part sympathy, part appraisal.

'They said if Mr Walker called in the gendarmes they would take reprisals,' Tom said. 'Do you think they meant it?'

Bouillot glanced at his computer screen while he considered his answer. 'I think it's a threat they were bound to make,' he said, turning back to Tom. 'They could hardly encourage him to go to the authorities, after all. On the other hand these are not entirely rational human beings we're dealing with here.

We shouldn't forget that.' Seeing the alarm on Tom's face, he qualified his statement. 'But on the whole I believe they want that money more than anything. They may change their terms but I think they will try one more time.'

'Only one? What if there's another catastrophe?' Tom said.

Bouillot wagged his forefinger. 'Ah no,' he said with a reassuring smile. 'One maybe, when the totally unexpected happens. Two, never. Absolutely never.'

Tom looked at Daisy, who mouthed 'show him'. Taking the enlargement of the crest out of a brown envelope, together with the drawing, Tom laid them on the table.

'What's this?' Bouillot said with a frown.

Keeping the story as clear as he could, Tom recounted what little there was to tell.

'It's curious,' Bouillot said when he'd finished. 'We'll see what we can do with it, of course. You were right to inform us.' His tone indicated more a willingness to appear helpful, than any positive interest. The interpretation was confirmed when he looked up at Tom and added: 'This Monsieur Viggars. He's an eccentric gentleman, isn't that so?' He touched his forehead with his index finger. 'A little bit mad?'

Tom smiled. 'I think it's just an impression he gives. I've a feeling he's no madder than the rest of us. He likes a drink, but don't we all?'

Bouillot managed a tired smile and summoned a colleague to photocopy the images at a nearby machine. When the copies had been returned to his desk, he handed the originals back to Tom and rose to end the interview. 'Well, thank you both for coming. I know how you must be feeling, but believe me we're doing everything in our power. It's nearly impossible, I understand that, but if you can just be patient a little while longer . . .'

Tom and Daisy were on their feet.

'Enchanted to meet you, mademoiselle,' Bouillot went on.

'And if either of you have any queries, any at all, you know where I am.'

'Bit of a charmer,' Tom said, as he and Daisy walked to the car.

'Imagine the Old Bill saying that: "enchanted to meet you"! I know it's all tosh, but it's very nice tosh,' Daisy said.

'He seemed on the ball. They all do. Let's just hope to God they nail these pigs today.'

Twenty minutes later, after a fast drive during which they didn't see a single other vehicle, they had their first view of the vineyards, in regimented descent from the crest of the hills to the valley road and beyond. In a few weeks, Tom was reminded, the slopes would be animated with pickers, and the miraculous, age-old transformation process would renew itself. The vines that had looked like gnarled, barren twigs in the early spring would yield enough fruit for an unimaginable output of some of the finest red wine on earth. Beyond lay Beaune, the wine's name and immediate destination, with its roofs, some of them conical, tiled in geometrical patterns of gold and maroon.

Parking in the Place Monge, beside the statue of the striding educator, Tom and Daisy walked to Quignard's house.

'Maybe we should have rung him first,' Tom said, remembering his reluctance ever to appeal to Quignard again.

'Think of mum, Dad. Nothing else matters.'

How wonderful it was to have Daisy with him, Tom thought, as he pressed the street bell. There was no response. He tried again. This time, after a delay of perhaps thirty seconds, a querulous voice replied.

'Who is it at this hour?'

'Monsieur Quignard, it's Tom Bellman again. I'm sorry it's so early but I've got a very great and urgent problem. Perhaps by now you've read in the newspapers . . . '

Before he could finish, to his surprise the buzzer sounded,

signifying that the door was open. More surprising still, Tom and Daisy had taken no more than ten steps into the courtyard when Alain Quignard appeared at his door. Wearing a purple silk dressing gown over yellow pyjamas, he looked as groomed and elegant as when he was fully clothed. This time he extended a long, pale hand in greeting.

'I'm so sorry,' he said. 'If you had told me last time . . . '

'I wanted to,' Tom said, 'but my instructions were to say nothing. It was very awkward. This is my daughter, Daisy, Monsieur Quignard.'

'Enchanted,' Quignard said, inclining his head. 'Come inside, won't you?'

They followed him through into his sitting room, where the severity of the bachelor's taste was somewhat softened by a demure floral fabric on the sofa and armchairs. His late mother's choice, Tom wondered? When they were seated, and Daisy had declined Quignard's considerate offer of refreshment, Tom once more ran through Roland's theory, showing the ex-schoolmaster the drawing. At the end of the brief explanation, Quignard put the tips of his fingers together and thought for a moment.

'You know, it's not my period,' he said at length. 'I have tended to interest myself only in notable families with deep roots. French families.'

Though Tom was sure he no longer intended to sound aloof, the habit was too ingrained to be dispensed with at a stroke.

'So you can't help us.' Daisy, conscious only of precious time, sounded abrupt.

Quignard appeared not to have noticed. 'In my view it could be an invention. A conceit,' he said. 'It is untypical, but France abounds in things that are untypical. It's part of her charm.'

Resisting the temptation to remind him of France's deep-rooted conservatism, Tom said: 'Last time we met, you thought you might have seen it before.'

Quignard inclined his head in a cautious nod. 'It does seem somewhat familiar, I confess, though where one has seen it . . .' His shrug was expressive of infinite possibilities, and none.

Accustomed by now to disappointment, Tom remained calm. 'Well, once again I'm very grateful to you,' he said, rising. 'We'd better get off. Sorry to have wasted your time.'

'Not at all,' Quignard said, getting up to show them out. 'I wish I could be more helpful. If anything occurs to me, I'll give you a call.' As he opened the front door, he added: 'And good luck. Soon the news will be good, I hope.'

Thanking him, Tom and Daisy made their way back to the Place Monge.

'Good lord; I've never seen such a change in a man,' Tom said. 'Last time he was horrible. You bring out the best in people, Daise.'

'No,' she said, 'it's mum who does that.'

On the way home they bought fresh bread and croissants from the baker in Bligny. Tom tried to persuade Daisy to have a *pain au chocolat* but she said it felt too much like a celebration. She'd have one when her mother was safe. Instead, in the kitchen, she spread fig jam on her croissant.

It was twenty to nine when Robert came in through the French windows from the garden. Taking out of his pocket three fresh, brown eggs, which he presented to Daisy, he welcomed her with a kiss on both cheeks. While he sat over a cup of coffee, Tom brought him up to date with the events of the morning. Listening without interruption, Robert seemed sceptical and distracted.

'We can't ignore anything,' he said, when Tom had finished.

'Are you all right?' Tom said. 'You seem far away.'

'Me. Yes, of course,' Robert drained his cup and rose. 'A lot to do.' Smiling at Daisy, he said he would see her again very soon, and went out the way he had entered.

Sensing from his manner that he had left things unsaid, Tom

followed him into the garden. When they reached the back gate, well out of earshot of the kitchen, Robert turned.

'Tom, I should tell you something. The gendarmes told me not to but I think you have a right to know.'

Tom stopped, already prepared for unwelcome news by Robert's tone.

'It doesn't change anything, you understand, but still there's no point in hiding it from you.'

'Just tell me, please.'

'The night we raided Gazin's house, remember?'

Tom nodded.

'I mentioned to you I told the gendarmes, but I didn't tell you I'd found something. It was at the back of a drawer in the kitchen. A woman's comb.'

Forcing himself to be calm, Tom was holding his breath. 'Not . . . ?'

'No. Absolutely not,' Robert said, understanding his fear. 'The name on the comb was Stéphane. I took it the next morning to the gendarmes, when you gave me a lift down to Bligny.'

'Why didn't you say?'

'Because at the time it proved nothing at all and I didn't want to alarm you. But this is what you must know, Tom. You've probably forgotten but Stéphane was the name of the girl I told you about who was murdered, on the common land at the edge of the village.'

Shocked, Tom tried to make connections but found himself floundering. 'So . . . so they think Gazin did it?'

Robert nodded. 'They made a thorough search of the house and they found something else. Under a floorboard, apparently. They wouldn't say much but whatever it is, it's been sent for tests. DNA.'

'And you think . . . they think that as well as that . . . ?'

'They suspect Gazin is one of the kidnappers. There. That's it.'

Tom leaned on the gate. 'Oh my God.'

'I thought for a long time about not telling you but in the end Yvonne said it wasn't the act of a friend, to leave you ignorant.'

'Two women . . . ' was all Tom could say. 'He's taken two women.' He looked at Robert. 'What if this thing's not about money at all?'

'Hold on a moment. Even if the gendarmes are right, he doesn't need to kidnap for that. Also he's not alone. He couldn't have done this without accomplices. They wouldn't all have gone this far just for . . . if it wasn't for money.'

'But what if they get desperate, after last night? What if they think they're not going to get the money?'

'What did the adjutant say about that?'

'He said he thought they'd give it one more go.'

'I agree,' Robert said.

'So this guy's voice must be on the tapes,' Tom said, his head beginning to clear.

'They've played them to people who know him but often the voice is muffled. They know Gazin can't have been at the farm for a while now. The animals were in a terrible state. And before that we knew he was coming and going at night.'

Tom thought for a moment. 'You were right to tell me,' he said. 'If I'd found out later you'd known all along . . . '

'What about Daisy? Will you tell her?'

'I don't know. I can't at the moment; she must be exhausted, poor love. I'll have to think about that.'

'With any luck it will all be over before you have to.'

'Do you honestly think so, Robert?'

'Yes,' Robert said. 'I believe it.'

'What about the number plates on the car that got away? Have they had any luck with those?'

'The Beaune area, apparently. Now they're making progress.'

* * *

Félix lay silent on the camp-bed. Henri had closed the eyes which had been open even while resting. Why was Félix sleeping so much? It must be the strain of the past few days; the tension of last night. In his own time he would wake and they would finish this thing. Get him to a doctor if he needed it. Drive a couple of hundred kilometres south and pull into a small town somewhere. Round Lyons, maybe. There'd be plenty of money to keep the doctor quiet. They made out they were like priests, but it all came down to money in the end. Rest up for a couple of days – longer if need be – and then drive away to a place where nobody would ever find them. Maybe avoid the A6, on second thoughts. Maybe keep to the D roads, where there wasn't much traffic and nobody paid attention to it anyway.

But things needed doing now and with Félix asleep, Henri would have to make the decisions himself. Above all, one thing was clear to him. He couldn't bear for this to end without the ransom. He would call Walker again. He'd raise the price to . . . what? Fifteen million? How long would it take Walker to get hold of the extra? The lying creep would pretend it was difficult. He'd ask for more time, as if he cared more about the sous than he did about his daughter. No. That was hopeless. No more time. Henri couldn't stand any more of this. It had to be today. Pick a place for the handover and get on with it. Make it ten million, like before. That would have to be enough. There was no need to give Paul any. Just drive him somewhere and tell him the share-out would come at the other end. Then dump him by the road, a long way from home. He might squeal but who was going to listen? A village idiot with a stutter, ranting on about being cheated? Anyway, if Paul said that, they'd know he'd been part of it. The moron would finish up in gaol. Or worse; a madhouse.

Henri was so pleased with the plan he felt like celebrating.

The trouble was, Félix had hidden the booze and he hadn't been able to find it. Send Paul out for some. He could get some fresh bread while he was at it. And butter. Henri hadn't tasted butter in days. Thick and yellow, like his mother had made. And sometimes she would spread it on the crisp loaf and sprinkle sugar on top. He could taste the sweetness now, the way his teeth sank into the creamy surface, with the granules to make it more interesting. And then the bite into the crusty shell of the bread. Yes, he would breakfast on that and then make the call. But what to do about the women? Should he feed them? No, why bother? A few more hours and it would all be over. The Englishwoman hadn't shown any interest in food anyway. And the American was young enough. She'd survive. That was a point though. Why hang on to both of them? Right at the start he'd told Félix they didn't need the Englishwoman. He no longer remembered what Félix had said, but Henri had let it go. Now it didn't make any sense at all to keep her alive. She wasn't good for any money because they didn't know who she was. When they'd put her back in her cell last night, she had just lain there like someone in a trance. And with Félix out of action for the moment, two prisoners were more than Henri and Paul could cope with. No, better to make it simple. Henri could have it done before Félix recovered. Maybe dig a hole first, like he had before. That wouldn't take long. It didn't have to be deep. He could make a start and then get Paul to finish it when he was back from the shop. No need to tell him what it was for. And Félix would understand. He'd even be pleased. It was another thing he wouldn't have to worry about.

Feeling stronger and more certain than he had for a while, Henri went to the top of the cellar steps. 'Paul,' he shouted. 'Leave them and come here. I need something.'

The longer the morning wore on, the more Tom dwelt on what

Robert had said about Gazin. Helen was in the hands of a killer. Well, it wasn't proved but it seemed almost certain. A killer whose victim had been a woman. Tom tried everything he knew to keep a grip on hope. Most murders were in the family; perhaps Gazin and the girl had been related. Perhaps he had killed her in a fit of jealousy. Maybe he hadn't meant to go that far but had underestimated his own strength. Maybe, perhaps, suppose . . . But soon Tom conceded it was pointless. There was no getting round the fact that Helen was in mortal danger. And somehow, God knew how, they must get to her before the kidnappers had second thoughts.

Tom had decided not to tell Daisy. The truth, he felt, could tip her into despair. She might blame him afterwards for keeping the information to himself, but that was a chance he would have to take. Meanwhile, unable to remain inactive a moment longer, he suggested they go for a short walk. To his relief Daisy agreed and, having told Robert they would take the mobile with them, they set off in the direction of Charmoy. The pace was brisk. Both wanted to be absorbed, if only in physical effort. They needed to exhaust themselves; to be too tired to think. Not yet tired enough, however, each was too preoccupied to say much. It was as though, for the sake of sanity, they had made a silent pact to avoid the one subject that both burned to analyse. Tom tried asking about Daisy's job in the London saleroom, but her answers were unengaged. She wondered whether they might be able to contact Frank through an embassy, but Tom said he had no idea which to approach. This was a concern he had managed to edge from his mind. As yet Frank knew nothing of this entire episode. Tom prayed that he wouldn't find out via some newspaper headline, a long way from home.

Passing the sign that marked the boundary of the village, they began to climb the gentle gradient that led to Charmoy. For some while their thoughts had been accompanied by irregular bleating from the field to their left. Now the sound seemed to take on a new urgency and, glancing in its direction, Daisy tugged at Tom's sleeve. At the far side of the field, beside a hedge bordering an orchard, a sheep was caught in the barbed wire fence.

'Poor thing,' Daisy said. 'We'd better tell somebody.'

'Won't take a minute,' Tom said. 'We'll do it.'

Tom climbed over the metal gate, next to the water trough, and crossed the field, almost grateful for the distraction. While Daisy wrestled with the uncooperative animal's hindquarters, in an attempt to stop it pulling away and tearing its flesh, Tom identified the point where its neck had been speared, and freed it. Bleating even louder than before, the sheep ran off to rejoin the flock.

Before turning back and resuming the walk for which he had little real appetite, Tom looked into the orchard, noticing for the first time that beneath the trees were parked a number of pieces of agricultural machinery. Ploughs, harrows, balers, even an old wooden-sided threshing machine. Some had the metal seats, pierced with holes, that he remembered from childhood. Others were so choked with undergrowth it was almost impossible to guess their function. The range of their ages suggested that this was more than a mechanical graveyard. Instead it seemed to be a haphazard collection, built up over years by an enthusiast, either with an eye to future value, or an affection for the past.

Unable to resist, Tom ducked under the top strand of wire, squeezed through a gap in the hedge and entered the open-air museum. In a sense it couldn't have been better planned. The fact that it was random and claimed by the grass was much more fitting than any urban installation. Here the rusting metal was reunited with the soil. If undisturbed long enough, the two would become one again.

'You going to be long, Dad?' Daisy called

'Back in a minute,' Tom said. 'It's fascinating, this.'

'Riveting,' Daisy muttered.

As Tom passed ploughs, he grasped their handles, imagining the straight furrows ahead, and the broad backside of the horse between the shafts. His grandfather, Joe, had worked with one of these, cultivating eleven acres in Cheshire, on the edge of Delamere forest. Tom remembered the foamy lather the horse worked up where the harness was in contact with its flanks, like froth on beer; the way its nostrils flared before it whinnied; and the neat, deliberate placement of its shaggy hooves. Joe would have loved this. But how would he have reacted to Helen's plight, Tom wondered? His sense of outrage would have been terrible and unquenchable. He would have rounded up an elderly posse and gone looking for the kidnappers himself. And God help them if he'd caught them. Joe's had been an uncomplicated view of the world.

The memory of the indomitable old man made Tom wonder whether he'd done enough. Had he been guilty of sitting back and waiting for developments? Could he have done more to trace Helen or put pressure on the kidnappers? But how? That was the worst of it. How did you get to grips with an invisible enemy who left no clues? As Tom felt the burden of his inaction, he reached the old threshing machine, faded now to a dusty rose colour, and buried to the axles in weeds. Better be getting back. Daisy would be worried and impatient. He looked at his watch. Ten past eleven. Just a quick glance at the other side and then straight home. It was rare to see these things now. He wished he had his camera with him. Instead, photographing the details in his mind, he noted the perished drive-belt, green with algae, and the rusting wheels which it had once worn to a shine.

Then, turning the corner, he stopped; all his faculties focused on the half-obliterated design that occupied a discreet panel low and to the right on the wooden bodywork of the thresher.

Though bleached by time and weather, it was unmistakable; the horse and chevrons Roland had sketched in Tom's kitchen. Just as the puppeteer had predicted, the horse was prancing, forelegs in the air, its generous mane flying like a romantic pennant. Tom felt choked with excitement.

'Daise!' he yelled. 'Daise, come here quick!'

'We'd better get back, Dad. Come on.'

Tom ran to where she could see him. 'Darling no, come here please. It's important. You've got to see this.'

'What?' she said when she joined him.

'Look!' Taking her by the arm, he guided her to the crest.

'How amazing! It's exactly the same as that other thing. Look there's something underneath. Some writing.' Squatting, she peered at the faint, hand-painted script which Tom had failed to notice.

'I'll have to get my eyes fixed,' he said. 'What is it? Can you make it out?'

'Something "*et fils*" – "and son". Looks like something something "s-q". " . . . o-s-q" that's it. " . . . o-s-q", then it must be a "u" after that. " . . . o-s-q-u". What's that at the beginning? "C" isn't it? "C-o-s-q-u . . . ", and an "n" at the end. Do you think? "Cosqu" something "n"? " . . . i" presumably. "Cosquin and Son." Then there's an " . . . e-a-u-n" with something missing at the end . . . and the beginning come to that. "P" is that? "P-e-a-u-n . . . "?'

'Beaune!' Tom said. 'Not a "P", a "B". "Cosquin and Son, of Beaune."'

'Yes!' Daisy said, her small fist raised in celebration. 'Cosquin and Son of Beaune. Gotcha! But where do we go from here?' She stood up. 'Ask the farmer, do you think?'

Tom shook his head. 'Better get back. We can always ring him. Robert'll have his number. So that's why the horse,' he went on, as they crossed the field. 'Agricultural machinery. Either manufacturers or dealers, presumably. Horsepower!'

'Not a regular coat of arms at all but just a commercial logo.'

'I had a funny feeling it was new money,' Tom said. 'I'm not sure where it gets us, but at least it's something.'

'Tell the gendarmes?'

'I'll do it now,' Tom said. 'Damn, I've left the Bligny number at home. It'll have to wait a couple of minutes.'

'Do you think they'll take it seriously?'

'Bouillot seemed a sensible bloke. I'm sure he'll check it out. Maybe we'll get there first.' Tom took her hand. 'Either way, love, we're going to beat these scum.'

The revelations of the night before and a consequent lack of sleep had left William Walker in an uncompromising frame of mind. He knew it was a dangerous one. Even now, after the debacle, he should be prepared to be reasonable. The only thing that mattered was getting Julia back, even if it meant grovelling. But whatever common sense dictated, he was no longer in the mood for that. His wife's lover had hatched a plot behind his back based on her information, however unwitting she had been, and the time for conciliation was over. When the kidnappers rang he was determined to be firm. They must be made to understand that this was their last chance. From here on in, any demands would be his.

The telephone in his study rang at five minutes to twelve. The voice at the other end of the line was rough and impatient.

'Tonight. The stone cross outside Chazilly; the road to Ste Sabine.'

'Time?' Walker said.

'Just leave the money in the hedge by the entrance to the side road.'

'And my daughter and the Englishwoman? Where will they be?'

'Shut up. Who do you think you are? You think you're a

big man? You're just a . . . you're nothing.'

'Tell me when and where you will release the hostages or . . . '

'Find out,' the caller said. 'If you're so clever, find out. Any tricks and this time I'll blow their heads off. Understand? Any sign of a gendarme – I mean even one – and I'll put it in their mouths and blow their heads off.' With that he hung up.

Walker put down the receiver. He had never felt so angry. Or so useless. This kidnapper sounded volatile, unbalanced. Since they now saw Walker's side as untrustworthy, they could no longer be trusted themselves. This time the situation was much more unstable and unpredictable than before. Damn Charbonneaux! How could he have imagined he'd get away with it? And damn Madeleine. Damn her. All the sophistication in the world, the utmost willingness to try and understand, couldn't rationalise the terrifying consequences of her betrayal. When he looked up, she was standing at the door.

'What did they say?' Her voice sounded weary and resigned. After their bitter conversation, she had spent the night in a guest bedroom.

'Tonight. A stone cross outside Chazilly. It was a different one this time. He sounds more dangerous.' Why should he spare her the anguish, Walker thought?

'Do you want me to leave?'

'What do you want?'

'I want it not to have happened.'

'You've had what you wanted. That's one thing you can't have.'

'Shall I go?'

Walker looked at her, pausing before he answered. 'Stay for Julia,' he said. 'After that . . . I don't know.'

As Tom and Daisy turned into the courtyard in front of the house, Robert ran towards them from his front door.

'Quick,' he said as they got out of the car. 'I've just had a telephone call.'

'Quick what?' Tom said.

Robert indicated his car. 'We have to get going.'

'Where?'

'I'll tell you on the way.'

As Tom broke off to join him, Daisy looked confused.

'What shall I do, Dad? Shall I come with you?'

Tom paused to think. 'It's probably best if you stay, love, if you don't mind. Chase the other thing up. Tell Bouillot, and find out as much as you can about Cosquin and Son. Whether there's any big house associated with them. God knows what this is going to turn out to be,' he inclined his head towards Robert, who was getting into the car, 'but I'll be back as soon as I can. You've got the mobile number?'

Nodding, Daisy disappeared into the house while Tom got into the passenger seat, and Robert swung out of the courtyard, scattering the gravel.

'What is it?' Tom said.

'I just had two calls. One was Walker. The kidnappers say the money's to be left at Chazilly tonight. By the cross, behind a hedge. This time it was a different one. Probably Gazin. And then Michel rang from the garage bar at Foissy.'

'What did he say?'

'He said there's a young man there. Came in about three-quarters of an hour ago. Sat at the bar on his own. Nothing to say for himself. Started drinking Ricard. Began to open up a bit. Obviously not used to alcohol. Started talking about his friend who was making him do things. He was fed up, he said. He'd had enough.'

'What sort of things?'

'Michel asked him that . . . Get out of the way you stupid animal!' Robert thumped his horn several times, sending an elderly sheepdog scampering for the safety of the grass verge.

'He tried to draw him out,' he said, resuming his account. 'The young man mentioned money. He said he was only hanging on for the money. Then he'd be out of there, because his friend was mad.'

'Has he gone? Where's he gone?' Tom said, his mind racing.

'He's still there,' Robert said. 'At least he was when I put the telephone down.'

Tom's expression was a mixture of anxiety and anticipation. 'Can't she go any quicker?' he said. 'We should have taken mine.'

'If you insult her, she'll stop altogether,' Robert said.

'Was he on foot, this man? They must be very close if he is.'

'No,' Robert said. 'He has a scooter. Apparently he stopped for two-stroke and then he found he had a slow puncture. So he fitted the spare wheel and then he had a drink. And then another, et cetera, et cetera.'

'It must be one of them, mustn't it?' Tom's hopeful tone invited only one answer.

'I can't believe it's a coincidence. You do get hoaxers in cases like this but Michel's intelligent. He wouldn't be taken in easily. Ah! I forgot. We left so fast I never rang Granier, or your friend Bouillot. Stupid. Better ring them now, Mr Professor.'

Tom made the call. Bouillot, who said that Daisy had already been on to him, noted the details and promised to send men at once. At the crossroads, Tom craned forward to see if he could make anything out on the garage forecourt, but his view was obscured by an outbuilding. When they turned the corner and got their first view of the pumps, however, there was no sign of a scooter.

'What does that mean?' Tom said.

'I don't know.'

Robert skidded to a halt and the two men ran to the café. In the short, dark passage behind the bar, Michel, the proprietor, was on the telephone.

'What happened? Where is he?' Robert said.

Michel replaced the receiver and joined them. 'I was just trying to get you again,' he said. 'He left. Maybe five minutes ago. I think he saw me calling you and even though he was half pissed, he must have thought something was wrong.'

Tom put his elbows on the bar, his head slumping forward. 'Did you see which way he went?'

Michel nodded. 'I ran out after him, naturally. He took off that way. The Ste Sabine road. I had a funny feeling I'd seen him before, but I can't remember where.'

'Thanks, Michel. The gendarmes will be here any minute. Tell them we're after him.'

Back in the car, Tom's disappointment gave way once more to hope. 'They're not very quick are they, scooters?' he said.

'No match for this,' Robert said. 'We'll eat him.'

'Do you think this is finally it, Robert?'

'Patience, my friend. Just a little more patience. We deserve some luck now.'

At the junction with the Painblanc road, Tom raised a sudden doubt. 'He could have branched off anywhere, couldn't he? He needn't necessarily have stuck to this road.'

'I wasn't a traffic cop for nothing,' Robert said. 'You get a feel for these things.'

Tom turned the assurance over in his mind. Could that be true, or was Robert just trying to encourage him? Either way, he needed to believe it.

A few hundred metres after they had passed the village boundary of Chazilly, Robert pointed out the stone cross which was to be that evening's pick-up-point. Standing in the shade of a tree, the cross bore the inscription: '1937. Fiat Voluntas Tua.' If God's will had been done in the ten years of suffering that followed, Tom found himself thinking, He must have a strange sense of humour. But how could it have been His will, any more than He could will anything but Helen's safe return?

At the base of the cross, the road forked. To the left was a narrow lane bordered at first by the hedge, where the money was to be placed, and then flanked by cornfields on both sides. The way ahead, meanwhile, was the main road to Ste Sabine. Braking, Robert weighed up the alternatives and opted for the lane.

'Are you sure?' Tom said. 'Why wouldn't he have stuck to the major road?'

'You learn to think like they do,' Robert said. 'I think this animal said to himself: "If there's anybody following, they'll never think of going down here." But we did, you slug, and you'll never stop us now.' Robert's face reflected his determination.

A short distance further on the lane began to fall away towards the canal and the A6. High on the hill beyond the motorway stood the mediaeval castle of Châteauneuf, close to the spot where Tom and Robert had found the envelope containing the Polaroid. To Tom it felt like a month ago. Since then he had known such extremes of optimism and despair that he might have fought a war; except that he had been unable to find the front line. The fact that, after all this, ending the agony might depend on catching a drunk on a scooter seemed absurd, but what did it matter as long as Helen slept at home tonight?

'There!' Robert said, as they rounded bend. 'He must have come off.'

The scooter had somehow left the road and landed in a ditch. There, riderless, it lay on its side. Robert pulled up beside it and he and Tom jumped out to investigate. A bottle of light brown liquid had worked loose from the pannier and had smashed on the metal frame. From the pungent smell Tom could tell it was cheap brandy. Above the ditch was a dense, extensive wood, which had not been visible from the cross.

'Let's get at him,' Robert said, scrabbling up the steep side of the ditch. 'Just let me get my hands on him.'

Tom followed him into the green fringe of trees, making a further, hurried call to Bligny before the signal was interrupted.

'He can't have gone far,' Robert said. Then he shouted the same message, which was returned by a slight echo. 'Listen to me, pigface!' he went on, bellowing now. 'We're coming to get you. Nothing can save you. Nothing. You might as well come out, then you've nothing to fear. If you make me find you, you'll be very, very sorry. The gendarmes are on their way. Be sensible, pigface. Give yourself up.' The effort of shouting and running at the same time left Robert so winded that he had to stop, bent double, to get his breath back. 'Hell,' he muttered. 'I'm like an old balloon. Let the air out and I collapse. Bravo, Mr Professor. Catch the swine. I'll be with you in a moment.' After a respite of perhaps twenty seconds, Robert straightened and resumed the hunt.

Continuing on his own, Tom tried to listen for tell-tale sounds as he ran, but it proved impossible. His own panting obliterated everything. Minutes later he was distracted by a siren from the direction of the road, which he assumed signalled the arrival of the gendarmes. The search had become almost impossible. There was so much cover on every side that, given his head start, the kidnapper, if it really was him, held all the cards. Drunk or sober, he could hide more or less wherever he chose. It was true that when the gendarmes were deployed, his options would be more limited, but by then he might be out of the wood and into a hijacked car, or a safe house, or anywhere. If only this had been open land, he would have stood no chance, but fate had provided him with the perfect camouflage, and it would take a major stroke of luck to flush him out. All the luck had gone to the kidnappers up to now, Tom thought, with the exception of the crest on the old thresher. He wondered what sort of progress Daisy was making with that?

Stopping for a breather, he was rejoined by Robert, still puffing from his exertions.

'Dogs are what we need,' Robert said. 'Sniff his trail and shake him like a rat. But the nearest dog section's probably in Dijon. Fat lot of good that is. We're so close too. He can't be more than five minutes ahead of us.'

'He's younger than us, don't forget. He can cover a lot of ground in five minutes.'

'We've given him a big fright, though. And now he's got to get back on foot he'll be conspicuous. He'll probably wait till it gets dark, and by that time the others will be in a muck sweat.'

'What will that mean for the handover?'

'Shouldn't affect it. They won't know what sort of trouble he's in until it's too late. Come on, we're wasting time. You take that side. I'll take this. We're not giving up until we're sure he's not here.'

Joined by an advance party of six gendarmes, and later by five more, Tom and Robert searched the wood for another hour. When Adjutant Bouillot arrived, he advised Tom to go home and leave the hunt to the professionals. It was important, he said, that Tom should be ready to react to the events of the evening. Thanking them for their prompt action in notifying search headquarters, Bouillot walked back to the road with Tom and Robert. On the way he revealed that the tape of that morning's telephone conversation between Walker and the second kidnapper had been played to villagers in St Luc, three of whom had identified the speaker as Henri Gazin, the missing farmer. Tom noted with some relief that Bouillot still did not touch on suspicions about Gazin's involvement in murder.

As they reached the ditch beside the road, a young gendarme wearing gloves was making a preliminary search of the scooter's pannier. He had removed the remains of the brandy bottle and, as Tom drew level with him, was drawing out a packet of butter. Next came two compact cardboard boxes stained with the spirit. He opened one, revealing orange-coloured shotgun cartridges. Seeing Tom's expression, he said: 'Well, at least if they're here he can't be using them.' He laid them beside him and withdrew a fresh oval-shaped loaf, one end of which was also soaked in the alcohol.

'This must be his lunch,' he said. 'He's going to be hungry.'

Tom watched as he placed the bread on the grass. Delving into the pannier again, the gendarme now withdrew a short, silver torch. Tom paid little attention to this until the gendarme adjusted his grip on the barrel and revealed a piece of soiled sticking plaster round the middle. All of a sudden, Tom felt the stirrings of recognition.

'Excuse me, could I see that?' he asked.

'I'm afraid I can't let you handle it, monsieur. There may be prints.'

'I understand that, but can you just hold it a bit nearer so I can see?'

The gendarme did as he asked.

'Could you turn it a little?' Tom mimed the direction with a roll of his finger.

Again the gendarme complied. Tom leaned forward. Written on the plaster in biro, indistinct to anyone but him, was a single word made up of uneven capital letters. The word, which made Tom feel light-headed for the second time that week, was 'BELLMAN'.

CHAPTER SIXTEEN

Beyond the wood Paul had broken through a hedge and, shielded from his pursuers, had made rapid progress towards the canal. Forcing himself to run half-crouched, despite the pains in his chest and side and the fuzziness caused by the Ricard, he aimed for the lock-keeper's cottage beside the road to Pont d'Ouche. His aunt Edith lived there. Though she wasn't a comfortable woman, at least he knew she wouldn't give him away. He hadn't seen her for months now. What if she was out? Then he'd hide in an outhouse until she got back, or cross the footbridge and lie low somewhere on the other side. They'd never find him there, those bully-boys in the wood. All that shouting. Still, they hadn't been far behind. At one point, when he stumbled, he'd thought they were going to catch him. But he knew this country better than they did. He'd known it from childhood, when he'd come birds'-nesting with his cousin, Bernard, and learning about sex with Julie from the little shop at Ste Sabine. She was luscious, Julie. How come she'd known so much more than they did? She must have learned it along with the alphabet. What had happened to her, he wondered? Fat with three kids, he supposed. Anyway, it had been great while it lasted. After that he hadn't had much luck with girls.

It was the spots that did it. They'd left his face looking horrible – all pasty and pock-marked. He'd tried to be funny instead, but he didn't seem to have the knack. The stammer hadn't helped, either. They laughed at that, but not for the right reasons.

Why the hell was he thinking about Julie when he was running for his life? It was the alcohol. He wasn't used to it. For a while it had been good. In the bar he'd forgotten Henri for a few minutes, talking to that nice guy. Then he'd seen the barman on the phone and even though he was a bit pissed by then, he'd known something wasn't right. So he'd put his foot down, but the fresh air got to him and within a few hundred metres he'd had trouble keeping the scooter straight. Two or three times he'd run up on the verge and then, taking a bend too fast and skidding on fresh cow-shit as he braked, he'd ended up in that ditch. Stupid thing to do. The smell of the brandy was the first thing he'd noticed. Henri would kill him. Already he'd been away much longer than he'd said and now he'd be coming back empty-handed. No bread, nothing. God, Henri *would* kill him, no question. He'd seen him kill Félix, though Henri was too thick to realise what he'd done. Poor Félix. Lying there dead and the stupid sod thought he was asleep. Félix had been decent. Being with him had made Paul feel part of a team. He liked that. And Félix would have seen to it that he got his fair share of the money. But the other lunatic wouldn't. He'd keep the lot, just like the American said. Shoot him and keep the lot.

Since there was no sign that his pursuers had left the wood, Paul stopped for a moment and held his side. The stitch felt like his appendix was bursting; a sharp pain that seemed to get worse with every step. His breath was coming in great heaving gasps and his forearms were bleeding from the brambles. Still, just to be free was something. That dungeon he'd been in for what felt like a year had begun to get him down. It was like he was a prisoner. Hours and hours of boredom, crap food, no booze, the only decent man dead, and a maniac in charge. When he looked at it from here it seemed crazy. Why go back at all? He'd managed all right without much money before he met Félix and he'd manage again. Maybe get a job at that bar. He fancied that. People to chat to and a free drink now and again. Girls went for barmen. He'd get expert at polishing the glasses, and that stuff, and sometimes maybe he'd forget to charge them. Just wink and smile, so they'd know.

The pleasant prospect was interrupted by a sudden wave of nausea. Putting his head between his knees, Paul vomited, smelling again the sour spirit. Blast. There was some down his shirt, which was already soaked in sweat. What would his aunt say about that? He could give it a quick wash in the canal before he got there. Hearing faint voices from the direction of the wood, he straightened and jogged on. Now there was a sharp ache in his head, which made him grit his teeth and wince at every step. What about the American and the other woman, he thought? What would happen to them if he stayed away? Would Henri care about the ransom enough to keep them alive? Would he claim it and kill them anyway? Who could say what the loony would do? Paul hoped they'd be safe. He'd had little to do with the other one, but he liked the American. She was a great looker and she'd taken a real interest in him. She didn't deserve to die. Besides, if he helped her, she'd see that he got money. She was rolling in it. Two hundred thousand francs, she'd said; all in used notes. It was hard to imagine that much. He could get some sharp clothes and a decent motorbike. But how could he do anything for her without risking his own life? Just tell somebody, maybe. Ring the gendarmes and tell them where to find her, without saying who he was. That might not be a bad idea. Then, later, he could contact her and she'd see him right. Or would she? Félix had warned him that people say anything when they're frightened; then, when they're free, it's all different. And Félix wasn't a liar. So maybe it was best just to forget the whole thing. Get somewhere safe and wait for it all to blow over. Anyway, whatever happened he'd done one thing for the American. At least he'd thought to take the shotgun cartridges before he left the château. He was glad about that. And come to think of it, that was another reason he couldn't go back. Even Henri would have worked that one out. But when it was all over, what a story Paul could tell! If he met a woman he trusted over that bar, he wouldn't half impress her with his adventure. He could even make bits up and she'd never know. Swear her to secrecy and say he'd saved the hostages single-handed by taking the ammunition. Well, he had, in a way.

Ever since he'd left the wood, the sky had been growing darker. Now, as he reached the road that bordered the canal, he felt the first drops of rain and heard them putt-putting on the dry leaves. This was still a fair way north of where he wanted to be, and he didn't fancy getting soaked on top of everything else. Best to sit it out for a while. He looked around for shelter and spotted a worn tarpaulin lying in the ditch. Lifting the edge, and ignoring the musty, rubbery smell which was in any case overpowered by his own stench, he slipped underneath. It reminded him of camping when he was a kid, that night he'd woken up with his head out of the tent, when the lightning was like a firework display. He would stay here until the rain stopped. The rest would do him good too. Then, when he felt stronger, he would make his way parallel to the canal and slip into the house unnoticed. Meanwhile, as he closed his eyes, he gave himself over to the pain, knowing that when he drifted into sleep, it would go away.

By three o'clock, Henri was in such torment that the only way he could find relief was by pounding his fists once again on the stone wall. The scars on the knuckles opened and the blood

oozed. He licked it, remembering the brandy he had asked
Paul to bring. But Paul had never come back. The traitor. And
Félix lay there, still, with his eyes closed, saying nothing. Henri
couldn't bear it any longer. He needed to hold him. Everything
was wrong. He couldn't keep up with the thoughts in his head.
They were like lights in a village at night, being switched on
and off all the time, as though children were playing games.
When he tried to concentrate on one, it went out again and he
couldn't tell which would come on next.

Walking over to the camp-bed, he sat beside his friend and
cradled his head. Félix was so cold. That must be why he needed
the sleep. It must be the sort of fever where you went cold
instead of hot. He'd be all right later. But Henri needed him
now. Just to feel that warmth he'd only known from two people
in his life – his mother and Félix. It wasn't a lot to ask but
without it, living was just getting through the day. And the
night. That's what had made Félix so important. Not being
alone any more. Well, he wasn't alone now, but with Félix so
ill it wasn't the same. He held his cheek to his friend's face,
feeling the bristles against his own. They both needed a shave,
and a bath, and that bread and butter. Paul must have eaten it
himself. And drunk the brandy. Bastard. Maybe he'd go to the
flics, the little runt. Tell them where the women were. No,
he'd never do that. He hadn't the guts. But if he did, Henri
would find him and pay him off with the shotgun. He didn't
even have second thoughts about using it any more. It was just
like potting rabbits. Squeeze the trigger and bang, it was all
over. But thinking about it brought his father back, and that
time in the cowshed, and the sudden explosion, and his face
flying apart, and he wanted to scream until his lungs hurt.

Getting to his feet, he walked over to the fireplace and
looked at himself in the big old mirror. He had a vague memory
of the American standing here for the photograph. Fat lot of
good that had been. All those plans, and somebody just stepped

in and screwed the whole thing. What they should have done
was stop Walker himself, maybe when he was out in his big
black car, and frighten the money out of him. All this stuff
with the women had been a complete waste of time. Feeding
them, making phone calls, the worry of guarding them . . . He
couldn't bear to spend another night in this place, with no one
to talk to. It was spooky in the dark; all those high ceilings and
long corridors. Sometimes he thought he could hear voices.
Nothing you could understand, just snatches of talk. He couldn't
even tell what language they spoke. But he had the feeling
they were muttering about him. Ganging up on him in corners
and empty rooms. He couldn't stand that on his own, with no
lights. When he'd looked earlier he couldn't even find the torch.
That stupid oaf Paul must have taken it with him. So what was
he going to do with the women? Try to think. Try to just work
this out and then there'd be no more worries. Take the money,
lay Félix on the back seat where he could rest, and point the
car towards Lyons on a quiet road. What could Walker do
about it? Nothing, for the sake of the women. With the cash
gone there'd be a chase, but Henri had already shown he was
more than a match for those stupid gendarmes, even in a van!
When he was in the car they'd have no chance.

So that was it then. It all seemed so simple now. Finish the
women, make the pick-up at Chazilly, and off. And the beauty
of it was that using the shotgun on both of them might stop
that voice in his head once and for all. He could imagine feeling
calm for ever after that. No need for any more. He could see
his mother smiling. At last she would be satisfied. For a few
moments the flickering lights of his thoughts no longer
tormented him. Drawing closer to the mirror, he peered at his
reflection. The image he saw disturbed him. It was the face of
a stranger. A week's growth of beard, the dark, greasy hair
sticking up, the deep shadows under the eyes, all made it look
wild and hunted. But the strangest thing was that the two sides

didn't seem to match. It was as though a child's drawing had been ripped down the middle and stuck together wrong. That was horrible. Henri shut his eyes to keep it out. This wasn't him at all. This was somebody looking through from the other side. He'd have to destroy it. Turning, he re-opened his eyes and looked for something heavy. Down by the camp-bed he saw the small gas canister. That would do. He wouldn't need it any more anyway. Running across the room he picked it up and, racing back, hurled it at the mirror. The old glass shattered, and some fell out of the frame, but the face was still there. It was still staring at him from the space where the reflection had been. He had to get out of here. Get the shotgun now and do the thing. Then take Félix and wait somewhere in the car if need be, until it was darker. But where had he left the twelve-bore? He'd taken it with him down the cellar, hadn't he? But where had he put it when he came back up? What had happened to his memory? He couldn't remember things he'd done minutes ago. Must be because he was hungry. Damn Paul. This was all his fault. Try the next room, where the door to the cellar was. Yes, there, leaning against the wall! Just break it first, make sure there were cartridges. Funny. It was empty. He could have sworn he'd put a couple in before Paul left. No problem. Plenty more in the van.

Exhilarated now, Henri ran into the stable yard and searched in the glove compartment. Nothing. Must have been mistaken. Must be in the car. Wrenching open the door of the saloon he searched everywhere. No sign. Growing more agitated, he raced back into the house and scoured every ledge and shelf in the few rooms they had used, without success. Sweating now, he sat on the floor beside Félix with his head in his hands. His arms and legs were shaking, and still he didn't dare look at the mirror. 'Tell me!' he screamed at his sleeping friend. 'For Christ's sake tell me! I don't know! Tell me!'

A rumble of thunder interrupted the cold silence.

* * *

When Tom and Robert got back to St Luc, Daisy was on the telephone. Waving a welcome, she carried on talking as, eager to hear what progress she had made, they hovered beside her. After another minute of animated conversation, she put down the receiver.

'Well,' she said, with a smile on her face, 'it's coming. How about you, first?'

Tom sat on the arm of the sofa. 'We were so close,' he said. 'But not close enough.' He gave her a brief account of their pursuit.

'And are they sure he really was one of the kidnappers?' Daisy said.

Tom nodded. 'Mum's torch was in his saddle-bag. Theoretically he might just have got it some other way but it's not very likely. It was him all right. Otherwise why would he take off like that?' For Robert's benefit he explained in French what he'd said.

'So what do they think he'll do now?' Daisy said.

'If they don't nick him he'll probably go back and tell his mates. And if they get nervous they might move the hostages.'

'Oh, no. All this is useless then,' Daisy said, pointing to the telephone directory, open on the windowsill.

Remembering that, in the heat of events, he hadn't told Robert about the discovery of the antique threshing machine, Tom sketched in the details.

When he'd finished, Robert said to Daisy: 'It isn't necessarily useless. He's very young, this pigface we chased. He may not go back to the others for fear of leading us there. He may be caught. It's quite possible.'

'At least we know the place must be in this immediate area,' Tom said. 'You'd hardly send a boy out on a scooter if it was more than a few kilometres. Anyway, love, did you manage to get anything?'

'A bit. First I got on to a main dealer in Dijon; young executive type. He said he'd never heard of Cosquin & Son; said I must understand there had been huge changes in the agricultural machinery business since the war and the age of the little man was long gone, blah, blah, blah. It was like a lecture. You could just see him in his Hugo Boss suit, laying down the law. Then he said I must excuse him but he was very late for an important meeting, and that was it. Have a nice day!'

'I wonder what her name was, this important meeting?' Robert said.

'Exactly. Anyway, then I had a chat with your wife, Robert, and she was a thousand times more helpful.'

Robert was surprised and pleased.

'She put me on to a local bank manager, of all people. Monsieur Dauvergne. Martin Dauvergne. Runs a branch in Arnay. His special interest is the social history of the area. Yvonne told me he has a column in the local paper, which she enjoys very much. Anyway, he was extremely co-operative. Not only had he heard of the firm but he knows the son of the Son, in Cosquin & Son.' Daisy smiled at the complication. 'Are you with me? So in other words Cosquin's grandson. He's an acquaintance of Dauvergne's. Lives just outside Beaune, in a village called Levernois. Right? So I called him and I got the housekeeper. That's who I was talking to when you came in.'

'And?' Tom said, both anxious and hopeful.

'He went into Beaune for lunch. She doesn't know where and she doesn't know what time he'll be back.'

Tom couldn't disguise his frustration. A thunderclap made him glance up at the window. 'It's getting as black as a bag out there,' he said.

'He must have a favourite place,' Robert said.

'She hasn't been working for him long; she's obviously not all that familiar with his habits.'

Robert looked at the books in the alcove by the fireplace and took out a three-year-old Michelin guide. 'We'll ring them all,' he said. 'He may be somewhere that's not in here, but it's worth a try.'

'There won't be time to go down there,' Tom said. 'With the light going, the kidnappers might make the pick-up sooner rather than later.'

'We don't have to go down,' Robert said. 'My friend Dédé is on the spot. When I've tried the well-known places I'll get him to check the little bistros and bars. He's like a ferret. He knows the holes where the tourists never go.'

'This bank manager, Daise. What exactly did he say about the firm?' Tom said.

'He said they'd been very well-established and old man Cosquin made a lot of money in the Thirties. He had the foresight to do a deal with some big American manufacturer and bring in those huge combine harvesters they use over there. Cosquin was one of the first to see their potential for Europe, apparently. But when the war came it all got a bit complicated.' Daisy looked at Robert before going on, wondering how much she could say without offending sensibilities. 'It seems that Cosquin was a pragmatist. I suppose he didn't want to see what he'd built up disappear.'

'Pragmatist? What's that?' Robert asked.

Still hesitant, Daisy said: 'Well, he wasn't exactly in the Resistance, put it that way.'

'A collaborator, you mean?' Robert said. 'The day the Germans left my father's village they shot eleven innocent people. Eleven. And the Cosquins of this world wanted to ask the Germans to dance.' With an emphatic gesture he picked up the telephone and tapped out a number.

Tom opened the front door. The sky was even blacker now and the torrent from the down-pipe at the corner of the house deflected off an angled roof tile on to the gravel of the courtyard. After a moment, listening to Robert's animated telephone manner, Daisy joined her father, linking her arm through his.

'I wonder where mum's watching the rain from?' Tom said, remembering what Robert had said about Gazin and the murdered girl.

'She'll be watching it from here soon. It'll be over today, Dad.'

'She likes rain. Sometimes in summer we go for walks in it. Did you give the housekeeper our number, by the way, so she can call us if Cosquin comes back?'

Daisy nodded.

' . . . Manager! You couldn't manage a horse butcher's,' Robert bellowed, slamming down the receiver. 'In the army we had ways of dealing with these people. Give them a black jacket and they think they're the President of the Republic.'

'Any luck?' Daisy said.

'Not yet,' Robert said. 'But soon, I'm sure of it.'

Daisy smiled at Tom. 'Come on. I'll make us all a *croque-monsieur*, with Robert's fresh eggs on top.'

Under the tarpaulin, lulled by the sound of the downpour and the effects of the Ricard, Paul had slept for half an hour. His dreams had been vivid. Time and again the faces of the hostages had appeared to him, white and pleading. The American had held his head in her hands and kissed him on the lips; sitting by the embers of a fire, at night. She had tasted sweet and warm. He could smell apples in her hair as she moulded her body to his. When he spoke to her there was no trace of a stammer.

Peering under the flap of his temporary shelter he saw that although the sky was still dark, for the moment the rain had turned to drizzle. Though his head was still muzzy, he had a strange sense of purpose. The confusion he had felt as he fled the wood had been replaced by a sureness of what he must do. Since he couldn't go back to Henri in any case, he would call the gendarmes and tell them where the women were. Then, later, when things were back to normal, he might contact the American; see if she was as good as her word. No hope, he supposed, of her being as good as the dream. You couldn't always tell though, with women. And if Henri tried to shop him, it would be his word against Paul's. Who'd believe a lunatic? And what proof was there that Paul had ever been anywhere near that pig-sty of a prison? Unless the American ratted, and the girl by the dream-fire told Paul that she wouldn't.

As he eased out from under the tarpaulin, he caught the stench of sweat and vomit from his clothes. If he smelt bad to himself, what would other people think? With any luck there wouldn't be any. Maybe he should head for his aunt's first? Have a bath before he made the call? No. Get this thing done and then he could relax; feel good. He'd never gone out of his way to help anyone like this. Never. It was a good feeling, like winning something and having a drink with the lads. Knowing you'd made a difference. He tried to remember whether there was a telephone box between here and the house by the canal. The nearest he could think of was in the other direction, at Vandenesse. It meant going maybe half a kilometre out of his way but what did that matter now? If it saved two lives and put Henri in gaol, it was worth it every time. Then, after that, he could have a good soak, dry off, and think what to do next. He could soon make up a story to satisfy his aunt.

Keeping as much as possible to the cover of the hedge, though it meant loping at an uncomfortable crouch, he headed north. But when he reached the junction of the canal road and the route from Ste Sabine to Châteauneuf, close to the lock, he was forced to emerge from hiding. With a careful check in both directions, he crossed the road. For a hundred metres or so the house on the corner, its outhouses and straggling

vegetable garden, made it impossible to re-enter the fields.
But the roads were deserted, and in the poor light and drizzle,
which was now getting heavier again, Paul began to feel more
confident. Perhaps there was no need to leave the tarmac at
all. Walking on this hard surface was so much quicker. Within
fifteen minutes or so he should reach Vandenesse and then he
might go back to his aunt's house via the towpath on the other
side of the canal. Meanwhile, if a farmer drove by and spotted
him, what did it matter? He'd just assume Paul had got caught
in a shower. Quickening his pace, Paul passed the lock where
often in summer he saw tourists lounging on the cabin roofs of
hotel barges. Deserted now, the dark recess looked sinister.
He thought again of his dream, and fantasised about the
American girl's gratitude when she found out what he'd done
for her. He didn't have to make a big thing of it. Perhaps he
could wait and surprise her one day when she was out shopping.
Just tell her the truth. Or maybe the gendarmes would have
told her already about the mystery caller. She'd know who it
was at once. It couldn't be anyone else. She'd be excited to
see him. She'd give him money; the man who'd saved her life.
She'd want to see him again. But the pride he felt in doing it
for her was almost enough in itself. The last rotten week had
been worth it just for this. Stride on. Faster. The stitch didn't
matter. The weather didn't matter. Just get round this bend
and he'd be able to see the church spire that marked journey's
end. Tilting back his head for a moment, he shut his eyes and
smiled, welcoming the warm rain on his face.

When he reopened then, startled by a sudden scream of
brakes and a horn that wailed an unending note of alarm, he
saw yellow headlights that seemed so huge they blinded him
and shut out the dark sky. A second later the car hit him with
an impact so terrifying that it swept him away, with a roar like
the sea.

* * *

'There's been a fatal accident,' Robert said, putting down the telephone. 'On the Vandenesse road. A young man.'

'Poor fellow,' Tom said. 'Visibility's bad I suppose.'

'The driver was a gendarme. They're swarming like hornets now. He just came round a bend and paf! The guy had no chance.'

'That's terrible,' Daisy said. 'What a terrible waste.'

Robert gave Tom a level look. 'They think he might have been the boy on the scooter.'

Daisy reached out for her father's hand as he tried to calculate the implications.

'No information then?' he said, his voice dull and accepting.

'If they're right, no. Not from him. They think he was killed instantly,' Robert said.

For a moment Tom was speechless at this new body-blow. Then, his eyes reflecting his incomprehension, he said: 'When do we get a break? He could have told them everything.'

'If, Dad. It's only if,' Daisy reminded him. 'It might not be him at all. How can they tell from a dead body?'

'He'd obviously been in fields,' Robert said, 'there was mud on his shoes. There were grazes on his arms, scratches, as well as the more serious injuries of course. There'll obviously be prints on the scooter, and Michel's on his way from Foissy to see if he can identify him. But Daisy's right. It's not proof yet.'

As Tom rose to pace the room, the telephone rang again.

'Yes,' Robert said. 'Yes, I'm a friend of hers. Tell me.' Even the hardened veteran looked excited. 'Well, can I speak to him please?' Beckoning to Tom and Daisy to draw closer, he tightened his grip on the receiver. 'Monsieur Cosquin, thank you for calling. I'm putting Monsieur Bellman on the line. Thomas. It's his wife that the gendarmes are searching for, with the American. A moment.' Handing the telephone to Tom, he stepped aside.

Tom felt hollow with nerves. 'Hello?' he said, his voice weak and hesitant. Then, clearing his throat, he repeated it, this time with more weight. 'Hello?'

'I believe you wish to talk to me, monsieur. I regret that it's taken so long but I had to make an unexpected visit to Autun. I have read about the incident of course, and I offer you my sincerest sympathy.'

'Thank you. Monsieur Cosquin, I think my daughter told your housekeeper something about your grandfather's emblem that turned up on the photograph sent by the kidnappers. What I was wondering, quite simply . . . ' Tom found himself listening to his own voice. After what seemed like half a lifetime, here he was confronting someone who might at last have the key to Helen's whereabouts. The question he needed to ask was both momentous and mundane, and on the reply might hang his only chance of saving her. What if the crest proved irrelevant after all? Tom fought a sense of rising panic.

'Yes, monsieur?' Cosquin said, puzzled by the delay.

Once again, Daisy reached out for Tom's hand.

'What I was wondering was,' Tom repeated, 'might your . . . did your grandfather have a house, a largish house near here, a place where he might possibly have used his own crest as a decoration?' It sounded absurd, Tom thought, now that he heard himself describe it; such a petty domestic detail.

'But of course,' Cosquin said, without hesitation. 'He was building himself a mini-château overlooking the A6. It wasn't a motorway in those days, naturally . . . '

Overwhelmed by the ease of the confirmation, Tom struggled to concentrate on what Cosquin was saying.

' . . . It was all open country then. Yes, he had big ideas. And business was good. Really it was a sort of temple to Cosquin & Son, to his considerable success. And why not?'

'You say he "was" building. Didn't he finish it?'

'Unfortunately not. Before it was completed my grandfather

died. This was at the end of the war. My father was not at all so flamboyant. He sold the property to an entrepreneur who planned to make a hotel, but he went bankrupt. And after that, I don't know.'

'Monsieur . . . ', clearing his dry throat, Tom put the question he had been desperate to ask ever since seeing the Polaroid image enhanced on that morning of revelations in Dijon. 'Monsieur, can you possibly tell me where it is, your grandfather's house?'

'It's not a secret, monsieur. It's just outside the little village of La Forêt, near Châteauneuf.'

Tom was silent for a moment. How many kilometres? Twenty at the outside. Twelve miles or so. If he was right, and he prayed that he was, all this time Helen had only been twelve miles away. It seemed almost absurd; such a short, straight line. It was walkable. Throughout her ordeal, she had just been a walk away!

'Monsieur?' Once more Cosquin was puzzled by the silence.

'I'm sorry, Monsieur Cosquin,' Tom said, recovering. 'It's just that . . . I'm extremely grateful to you. Perhaps when this is all over we might meet? I'd like to thank you in person.'

'With pleasure,' Cosquin said. 'And good luck, monsieur.'

When Tom replaced the receiver his hand was shaking. In three sentences he explained what Cosquin had told him. Before he had even finished, Robert was calling Bouillot on the mobile. Listening, Tom put his arms round Daisy and hugged her.

'Tell Mister Walker, Dad, right now,' she said. 'Oh please, please let this be the end.'

Tom rang Walker, who was unable to disguise his excitement.

'Will you go, Tom?' Walker said.

'There's nothing on earth could stop me.'

'Me too. I'll make my own way, to save time. See you there.'

'Let's go,' Robert said, as Tom ended his call.

'Daisy . . . ' Tom began.

'Forget it,' Daisy said, sensing that he was about to ask her to stay behind again, perhaps for her own sake, perhaps for her mother's. 'I'm coming and that's that.'

This time Tom took his own car, driving fast but with great concentration. What he must do now, he told himself, was focus on the single objective of freeing Helen. He must try not to look forward or backward from that point; not to indulge in thoughts of revenge or to plan beyond today. Otherwise the swarm of possibilities might obscure his judgement. One possibility, however, refused to go away, an echo of his earlier fear. If the kidnappers had grown suspicious at the increased gendarme activity in the area, or at the non-appearance of the man on the scooter, they might have moved the hostages. That could prolong the search by days. But even if they had, Tom consoled himself, Cosquin's unfinished château must yield clues. Thinking of Bouillot's men, and Walker, racing for the target, blocking every escape route, he looked at Daisy in the rear-view mirror. Tired but elated, she was intent on the road ahead, her eyes bright in the unseasonal gloom. Tom reached back with his left hand, which she held for a moment.

The one car they passed before the crossroads at Foissy had its headlights on – a reminder to Tom that he should do likewise. The thunder grumbled but the rain was easing off again. It might yet be a fine evening, Tom thought. After the downpour, the garden would smell so rich and alive. Helen's garden. He wondered whether Michel had identified the victim of the accident, but, anticipating him, Robert made a call on the mobile and was told that the proprietor of the bar wasn't back yet.

A spade would do, Henri thought. He didn't need a shotgun. One crack each. They wouldn't even see it coming. Then drag them out and throw them in an outhouse. Or maybe dig a hole, if there was time. How long would it take? No. On second thoughts even after the rain the ground would be like a rock. No, to hell with it. Do it and leave them where they were. By the time they were found, if they were found, he and Félix would be hundreds of kilometres away, with a big drink in their hands, and plenty more where that came from. Put Félix in the car first. Make him comfortable on the back seat, ready for a quick getaway, then do it and go. Oh, this bitch of a place. How he hated it. How he hated the greyness and the thick walls and the darkness. He roared his hatred, hearing the echo back from the stone. Still he daren't look at the broken mirror, in case that other devil was staring back at him. Pick up Félix. Be careful. Hold him here and here, under the neck and the legs. How limp they were, and how heavy he seemed now. He was slight but he felt as dense as a sack of grain. When his head fell back, showing the tide mark on his pale neck, you could see where the line of bristles ended; where they gave way to soft flesh they were reddish. Perhaps Félix's mother had been a redhead. Tomorrow, in a guest house far from here, he would shave his friend; bathe him; sponge his tired body; wash his hair and make it fresh again. That would revive him. Lie him in the sun on those hills, watching the buzzards; see him grow stronger every day. And then, in a few weeks, the circuits! Smell the rubber and the fuel. Feel they had come through something just as dangerous as the rich drivers.

Laying Félix on the back seat, Henri wound down a window to let in some air. The rain had stopped. At last the storm was moving on. Taking care not to wake Félix when he shut the door, he opened the boot in the hope of finding a spade. There was nothing except an old sack and a jerry-can. Maybe there'd be one in the stables. Have a quick look. If there wasn't one here, maybe he could go home and get one. But as he wrenched open the door of the second stable, a thought struck him. What if Paul had been to the gendarmes? They'd be watching the place. They might even be on their way here. And what about Félix's office? They must be missing him by now. The complications made his head ache. Félix had been the one who dealt with these things. He was the brains. Maybe that was why he was so quiet. Maybe he was exhausted with all that thinking and planning. But whose was that face in the mirror, watching Henri as though it already knew what he was going to do?

This was dark, this stable. Horrible. What was that, touching him, touching his face? It was like a bony finger, stroking him. Get out of here, quick. Get out and do it, do it, do it. Never mind the spade. Shut your eyes and put your hands round their scraggy throats. Think of them like cats. Don't think about the warm skin and the fat lips, grinning. Think of turkeys. One twist and that was it. Think of them like the animals they were. Deliberate now, as he re-entered the house for the last time, he had no difficulty in believing that on this cursed farm, the beasts were due for slaughter.

At least he wouldn't have to face the mirror again. Running towards the cellar door he felt sick at the thought of its lopsided stare. But it couldn't hurt him now. Now he was in control. Down the steps and into the half-light of this horrible tunnel. He hated the dark. And the touching. If only he didn't have to touch them. All at once he was a kid again, standing in the cowshed that hadn't been mucked out for days. He was seven, maybe. And his stepmother was standing over him. Saying things. Taunting him. And her hands were on him. Her hands were on his face and moving down. And her lips were red like a cut and her hands were undoing his buttons. He squirmed and struggled to get away from her but she put one hand over his mouth so he couldn't call out. Who was there to call to, anyway, she said? Only the hens, and they didn't care. And the buttons were undone and her hand was on him down there, gripping tight and hurting him; and she was grinning to see the pain. He screwed up his face so she wouldn't see him cry but she hurt him so much that he couldn't help it. And he was wet now, standing in the stink of the cold cowshed and she threw her head back and laughed at him. And the hate began to be like a sharp sickle. That's what he needed now, but all he had were his hands. Think of something else while he did it. Think of Félix. Do it for him. What was that? Sounded like faint voices, somewhere above his head. Must be voices inside his head. Must be those same voices he hadn't heard for a while, trying to trick him. The strange thing was, his mother's wasn't one of them. She wasn't telling him to do it; not like the other times. But he knew all the same.

Turning the key in the lock at the end of the passage, he just stood there for a moment, looking at the American. Better do it here, not take her upstairs where it was lighter. He'd rather not see her skin. She stared back at him, not moving. She didn't seem frightened. He could smell her; sweat, but not like a man's. And her hair. That frightened him most. The hair that turned to grass snakes. He took a pace forward and still she didn't move. If only he could get behind her he could strangle her without seeing her eyes. But as he moved to do that, she darted for the door with a force she must have been saving up, and before he had time to recover she was out in the passage. No, not again! Now he was after her. Chasing her, he wasn't frightened any more. Now she'd made him angry and that was all he could think of. That and the screaming in his head that had started again and seemed to be getting louder. It seemed like someone was shouting his name, over and over. His family name at first, then both together. The American seemed to be calling too, and he wasn't sure but he thought a voice answered from one of the other cells. It didn't stop him though. Nothing would stop him now. At the bottom of the steps he caught her and, leaning back so he wouldn't feel her hair, he gripped her round the waist and hurled her against the wall, to stun her. Maybe that would be enough. Head cracked like an egg, dropped on the cold yard. Yolk dribbling yellow on the wet stones. Crush it under his boot. Hear the shell crunch under the studs. Look back and it was nothing. Part of the earth again.

Twice misdirected by passers-by they had mistaken for locals, Tom skidded to a halt in front of the unfinished château only to find that the massive double door at the front wouldn't open. Robert took out his service revolver and fired three shots at the lock but still there was no movement. Daisy, who knew nothing of the weapon, was startled. Racing back to the car, they drove round to the rear entrance and found themselves in the neglected courtyard where the car and the van were parked. As Tom and Daisy ran across to check them, Robert called out:

'No time for that. Let's go.'

Daisy paused long enough to look through the side rear window of the car, and saw the body on the back seat. 'Dad!'

Tom shouted: 'Robert! There's one of them dead in here!'

'He'll still be there when we get back then. Let's go.' Robert was already half-way up the stone steps.

Panting now with effort and excitement, Tom and Daisy followed him into the ante-room with two doors leading off it; one revealing a much larger chamber beyond. As they entered this vaulted space, with its two camp-beds side by side in a corner, and a large broken mirror that was at once familiar from the Polaroid, Robert pointed to the ceiling.

'There! The horse!'

Tom looked up and saw the original of the image which had tantalised him since his first sight of the Polaroid. 'That's it all right,' he said.

'It is. It's Cosquin's horse,' Daisy said.

'They'll have heard us or seen us,' Robert said. 'We have to move fast.' He pointed to the room they'd just left. 'You try that door we saw in there. Try to be methodical. I'll keep going. I doubt if they're above the ground floor. There's no reason. Yell when you find something. And good luck, Mr Professor.' With that he was on his way to the entrance hall.

Tom and Daisy turned back and approached the door they had already passed. As Tom pushed it open, he heard more vehicles arriving in the yard, and doors slamming. Must be Walker and Bouillot's men, he thought. Should they wait for them? No, he decided; if the remaining kidnappers were nervous, moments might be crucial. How many could there be of them anyway, if the man in the accident and the body in the yard were two? Any minute now he would know the answer. It was shadowy down here, and silent. He paused for a moment to get used to the gloom. Was that irregular breathing he could hear, from somewhere beyond the bottom of the steps? Beginning his cautious descent, followed by Daisy, he called: 'Helen! Julia! Helen, it's Tom! It's me!'

Now, from the other side of the passage, he could hear a faint but definite response. A small voice called: 'Here!'

Before he could react, Tom was aware of a violent struggle somewhere in the near-darkness. With a glance behind to check that Daisy was still with him, he reached the last step, aware of more than one door in the wall to his left. And there, for the first time, he confronted the face of his enemy. No, he thought, with a confused mixture of horror and astonishment. Not the first time. The meal he'd shared with Robert and Yvonne at the Terminus. The couple in the corner. The nervy, thin one, and this animal. Moving out of the shadows was a dishevelled figure with several days' growth of beard, and wild eyes that saw Tom but seemed to look beyond him. At his feet was the body of a young woman with fair hair whom Tom recognised, even like this, as Julia Walker. She had fallen in an awkward position, and there was blood on her face, but she was alive – breathing hard, as though she had almost choked. Absorbing this with a sense of relief, Tom watched transfixed as the man he should hate began to walk past him. What should he do? Throw himself at him and take out all the loathing on that pudgy, dislocated, dingy face? Take out all the heartache on what, at close quarters, looked like anyone you'd see in the Café du Nord? Beat him until he fell; make him fear, just as he must have terrified the women? He seemed too unresisting for that; broken already. In any case, Tom must get to Helen. Nothing else mattered.

'Don't, Dad,' Daisy said, as if reading his mind. 'Let them deal with him.'

As she spoke, three gendarmes appeared, followed by Bouillot. Shining a powerful torch, Bouillot picked out the face of the kidnapper.

'Right, that's it,' he said. 'Don't try anything. It's over.' To the men he said: 'Take him. The medics will be here in a moment. Don't move the young woman until they arrive. There may be injuries.'

As though responding to this, Julia stirred and tried to sit up.

'I'm all right,' she said. 'If someone can just give me a hand.'

Touching Daisy's arm, Bouillot urged her to go back to the ante-room. 'If you don't mind, mademoiselle.'

'I want to see my mother.'

'Two moments and you will. Please.'

Daisy shook him away. 'I'm seeing her. You can't stop me.'

As the gendarmes took hold of the kidnapper, who made no attempt to resist, and the medical team made their way down to help Julia, Tom saw Walker framed in the doorway at the top.

'She'll be fine in no time,' he called up. With attention focused on the visible hostage, he made for the door with a large key in it, followed by a defiant Daisy.

The voice had said: 'Here!' The voice had been English. Only a width of wood separated him at last from Helen. Turning the key, the background noisy with excitement, he was glad that the three of them would share this moment. So much to say. So much love, and gratitude. So much that he knew the words wouldn't come. Just to hold her, feel her warmth, make her safe. He had never wanted anything more than this.

He pushed open the door, looking down at the figure sitting with her back to the wall, her head resting on her arms as though even now, she had no energy to rise. Standing in front of her, sick with relief and concern, Tom lowered himself to a crouch. At her level now, he put out his hands to her face. As she raised her head, Daisy, silent until now, let out a gasp.

Even in this uncertain light, Tom saw with a piercing sense of loss that this was not Helen. The face that seemed to plead with him, exhausted and tear-streaked, was that of her sister, Nancy.

CHAPTER SEVENTEEN

After Gazin had been arrested, Tom and Daisy had driven to the hospital in Arnay, where Nancy and Julia were to be detained overnight. Robert, who knew their need to be alone, had been given a lift to St Luc by Bouillot. Inconsolable, Daisy had sat on the back seat, looking out of the window with tearful, unseeing eyes. At the wheel, Tom went through the motions of driving without recognising anything they passed. All the longing, the hoping, the searching, had ended in despair. During the endless night ahead, devastated and fearful, they would ask a hundred questions, and understand nothing. And far, far worse was to come.

The following morning, when they had again visited Nancy, who was still too shocked to say more than a few words, and called in on Julia, beside herself with happiness at being reunited with her father, they had returned to St Luc. For several minutes they had stood together in the main room, where in their consciousness Helen was still a presence, and held each other tight for the comfort of human contact. Twenty minutes later, while they were still unable to speak their grief, a car had drawn up in the courtyard. It was Granier, alone. Tom had invited him to sit down, but the major had said he preferred to stand.

'What is it?' Tom said.

'It's terrible news, I'm afraid. I'm so sorry.'

Prepared now, Tom lowered his head, holding his hand out to Daisy.

'Madame Bellman. Her body has been found. Here in St Luc, at the boundary of the village.'

Tom felt hollow, without resistance. Daisy left his side and lay on the sofa in the foetal position, her hands covering her ears. The words leapfrogged each other in a meaningless procession. 'Body' ... 'Helen' ... Tom's Helen? The Helen who had laughed, and been angry, and courageous? The Helen who helped people, who couldn't stand apathy, who filled her life with colour? The Helen who had told him he was getting fatter than an old labrador, and sang all over the house, and put flowers in every room? The Helen he had learned to please in lovemaking, so long after youth had gone? Unable to break down in front of Granier, Tom had meant to enquire when this had been reported, but instead found himself asking: 'Why?'

'I'm afraid I can't answer that question, monsieur. Very soon we should know more.'

'Where is Helen now?'

'She's in the mortuary, monsieur. In Beaune. I'm afraid I must ask you if you will identify her for us?'

For five minutes after Granier had left, Tom and Daisy had sat in the sunlit room, still seeming to hear the echoes of what he had said. Then, together, they had taken the most terrible journey of their lives.

Now, six days later, as they prepared to leave St Luc for England, Granier had called to say goodbye.

'Home then,' Granier said.

'Yes,' Tom said. 'We'll be heading back shortly.'

Granier turned aside. 'I'm so sorry, monsieur. I ... ' Accustomed to grief, but too sincere for glib expressions of sympathy, he was unable to complete the sentence.

'Thank you,' Tom said. 'You've been very good.'

'Perhaps, when you visit us again . . . ' Granier hesitated. 'You will come again?'

'Oh, yes. It's . . . it was Helen's favourite place. I'll be back.'

'I should like to see you again.' Granier turned to Daisy. 'And you, mademoiselle.'

Daisy acknowledged the courtesy but didn't trust herself to speak. When Granier had taken his leave, she went upstairs to pack and Tom wandered out to the garden. The air was shrill with swallows and crickets. The young cat from the farm beyond the ruined bakery was sparring with a feather, and the church bells tolled eleven. Here, nothing marked this tranquil day from any other. Farmers were at work in the fields; mothers suckled their babies; the yellow post van was on its rounds. But for Tom the world was altered. The death of Helen had made its mundane patterns seem comfortless; without meaning. They were no more than a river running by; close, but remote in its mysterious urgency. He was left with a sense of emptiness so profound that nothing else had any reality for him, except his pity for Daisy's suffering, and his dread of breaking the news to Frank.

Sitting in one of the chairs by the wall, where he and Helen had often talked until the sun went down behind the dark hills, he relived the horrors of the past few days; the discovery of Nancy, and the story she had told when, nourished and rested, she had been able to gather her thoughts, encouraged by the kind nurses at Arnay. After her recent divorce, without announcing her departure to anyone, Nancy had taken herself off to camp, alone, in the Auvergne, and to do some painting. From there she had gone on to Lyons and, out of impulse one evening, feeling restored after several weeks in the sun, she had telephoned Helen. Nancy's plan, she said, was to come up to Beaune the next day and pay her a visit. After that she thought she might go on to Alsace, which she had never seen in summer.

Delighted, Helen had asked if she would do her a favour. The car was ready for collection. Would Nancy get a taxi to the garage and drive the 2CV home for her? Nancy had agreed without hesitation, but a few kilometres short of St Luc she'd had a puncture and, seeing a car parked outside a nearby cottage, had gone in to ask for help . . .

Throughout the first few days of her captivity she had alternated between unconsciousness, an overwhelming need to sleep, and moments of terrified lucidity. It was now clear that she had been concussed. Later, when she was still weak and often felt faint, but was a little more in control of her faculties, she thought it best to pretend illness. Perhaps the kidnappers would show some pity; even get medical help. They hadn't of course, but at least, assuming she was half-dead, they hadn't pestered her with threats. She had longed to know more about the American but the only kidnapper she had asked, whom she now knew had been Paul, the victim of the road accident, had told her to mind her own business.

Tom had spent many hours every day at Nancy's bedside, though he feared he had been poor company. Not until last night, however, had he told her the heartbreaking news. The morning after Nancy's release, Helen's body had been found covered with earth and leaves in a dry ditch close to the wooden cross on the Lacanche road. It appeared that she had been killed with a single blow to the head. Tom supposed that after her conversation with her sister, she had gone for a late evening walk, alone. He found the thought of that last walk unbearable. Helen would have been brisk. She hated to dawdle. As usual she would have been thinking of a dozen things at once: *A Midsummer Night's Dream* at the château, Nancy's unexpected arrival, the days to go until Tom came . . . Unaware of her vulnerability, she would have passed the war memorial and the church, and the field where the fête was held on the last Sunday in August, and then the last houses at the edge of the village. Another three or four hundred metres and she would have turned for home, as they almost always did when they walked together. But her journey had ended by the cross; and now Tom faced the long road alone.

With tact and consideration, Granier had told him as much as the gendarmes had so far discovered. In a rambling confession, sometimes in the first person but often in the third, Gazin had confessed to Helen's murder. A voice had made him do it, he said; a voice that was not his mother's but which spoke for his mother. What Granier knew, but did not reveal to Tom, was that Gazin had caught in Helen's face a fleeting likeness of his hated stepmother that night. He had gibbered something about full lips and dark hair. Meanwhile the DNA tests had indicated that he had also been the murderer of the girl, Stéphane; but he still refused to accept that he had killed his friend, Félix, and kept asking where he was. He was regressing more and more into a childlike state of terror and confusion. Efforts had been made to find his stepmother, but without success. Even the mention of her name made him unmanageable.

Tom had felt unable to visit the château, but Walker and Julia had twice called at St Luc. Delighted though he was for them, he found that their pleasure in each other's company made the loss of Helen harder to bear. Nevertheless, he admired Julia's courage, knowing that she had done what she could to find out about Helen's condition, and had risked reprisals by wearing the bracelet in the photograph. According to Robert, her stepmother, Madeleine, had left the château the morning after Julia's release. She had gone early, before most of the staff were up, and had not returned. Nobody had been able to give Robert a reason. Perhaps she was keeping a long-standing engagement, but it seemed strange that she had taken most of her clothes with her in three large suitcases.

Madeleine was, however, to make one more appearance.

Tom had not invited Walker and Julia to the memorial service at the crematorium. He and Daisy, Robert, Yvonne, Monique, Zazie and Roland were the only official mourners. The puppeteer had driven through the night from Genoa to be there. A few minutes after the service began, something made Tom look round and there, on either side of the aisle at the back, by the door, were the unmistakable figure of Madeleine Walker, wearing dark glasses, and the even more unexpected sight of the wood merchant from Arnay, Monsieur Vauliquet, head bowed and hands joined in prayer over his dark blue suit. Tom was moved by this sincere, unbidden tribute, and tried to find Vauliquet afterwards to thank him, but the old man had gone. Madeleine too had driven away without a word. Tom wished with all his heart that Helen could know they had been there.

On their return to St Luc, he and Daisy had sprinkled Helen's ashes at the base of the glorious white rose that climbed ten metres into the grizzled branches of the old pear tree at the bottom of the garden. Helen had always said that was where she wanted to be, when the time came.

Tom's reverie was interrupted by Daisy. In silence she came and sat beside him, in the wicker chair Helen had bought for sixty francs at Emmaus. Tom remembered her delight at having found yet another unbelievable bargain. Others would haggle with the man who ran the charitable community, even at those absurd prices, but Helen never did.

Leaning back, Daisy surrendered to the heat of the sun. 'I'm ready when you are, Dad,' she said after a while.

'All right, love. I'll put the stuff in the car and lock up. The hospital rang. They'll have Nancy ready when we call by.'

As Daisy rose, he remembered something else. 'Oh, hang on, Daise. How stupid of me. Major Granier gave me something. He wondered if you might like it.' From his pocket he took Helen's battered bracelet, recovered from the château at La Forêt. With slow, tender reverence, she leaned over and picked it up. Overcome by the inexpensive, precious object, tarnished by neglect, she slipped it on to her wrist and went into the house.

Tom got up, reluctant to leave the garden. On his way through the kitchen he saw Helen's sketchbook, open on the sideboard at the happy painting of the daisy: 'The eye of the day' Beside it was the computer enhancement of the prancing horse, which, in the event, had led them to cruel disappointment. Nevertheless, it had helped save the lives of two people, and Tom was thankful for that. He closed the book and took it with him.

When he had turned the long brass key in the front door, he swung the grey shutter across the window of the main room, securing it to a screw in the wall with its loop of wire. The house was enclosed again, left alone with its echoes of warm content and infinite sadness. Neither would ever leave it. As long as the fabric stood, the memories would be there, in the wood and the stone, to be relived and sorrowed over.

Daisy had the engine running. As Tom walked to the car, Robert emerged from his door and came towards him down the courtyard. In his hand was an open box, filled with lettuces and tomatoes.

'In the spring I'm planting potatoes for you, Mr Professor,' he said, holding out the gift. 'So you'll have to come back. If you don't, I'm coming to fetch you.'

Tom put the box on the back seat and turned to shake Robert's hand. The words were hard to find. 'I'll be back. I don't want to leave, but I have to.'

'Of course,' Robert went round to Daisy's window. 'Mademoiselle, good journey.' He kissed her on both cheeks. 'Look after him.'

'You've been so kind, Robert,' she said. 'Thank you.'

Robert held up his hand to disclaim gratitude. '*Au revoir*,' he said. 'Till the next time.' They could still see his arm, raised in farewell, until a bend in the road lost him to view.

Lying awake in the early hours, Tom had wondered whether the ache of loss would make him glad to go; to put the tragedy behind him. But as he drove towards the old Paris road leading to Arnay, past the field of maize and Monsieur Poinsot's farm, he felt that he was leaving home; that now, more than ever, this was where he belonged.